Death In The Last Reel

Margaret Demeray Book Two

Paula Harmon

January Press

This book is dedicated to the memory of May Clark (1st June 1885-17th March 1971), an English silent film actress turned cinematographer who played Alice in the first film adaptation of 'Alice in Wonderland' in 1902, and to all the early silent film actors and actresses whose names were never published.

One

London - January 1911

London An hour into the new year, the dances slowed.

Dr Margaret Demeray waltzed in Fox's arms, eyes closed and head against his shoulder, glad that he had been able to come to the ball as if he were an ordinary man; forgetting for a few hours that he was an intelligence agent with two missions to complete.

They spun and whirled... then Fox's embrace loosened and they stopped, an island in a sea of dancers.

Margaret raised her head, but Fox wasn't looking at her but across the ballroom.

His friend and colleague Charles Craven was beckoning, face solemn.

'I think I might need to leave.' Fox kissed Margaret lightly then led her across the floor. 'I'm sorry.'

'Do you think they've traced George Gardstein's accomplices?'

'With any luck. We can't have murdering anarchists like them running loose. The other thing can wait... I hope.'

He stopped speaking as they reached Charles.

'Hare's on the telephone,' he said. 'He's given me my orders, now he wants to give you yours.'

'Very well.' Fox kissed Margaret again and went to the foyer.

Charles contemplated Margaret. 'Try not to fret.'

'I can't help worrying every time he disappears. Or you.'

'It's part of our job, Margaret. You know that. If I hadn't had to disappear last summer, Fox might not have needed to make acquaintance with you.'

'And even then he nearly...'

Charles squeezed her hand. 'It's our job.'

'Is it Gardstein's men or—'

'Gardstein's common knowledge.' Charles frowned. 'You shouldn't know about any "or".'

Fox had returned. He held her close briefly. 'We'll be back before you know it.'

'Take care,' she whispered, the words feeble. 'They gunned down three policemen two weeks ago. They won't stop at—'

'We've got the upper hand this time,' Fox whispered back. 'You'll know when we're successful.' Then he let her go, kissed her once more and left.

But after that Margaret heard nothing, and the only news reported was that an unnamed man had been murdered and mutilated and left on Clapham Common a few hours after that hurried goodbye.

**

The following day, Margaret went to work at St Julia's Hospital, her heart full of dread, struggling with the newspaper to find the latest information.

People bumped into her, making the pages slip in her hands. Oblivious to their grumbling, Margaret found an article buried on page eleven. She skipped the first lines which repeated what she already knew to read the latest information.

A torn letter found on the body, indicated that the crime might be connected with the atrocity committed by George Gardstein and his men in Houndsditch two weeks ago.

Margaret held her breath. Connected how? An informer, a police-man, an undercover agent killed by someone they were trying to arrest? *Please God don't let it be Fox or Charles.* She stepped out of the flow and manhandled the paper into submission.

However the body has now been identified as a well-to-do Russian from Stepney who simply fell foul of a violent robber. The police are sure of an early arrest.

Margaret breathed out. Sad and shocking as it was, the victim was no one she knew. Folding the paper, she hurried up the steps into the mortuary wing. *But it didn't stop the fear. Where are you Fox?*

'Happy New Year, doctor,' said the desk clerk cheerfully.

'Happy New year to you too, Mr Holness. Are there any messages for me?'

'Only that Dr Jordan wants to see you and Mr Hardisty's sent word that he'll be little late.' The clerk winked. 'Medical students eh, doctor? They never know when to stop celebrating.'

Margaret rolled her eyes a little. 'I hope he'll be in a fit state to assist me later.'

The clerk chuckled. 'Shall I have some coffee ordered when he arrives?'

'Good idea. And please let me know if anyone else wants me. I'll be in Dr Jordan's office.'

'Of course.'

Dr Jordan rose from his desk as she entered and shook hands. 'Happy New Year my dear. It's nice to see someone early and sober.'

'I hear Algie's suffering.'

'Young men were ever thus,' said Dr Jordan with a grin. 'But beer aside, he's a credit to your tutelage.'

'Thank you sir.'

'In consequence, I have something to discuss, but before I forget, Matron asked if you'd speak with Mrs Balodis. The tuberculosis is confirmed, so she'll go to Frimley Sanatorium this morning. At least she can spend her last few weeks in something approaching comfort.'

'That poor woman.' Mrs Balodis was a fighter; barely over forty-five, sharp and witty. But she'd left it too long to have a persistent cough diagnosed. 'Why does she want me?'

Dr Jordan picked up a note and squinted. 'To explain matters to her grown up children. They live in... Myrdle Street.' He pulled a face. 'Whitechapel's not the best place to visit just now. You'd be wise to have someone escort you.'

'Of course,' said Margaret, determined to do nothing of the sort. 'What else did you want to discuss?'

'Ah yes,' Dr Jordan settled more comfortably in his chair, a broad smile on his face. 'Your work. Not simply your pathology, but your teaching. All your students do well and Algie has been working under your close supervision for nearly two years and is far ahead of his peers. I've convinced the board to credit you instead of me for his training in post-mortems.'

'I appreciate that very much. Didn't anyone complain about my helping with Fox... I mean Special Branch on occasion?'

'Superintendent Fox's superior explained all that to the chairman some time ago,' said Dr Jordan. 'It just proves your worth.' He leaned forward. 'But this is my news: I'll be bringing you to board meetings. I recommend a cushion and some deep breathing exercises, and a nice brick wall to bang your head against afterwards, but it's all part of the job.'

'What job?'

'Mine, when I retire. St Julia's may be the first London hospital to have a woman as senior pathologist. You're suitable in every way.'

'That's wonderful!' Margaret restrained herself from rushing to hug him. 'Although I hope you're not planning on retiring soon.'

Dr Jordan removed his glasses and polished them. 'I'm delighted you're keen. Now then, what shall we find to tax Algie's brain when he arrives?'

The morning allowed little time to think about anything but work, but at lunchtime Margaret sat in the café across the road from the mortuary wing with a later edition of the paper. The murdered Russian wasn't mentioned but Gardstein's gang was.

In a dingy dwelling, H division found the ingredients for several highly effective bombs, with more lethal potential than dynamite. How many other arsenals are there in similar squalid rooms and what crime is planned? Should we not fear the anarchist more than either Fenians or German spies? They must be stopped.

Bombs.

Fox didn't always tell her details of his missions, but whether or not Charles approved of her knowing, she knew that apart from hunting down Gardstein's accomplices, he and Charles were working on something else.

Intelligence received indicated a bomb attack on London planned for spring. Exactly where, how and by whom was unclear. Fox's information pointed at Germans, while Charles's Whitechapel contacts hinted at Russians or Latvians. But the name of the man given by both informants was the same: Anderson. Charles suspected he was a small time criminal after someone else's turf rather than an anarchist.

Fox remained convinced Anderson was part of the war machine. Until they could establish who Anderson was and what he was planning, they wouldn't know. And if there were two men with the same name and they could apprehend one of them, they could seek the other together.

There was nothing Margaret could do by worrying. Paying her bill, she returned to the mortuary wing prepared to bury herself in work. In the laboratory, Algie was looking down on a covered body. That much wasn't surprising.

The young police constable standing with his back to the door, however, was.

'Good afternoon,' said Margaret.

The policeman looked wary. There was something familiar about his face, though not his demeanour.

'Remember me?' he said. 'Constable Harris.'

Margaret contemplated him. He brought to mind stifling summer heat, flies, the smell of pig and unspecified litter, a shadowed courtyard behind a rough public house and an expression of mocking disdain. 'Lemon Street last June. Are you waiting for a *proper* doctor again?'

Constable Harris ran a finger round his collar and went scarlet. 'Er...'

Algie frowned. 'He insisted this corpse was brought to St J's. He asked for you especially.'

'Really?'

'Yes madam, I mean doctor,' said Constable Harris. 'I've wanted to say sorry for some time, but wasn't sure how.'

'Isn't being able to write a prerequisite to joining the police?'

'Yeah, but I wanted to bring you something to *show* I was sorry. A murder victim, that is. Only it's taken this long to get anyone to agree to it coming her rather than St Barts or St Mary's.'

Margaret raised her eyebrows. 'And to think some women get flowers. All right, apology accepted. What changed your mind?'

'When I thought about it afterwards,' said Constable Harris, 'I realised I'd never seen what I called the "proper" doctor take as much care as you did to work out what killed that poor cove. I'd like to learn from you, so when we come across an unexpected death' – he waved a hand at the corpse – 'maybe I'd have more idea if it was an accident or deliberate.'

'Very well.' Margaret donned her rubber gloves and reached for the sheet. 'It's a grim process if you're not used to it.'

'I know,' said Constable Harris. 'So small steps, hey?' He pulled a face.

'I'm glad you've brought the body here.'

Constable Harris shrugged. 'The sarge hopes I'm not wasting time. We're up to our ears, what with trying to find Gardstein's gang.' His face grew grim and his hands clenched.

Margaret paused, filled with pity. 'I suppose you knew the victims.'

'Yeah. Coppers don't deserve to die doing their duty. Anyway—' Constable Harris closed his eyes, took a breath, and continued in a calmer voice. 'What do you reckon to *this* bloke?' He nodded at the covered corpse.

A sudden fear made Margaret's heart thump and she told herself to be rational. The form under the sheet was the wrong build entirely for Fox or Charles. 'Go on.'

'This is Mr Green. He was found drowned in the bath.'

'It happens.'

'I'm not convinced. The neighbours heard him and his missus arguing last night. And I've seen people drug out the river straight after drowning, and Mr Green seemed deader somehow. I found a sodden apron with a bit of blood on it shoved in a neighbour's ashcan. The neighbour swears it's Mrs Green's.'

'Let's see,' said Margaret, pulling back the cover to reveal a short, plump man in his forties. There was bruising on the inside of his arms and a slight cut on one.

'I think that's what he'd have got from the edges of the bath if he was trying to get a hold,' said Constable Harris. 'There's a sharp bit on the left side of the bath where the enamel's chipped.'

'There seems to be more bruising on his chest,' said Margaret. 'Why do men have to be so hairy?'

'Yes. I mean, I dunno.'

Algie turned the body over. The back was dark with blood which had settled internally, suggesting the man had been dead for several hours. Despite the lividity and the thickness of his hair, Margaret was sure there were bruises on the back of Mr Green's skull.

She lifted his hands. 'Look at this. The nails of the thumbs and little fingers are clean, but under the others there are fragments of what look like skin and blood. If I were you, I'd check the wife's forearms.'

'To look for scratches where the poor wretch tried to fight her off?'

'Deep ones.'

'Blimey.' Constable Harris swallowed and looked at Algie. 'It's enough to put a man off matrimony, ain't it?'

A dreamy expression crossed Algie's face. 'My girl would never drown me.'

Margaret rolled her eyes. 'No, but I might if you don't concentrate.' She smiled at Constable Harris. 'After the post-mortem, we'll have a better idea of whether this might have been deliberate. But...'

'But in the meantime, check Mrs Green's forearms before she "accidentally" burns them on the stove or something,' said Constable Harris.

'If she's done this once, she could do it again.'

'Righto, I'll go and see. Let me know what you find.' He donned his helmet and left the laboratory.

Four hours later, Margaret walked towards the tube station. Before going home, she wanted to visit Wesdon Street police station and give Constable Harris the results of the post mortem, then after that she'd go to speak with Mrs Balodis's children. But outside in the dreary January dark, her skin prickled.

Away from the street lights, shadows moved, periodically spotted with the red lights of watchers' cigarettes. Margaret felt very alone. If it were like this nearer to central London, what would it be like further east? After a brief hesitation, she returned to the mortuary wing and telephoned the police station.

The call was answered almost immediately, the desk sergeant audibly breathing in relief when Margaret gave her name. The usual noises in the background of a police station - arguing, shouting prisoners - seemed muffled, subdued.

'Dr Demeray?' said Constable Harris a few moments later. 'Is this about the post mortem?'

'Yes. I was going to bring the results as I passed through, but—'

'Passed through? Where to?'

'Myrdle Street. I er... I actually wondered if you might be able to come with me and I can explain the post mortem in more detail.'

Constable Harris grunted. 'Not Whitechapel. Not tonight.'

'Never mind. I'll go alone.'

'You can't!' The force of his response startled her. 'I mean - sorry doctor. I mean what's so important you're thinking of going *there* after dark?'

'A dying woman's asked me to speak with her children.'

'How long's she got?'

'Weeks. But—'

'Little kids?'

'Grown up. But—'

'Please take me seriously, doctor. I can't explain, but tonight is not the night.'

Margaret blinked. Even through the wire she could sense a prickliness, an anticipation - it was what sparked from Fox when a hunt was nearing its end.

Constable Harris sniffed. 'Er ... was I right about Mr Green?'

'I believe so.'

'Thanks.' There was a pause. 'Good night, Dr Demeray. Best go home where you're safe. Take a cab. If you've got to come to Whitechapel, do it in daylight.' He added in a whisper, 'Not before the weekend. Goodbye.'

Margaret replaced the receiver and stood at the desk, anxiety prickling through her senses. She hadn't noticed the telegram boy standing along side her.

'It's for you, doctor,' said the clerk.

She handed him the telephone and took the telegram.

Out of contact for now. Remember I love you. Say your prayers tonight like a good girl. Hope your red-headed sixth sense isn't tingling. Don't reply. Fox.

God, prayers, love? They weren't words Fox used lightly. If it hadn't been for the reference to tingling, Margaret would have thought he was playing a joke.

But the truth was that not only was her sixth sense troubling her, but down the telephone, she'd heard Constable Harris's voice tremble. Now Margaret was trembling too and more than ever, she wondered where Fox was and what he was facing. And there was nothing she could do to find out.

Two

On Wednesday morning, there was still no word from Fox. Margaret stayed in her Bayswater flat as late as she could and then spent her journey looking out for two of Fox's colleagues: Bert who sometimes chauffeured him, or Pigeon who brought messages by motorcycle. One or other of them often let her know that Fox was safe without necessarily addressing her directly. Neither were to be seen anywhere.

When Margaret finally emerged from the tube station near the hospital, it was to an atmosphere of tension. Men were whispering on corners.

'Where have all the coppers gone?'

'Reckon it's true?'

'Shall we go and see?'

'How many gonna die this time?'

'They're anarchists. What if they use bombs?'

She rushed to St Julia's, trying to shake the last words from her mind. It was ten to eight. The desk clerk was on the telephone, his face grim. 'Yes ... yes ... understood... I'll tell them.'

'What's happening?' asked Margaret as he replaced the receiver. Algie, who had entered just behind her, stopped at her side.

'We're on alert for casualties, doctor,' said the clerk. 'If the London and St Mary's can't manage, we're next on the list. The main desk's asked me to tell all doctors to be ready in case we're needed to help.'

'Casualties?' Margaret tried to keep her voice steady.

'There aren't any yet that I know of,' said the clerk. 'But the police have that Gardstein's accomplices under siege in Sidney Street.'

'That's less than two miles away!' Algie cried.

Surely Fox and Charles aren't there? 'I'll tell Dr Jordan,' said Margaret, hoping her voice sounded calmer than she felt. 'Come along, Algie. Nothing's happened yet and we've work to do.'

The orderly brought more news at nine. 'Word is there's police all over. Coppers, detectives, the whole shebang. The whole area's blocked off. Gawd, I hope they're armed properly. Them anarchists have semi-automatics.'

By eleven, the clerk asked them to come outside. Over the noises of the city came distant pops and rattles. 'The Scots Guard has gone in. Everyone's firing at everyone else from either end of the street,' he said. 'Place is swarming with onlookers. Everyone's going for a look-see.' He glanced sideways at Margaret hopefully.

'Like tourists?' growled Algie, voicing Margaret's thoughts. 'If the hospitals have to waste time treating one of them instead of those trying to do their duty...'

'Oh yes, yes, of course. Very irresponsible.' The clerk heaved a sigh before going back indoors.

Margaret returned to work and tried to concentrate until it was time to collect her lunch from the café across the road. The gunfire seemed to have paused and the news was garbled.

'They've set fire to the building,' said a customer at the counter.

'Who?'

'Dunno. But you can see the smoke.'

Everyone peered out of the doorway and windows. To the east, above hundreds of spewing chimneys, the sky seemed a little thicker, a little more noxious.

'And that flaming Churchill's there.'

'*Mr* Churchill,' admonished a man near the window. 'He's the Home Secretary.'

'Huh,' said the other customer. 'He's to blame for all them foreign anarchists, ain't he? "Ooo let 'em in?" That's what they're shouting.'

'Who?'

'Them what's watching. Hurry up with that sandwich, will yer? I wanna go join in.'

Just after three p.m. the orderly came in, looking grim. 'Here's the latest. They took in a Maxim and—'

'What?' said Margaret, feeling the blood drain from her face. She imagined the machine gun rattling off rounds in that narrow street, bullets ricocheting off the overcrowded buildings and the guilty and innocent: police, soldiers, adults, children, Fox, Charles mown down in fragments of brick and mortar. She tensed. 'How many are hurt? When are they coming?'

'They ain't,' said the orderly. 'It was never used. The gunmen are dead and St J's has been stood down.' He shook his head. 'But the building's still on fire and a wall collapsed on a bunch of firemen. They've been taken to the London. If anyone dies, then the gang's as good as murdered him.' He heaved a sigh. 'What a day. It feels like this whole place has been on tenterhooks. I swear even them on their last legs on the wards haven't felt able to die. I feel like a stiff drink and I weren't even there.'

The clerk had slipped into the room. 'We'll get to see it for ourselves soon.'

'See what?' said Algie.

'The siege. There were people filming it for the newsreel, so it'll be in the cinema. Wonders of modern technology, eh? Anyway, telegram for you, Dr Demeray. The lad says it's urgent.'

Margaret tried not to run to the front desk. Her hand shook as she took the envelope and scanned the contents without reading them, seeking the signature first. It was from Bert.

Read it, she told herself.

He says tell the medic the prayers did the trick. Should be fit for the cinema and dinner on Thursday night.

'Any reply, madam?' said the telegram boy.

'Yes, please.' She scrawled *Thanks* on the back of the telegram, handed over the fee, then said to the clerk: 'Mr Holness, if I give you the money, would you go to the baker's and buy a selection of cakes? I think we all need them.'

On Thursday, Margaret sat in the cinema, holding hands with Fox. The newsreel of the events in Sidney Street was being shown again. She'd seen it twice before. Watching it the first time with her close friend Phoebe and the second with her older sister Katherine, Margaret had squinted at the men she thought were plain-clothes officers to see if any of them were Fox or Charles and failed. Even the third time, she still couldn't see them.

'You'll look till your eyes pop and won't spot Charles and me in that crowd,' he whispered.

'Were people really jeering Mr Churchill?'

'They were certainly jeering him in my part of the crowd. Another faction was cheering. Whether it was to show support for his policies or to cause trouble is anyone's guess.'

'Shhh,' said the person behind them.

'Let's go,' said Fox. 'I'm tired of watching this and I'm hungry.'

He stood, offered her his arm and they made their way to the aisle, annoying everyone in their vicinity, then left the cinema and drove to the hotel where Fox lived.

It wasn't until the end of their meal, that Margaret told him about Mr Green and Mrs Balodis. She gabbled through her planned visit to the police station, hoping that Fox wouldn't work out that she'd nearly gone after dark. But it was a failed hope.

'I sometimes wonder if you leave your brains in a jar,' he said. 'And you think you have the right to worry about me. Never mind: even if you'd forgone the police station, you'd have been turned back before you got much further.'

'I've worked that out since.'

Fox grinned at her over his wine glass. 'Now the area's clear, you can visit the Balodis offspring tomorrow lunchtime like a sensible woman.'

'Hardly,' said Margaret. 'They both have jobs. That was the whole point of going in the evening. It'll have to wait till Sunday.'

She waited for him to offer to go with her, but the waiter had brought the brandy and while it was poured, Fox stared out into the blackness beyond the windows. The hotel only ran to an orchestra at weekends, so someone had put a recording of a schottische on a gramophone. Fox's fingers tapped his glass to the rhythm. He still seemed on edge.

'You say Charles didn't come back with you,' said Margaret. 'Why not?'

'He's following a different lead,' said Fox. 'I'm certain that Anderson will keep away from the anarchists for now and my part of the investigation is effectively digging through paperwork.' He pulled a face. 'But just in case he doesn't, Charles is deep in among the locals. At the moment a lot of them are keen to distance themselves from Gardstein, and they're more likely to talk to Charles as he knows several languages.'

'So do you.'

'I don't know Russian, Polish, Hebrew and Yiddish anywhere near as well as someone whose parents came from Lemberg and changed their name in the sixties.'

'I always forget that about Charles.'

'Because he wants you to,' said Fox. 'You know him as a suburban solicitor's son with journalistic ambitions. That's partly who he is and partly his cover. But he can just as easily play the newly arrived immigrant and merge into the background in the East End and people would say "I never knew he was English born and bred".' Fox fiddled with his glass and cleared his throat. Three other couples were spinning elegantly to the music. 'Let's dance.'

He led her onto the floor and drew her into his arms. To her surprise, he was trembling. She could feel his heart thudding against hers. 'Are you worried about Charles?' she asked.

'What?' said Fox. 'Oh. A little.'

'He knows what he's doing,' Margaret squeezed his shoulder. 'He'll come back a bit grubbier than before, just like you do.'

'Of course,' said Fox, pulling her closer still. 'It's a tricky job, though. It's why he thinks he should stay single.'

'That's a shame,' said Margaret.

'He thinks, given our work, that a wife would have to put up with absences, silences, possible threats and danger, and it's not fair.'

'Then he ought to ask the potential wife if she's prepared to take the risk.'

'Would you be?'

'What?' Margaret leaned back and looked up into his face. His usual nonchalance was gone. His expression was blank, but it was a wary blankness.

'I'm so in love with you,' he said. 'Even though you thought about going to Whitechapel in pitch darkness when there's a criminal gang running loose.' A grin flickered across his face then faded. 'But I'm a man who might lead danger to your door, and that terrifies me.'

'You brought danger to my door last summer and I survived.'

'I'm being serious. I can't always tell you where I'm going or where I've been and one day… One day Bert may come and tell you that I'm never coming back.'

'Fox, whatever are you talking about? I've known all this since last June.'

'Then let's get married.' His tone was casual, but she realised they'd stopped dancing and her mouth had fallen open.

Fox looked into her eyes, his face full of doubt. 'Doesn't it appeal?'

'More than you can imagine,' she said.

'Damn,' said Fox. 'You said yes. Now I'll have to do it.' But his face shone and he kissed her full on the lips despite the disapproving dancers who were colliding with them. Then he drew back with a frown. 'Should I ask your father for your hand?'

'I'm about to turn thirty-seven. My hand is my own responsibility.'

'I haven't bought a ring. And I'll have to tell you my proper name.' He pulled a face.

Margaret blinked. 'Isn't Fox your name?'

'No, and very much yes. I'll keep it a surprise till we tell the vicar.'

'It can't be as bad as my middle name.'

'It'll be worse. My parents were Scots. My maternal grandfather had a strange sense of the romantic and Scottified his English-sounding surname. My mother added it to to my father's when they married and decided to give me a middle name that's, well, unusual. But the surname's worse. You can change your mind if it puts you off.'

'I'm fully intending to keep my own surname. Yours is your own concern.'

'You'll have to pronounce it in public when we marry,' said Fox. 'Stop laughing. I thought you'd say no. I've been hinting for months, but you've been so oblivious that I thought you were trying to let me down gently. Are you really sure? Despite everything you know about me and my job?'

'Of course I'm sure,' said Margaret. She was shaking with happiness. She wanted to hold him and kiss him and never let him go. She could have fought a dragon if one had been handy. 'And if Bert ever tells me he thinks you might not be able to come back, so help me, I'll go and get you myself. You're not getting away that easily.'

Three

Myrdle Street at ten a.m. on Sunday was busy. With the police presence in the area higher than normal, Margaret felt less uneasy than she might have, although part of her wished that she'd asked Fox to come with her. But he needed to be away with his mission until Tuesday and it had seemed pointless mentioning it again. In broad daylight, she convinced herself there was nothing to fear except feeling conspicuous.

Under a chilly but blue sky, women gossiped in doorways and men came in and out of a public house, or loitered in idle groups sharing cigarettes. There were few signs that a siege had taken place only a short distance away.

Small boys chucked stones at the remaining glass on the street lamps, or flung ropes around their curlicues to swing from them. Other children, half of them barefoot, kicked cans, rolled marbles and bowled misshapen hoops. Several narrowly missed Margaret's ankles, to derisive laughter and cheers from the adults looking on.

Even in daylight it was hard to find the address, and while the locals watched her they didn't speak to her, chattering and shouting at each other in a rapid, almost indecipherable dialect combining rhyming slang, rogues' cant and Yiddish. Margaret understood only a few of the words and knew it was being done to exclude and intimidate her.

Sooty buildings loomed on either side, with peeling paint and windows curtained with ragged blankets, but the street seemed tidier than was usual. There was no litter in the gutters, no horse droppings on the road. It looked as if it had been cleared for a performance. Margaret was wondering if they were expecting a Salvation Army band to appear, and what reception it would get if it did when a tiny woman of indeterminate age asked what she was doing.

'I'm looking for Mrs Agnes Balodis's children. I'm from the hospital.'

'You the lady almoner? You gonna chuck her out after all unless she coughs up?'

'No,' said Margaret, wondering if the woman had any idea of the irony of her terminology. 'I'm here to let them know their mother's been taken to Frimley Sanatorium.'

'Where's Frimley?'

'Surrey.'

The woman looked blank.

'South-west of London. In the countryside.'

'Gor, things people will do to get an 'oliday.' The woman's sorrowful expression belying the joke. 'Come on, then.' She stomped down the street, shoved open a door which looked as if it would disintegrate under the force and yelled up into the darkness. 'Annie! Visitor!' She turned to Margaret, holding the door open. 'Up two flights o' stairs, second door on the left.'

The air inside the building seemed a solid, malevolent entity, concocted from rising damp, black mould, cabbage, sweat and mice. As she climbed the pitch-dark stairwell, it was only the sudden added element of ammonia that stopped Margaret putting her hand on some badly laundered babies' napkins draped across the peeling bannister rail. She held her skirts as high as she could to avoid them brushing the stairs. Several steps were spongy underfoot; she imagined herself putting her foot through one and ending up trapped with a broken ankle in this dingy, nameless building, peered at by its innumerable, invisible inhabitants as dogs might contemplate a rabbit in a snare.

On the second floor, light shone from a door and a young woman stood waiting, arms folded. 'You the doctor what wrote?'

'Dr Demeray,' said Margaret, holding out a hand. 'And you're Miss Balodis.'

After a second's hesitation, the other woman shook hands. 'Yeah. And it's Anna,' she said. 'That ole bat calls me Annie just to rile me. Come in. Pardon the mess, the parlourmaid's orf sick.'

She led Margaret into a room which overlooked the street. Squeezed into it were a double bed, a small disintegrating wardrobe, a table with two mismatched chairs and a low cupboard on which stood a one-ring kerosene stove bearing a boiling kettle. 'Cuppa?'

'Yes, please.'

'You'll have to sit on the bed. The chair legs ain't to be trusted and I can't have a lady falling on her arse.' If Anna was joking, it was hard to tell. She was small like her mother. Dark heavy eyebrows frowned over small blue eyes and her mouth was narrowed in ... Suspicion? Disapproval? Wariness? She wore a simple dress which was in the latest fashion, but unusually constructed. The bodice, sleeves and skirts were from different but complementary fabrics, from pearl grey to dove grey to smoky grey, and those elements were made of multiple patches sewn together so that the joins were barely discernible, giving the impression of facets on a gemstone. Her straight dark hair fell to her waist, held back by a simple band made from the same pearly fabric as her sleeves.

'That's a pretty dress,' said Margaret.

Anna shrugged. 'Got to be some advantages to working in a sweat-shop, only don't tell ole Sullivan. We ain't s'posed to take the remnants home, but we all do. I only wear it Sunday.' She spooned tea into a brown metal teapot, filled it with hot water, then extracted two cups from the cupboard. 'Hope you don't want milk. We ain't got none.'

'It's fine without.' Margaret scanned the room, noting a curtain across one of its corners behind which might be a narrow bed.

'That's the west wing of the castle where my brother sleeps,' said Anna. 'Here's your tea.' She slammed herself down on one of the chairs, making one of its legs twist in an unnatural manner. 'Cut the cackle. When's Ma coming home?'

'She's gone to Frimley Sanatorium. It's in the countryside to the south west of London.'

'Ain't she the lucky one.' Anna's scowl deepened. 'Is that it?'

'Your mother asked me to come and speak with you.'

Anna's expression of belligerence quivered. 'She ain't coming home, is she?'

Margaret shook her head. 'I'm sorry. She's terribly ill. The best the sanatorium can do is make her comfortable and give her plenty of clean air and fresh food.'

'I knew it.' Anna slammed her free fist on the table. Tea spilled over its scrubbed surface. 'It's the bloody sweatshop. Most of the older ones have got cotton lung. It's no wonder, what with breathing in dust and bits of thread all their lives. We all got a cough, and Ma's been working there thirty years. I'm gonna...' She drew a deep breath. 'Why couldn't she stay at St Julia's? It's a chest 'ospital, ain't it?'

'She's dying from consumption, Miss Balodis, not cotton lung. We're not allowed to keep TB patients in a London hospital: it's too contagious. If you and your brother come in to St Julia's to be examined, it will put your mother's mind at rest.'

Anna sniffed. 'So it's not ole Sullivan's fault, then.'

'Your mother's diagnosis includes cotton lung, and that's made it worse. If you tell me which sweatshop employs you, I can report it to the authorities. Your mother wouldn't. But chest diseases come from more than just that.' She tried not to look at the damp in the corner or the musty bed on which she sat.

Anna was not a fool. 'One day soon, men like Sullivan will be put asunder and everyone will have decent housing and working conditions.'

'If you had the vote, that could help,' said Margaret. 'The suffrage movement aims to get it for everyone, whatever their sex, whatever their rank, and regardless of whether they have property.'

'The whole system's corrupt,' said Anna. 'Why be part of it? We need something new.' She swallowed. 'But thank you, doctor. A lot of people like you wouldn't bother. Can we go and see Ma?'

'Here's the address,' said Margaret, handing it over. 'It's probably best to write. She asked if you had a photograph you could give me to get copied.' She glanced at the mantelpiece, where a framed picture of four people and a baby stood between a clock and a china shepherdess.

'We'll get it done. No need to trouble you no more.'

'If you're sure,' said Margaret. She rose to her feet just as a cheer came up from the street below.

'They're here,' said Anna. She went to the window.

Margaret waited to hear the sound of the Salvation Army band, but there was nothing. Just cheers and shouting.

Anna snorted. 'More capitalist nonsense. They say they just want to make people happy. But is it happiness if you stop realising life's so bad you have to do something about it?'

Curious, Margaret put her cup down on the table and went to join Anna at the window. On the street below the locals had formed a semicircle, leaving the street ahead of them clear, and to Margaret's immense surprise, a film crew was there. One man operated a camera, another shouted directions while a woman in a blue hat pointed, and two young men in suits made exaggerated gestures as a motor car bore down on them, in the back of which a young woman struggled in bonds that a six year old could have undone.

'The cinema is as much of a drug as religion,' muttered Anna. 'Maybe it's worse. People think it's all true cos it's photographs. But see here.' She snatched the photograph from the mantlepiece and stabbed a finger at the toddler lolling in her mother's arms, eyes wide, curls arranged prettily round a happy face. 'My little sister looks full of life, don't she? But she was dead when this was took; they painted her eyes and smile on. It was the only way we could remember her. So it's a lie, and moving pictures is just the same. What's the point of them?'

Margaret peered down into the crowd.

Anna turned from the window. Her eyes sparkled but her head was high. 'I'll show you out. Not sure how long we can afford this place without Ma's wages, though.'

They made their way down the stairs and into the street. Someone with a megaphone was trying to keep the onlookers quiet while picking out children to take part in the scene.

'It's like we're zoo animals,' muttered Anna. 'I bet he's only picking the raggedest but prettiest ones. He wouldn't pick me.'

'I know a dressmaker who could make good use of your skills,' shouted Margaret over the noise. 'She's very strict about good working conditions. I could give you her details.'

'I got my own plans,' Anna shouted back. 'I don't need another toff offering work.'

'If you change your mind, contact me at the hospital.'

'Maybe.'

'And think about finding a suffrage group.'

'Like I said, I got my own plans.'

Anna stood with her back to the crowd, hugging herself in the chilly air. 'Best get out of here before it gets rowdy.' Her scowl softened into a half-smile. 'Which it will once they realise not everyone's gonna be in the film and the kids get a penny each tops.'

They shook hands and Margaret headed towards the tube. She knew she was being observed, and once she was nearly beyond the crowd, Margaret heard footsteps behind her. They sounded too heavy to be Anna's. The sense of being watched became menacing. *It's because of the siege. It's because Fox will disapprove of my coming alone. It's all in my head.* But the feeling increased. *Should I turn and confront them or should I just run? The main road's not far.*

More footsteps, this time lighter and faster.

'Here,' said Anna, running up beside her and hooking arms. 'You need an escort.' She looked over her shoulder. 'Does she look that sort to you, or don't yer care? Bastards.'

Margaret looked, too. On the pavement a small group of men stared, arms akimbo, uncertainty mingling with irritation. Had all of them been following her, or just one? Then, with a sickening shock, Margaret realised that one of them was Charles. He frowned, put his hands in his pockets, then pushed his way through the others and melted into the throng.

Four

Monday morning brought icy rain. The afternoon brought Constable Harris with another corpse. 'Mrs Green is safely in custody.'

'That's good news.' She pointed at the covered body. 'Who's this?'

Constable Harris scratched his nose. 'A puzzler.'

Margaret turned down the sheet to reveal a man in middle years, his grizzled grey hair cut very short, his skin heavily lined. Dried blood from a recent cut on his scalp had filled his left ear. He had been tall for a working man, nearly six feet in height, and his body strong and lean. With Algie's help, Margaret turned him over. There were no other wounds visible on the body except a contusion on the back of his head.

'His mate called him Dutch Jake,' said Constable Harris, 'but said his proper name was Jake Lang. We asked why Dutch, since Jake's Whitechapel born and bred, and he said, "Maybe his parents was Hollanders; you know what they're like for height". But in the dead man's pocket we found a letter from Hamburg addressed to Jakob – spelled with a K– Lang. Is that a Dutch name?'

'It could be from any number of countries,' said Margaret, 'including Britain.'

'Why get a letter from Hamburg, then? The sarge knows a bit of German, and he said it was Lang's auntie telling him to pray for his relations.'

'Perhaps Lang's parents were German,' said Algie. 'If they came here fifty years ago with poor English and said they were "Deutsch", it's might have been misheard or misunderstood.'

'What happened?' said Margaret, examining the wounds. The injury to the back of his skull, which was covered in bits of plaster and wood shavings, would have been enough to concuss him badly. Killing him was another matter. She straightened up.

'He was labouring with a mate over Duval Street way in a rat-hole of a boozer called the King's Head. The mate thinks Lang was shot at. Says there was a loud, sharp pop and Lang cried out. The mate looked round and saw Lang clasping his ear and tripping backwards over some rubbish. Banged his head good and proper and never came round. I've seen men die like that before. Usually after a drunken punch-up, almost always an accident. Some men's skulls are thinner than others, I guess.'

'It depends how the brain is injured by the fall,' said Algie. 'Once we get inside, we'll have a better idea.'

Constable Harris managed to turn retching into a cough. 'It could just be a lump of plaster falling off the ceiling for all I know. That gaff's a proper mess. But if there's someone out there shooting at people we need to know.'

Margaret ran her finger along the graze. 'I'll need to consult an expert. Is there any reason why someone would shoot him?'

'His mate hinted it might be mistaken identity,' said Constable Harris. 'Things are a bit heated round there, as you know. And here's Jakob Lang with a foreign name and a letter from Hamburg in his pocket. The sarge says we can't trust the mate's evidence, but Lang's dead either way.'

Margaret nodded. 'It could be the blow to the head, or it could be his heart, or it could be something else entirely which we can't see just yet. I'm sorry, Constable Harris. I can't give you an immediate answer.'

The young policeman heaved a sigh. 'I'll go back and see if anything else was found in the King's Head, even if it was just an accident.' With a nod, he left the laboratory.

'I'll ask Dr Jordan,' sighed Margaret. 'This just looks like bad luck to me.' But even as she said it, she thought of Fox's theory that the Anderson threat was German.

She rushed into the corridor and accosted Constable Harris before he left. 'Can you get me a copy of the letter and bring it with you this afternoon?'

Constable Harris raised his eyebrows. 'How will that help?'

'It - er - it might explain if it caused Mr Lang some worry which might have made him easier to startle and fall.'

'If you say so,' said Constable Harris, clearly nonplussed. 'I'll see what I can do.'

Margaret arrived home exhausted. She lived in the top half of what had once been a family home. Mrs Winson, the sweet elderly lady who'd once owned the whole house, lived on the ground floor, although she was being pestered by her son to sell up and move in with him.

Being upstairs Margaret's flat afforded a view over a little park and plenty of light, but this evening, even climbing the single flight of stairs to her own door seemed too arduous to make it worthwhile and Margaret felt unaccountably on edge without anything to account for it. Jakob Lang had died from a bleed on the brain caused by striking his head. There was nothing to prove what made him fall. A ballistics specialist had given his view that the graze was not a bullet wound and later explained it to Constable Harris who returned at two with a transcript of the letter from Dutch Jake's pocket and a translation made by a colleague with a German grandmother. Applying her own knowledge of German, Margaret was certain it was as accurate as it was innocuous. A religious Roman Catholic aunt listed Katrin, Bartholemäus, Thomas, Guido, Julia, the Saviour and several Marias, before finishing with an admonition that Jake must remember the days when masses should be said. '*Nowhere will there be a change of date. Yours with shared devotion, Tante Victoria.*'

The rest of the day had passed in the normal ward rounds seeing patients with various chances of survival, clinical work and finally a practical session in the laboratory with a group of conscientious female students. Now it was dark and the temperature rapidly dropping. Before even closing the curtains, Margaret knelt to light the sitting room fire but it took five minutes of fiddling with matches and newspapers to make it draw, and when it finally caught, Margaret felt grubby and even more on edge.

The telephone rang when she was in the bath. By the time she'd got to the receiver in the sitting room, it had stopped. She'd only had the apparatus for six months and it already seemed more of a curse than a blessing.

Margaret dressed in front of the fire, then sat in the armchair with a novel and her cat Juniper, waiting for something to happen. 'Why do I feel like that?' she said aloud.

'Prrp?' suggested Juniper, curling up into a tighter ball.

The telephone remained silent.

Unsettled, Margaret lifted Juniper and cuddled her as she looked out of the front window onto the street. There was nothing to be seen. The occasional motor car passed, but none stopped. There was no one on the pavement or in the park opposite, as far as she could tell. Besides, it wasn't that kind of edginess. She returned to the chair and her book and after a while became so enthralled with its plot that the doorbell made her jump.

On the doorstep stood Charles, supporting Fox, half-slumped in his arms

'What's happ—' Margaret undid the chain. 'Quick, come in,' she whispered. 'Be quiet or Mrs Winson will come out.'

Fox rolled his eyes. 'We're engaged.'

'It's not that. She'll witter. And I want to know what's happened.'

In the sitting room, Margaret reached for Fox. He made a tiny sound of pain as she hugged him.

In the light, Margaret could see smears of mud on his clothes, a graze on the hand he was nursing, and a bruise starting on his left cheek.

'I lost an argument with a motor car,' he said. 'Our medic patched me up and poured aspirin down my throat.'

'Have you any brandy?' said Charles.

'He shouldn't have brandy as well as aspirin!'

'The brandy's for you and me.'

Margaret waved a hand at a cupboard but concentrated on easing Fox's coat off his shoulders. 'I want to see.'

'Fox wanted to come to you rather than his hotel,' said Charles. 'Will your neighbours—'

'Hang the neighbours,' snapped Margaret as Fox flopped onto the sofa.

'I telephoned, but you didn't answer,' said Charles.

Fox closed his eyes. 'We were afraid you were out visiting anarchists with sick mothers in insalubrious places.'

Margaret was baffled. 'How do you—'

'I told him I saw you with Anna Balodis,' said Charles. 'I followed to make sure those men didn't do anything, but I couldn't let on we were acquainted so I probably looked just as predatory as they did.'

'You didn't look predatory, Charles. You looked ... well, appraising.'

'I was wondering how you knew Anna.'

Margaret briefly explained.

'Ah,' said Charles. 'I've been working as assistant janitor for an anarchist paper *The Freedom Press.* Her brother Andris works there as a print setter. He's planning something with her, but won't say what. For a while I thought he was Anderson, but he's far too young and hot-headed. All the same, as anarchists, Andris and Anna Balodis are under observation by the police.'

Margaret recalled the furious young woman, defiant in the face of poverty, disease and prejudice, wearing a frivolous dress made of patches and scorning the moving picture crew. 'I understand her anger but I've no reason to see her again. What happened to Fox?'

'Someone tried to run him down. Another car appeared just as the driver was backing up, and then fortunately the beat bobby turned the corner, commandeered the second car and told the motorist to give chase. They'll catch him. We shouldn't have come and upset you. I can take Fox back to the hotel.'

'Over my dead body,' said Margaret. 'He's staying here. Telephone at seven, Charles and I'll say if he's fit to work.'

'But your neighbours—'

'As I said: hang the neighbours.'

Charles didn't move for a while, then snatched up his hat and left.

'It's only really my shoulder that hurts,' muttered Fox when he'd gone, wincing as Margaret removed his jacket and shirt to make a cursory examination. The injuries seemed slight, his body protected to some extent by his heavy winter coat.

She touched his head gently.

'That's nice,' he murmured, barely responding as she re-buttoned his shirt, put the blanket over him and held him gently against her breast. 'Is someone drumming a fandango somewhere, or is that your heart?'

'What would your heart be doing if I'd been knocked sideways by an idiot who can't control a car?'

'He could control it very well.'

'Please explain, Fox.' She couldn't quite keep the tremor out of her voice. He didn't answer. 'Charles doesn't want you to talk about this, does he?'

'He thinks it compromises both you and the mission,' said Fox. He struggled upright a little. 'But here goes. Anderson's planning to destabilise the whole country just as Britain is working on a treaty with the French.'

'And if France sees we're weak, maybe they'll make another treaty with someone else who will then put *us* under threat?'

'Exactly. Different sources say different things.' Fox paused. 'It started to look like anarchists, then agitators, and now spies. Every name, every address, every hint leads nowhere. I got home late last night from Dover. I'd intercepted some documents which shouldn't leave the country but they were nothing to do with Anderson.'

'You should have come here.'

'It was midnight. I planned to surprise you this evening instead.'

'Bravo. You succeeded.'

Fox laughed and then groaned in pain. 'First thing today, we received information suggesting that Anderson was operating in Glasshouse Street.'

'Off Piccadilly?'

'Yes. Charles and I went there. Nothing. We called back at the office and found the message might be wrong. So we went to Glass House in St Giles then Glass Street in Bethnal Green instead, but there was nothing there either. So we were back at square one. Then in the late afternoon, another message came in with a street in Hampstead. And in Hampstead, someone tried to run me over.'

'You're sure it was deliberate?'

'The driver had obscured the number plate and steered off the road towards me fast enough to knock me sideways, then while I was trying to get up, reversed and...'

'My God, Fox!' Margaret heard her voice falter. She wanted to say *Won't you give up, won't you find a nice quiet office job*, but couldn't. She must never influence his decisions even when she was his wife. And that wouldn't be until after Easter, to allow for arranging the big wedding that she'd imagined for since girlhood. *Why does it matter?* she suddenly thought. *Life is too short.*

Fox leaned in to her again.

Margaret held him close. 'Marry me,' she said.

'What?'

'Marry me.'

Fox lifted his head from her shoulder and frowned. 'I am. On April the twenty-third.'

'No. Now. Or very soon.'

'But you wanted a proper wedding to make up for the elopement with Owen.'

'I want you, Fox. I want to be able to go to bed with you without anyone muttering or me losing my job. I want to belong to you and have you belong to me. I want our lives to be the same life. I want you.'

Fox was dressed well before Charles rang on Tuesday morning. Pain made his face grey, but he refused any more aspirin and did his best to hide a slight limp as he paced the flat.

'Did you really propose to me last night?' he said

'Yes.'

'What did I say?'

'You said, "Just corner a man while he's down, won't you?"'

'I never pretended to be romantic.' Fox stared round the pretty room. 'I still haven't bought you an engagement ring, let alone found a house for us.'

'There's no rush. We have here until we find something.'

'Here's not quite big enough for the contents of the old family home I have in storage. And I need somewhere to go where I won't disturb you when work is chaotic. I'll keep the hotel room till we have a house.'

'We could manage.' Margaret followed his gaze. The flat was very much hers, very feminine. And she had no idea how much stuff he'd kept from the home he'd sold after his wife's death.

Fox nudged her out of her reverie. 'Did we choose a date?'

'My birthday: the twenty-first. Just over a fortnight away. We decided to book the Curzon in Brighton for a two night honeymoon.'

'Did we? What else did we do that I don't remember?'

'Nothing. You fell asleep and snored like a steam engine. Juniper was most affronted.'

'Tsk,' he said. 'I must have been ill.'

Charles telephoned just as they were finishing breakfast.

'Hallo?' said Fox. 'Yes, I'm fine to come in... You needn't bother, I'll take the tube... What? Really? The man's a blithering fool. I've a good mind to run *him* over. I suppose I should be relieved. Back to the cross-referencing, then.' He replaced the receiver and looked over at Margaret. 'Apparently Hampstead was wrong, too. We didn't need to be there.'

'But someone tried to run you over!'

'Someone tried to run *someone* over. The policeman who commandeered the other car found the one that hit me in a ditch. The driver was unconscious, but came round this morning and said he was hired to steal the car and scare its owner by knocking him down. It's a police matter. I was just in the wrong place and more importantly, wasting time. Which we're doing now too. Haven't you any work to do? Lungs to prod? Murder victims to dissect?'

'Oh don't.' Margaret explained about Jakob Lang.

Fox put down his coffee cup. 'A letter from Germany?'

'Hamburg. But it's just a religious aunt prompting about devotions. Here.' She extracted the transcript and translation from her handbag and passed them to him.

'Are those all real saints' names?'

'I'm far too low church to know for certain,' said Margaret. 'But I think so. Besides, I'm fairly sure there's a saint for every name you can imagine.'

'I bet there isn't for mine,' said Fox darkly. He refolded the letter back. 'As you say, there's nothing interesting. Just sad. Someone will be saying mass for Jakob Lang now.'

'I imagine so.'

Fox rose and bent to give her a kiss, with the tiniest noise of pain as he did so. 'Cheer up Margaret. I'm alive. And you're alive. Let's rush into a wedding.'

Five

On the afternoon of the wedding, Katherine and Phoebe arrived at the flat with their arms full of boxes. Margaret's other close friend Maude was waiting for them at the church since there would be no room in the car for her.

Before Margaret could protest, Phoebe swept up the outfit she'd laid out on the bed and put them away.

'But that's my prettiest suit and hat. I—'

'You don't need them,' said Phoebe firmly.

'Maria's dressmaking staff had a lull,' said Katherine, handing Margaret the largest box. 'Don't just stand there gawping, Meg, open it.'

Inside was a dress of ivory satin with a hint of pink. 'Oh Kitty. Is some of this material...?'

'Mother's wedding dress from 1864,' confirmed Katherine. 'The skirts then were made with enough fabric to make three gowns nowadays.' She chuckled, but both of them smoothed the fabric for a moment, remembering the woman who'd died thirty-one years earlier.

The new skirt was of smooth unembellished satin, crossing at the waist but cut away to reveal an embossed underskirt before becoming a short train. The bodice also crossed, with the right side and sleeve in sleek satin, the right in the same embossed fabric as the underskirt, and a fine lace modesty panel with a high neck under it.

'Maria thought she knew what you'd like,' said Katherine, her voice uncertain. 'Do you?'

'It's absolutely beautiful. I don't know what to say...'

'Your face says everything Margaret,' said Phoebe. 'Here are your shoes and veil. I've brought a shawl too. An evening wedding's all very well, but it's very cold.'

'Come on,' said Katherine. 'Let's get you dressed before Father and James arrive.'

It seemed rather silly to drive to a church which was five minutes' walk away, but at eighty-one, Father was none too steady on his feet in daylight, let alone after sunset. Margaret sat between Phoebe and Katherine, wrapped in the shawl, shivering from anticipation and cold.

The church looked beautiful in the evening darkness, with lights and candles twinkling through the windows, but it also looked huge, the spire disappearing into the night sky.

'Oh, my dear little Meg,' said Father, tucking her hand into his elbow and patting it as they made their way to the entrance. 'What a wonderful idea to marry at night! So magical!'

'There aren't many of us,' she whispered. 'We'll positively rattle. Fox is here, isn't he?'

'Of course he is,' said Maude, stepping out of the porch and taking her place with Katherine and Phoebe.

'Are you ready, Meg?' said Father.

'Yes.'

The doors opened. The organ stopped and after a short pause started playing Handel. At the end of the aisle, Margaret could make out Fox and Charles. Charles was peering round, but Fox wasn't. The aisle looked ridiculously long. Father's arm was trembling in hers and then they stepped into the church itself. Now she was nearly at the altar and now she was standing beside Fox. At last he turned and stared as if he'd never seen her before, his face flooded with joy.

The music stopped. 'Dearly beloved,' intoned the rector, 'we are gathered together here in the sight of God—'

His words washed over Margaret. She shivered, and she wasn't certain if it was from cold, nervousness or joy. Then the rector asked if anyone knew of any just impediment and her heart stopped. But there was no sound but the rustle of pages in prayer books and feet shifting on the stone floor.

The rector took a breath as he prepared to attempt Fox's full name. 'David Reynard Foxcroft-MacSionnach,' he mumbled, then raised his voice again, 'wilt thou have this woman to thy wedded wife, to live together after God's ordinance in the holy estate of matrimony? Wilt thou love her, comfort her, honour, and keep her, in sickness and in health; and, forsaking all other, keep thee only unto her, so long as ye both shall live?'

'I will.' said Fox.

'Margaret Calliope Demeray, wilt thou have this man to thy wedded husband, to live together after God's ordinance in the holy estate of matrimony? Wilt thou love him, comfort him, honour, and keep him, in sickness and in health; and, forsaking all other, keep thee only unto him, so long as ye both shall live?'

'I will.'

'Who giveth this woman to be married to this man?'

'I do,' boomed Father. 'I've finally managed to give a daughter away instead of them getting married without me.'

The rector blinked.

'Shh, Father,' said Katherine. 'You weren't supposed to say the last bit out loud.'

Fox grinned, but as they clasped hands and made their vows, either she was trembling or he was or both. It was impossible to be sure.

And finally the rector said, 'You may kiss the bride,' and Fox kissed her shyly as if it was the first kiss that had ever happened.

'Your mother was mad, Reynard,' she whispered.

'So is your father, Calliope,' he murmured through a second kiss. 'It was in the stars from the start.'

Arm in arm, they turned away from the altar. Margaret had somehow forgotten that anyone but her, Fox, and the rector was present, and found herself blinking at the rows of friends and relations smiling or dabbing their eyes in the soft light of flickering candles.

Katherine, Phoebe and Maude stood up to take their places with Charles in the aisle. 'I can't believe you're going to be Mrs Fox-thingy-McWotsit,' whispered Phoebe. 'As if your full name isn't enough of an unspellable mouthful.'

Margaret grimaced. 'I'm keeping Demeray thank-you. But how are my students ever going to take me seriously now they know my middle name's Calliope?'

'You know, Meg,' boomed Father as the organist stopped playing to reorganise her music, 'I really wanted to have you christened Boadicea, but your mother and the vicar refused for some reason. They weren't too happy with Calliope, either. Perhaps I should have chosen a different Muse. Polyhymnia, for example, or maybe— Ow! You trod on my foot, Kitty!' But his remonstrations were drowned out by the Wedding March.

As they made their way down the aisle, Fox leaned towards her. 'I'm sorry we can't have a proper honeymoon for a few months,' he whispered. 'It's your fault for rushing me into the noose.'

'Two nights in Brighton will be fine,' she whispered back. 'You'll have to surprise me there, as well as wherever you have planned for April.'

'I intend to. When can we— Wait a moment, someone's outside.' He slowed down and pulled her close.

Margaret peered out. She could see nothing but the parked cars, the solitary tree and a street lamp. It was possible there was a cat in its shadow, peeking out. The other side of the road was in darkness, the trees in the gardens opposite held in by fences. 'I'm sure—'

'Here they come! Quick!'

'That's Algie! What on earth are they doing?'

She stepped out of the porch and onto the steps of the church just as two rows of students on either side of her lined up, giggling. They were making an arch with various medical instruments from stethoscopes to forceps, and in Algie's case, a saw. Light from the church glinted off it, and the half-seen cat in the shadows slinked out of sight.

Fox leaned in to whisper. 'If I'd known quite how mad everyone connected with you is, I might have reconsidered marriage. I'm hoping you can convince me it was worth it later.'

'I will,' she whispered back. 'As long as you will, too.'

Margaret returned to work the Tuesday after the wedding, still dreamy and walking on air.

Constable Harris had written to say that the investigation into Jakob Lang's death had been officially abandoned. '*The mate's gone to ground, the pub has been redecorated and renamed the Dolphin. It's impossible to tell if there's a bullet in there and even if there is, it could be from another time entirely. It's that kind of place. Besides, it wasn't a bullet that killed him, just bad luck. If he hadn't fallen, he'd have been all right.'*

It was no great surprise but she hoped the constable's enthusiasm for detection hadn't been crushed. She would have to write an encouraging reply later, but first she needed to see Dr Jordan to find out what duties she needed to undertake.

She entered his office feeling warm and happy. 'Good morning. I hope you enjoyed the reception on Saturday and that Father didn't corner you for too long.'

She expected a cheery and perhaps slightly coy query after her short honeymoon, but instead there was a silence as chilly as November fog. A red flush started up from Dr Jordan's collar and he dropped his gaze, removing his glasses to polish them. Finally, without looking at her, he said, 'Your wedding was delightful, as is your father. But it's left us with a problem.'

Margaret felt her face go cold and then hot. 'Us? Who?'

'Technically, I suppose, only you. But I personally feel that it affects both of us.'

'I'm sorry, Dr Jordan, I don't follow.'

'My dear, don't you know?' He addressed a filing cabinet. 'It was quite hard enough persuading the board to promote you in the event of my retirement when you were single. They consider it quite impossible in view of your marriage.' Dr Jordan replaced his glasses and sighed, then looked into her face. 'In fact, the board feels that you should resign from your current position immediately.'

'But—'

'Nurses have to resign if they marry.'

'But I'm not a nurse.'

'Are you going to tell them that it's different for a doctor?'

Margaret was afraid to speak. Anger, humiliation and hurt grappled for the upper hand and she was scared of what she would say. She should have been prepared for this. She ought to have known.

'I'm trying to persuade them otherwise,' said Dr Jordan, 'but many feel it's a step too far and I can't think of another London hospital that would have a different policy. I'm doing my best to argue your case, Dr Demeray – Margaret – and I'll be very sorry to lose you. Despite being an old fogey, you know I don't think this is fair, but I can't see it changing for a long time.'

'Yes, sir,' Margaret had to force herself not to look away.

'Could your husband find more police work for you to assist with?'

'It's not quite that simple.'

'Not, I suppose you can't just conjure it up. Well, I have some alternative suggestions for you. You'd be ideally suited to teaching. Our medical school wouldn't take you, but another might. And of course there's private research. You'd just need a sponsor. Perhaps your cousin, Mr Lamont? Or you could see if a pharmaceuticals company will take a married woman.'

'I...' Margaret felt her voice crack and closed her mouth.

Dr Jordan pondered. 'I had a junior doctor several years ago who was once in a similar position. She had great promise, but married and had to resign. Fortunately her husband had enough money to set her up a small private practice. I lost touch with her some time ago, but recently saw in the Lancet that she's looking for a partner. You wouldn't get rich, but since I presume Superintendent er... Fox has sufficient means to support you, I imagine that's less important.'

Margaret didn't entirely trust herself to speak, but managed to choke out. 'May I address the board?'

'I'm sure that can be arranged. In the meantime...'

'In the meantime, may I go out for some fresh air?'

'Of course,' said Dr Jordan, patting her vaguely on the shoulder before removing his glasses again. His eyes seemed moist. 'And maybe addressing a board meeting *will* make all the difference.'

'Yes,' said Margaret. But even as she said it, she knew it was unlikely. The rules were the rules.

Sitting in the café regaining her composure, she felt tears prick her eyes. Then two of the more old-fashioned hospital governors passed, laughing, and she gritted her teeth. She extracted the Lancet from her handbag and turned its pages until she found the advertisement that Dr Jordan must have meant.

Dr C Fernsby, MD offers a partnership in her modern, centrally located practice near Shaftesbury Avenue. Patients are drawn from all ranks in the district and there is the opportunity to work with a wide range of medical conditions. Enquiries to 47 Glassmakers Lane.

It could do no harm to enquire. Dr Fernsby had found a way and Margaret was not prepared to give up the fight just yet.

Six

She arrived at the flat first that evening. After feeding Juniper, she contemplated the contents of the pantry, devoid of inspiration and longing for Fox to come home so that she could tell him everything.

He bounded in waving a bottle of champagne. 'Forget cooking, we're going out to celebrate. Let's start with this.'

She followed him into the sitting room. 'What are we celebrating?'

'We've got Anderson,' said Fox, popping the cork and pouring them each a glass.

'You have?'

'Well, Charles has. He was right all along. After all those months he's spent infiltrating the anarchist cells, he cornered the little weasel in Bethnal Green. He's just a shop-assistant with a sideline in burglary and consequently all sorts of other people's cash and valuables under the floorboards.'

Margaret frowned. 'To support the anarchist cause?'

'Anderson's not an anarchist. We didn't need to be involved. He really is a small-time criminal. I thought maybe there was a link to something bigger. He's not even called Anderson but Abolin. Changed it to sound less Latvian I imagine.'

'Aren't you worried there's still something else?'

'Of course there's still something else. But it isn't Peter Abolin.'

It was impossible to destroy this triumph with her bad news. 'You look as if a weight has lifted from your shoulders.'

'It has: this was a regular police job all along. If they'd had the gumption to have their constables learn the right languages, they could have done this themselves. Charles has been in the thick of it, risking his life for nothing.' Fox sat back with his champagne and Juniper jumped into his lap, rubbing her head against the bottom of the glass. 'Now we've established that there's no connection between what Charles has been looking into and what I'm investigating, he can get on with helping me.'

And that will involve both of your risking your lives, thought Margaret, but there was no point saying it out loud and making him regret confiding in her. 'Shouldn't you and Charles be celebrating together?'

'I wanted you to join us. He's inviting Phoebe, in case male conversation gets too much for you. And we're going to the picture house afterwards to bring it down to the female level of intellect. Did I say something? It's a joke.'

'I'm sorry,' said Margaret, smoothing the scowl from her face. 'A bubble went up my nose. So this Abolin was on his own?'

'It appears so,' said Fox sighed. 'A known local fence peached on him to the police. Said he'd been approached to buy goods, but he was far to respectable to buy things he thought questionable. That suggests that Abolin was trying to muscle in on someone else's operation and the fence had too much sense of self-preservation to get involved. The fence gave an address and said the lodger in question was ill.'

'Ill with what?'

'Pneumonia.' Fox's face clouded. 'As much trouble as he's caused, it's no pleasure to see him like that. He's barely conscious now but the police surgeon says he'll recover enough to be questioned in a day or so. You might have a different professional view of course.'

Margaret downed her champagne.

'Hey, slow down,' said Fox. He contemplated her. 'Is something wrong? You look a little—'

'Tiring day,' said Margaret. *It's not a lie,* she told herself as she went to change out of her work clothes. *It's not the whole truth, but now is not the time. It can wait.*

The following day, Margaret addressed the hospital board.

She faced the seven men and one woman and paused before speaking, trying to gain the upper hand by appearing cool as she prepared to merge the calm, logic she applied when speaking at suffragette rallies with the righteous call to reason and justice she applied when speaking to landlords' associations. She didn't mind the board declaring her passionate. She didn't want them labelling her hysterical. With the exception of a few, the doctors, clergyman, aristocrats and laymen before her returned her gaze as if they were judge, jury and executioner and that sentence was already passed.

'I have worked at St Julia's for over five years,' she said. 'I was a widow when I arrived here and worked as a married woman at the Women's Free prior to my husband's death without incident.'

'I gather that neither the marriage nor the husband were known to that board,' said the vice chairman. 'We have done our research.'

Margaret felt the notes in her hand grow damp with perspiration. 'The chairman knew and thought it irrelevant to my capacity. My husband and I separated soon after the wedding.'

'If you make a habit of *that*,' drawled one of the aristocrats, 'we may be able to keep you on after all.' He chortled at his own joke and even though no one else joined in, Margaret wished she could melt him by force of thought alone.

'But, my dear,' said an elderly layman, 'now that you have reached the pinnacle for womanhood - a second time - I'm sure you'd like to avoid the same thing occurring. We all wish you the very greatest success for this marriage and a quiverful of sons for your husband. But you cannot apply yourself to that and work.'

'I very much can,' said Margaret. She felt her temper rising and wrestled it back under control. 'I have proved myself a sufficiently valuable pathologist that in the last month, the police have brought two possible murder victims to this hospital rather than St Mary's. Moreover, the students I've mentored passed at the top of their classes in pathology.'

'Police autopsies are nothing but a nuisance,' argued the vice-chairman. 'And I am concerned about women - married or otherwise - tutoring young men. I've long feared that women doctors sap their moral fibre by making them sentimental.'

'Not to mention,' said the aristocrat, 'that we had two not play for the hospital first eleven because of their insistence on working late on their studies or some cure or other. We lost to St Barts by ten wickets.'

'I'm proud that they think medical work's more important than sport,' snapped Margaret.

Several of the men exchanged horrified glances.

'But sport is how one gets on,' explained the vice-chairman. 'Appointments, faculties, partnerships, chairmanships, all that sort of thing. The backbone of the country depends on connections made at school and through cricket and rugby. This just proves the point that a woman simply can't understand every aspect of working life.

She can only remain focussed on one thing and if she marries, that one thing will be her husband - quite rightly.' He appealed to the only woman on the board. 'Surely you agree that Dr Demeray cannot stay, Matron Johnson. Nurses must resign once they're married; you've said so yourself. So surely you think a female doctor should.'

Matron pondered, her lips pursed. 'Nursing is a hard profession requiring intelligence and dedication, but, there's a steady supply of nice young ladies bored senseless by the thought of matrimony and interested in a nursing career instead.'

'Bored by the thought of matrimony?' gasped the clergyman. 'It's unnatural! The pinnacle of womanhood, the arms of motherhood, the...'

'Going back to the point,' said Matron firmly. 'Britain has far too few female doctors – especially senior ones. Dr Demeray provides reassurance to our female patients and empathy - not sentiment, not sympathy, not emotion, but empathy - to male and female, which is very much appreciated.'

'Thank you Matron,' said Margaret.

'Well,' said the chairman, 'How do you intend to work while running a home Dr Demeray?'

'I've run my own home for ten years.'

'It's not really a home without a husband.' He bestowed an avuncular smile. 'Your husband's needs will prove very distracting.'

'How do the married men on this board manage to work while distracted by their wives' needs?' said Margaret. 'Do tell.'

Dr Jordan choked into his glass of water and Matron openly grinned. Through a mist of fury, Margaret was aware of a sea of red faces.

'We will consider your request, Dr Demeray,' said the chairman, his voice cold.

'Thank you.' Margaret spoke through gritted teeth. It took all her energy to turn with head held high, walk slowly to the door and pass through without slamming it. Outside in the corridor, she leaned for a moment against the solid oak which seemed to stand between her and her ambitions. When she opened her palm to unfold her notes, she saw that they were blotched with ink. She willed her breathing to slow and her mind to refocus. There was work to be done and Algie didn't deserve her temper. If she needed to prove that she could work without letting other distractions stop her, now was the time.

That evening she and Fox went out for dinner.

'How was your day?' He said. 'What's wrong? You look pale.'

'You first.' Margaret wondered if she should invest in some rouge. 'You look paler.'

'I'm waiting for you to shout at me for obtaining some house details and orders to view on Saturday afternoon without asking your opinion.'

'We have to start somewhere. I shan't shout unless they're horrible.'

'Good. So what's —'

'Honestly, I do have something to discuss but I'm keen to know about Peter Abolin.'

The waiter came to take their order, then Fox pondered. 'The trial can't start for a few weeks. Charles gave the police a great deal of evidence to wade through, so they've released Abolin on bail for the time being.'

'Aren't they worried about him absconding?'

'Apparently not. He's living in a house they staff and monitor for the purpose and he's keeping himself to himself, accepts his guilt and seems to want it all over with. He's vague as to whose money and goods he'd garnered.'

'But it's a police case now and you aren't involved any more,' said Margaret.

'Yes, but Charles can't quite let go. Something's still bothering him.'

Margaret sipped her sherry. 'And you?'

'Nothing suggests Abolin is a threat to anyone but householders and perhaps local criminal gangs, although from what I hear, I doubt he has the personality to succeed. I think Charles just has a bee in his bonnet and the sooner he gets it out and helps me the better.'

'What will become of Abolin?'

'A long prison sentence I expect.'

'Doesn't it bother him?' Margaret imagined a lifetime in prison: the boredom, the cold, the repetitive breaking of stones or picking of oakum till the prisoner's hands, spirit and perhaps mind were destroyed.

Fox shrugged. 'You'd have thought so, but he seems content, or at least relieved. But that might be because he stepped on the toes of criminals who know what they're doing and thinks he'll be safe from reprisals in prison. He'll be lucky. But that's enough about him. What's wrong with you? Something is.'

Margaret took a gulp of wine. 'I'll probably have to leave St J's.'

'Why?'

'Because a married woman has to resign.'

Fox exploded. 'That's ridiculous!'

The couple on the nearest table tutted and glared.

'Shh,' said Margaret. 'It's normal. Don't the female employees in your organisation have to leave?'

'But...' He reached for her hand. 'When did you find out?'

'The day Abolin was arrested.'

'Why didn't you say?'

'Because I didn't want to spoil the moment and because... because I feel something of a failure.'

'You aren't a failure. They are. I've a good mind to—'

'To what? Prove their point by going round and demanding as a husband that they treat your chattel with respect?'

'I don't think of you as—'

'I know. But apparently I'm going to be distracted by your needs and should concentrate on giving you a quiverful of sons.'

'I'm quite sure you're capable of doing both without failing at your job. And I don't want a quiverful, however many that is. I want two quiversful.' His mouth twitched and Margaret's self pity started to fade. 'So what are you going to do?'

'I've written to some pharmaceutical companies and sanatoria. And there's a female doctor looking for a partner. It could work, though I never planned to go into private practice.'

Fox squeezed her hand. 'I can see if there's more ways you can help us.'

'That's not paid though,' said Margaret. 'I always swore I wouldn't be dependent on any man for money.'

'Whereas I'd be quite happy if you supported me.'

'No you wouldn't.'

'I'm sorry,' said Fox, his scowl returning. 'I wish I could help. St J's would be fools to let you go.'

'Fools or not,' said Margaret. 'They might. But I'm blowed if I'm going quietly.'

Seven

On the morning of Saturday 11th February, Margaret went to meet Dr Fernsby in Glassmakers Lane.

Not far from Leicester Square, the neo-classical cul-de-sac ran parallel with Shaftesbury Avenue. Situated midway between the unimaginable wealth of Piccadilly and the desperate poverty of Seven Dials, Glassmakers Lane was equally midway in terms of social status, containing a number of average sized private residences and a mix of small businesses including Madam's Modes, Soffiato's Licensed Restaurant and Burton's Dispensing Chemist. At the very end, near a twenty-foot wall were two much older buildings, one of which was a grimy-windowed property with a rusty sign declaring it was called Nierling's. It appeared to sell old books, although it was doubtful it would be worth risking dust and spore inhalation to find out what sort. One way or another, they were likely to be grubby.

Between Burton's and a private lodging-house was what looked like an old grain store. It had recently been refurbished and bore a neat sign declaring that it housed Dysart's Film Studio. Turning her back on it, Margaret saw what she was looking for: a narrow building with a red front door and spotless windows brightened with boxes full of optimistic foliage. The paintwork gleamed, as did the doorstep and the brass plaque: Dr C Fernsby, M.D. In any other set of circumstances, it would have made Margaret's heart leap to see a woman doctor with her own private practice, but today, it sank lower than ever.

A young maid ushered Margaret into a waiting room and introduced her to the young receptionist, Miss Hill. Miss Hill rose with a smile and took Margaret through to Dr Fernsby's consulting room.

Dr Fernsby, a woman in her mid forties dressed in plain grey, was seated behind a folding typewriter, frowning at whatever she'd written. Her scowl vanished as Margaret was introduced. 'Delighted to meet you,' she said, rising to shake hands. She was in late pregnancy, her dress tight across a bulging waist. 'Do take a seat, Dr Demeray. It's nice to greet another woman doctor.'

'Have all the other interested parties been men?'

Dr Fernsby wrinkled her nose. 'I'll be frank, doctor, there have only been two. Yes, both men: one a wet-behind-the-ears, straight-out-of-medical-school puppy whose father came too and expected me to be glad a man would be taking charge. The other... Quite unsatisfactory.' She sniffed but said no more in explanation, briefly looking down to tidy her already tidy desk.

Margaret took the opportunity to scan the consulting room. It was uncluttered but not impersonal. A couch for examinations was set in a curtained alcove. There were bright, cheerful pictures on the walls and a set of funny wooden cats set out on a low table, carved and painted to look like a family.

Dr Fernsby followed her gaze. 'If the patient is a child, those help them feel less frightened. Sometimes they help them explain what's wrong. It can be depressingly revealing on occasion.' Her face darkened. 'I shan't pretend this is a wealthy practice. You can see where we're situated. The rich gravitate to Harley Street, so I have very few regular patients paying high fees, although there are a few senior civil servants and businessmen. Then I have several ladies of independent means who prefer a female doctor. Most patients are clerks, shopkeepers and senior servants, but I do have a large number of those who are lower ranking and generally pay in instalments, and quite a few below that, who pay into a fund in case they need a doctor when they don't have the wherewithal.'

'I see.'

'Tell me about yourself, Dr Demeray.'

'I trained at St Kimbrose, then worked in a private practice in Poplar until 1902 when I decided to specialise in pathology. I worked at the Women's Free until I obtained a more senior position in St Julia's a few years ago.'

Dr Fernsby stifled a yelp, winced, and shifted position, her hand on her bump. 'This wretched baby is trying to tunnel out through my ribs.' She contemplated Margaret with a grimace. 'My older children are in their teens. In case you're wondering, I'm forty-seven and quite aware of the risks of a pregnancy at my age. To be honest, I thought the likelihood was so negligible I didn't take the care I should have. Consider me a lesson in complacency. As you can imagine, I'm becoming desperate to find someone who's competent enough to manage alone for a few months.'

'I see.'

'Enough about me. How do you find pathology?'

'I love it. Our work will help us find cures for the conditions that now kill. We're getting more police work, too. I...' Margaret cast her eyes round the room. It was so very different from the mortuary wing.

'I can sense your passion. Would you feel the same here?'

It was pointless to prevaricate. 'You've been frank and so shall I. I didn't enjoy private practice when I was younger. I was sometimes too direct, and perhaps I still am. I found it annoying that some patients could afford to be "sick" when they really weren't, while so many others needed help but were unable to find the money. I feel more at home in a hospital laboratory.'

She expected Dr Fernsby to look irritated, but instead the older woman leaned forward as far as she was able, a twinkle in her eye. 'What changed? Are you tired of the dead?'

'I work with the living too,' said Margaret, then realised she sounded defensive. 'I really don't mean to waste your time. The absolute truth is that I got married. The hospital board believe a married woman shouldn't work. I've appealed to them and Dr Jordan supports me, but I'm looking into my options in case I have to leave.'

Dr Fernsby nodded. 'What are your others?'

'Private research. A sanatorium perhaps. Or finding a hospital with a different policy.'

'Mmm,' said Dr Fernsby. 'I find your openness and honesty refreshing. Why not ask Dr Jordan if you can spend two days here each week without commitment and then decide? That would make my life easier. I'll pay you for them. Besides...'

'Besides?'

'Being away some of the time may put remind the board of your worth.' Dr Fernsby extracted her typescript and locked it in a drawer, tucking the key into her purse, then folded and clipped the case around the typewriter. She collected her outdoor things, then ushered Margaret out into the foyer, took a list from Miss Hill and perused it. 'I'm about to go on my rounds. Perhaps you could come too and gain a feel for the practice. These are all within brisk walking distance and shouldn't take more than an hour. I have a retired clerk with an infected leg, a perfectly healthy rich widow who needs her hand holding every few months, and a woman in the poorer part of the district with suspected pneumonia. That would be right up your street, wouldn't it?'

Margaret pondered briefly. 'Thank you,' she said. 'I'd be delighted to join you.'

That evening, after she'd told him about the visit, Fox suggested they go to a cinema. 'Charles says there's a film you'd be interested in which unnerved him a little. He's gone to interview Abolin again even though it's a police case and there are more important things to do. He's irritating me to be honest, and you seem upset, so we might as well cheer ourselves up with some frivolity.'

The programme, was the usual mixture: some newsreel, a visit to a Moroccan bazaar, a rather alarming film about an aeroplane crashing and then the items that everyone was waiting for, a series of short dramas and comedies including *Dr Mesner's Fatal Prescription*, *Wilful Peggy*, *The Lobster Nightmare* and finally *The Cockney Connection*.

'This must be it,' said Fox, as the first title cards came up. 'Dysart Studios? Never heard of them.'

Margaret frowned. 'Oh! I passed it today! It's opposite Dr Fernsby's surgery.'

'Shhhh!' The person behind jabbed her in the back.

The film started in what the title card described as a 'lowly but honest and happy cockney home' with a set created to depict a poor London room of a spaciousness that Anna Balodis could only dream of. At the climax of the film, which up until that point had been shot indoors, the girl was tied up and bundled into a car driven by the criminals and closely followed by her beloved. This led to a car chase through London streets which were in reality nowhere near each other.

'Good grief!' exclaimed Margaret. 'It's Myrdle Street on the day I was there.' She leaned forward, wishing there was a way to pause the film.

There was the car she'd seen, rattling down the street. She knew there was a crowd of locals watching, but they were unseen, behind the cameraman. Another car barrelled along in pursuit and as both cars came to a sudden and illogical halt, the drivers started firing guns at each other. At that moment, small, ragged children came running out of nowhere to rescue the girl. While the hero stopped firing to avoid hitting them, the villain didn't, shooting a final bullet to strike the hero down. The camera drew back to show that a crowd had formed, then closed in on the scene as the girl, with the help of the cheery cockney children, freed herself and rushed to her beloved just as two actors pretending to be passers-by, overwhelmed the villain and the crowd came closer.

It was impossible for Margaret not to look for herself in the throng, even though she knew well enough that scenes not only filmed more than once and different pieces of film edited together to make a narrative, but that she hadn't been in front of the camera at any point and the gunfight must have taken place after she'd left the street.

The editing had evidently been hasty; while most bystanders were peering intently, two men were paying no attention whatsoever to what should have been a thrilling spectacle. They were at the very edge of the shot, talking intently. One was fair and appeared well-dressed while the other, turned away from the camera, was tall and dark, wearing shabby clothes that hung badly. Anna Balodis, or someone who looked identical, was also there, conferring with a young man of similar build and colouring.

Before Margaret could be certain, the scene changed and as the hero recovered and his parents gave their blessing to his marriage to the cockney heroine, the story ended.

'Apart from the fact that was the day we were both there when it was filmed,' said Margaret once she and Fox were settled at home. 'I don't know what would have bothered Charles unless he's worried that he was in shot. I didn't see him, though, did you? Perhaps we should go to another showing.'

Fox refilled their glasses. 'Perhaps. The only hint he gave was muttering about Piccadilly being more important than he'd thought.'

'What does Piccadilly have to do with anything?'

'It might not be the place but a person. Charles had a source with that nickname.'

'You're tingling, aren't you?' said Margaret.

'A little. I wish he'd let that investigation go. Did you say Anna Balodis was in that film?'

'I'd put money on it. But—'

The telephone rang.

'I bet you anything this'll be Charles with his latest theory,' said Fox, reaching for the receiver. 'Hallo?... Oh! Good evening, Hare. Yes... Go on.'

Margaret sat back with her wine and waited, irritated that no one would believe that Anna Balodis was nothing but an unhappy young woman and that Fox's senior thought it all right to ring this late.

Fox frowned, glancing at Margaret. 'What?'

As she watched, his face grew pale and his eyes darted around the room as if he were trying to see something just out of sight. Finally they settled on Margaret, full of horror. She put her glass down and reached for his arm. 'What is it?' she mouthed.

'Surely there's a mistake,' he said. 'Surely... Yes, I'll be there. Good-bye.'

He replaced the mouthpiece on its rest and put the telephone back on the table. He seemed to be looking through rather than at her. 'They've found a body on Primrose Hill. They're taking it to St Mary's for a post-mortem. It's...'

'Can I help?'

Fox focussed on her then. 'Oh God, no. You couldn't. It's Charles.'

'Then I'll come with you.' She reached for his hand.

'I—' Fox closed his mouth and after a while, entwined his fingers in hers and nodded.

Eight

A t St Mary's, the remains of Charles lay staring up in surprise with empty eyes. The shell which once been a man seemed like a poor copy of the original.

There was neat bullet wound in his left temple and a mess of shattered bone and tissue behind it.

'This gun was in his hand,' said the detective sergeant, holding out a revolver. 'Does it look like his?'

Fox nodded.

'I don't think it's suicide,' said the pathologist. 'The residue you'd expect on his left glove is missing even though his gun was in that hand.'

'Charles was right-handed,' said Fox.

'I see. Well that backs up my theory. We'd need to consult a specialist, but to me it seems that Mr Craven's wrist would have to be twisted at a really uncomfortable angle to achieve the shot to his head.'

'I can give you the details of a ballistics expert,' said Margaret.

'Thank you, Dr Demeray.'

The sergeant glanced at her with an expression that was a mixture of dismay and disapproval, waiting presumably for her to come over faint. But he said nothing.

All that Charles had ever wanted was to stop the people that might destroy our world, thought Margaret. *Is it because of that he's dead?*

'There's a note,' said the sergeant and handed over a blood-stained scrap of paper with the single word '*neizdošanās*' written in continental script. 'Is it his writing, Superintendent? Any ideas what it says?'

Fox's frown deepened. His face was cold, closed. 'It's Latvian I think. And Charles could disguise his writing. But I doubt he'd do it for suicide. Or write in any language but English.'

'That may explain it then,' said the sergeant. 'Mr Craven turned up to the bail house to speak with Abolin. They went out together and neither came back. There's no sign of Abolin now. And just so you know, since Mr Craven handed him over, we'd been doing more digging. Abolin's only been sneaking about under an English name for a few months. He moved from Spitalfields to Bethnal Green a year ago, but only became Anderson when it suited him. Savages the lot of them. They can change their name and move outta the slum, but they're the same underneath. Oughta be sent back where they came from. So help me, if there's another bl-, I mean flaming siege, I'll—'

'I take it someone's looking for him,' said Fox.

The sergeant was affronted. 'Acourse. A warrant's out for breach of bail and it looks like there's enough to add murder now. We thought your Mr Craven's notions that Abolin was an anarchist were a load of cobblers, but maybe he was right. Leave it with me, Superintendent. You can see the file tomorrer if you want.'

'Thank you.' Fox put the note into his pocket and looked down at his friend for the last time. 'Sleep well, old chap.'

After leaving the hospital, Fox drove westwards out of London for miles without speaking. The sun had long since set and the headlights caught the eyes of creatures in the road, reflected off windows, illuminated walkers. It seemed he might not stop unless forced to, but eventually he turned back to his hotel, collected the keys and took her to their room.

Margaret watched him pace for a while, then caught his arm. 'Stop.'

Fox pulled her down to sit on the window seat with him and stared out into the darkness. After a while she put her arms around him. He seemed unresponsive, cold, inflexible, but she drew his head close to hers and he relaxed just enough to rest against her. 'I wish men could cry,' he whispered.

'They can.'

'I can't. I haven't since I was told to stiffen my lip when Mother died.'

'But that's terrible. You were only six years old! And surely when you lost Cynthia...'

He shook his head. 'I became stone and practicalities. It felt like I was outside it all, watching a man holding his dead wife's hand as if we were in a painting of other people. It boiled up inside, but it wouldn't come out. And now I want to remember Charles laughing, dressed up to the nines or down like a tramp, clinking beer glasses, making rude jokes, those times when he danced with Phoebe, teasing her and playing the fool... But when I close my eyes all I can see is his body laid out under a sheet on a sterile slab.'

'That will pass. One day you'll remember him the way you want to. At the moment...'

'I know. But now he's a naked stranger with a hole in his head and a look of utter surprise on a face I could once read like a book. It was an execution. I met Anderson ... Abolin or whatever he's called. I couldn't imagine him crushing a beetle...'

Margaret held him closer, smoothing his hair.

Buried in her shoulder, Fox's words were bitter. 'Charles went to see him, and now he's dead. Oh God, Margaret...' He drew a breath that was almost but not quite a sob. 'I should have gone with him. If I had, maybe...'

'Shhh,' whispered Margaret. 'Shhh. You mustn't think like that.'

'Oh God, how can I explain to his parents?'

'I'm so sorry.' Were three words ever so inadequate?

Fox didn't answer, but brushed Margaret's face with his fingers then drew her nearer, tracing her curves, unbuttoning her blouse, unlacing her bodice, his touch setting tingling fires along her skin. He kissed her neck, her mouth and her breast as he pulled her closer. 'I need you.'

His hand cupped the fullness of her breast, his kisses insistent, his fingers tender. Their clothes slipped to the floor and they embraced on the window seat, ignoring the darkness beyond the pane and clinging to the warmth and love within.

Without speaking, they made love as if it was their first time, their only time, their last time.

And when they were both spent, as he lay trembling in her arms, Fox nestled against her neck and she wasn't sure whose silent tears soaked into her hair.

Early next morning, Bert telephoned to say that Abolin had been found in a grimy alley in Whitechapel. He'd taken poison, and in his pocket was a scrap of paper on which he'd scrawled in Latvian 'I'm sorry. I cannot face prison. If you'd left me alone, all would be well.'

Fox took Margaret back to her flat and left for work, saying he'd return when he could. Later, after a lunch neither of them wanted, Fox took papers from his briefcase and spread them across the table, tapping each in turn, starting with the bloodstained note. His pallor and lack of appetite were the only signs of grief. '"*Neizdošanās*" means failure in Latvian,' he said. 'Our expert doesn't think it's Charles's writing and in fact, the writing appears to be the same as in Abolin's note and the piece of paper torn from it. These are Charles's notes about the case. Not the stuff we gave to the police, but the stuff we don't normally show anyone. Abolin was first cousin to the father of Andris and Anna Balodis. He came to Britain in '98 and naturalised in '02. Charles's intelligence came from a man known locally as Piccadilly - a man of no fixed abode who spoke well and seemed to have come down in the world.'

'In that part of Whitechapel pretty much anywhere else in the world is "up".'

'Exactly,' said Fox. 'So Piccadilly might not have been as posh as the name makes him sound. And you know what it's like - a short man is nicknamed Lofty, a thin man Porker. Names don't always mean anything. Charles said Piccadilly's accent seemed "put on". He seemed healthier and taller than the average local which might mean a number of things or nothing. But through him, Charles discovered that at some point the man now called Anderson had worked for *The Freedom Press*, and Charles was already undercover there to see if Andris Balodis was linked to the plot we've had wind of and/or to the likes of Gardstein and he found out that a cousin of Andris had worked there once and he was called Peteris or Peter Abolin and from there...'

'But as far as I understand it, *The Freedom Press* strongly condemned the murders in Houndsditch.'

Fox nodded. 'Charles decided that Abolin might be an anarchist but not connected to the Gardstein gang who, let's be honest, were more opportunists than idealists. Abolin had long moved on from the *Press* and out of the immediate area, which was why he was hard to find. For someone who - according to the immigration records -

arrived in London unable to speak English, he'd managed to greatly improve himself - Workers Education evening classes and so on, hence finding a job with *The Freedom Press* in '05. He was doubtless a highly intelligent man, perhaps bitter at how difficult life is for the poor. But I maintain my view, that however appalling that is, it's not an excuse to plan an attack on the country that gave him sanctuary.'

'Do you now think Abolin was planning one after all?'

'Charles thought so. I didn't. Hare doesn't. Nothing adds up.' Fox lifted a different file. 'This is what the police have compiled. They found all those stolen goods under the floor boards in Abolin's rooms. They reported that Abolin seemed surprised to see them, then scared, then resigned, then admitted everything. It's not an unknown response, but pretty odd, especially when you consider that Abolin said he didn't know where anything came from. The police wonder if he had some sort of nerve-storm.'

'Nerve-storms don't lead people to burgle houses.'

Fox ran his finger down a medical report. 'This suggests maybe he sleep-walked or was hypnotised.'

'That's ridiculous.'

'You're the doctor, but burglary certainly appears to be out of character. It's partly why they granted bail. They found a very organised filing system in his rooms.'

'For his burglaries?'

'No. Once he'd learned to read and write English, he discovered his passion. He wrote articles for *The Freedom Press* for a while and then other papers. Then he obtained a job in a bookshop.'

'It's not called Nierling's is it?'

'No. Why?'

'Never mind.'

'As well as that, he ran a kind of lending library. He bought good quality second hand books and lent them through a kind of subscription service. He was doing quite nicely out of it too. And he was writing an account of his experiences as an immigrant which a social reform paper offered to serialise. Nothing in it suggests anything dangerous at all.'

'When did he have time to burgle houses?'

'Quite.' Fox picked up an old photograph. 'This is Abolin with his old mum back in Latvia. He seemed to want a quiet life. He doesn't seem like a burglar. He doesn't seem like someone who knows how to kill someone cleanly and make it look like suicide.' He placed the photograph back on the pile of papers and put his head in his hands. 'If I'd just gone with Charles,' he said. 'Neither of them would be dead.'

'You don't know that,' said Margaret, reaching for his hands, pulling them from his face and holding them. 'It might have been you. And did Charles ask you to go with him?'

'No. He just said he wanted to work it out alone and I should take you to see that film. Perhaps he was as irritated with my disbelief as I was with his obsession.'

Margaret thought back to the evening at the picture-house and further back to that day in Myrdle Street when she'd met Anna. If Abolin had moved from the area, why was Charles there? Who was he hoping to meet? Piccadilly? 'We'll go and see the film again,' she said. 'Maybe something will jump out at us.'

'I'm not sure I can bear the thought of all the silliness.' Fox let go of her hands and rubbed his temples. 'Charles's inquest is tomorrow but it'll be a mere formality. The funeral's on Tuesday. Will Dr Jordan give you leave?'

'I'm sure he will. And I'll go and see the film on my own and see if there's anything to note.'

'Thank you. Hare's on my back about the other thing and wants me to leave Charles's murder with the police.'

'I can find a way to talk with the Dysarts if necessary,' said Margaret. 'I've decided to ask Dr Jordan if I can work with Dr Fernsby two days a week.'

'I thought private practice wasn't what you wanted?'

Margaret hesitated. 'It isn't. But so far I don't have any other alternative. I'd rather do something. I don't want to have nothing at the end of April.'

'What a mess everything is.'

She went to put her arms round him and he rested his head against her. 'It is Fox. But we'll prevail. I know we will.'

Nine

While the news of Abolin's crime and suicide were in the paper, with calls for the bail act to be abolished, his victim wasn't named. The weekend passed in grief and sleeplessness, and any hope Margaret had that she didn't look drained when she arrived for work on Monday was in vain.

'Good morning, Dr Demeray,' said Dr Jordan, when she entered his office. 'You - er - you look a little wan.'

'A close friend of my husband's died at the weekend.'

'Oh my dear!' said Dr Jordan. 'I'm so terribly sorry. Please pass on my condolences.'

'I'd be grateful for time to attend the funeral. I know that on top of everything else it seems presumptive but—'

'Of course you may.' Dr Jordan contemplated her fully. He grew red about the collar and his shoulders drooped. 'I imagine this is adding to your worries about your work here. Please be assured that many board members support my view that your marriage should make no difference. Although of course,' Dr Jordan paused as the redness reached his cheeks to remove his glasses and wipe off an invisible speck, 'if you stay but then, erm, have a child, we'd need to review matters.'

'Madame Curie has two small children and is nevertheless a professor at the University of Paris.'

'Madame Curie is, er, widowed,' pointed out Dr Jordan, 'and also Continental, and Paris is not only Continental but French.' He managed to make all these things sound at best undesirable and at worst infectious. 'But let us get over the first hurdle.'

'I went to see Dr Fernsby as you suggested,' said Margaret. 'Would the board allow me to be seconded for two days a week from next Monday? I know my absence might be a nuisance, especially as I have a week's unpaid leave in March to visit a sanatorium in Switzerland. But Dr Fernsby would reimburse S J's for my salary.'

'Mmm,' said Dr Jordan consulting a diary. 'Would a Monday afternoon, a Tuesday and a Thursday morning be acceptable to you and Dr Fernsby?'

'Yes.'

'I'm sure I can persuade the board.' He heaved a sigh. 'I'll assure them that the time when you're away will be a great loss to St Julia's and that you won't be easily replaced. I'm sure it'll work out somehow.'

Charles was laid to rest in quiet, subdued dignity. The reporters at the inquest had been ordered not to name him and few of them bothered to try and attend the funeral, concentrating instead on writing up the details of Abolin's demise.

'I'm so sorry,' said Margaret much later over dinner. 'I wish I could...' What was there she could do? Charles was dead. His murderer was dead. Margaret could cut out disease. Nothing but time could excise pain and grief.

'I know what you're trying to say,' said Fox. 'But latent murderous tendencies or brainstorm, either way Abolin killed Charles because he couldn't face a long prison term and then panicked and did for himself. Why Charles went to see him is a mystery but Hare won't let me investigate further.'

'Because you can't be objective?'

'Because it's unnecessary and he needs me for other things. Let's talk about something else. Are you sure about joining Dr Fernsby's practice? You love your job at St J's.'

'Hopefully the board will realise I'm critical.'

'Or they'll manage without you from spite.'

'Don't say that Fox.'

'I'm just angry for you.'

'Who knows what visiting Gil's Swiss sanatorium in March will bring?'

'A decision about whether to move to Switzerland I imagine.' Fox sipped his brandy then sat staring into it, gold reflecting on to his face as he swirled the glass. 'It's not what I envisaged, but on the other hand, getting away from everything...'

'It's not what I envisaged either.'

'Come on let's dance.'

Holding him close, Margaret whispered in Fox's ear. 'What does Hare want you to do.'

'Go to Scotland. I can't explain. But you can tell your friends I'm inspecting my family lands in Ayrshire.'

'Do you have any?'

Fox shook his head. 'Not unless you count where my ancestors are buried. And I don't think graveyards will be on my itinerary.'

Margaret knew not to ask more. He couldn't always tell her where or why he was going when he had a mission, and the chances were she'd never find out. But each time her mind flew into a flurry of possibilities and those thoughts grew darker each time. Now, she tried to shut Charles's body from her imagination and keep her voice light. 'Will you be away long?'

'Two weeks perhaps. Hopefully less.' He squeezed her closer. 'I'm sorry I won't be here when you start a job you don't want.'

'It doesn't matter.'

He leaned down to kiss her. 'Since I'll be away for a while, let's give up the dancing and say goodbye to each other properly.'

The first week at Glassmakers Lane passed without incident.

The patients were as expected: several on middle incomes, some rich women, and a few people in desperate poverty as terrified of a doctor's bill as they were of illness. The weather was generally fine and the street bustled. Soffiato's was busy even though its menu seemed distinctly un-Italian, specialising in coffee, apfeltorte and schnitzel. Dr Fernsby chuckled when she mentioned it and explained that the Aldinis who ran Soffiato's had changed their name from Altman a few years earlier, when anti-German feeling started to increase and chosen a name for the restaurant which they thought sounded Italian. They had yet to master the cuisine.

There was no word from Fox other than daily messages from Bert or Pigeon to indicate all was well.

And Dysart's studio seemed closed.

'They'll be filming outdoors while they can,' said Dr Fernsby when she noticed Margaret looking. 'I believe they'll be going somewhere for a longish period shortly to film something special. Perhaps they've already gone.'

But the following Thursday, when she and Margaret drove back to Glassmakers Lane, the woman Margaret had seen directing the filming in Myrdle Street and a tall, blond man much like the one she'd seen talking to the man in rough clothes in *The Cockney Connection*, were standing in the middle of the road pointing at the sky and buildings.

'Ah,' said Dr Fernsby. 'They haven't gone. Good morning, Mrs Dysart, Mr Dysart,' she called as they pulled up alongside. 'May I introduce Dr Demeray? She's been working with me for a while and we thought we'd missed you.'

'Pleased to make your acquaintance doctor,' said Mrs Dysart as they shook hands. 'My husband thinks we can use the street for a film, but we've used it rather a lot for other things. I often wonder if people notice. And will anyone believe it's Paris? What do you think? I presume you watch moving pictures.'

'Yes,' said Margaret. She climbed out of the car and followed Mrs Dysart's gaze. 'I'm afraid I don't know Parisian architecture well enough to judge. But I've enjoyed one of your films.'

'Really?' Mr Dysart grinned in delight. 'Which one?'

'The *Cockney Connection*. That wasn't shot here though was it?'

'Gosh no,' said Mr Dysart. 'When did you see it?'

'The day it came out I think. And twice since then. It was good fun.'

'Thank you,' said Mrs Dysart. 'Although I hope you *didn't* see it on the day it came out. The editing wasn't up to standard.' She gave her husband a sidelong frown.

Margaret lied carefully. 'I can't say I noticed anything different when I saw it the second time.'

'Good.' Mrs Dysart's nonchalance returned. 'Sometimes people on the team get in the shot and the editor forgets to cut them out, even though they're standing round doing nothing but being accosted by drunks, beggars and tramps.' She glanced at Mr Dysart again. 'Fortunately, much like pruning unwanted weeds, it's easily rectified. Snip snip.' She made scissors of her fingers, giggled and looked at her husband who blushed. 'Come along Rupert, we have work to do and I'm sure these ladies do too. Lovely to meet you Dr Demeray. Do come and see me soon so we can organise a tour.'

'I'd be delighted,' said Margaret, with as much indifference as she could muster. 'Perhaps you can show me the editing suite and what happens to the edited bits.'

Mrs Dysart snapped her fingers and blew on them. 'Gone in a breath,' she said. 'Like dandelion seeds.' She peered around at the buildings again. 'No, they won't do for Paris. Perhaps we need to alter our plans a little.' With a small bow, she bade them goodbye and led her husband towards the studio.

Margaret checked her watch. She was at risk of being late for her afternoon's work at St Julia's.

'I suppose you can't stay for lunch,' said Dr Fernsby. 'It's a pity since you've yet to meet Leopold and for a wonder, he may be home.'

'Perhaps next week.'

Dr Fernsby waved a hand vaguely. 'Possibly. Leopold prefers the regularity of knowing when and what he'll be eating, because I'm not terribly reliable – look how late we are today for example – so he generally lunches at his club. And then of course, he's sometimes at his estate in the country. Like your husband.'

'Mmm,' said Margaret. She'd been as vague as possible about Fox, referring simply to private means and in an unguarded moment referring to him being away inspecting family lands as he'd suggested.

Now she hurried back to St Julia's, arriving at the café nearby with just enough time to spare for lunch and sat at the only table available, propping her book up against the coffee pot but not really taking in any of its words.

It was disappointing that she'd been unable to find out more about the edited film. Given what Mrs Dysart had hinted, Margaret's suspicion Mr Dysart was the fair-haired man in the tiny snippet that had been removed seemed more likely than ever. Which meant the person whom she referred to as a 'drunk, beggar or tramp' was the other man, standing with his back to the camera, hunched in a sagging coat. And he might possibly be Piccadilly.

And Dr Fernsby's assumptions about Fox had rattled her. What would she do if they went into partnership? That sharp-eyed woman might not be as easy to misdirect as Dr Jordan, who didn't really care what anyone did as long as the mortuary wing ran smoothly. Margaret half-wished that Fox really was striding a country estate rather than doubtless doing something dangerous. According to newspapers of varying reliability, an alleged German spy had been arrested in Aberdeen dockyards, a shipment of explosives had been found on an Inverness fishing vessel and a man of 'foreign demeanour' had been caught with local maps in an alley in Glasgow. Any or none of them could have involved Fox.

Someone stood beside her, casting a shadow. 'That's a deep sigh. Is the book so bad?'

'Fox!' Margaret leapt to her feet and flung her arms round him.

'Control yourself woman. You're putting people off their soup. Maybe this book will be better.' He handed over a small parcel wrapped in brown paper and tied with string.

'Oh. Er. Thank you.'

'It was at your flat. I arrived just after you'd left and when the postman handed it over, I thought it might be important.'

'Why should it be?'

'The writing and the postmark.'

'I don't recognise the former, and the latter... Hendon? I don't know anyone there.'

'I do. Will you open it?'

'Can't it wait? I've been ...' Margaret bit back her words. She'd promised herself that she wouldn't burden him with her worry every time he went away. 'I've been hoping you had a successful trip.'

'Very. One small neat package retrieved, another rather more awkward one safely - if so far silently - stored away.' He squeezed her hand and gave an apologetic smile. 'I've been looking forward to seeing you too but you'll need to be at work shortly won't you? And we've got all evening to catch up on news. It's just that I have an odd feeling about that parcel and it was all I could do not to open it.'

A sudden misgiving came over Margaret. 'Is it safe?'

'If I thought it might go bang, I'd hardly give it to you or bring it to a café.'

Margaret untied the string and unwrapped the parcel. Inside was a slim volume written by F.H. Hatch entitled *Mineralogy*, and a letter. Frowning, she opened it.

Dear Dr Demeray,

Thank you for attending our dear son's funeral and for your letter of condolence. We are still finding it hard to believe he is gone. He visited us on that last evening, went to his old boyhood room for a while and afterwards asked that if something happened to him, we would not turn it into a shrine. We have only recently had the heart to go through his things as he requested. It appears he wanted this sent to you although we can't say why.

With our very best wishes,

Mr and Mrs C Craven

'Now I'm even more confused,' she said.

'I knew it,' said Fox. 'What's inside the book?'

There was another note, this time in a more familiar hand.

Dear Margaret,

I'm writing to you rather than Fox, as he might move hotels. I know you'll show him anyway.

If you're reading this, then my visit to A went awry and I want you to ask you to do three things:

Persuade your 'old man' not to give up. He's right about where the threat is from. I was wrong. The A I found was the wrong A, but the right A is using him. I was wrong to trust P. This is not about burglary.

Tell him to acquaint himself with wrong A's filing system. Not just books but letters. Where did the former come from? Where did the latter go?

Don't either of you forget me, but don't mourn me. Go to the music-hall, get a little drunk, go dancing, find justice, then dance some more. Life is too short for weeping.

If you don't do these things, I shall haunt you both.

Charles

Ten

I n the weeks before Margaret was due to go to Switzerland to visit
Gil's sanatorium and join one of the Women's Day marches, she
and Fox did their best to follow Charles's instructions, even if they
often danced with heavy hearts.

Hare's staff worked their way through Abolin's filing system with
marginal success, tracking down the shops from which he'd bought
books with ease, but street traders with difficulty. Tracing the library
clients and what they'd borrowed was also straightforward. But there
were a few books, F.H. Hatch's *Mineralogy* included, that had been,
or were about to be delivered to a recipient and address that couldn't
be identified. And while Fox's source established that a man called
Anderson provided the capital for Abolin to start his library before
Abolin took on the name himself, it was unclear why either had occurred. It seemed doubtful that it was simply to do with hiding stolen
goods.

The real Anderson remained elusive. And the bomb threat,
whether anarchist or otherwise, remained.

Fox felt he was on the verge of something concrete when Hare
gave him and Pigeon an unconnected mission of higher priority. The
only positive thing about it was that it required them to travel Austria by motorcycle, so Fox was able to gain leave to join Margaret in

Switzerland on the way. Those few days turned into a strange kind of honeymoon - an oasis of happiness in a desert of frustration and grief.

On Tuesday the twenty-first of March, the last morning they would have together for a while, Fox hired a car and drove Margaret into the mountains and they sat on a blanket on the snowy grass. Margaret's feet were still sore from marching two days earlier. The weather was beautiful, the sky overhead the cleanest, deepest blue she'd ever seen. Rich enough to taste.

'That blue...' said Fox.

Margaret waited for him to say the colour of the sky was like her eyes. Even though it wouldn't have been accurate, it was the sort of thing lovers were supposed to say. 'Yes?'

'I bet you're imagining a dress in that shade,' he said.

She laughed. Fox had a point. An evening gown as blue as that sky, cut so that the silk appeared to change colour as she danced, would be beautiful. 'What are *you* imagining?'

'I'd show you if you weren't wearing four layers of clothes and there wasn't a goatherd two yards away.'

'Is there?'

'Bound to be. There are goats. Can't you hear the bells clanking?'

Margaret scanned the slopes around them. A long way away, on a small farmstead, a brown creature ambled, swaying like a woman with washing on her hips. 'It's a cow.'

'You're London born and bred.' Fox's fingers trickled down to the base of her spine. 'Are you sure you know the difference?'

'Ho ho.'

He kissed her neck, then followed her gaze. The mountain tops were still thick with snow. Below, Lake Wohlen shimmered like jade-green satin scattered with tiny diamanté beads. Who'd have thought the sun would be so warm so early in the year? Or maybe it was just being with Fox. In his embrace, the scent of him made her blood throb. Going back to London without him would hurt as badly as a wound.

He kissed her mouth and pulled her closer.

A distant voice, hoarse with age, yelled '*Hör auf, meine Ziegen zu erschrecken!*'

'Damn,' said Fox, releasing her. 'I told you there were goats.'

'Easily frightened ones, at that.'

He stood up and pulled her to her feet. 'Come along, time's marching on. We've things to do before we leave. One thing, anyway.'

'Yes. I need to telegraph Katherine to remind her to collect me from the station and—'

'That's not what I meant.' He sobered and said, for the hundredth time, 'I'm sorry I can't come back with you.'

'There's no choice,' said Margaret. She squeezed his hand. 'It's your job.'

'Stay two more days.' He put his arm round her waist as they walked towards the car.

'I can't. I'm expected at St Julia's on Thursday and if I don't turn up it'll be one more mark against me as far as the board's concerned. Frivolous, uncommitted women, and all that. And then there's your mission. Hare will be cracking the whip. It's bothering you. Can you tell me why?'

Fox opened the car door, helped her in, then swore as he turned the crank. 'I should have brought my motorcycle instead and squeezed you on behind. It would have been less strenuous.'

'Not in this dress. And I'd want my own motorcycle.'

'I wish it were you and me motorcycle touring rather than me and Pigeon.'

'Stop changing the subject. You won't be touring and you're not happy.'

The Ajax rumbled reluctantly into life and Fox climbed in beside her. 'The intelligence was deciphered by the new man.'

'What's his name again? Squirrel?'

'Smith.'

'The idiot who sent you and Charles the wrong way in January?'

'That's him. One sight of intercepted letters – half English and half gobbledegook – and he's like a terrier after a rat. Hare's convinced that while Smith might be bad at taking telephone messages, he can't be wrong about deciphering a set of symbols, so here I am off to Austria. I wanted to see the gobbledegook for myself, but Hare told me to … do my job.'

'Which is?'

'Track down some British blimp designs which someone's stolen to sell to the Austro-Hungarian empire. They're to be shared with Germany, allegedly to prepare for Russian attacks.'

'Not again?'

'Quite. That bit is in English, only it reads like something copied from the sensational press. But the gobbledegook, according to Smith, translates into something more specific.'

'But it doesn't relate to Anderson?' Bern was getting closer and Margaret reached for Fox's hand. Time was moving too fast. She didn't want to leave him behind. Perhaps she could help. Perhaps he was right; she should ask for more leave – and lose her job. Joining Dr Fernsby permanently was a possible option; Gil's sanatorium another. She didn't want either.

'I don't know. I was always convinced that Anderson was involved in selling secrets, though how Abolin's wretched library fits in I've yet to discover. Smith says the letters he's deciphered are nothing to do with bombs but to do with blimps.'

Margaret frowned. 'I don't mean to sound unpatriotic, but aren't the German airships infinitely better than ours? Why would they be stealing our designs?'

'You've hit the nail right on the head. I knew there was a reason why I loved you.'

'I thought it was for my ankles.'

'Too hairy.' Avoiding her slap, Fox pulled into the hotel yard and stopped the engine. 'Here we are.'

Neither of them moved. A garage-hand hovered, ready to take possession of the car, and nearby a liveried driver checked his watch, shaking his head. Two ladies left the yard in a trap, their horse shying as it passed them.

'Stay,' said Fox as Margaret said, 'Come back to England with me.'

Then they both said, 'I can't' and fell quiet.

'You're right,' Fox said at last. 'You have a job to do, and so do I. Even if there is something wrong about this mission, I need to work out what, and it's not fair to ask you to wait for me and risk your job. Go home; I'll be back in a week or so.'

After lunch, Fox took Margaret to Bern station the long way round, pausing to stare into shops selling souvenirs and eventually leaving her on the pavement to dash inside one of them. He emerged with two small wooden bears and put them in her hand. 'Take the one that reminds you of me.'

'What?'

'I never did get you an engagement ring. I can go down on one knee if you like.'

'Please don't.' Margaret picked the one which seemed redder and had a forepaw outstretched. 'I'll have this one. All he needs is a pint of beer.' Her lip wobbled.

'Chin up. Mine looks rather determined. I can just imagine her wielding a scalpel.'

Hand in hand, they dawdled the last few yards to the station. There was just over an hour before the train left, and Margaret both wanted Fox to stay and wanted him to leave her to be miserable alone. Perhaps he felt the same. His pace slowed to a stop and he gave Margaret a lingering kiss before holding her tight.

She resented letting him go more than ever. 'I wish you could come back with me.'

'We've had this conversation.'

'I know, but—'

'It's only for a few weeks. I promise I'll give you plenty of notice of my return so you can prepare a fitting welcome.' He hugged her close again. 'Take care.'

'I'm just going home. I'm not the one risking their life.'

'All the same, keep your wits about you.' One last kiss, then he slipped into the crowd without a backward glance as he always did.

Half an hour later, Margaret was settled in the dining car of the train, being served tea and cake. She tried to read her book, but the words jumbled and made no sense. She put it down and looked round the carriage at the other first-class passengers, who were as predictable as usual, then stared through the window as they neared Kerzers. Her heart beat a little faster, half hoping to see Fox waiting on the platform ready to board. When, naturally, he wasn't, she cursed herself for being worse than an adolescent and returned to her book as the train pulled out of the station.

'Madame, madame...' A strange French voice drifted into dreams of mountains and goatherds and Fox's worried face, and she blinked herself awake to see a smiling waiter. 'Madame, we are just arrived at Neuchâtel. A connecting train is half an hour behind schedule; perhaps you wish to have a stroll in the fresh air while we wait. Never fear, madame, we will gain speed afterwards and arrive at Paris in time for you to catch the boat train if you need to.'

'Thank you.' Margaret stretched and went to the compartment for her coat.

On the platform passengers milled about, getting in each other's way. Some were rushing to board, others heading for the exit. Those like Margaret, who had been on the train for some time and were bound for Paris, simply ambled, taking the opportunity to breathe outside air even though it was full of engine smoke, tobacco smoke and smuts. Porters ran luggage trolleys over people's feet and passengers lugging their own cases about bumped them into other people's shins. *I may as well go to the café and see if they have a souvenir*, thought Margaret. But as she saw the crush of people heading in towards it, she walked away from the melée and smoke to make a quick sketch of the chaotic platform.

If it hadn't been for someone audibly exclaiming '*soûlarde stupide*' as they rushed for the exit, Margaret would never have noticed that the brown bundle she'd just passed on the platform was not luggage, but a woman. She was bundled in an oversized, heavy coat and a large hat hid her face, while strands of blonde hair straggled on her shoulders. A handbag was slipping from half-curled fingers.

It was far too early to be drunk, but the crush was enough for anyone to faint.

Margaret bent to the crumpled form, lifting the hat to give the woman more air and smiling so that she'd see a friendly face when she returned to consciousness. But the woman's eyes were already open and no amount of friendliness would be perceived by her ever again.

Eleven

Margaret had seen death so many times, but it never ceased to humble her. And the woman was very young; little more than a girl.

A tall, dark-haired man crouched beside her and gasped before raising his head to bellow, 'Someone get a doctor!' as a certain type of English-speaker does on the assumption that if he yells loud enough the natives will understand.

The Swiss and French around them muttered in offended disapproval, but the word *médecin ... doktor ... arzt* rustled along the platform.

'I'm a doctor,' said Margaret, feeling under the young woman's still-warm jaw even though it was pointless. 'And she's dead.'

'But you're a woman.'

'I'm still a doctor, and she's still dead.'

'Good lord,' said the man. 'Although I suppose you know about women's health.'

'How dead a human is has nothing to do with gender,' said Margaret. 'Although I'm not so sure about stupidity. We need the stationmaster and maybe the police, and someone ought to find out if she has a companion.'

'If you're wrong, they can always get a proper doctor. Heart, I suppose.' The man stood and stalked off, bellowing. 'Stationmaster! Police!'

'*Anglais stupide*.' Another man knelt next to Margaret, muttering with feeling. She could tell by the way he touched the young woman that he was a doctor too and apologised in French for her countryman, explaining who she was. He shrugged, rolled his eyes, and said in English, 'Is that idiot with you?'

'Good grief, no.'

'Is she?'

'I've never seen her before. I haven't had a chance to do an examination. There's no obvious—'

The guard blew the whistle.

'There's nothing you can do,' said the doctor. 'You'd best catch your train. Here comes the stationmaster and a police officer. I'll make sure the body is cared for.'

'Here's my card,' said Margaret, extracting hers from the depths of her handbag and exchanging it for the doctor's. 'Thank you, Dr ... Gilliand. Let me know what happens if you can.' She stood up and handed another to the police officer. 'Please do write to me at the hospital if you need a witness.'

'Miss Vale!' A grey-haired man was shouting from the steps of the third-class carriage and scanning the platform. 'Miss Vale, where are you? The train's about to go! Miss Va—' He caught sight of the group huddled around the girl and dashed over to them, followed closely by a younger man who looked at the body and paled, putting his hands over his mouth before muttering, 'So it happened.'

'*Qu'a t'il dit?*' said the police officer.

'What do you mean?' said Margaret. 'What happened? Has someone —'

'No, no,' said the older man. He seemed more annoyed than upset. 'She might have had a heart problem.' The man ran his hand through his hair. 'Idio hyper something something.'

'Idiopathic hypertrophic subaortic stenosis?'

'If you say so. Her mother went the same way, apparently. We hoped that if it was true, she'd taken after her father, but evidently not. What a mess.' He turned to the younger man. 'Get back on board and tell everyone what's happened. I'll stay here to help the authorities and come back on tomorrow's train somehow.'

The young man swallowed. 'Y-yes,' he stammered, then dashed back to the train. The older man lit a cigarette as he contemplated Miss Vale's body.

The guard blew the whistle a second time. Margaret hesitated. 'Please accept my condolences.'

Exhaling smoke, the man turned to Margaret and shrugged. 'She isn't family, and the truth is, this is bloody annoying. Pardon my French.' He shook his head. 'What a bloody mess,' he repeated and waved away her card. 'You've given one to this lot, haven't you?' He turned to the policeman and pointed at Miss Vale, little flecks of ash fluttering down to land on the handkerchief Dr Gilliand was putting over her face. '*Je suis* ... Miss Vale's boss. *Parlez-vous* ... English?'

There was nothing more Margaret could do. The guard was looking at his watch and gesturing frantically. Dr Gilliand gave her a kind, reassuring smile and with one last look at the huddled form, Margaret dashed for the train.

A few hours later, after dinner, Margaret retired to her compartment. The berth had been made up and she undressed, then sat by the window brushing out her hair, watching the twinkling lights of scattered farms and towns in the darkness as the train rattled north. Her focus shifted and she saw her own reflection as France flashed past ghostly and insubstantial. For a second it made her think of Miss Vale and she imagined the stranger's body, stripped and put in a cold place. She sighed.

I wonder why sometimes the death of a stranger breaks your heart almost as much as a friend's, she thought. *Miss Vale died so young, and it didn't sound as if anyone cared very much about her. Dr Gilliand seemed competent. I'm sure he'll be in touch. If not, I'll get in touch with him.* She plaited her hair and closed the blind. *I never want to stop caring.*

Settling into her berth, Margaret sketched a picture of Miss Vale, then wrote to Fox care of his hotel in Bern. She knew the letter would arrive too late and that he wouldn't see it for a week or so, but apart from missing him, it helped to write things down before trying to sleep. She summarised finding Miss Vale, then chewed her pen before continuing. *I wish we could both have stayed, but I plan to keep disappointing the board. I'll miss you every day. Do stay safe. I'll be thinking of you all the time. I know you fear this is a wild-goose chase, but keep your foxy wits about you. One day it really will be you and me touring together. With all my love, M.*

She sealed the letter and lay back, imagining being in his arms as the train sped into the night. She never recalled turning out her light or drifting into sleep, or even what she dreamed, but in the brief time they had at Paris before changing from sleeper train to boat train, she posted the letter and also sent a telegram, hoping the latter would catch Fox before he left for Austria.

At Paris after eventful journey. Be safe. Strange dreams. Can't remember anything except compulsion to tell you there were no goats. M.

She chuckled as she handed it to the clerk, wondering how they kept straight faces when people gave them odd messages to transmit, although perhaps he didn't have enough English to realise how odd it was. But as she reclaimed her luggage for the next stage of the journey, she suddenly wished that Fox were with her, more than she had for hours.

Katherine had taken care of Juniper and her flat while Margaret was away. The flat was warm and inviting when Margaret finally closed the door behind her, which was more than could be said for Juniper whom she found under the dresser with her back turned to show her views on Margaret's absence.

'Suit yourself,' said Margaret and collected the pile of post on her hall table and picked out a telegram which had arrived that morning.

Hope eventful doesn't mean dangerous. Keep bear in beer and he'll keep you safe. Wait for Bert. F.

Margaret smiled. It was, despite Fox's absence and Juniper's spurning, good to be home.

The following day, she woke after a dreamless sleep and found Juniper watching disdainfully from the foot of the bed, flicking her tail. Margaret waggled her toes, and after a very short period of feigned ignorance and dignified immobility Juniper caved in to temptation and pounced, then squirmed under the eiderdown to sink her teeth into the wriggling toes. With a muffled shriek, Margaret flung back the covers and hauled Juniper out. The cat was tense and focussed as a hunter, her eyes dilated into a bottomless, eternal black and her tail flicking a rhythmic beat against Margaret's bare arms. Then she softened, relaxed and butted her head under her owner's chin with a purr.

'You daft thing,' said Margaret. 'What are you going to do when I'm sharing this bed with Fox all the time?'

She rose to get ready for work. With a gloomy sky outside and only a tiny gap in the curtains where Juniper had come in through the open window, Margaret's bedroom was dark. It wasn't until she was padding about in stockinged feet that she stood on something small, cold and squashy and discovered that Juniper had brought her a dead mouse and screamed so loud that she almost brought the tiny creature back to life. It was nice to feel forgiven for a week's absence, but Margaret wished cats had a different way of doing it.

An hour later, she arrived at St Julia's. The sky was overcast and the day cold. The heat of the underground had dissipated within minutes of climbing to street level and Margaret hunched inside her coat. The sunny cleanliness of Switzerland seemed to have existed in another world.

Margaret paused at the entrance to the mortuary wing. At least Dr Fernsby had been happy for her not to work in Glassmakers Lane before Monday. There was nothing Margaret could do about Fox. He would have no way to get word to her without potentially putting himself at risk, and being busy would take her mind off things.

A movement made Margaret turn. A few yards away, a man in chauffeur's livery was polishing the lights of his car while apparently watching her. He touched his cap and gave a surreptitious thumbs up before bending to his task again. Bert, telling her all was well with Fox.

Feeling a weight lift, Margaret entered the hospital and greeted the desk clerk. 'Good morning Mr Holness. Is Dr Jordan in?'

'He said he'd join you after you arrive. I've put your letters on your desk.'

'Thank you.'

Margaret went to her office, hung up her outdoor things and settled in that familiar space to read her correspondence. It was too early for a letter from Switzerland and the letters were nothing out of the ordinary: reports, advertisements, requests for surgical instrument salesmen to visit and entreaties for endorsement on patent medicine. Dr Jordan entered as she put the final letter in its pile for appropriate response. 'Good morning Dr Demeray! Welcome back!' His smile was open and bright. 'I take it you weren't snatched up by the sanatorium.'

'I've been invited to apply.'

'Oh dear. I mean good. For you I mean. Is it?'

'I'm not planning on going anywhere till I have to.'

'Excellent,' Dr Jordan heaved a sigh of relief. 'How was your trip otherwise?'

Margaret frowned. 'Very pleasant. The scenery is beautiful, the sanatorium up to the minute, the food interesting. The board will be glad to know the Women's Day March was well regulated and I didn't bring either myself or St J's into disrepute. But...'

'What is it?'

'I came across a woman who'd died of subaortic stenosis when I was on the way back. It was very sad.'

'Really?'

'Or rather, I may have. She was a passenger on the train, aged about eighteen and possibly a governess. Her employer said she had the disease in the family. She'd certainly died suddenly from something. I had to leave her with a Swiss doctor to do the honours.'

'Is something bothering you about it?' asked Dr Jordan.

'There's no reason why it should,' Margaret answered, smothering her sense of disquiet.

'You've been dabbling with too many police cases,' said Dr Jordan. 'What you need is some straightforward pathology of a diseased lung. Let's see what we can find.'

Twelve

Thursday and Friday passed. Neither Margaret nor Dr Jordan mentioned her position.

There was no word from Fox other than encounters with Bert, when he tipped his hat and give Margaret a thumbs up from outside the tube stop or the hospital or in a corner of the café where Margaret ate her lunch. There was no point walking over to speak to him. He'd feign ignorance, and quite possibly he knew nothing anyway. It was the way things worked. Fox would have his own means of getting messages back and she mustn't in any way compromise him.

Nor was there any word from Dr Gilliand.

On Saturday, after finishing work at noon, Margaret made her way to the British Library to look for backdated copies of the *International Herald Tribune* in case there was any mention of Miss Vale's death. There was nothing. Margaret reluctantly admitted that her interest was largely sentiment with a small element of professional curiosity, and serving to distract her from thinking of Fox and what she should do about work.

Afterwards, she went to Fulham to give her father and step-mother their presents from Switzerland, show them her sketches and souvenirs, then take them to the nearest picture house. One of the short films was a Dysart creation. It was another fifteen-minute melodrama set, as far as Margaret could make out, in a composite of Dover and

Folkestone. The story involved a plucky captain's daughter and the secret suitor saving the family fortune from a confidence trickster before sailing off into the sunset on their honeymoon.

'I could write them a better plot than that,' grumbled Father.

'I think you're right,' said Margaret. 'Although I bet you'd put a sea monster in.'

He mumbled into his pipe and she couldn't quite catch what he said. It sounded worryingly like, 'Let's find out shall we?'

She overslept on Monday and had to rush to be on time for work, only briefly pausing at the mortuary wing desk to ask if there were any messages.

'No, doctor,' said the clerk, 'but the police just this minute brought a body. They're in Dr Jordan's lab with Mr Hardisty.'

'That's the best news I've had for days,' said Margaret, unpeeling her gloves and stuffing them in her handbag.

The clerk chuckled as she hurried away. 'Comes to something when a corpse is what makes a lady happy!'

Constable Harris was there again, this time with another policeman and the body of a man short enough to look like a child under the covers, but clearly over forty when revealed. The covers were damp and the deceased, still fully clothed in a collarless shirt and mismatched suit, was drenched and smelled of wet dog, rotten vegetation, oil and worse.

'We drug 'im up outta the Thames,' said the second policeman unnecessarily. He scanned the laboratory, unnerved more by the instruments and jars than the corpse. 'This is a waste of your time, but 'Arris insisted. A five year old could say what 'appened.'

'Ah, you're an expert, how wonderful,' said Dr Jordan, with apparent sincerity. 'We'd be delighted to hear your theory and save ourselves some time.'

The policeman, oblivious to the others' smirks, pointed at the corpse's pallid head and a hole in the pocket of his threadbare jacket. ''Arf garrotted, 'biffed on the bonce, 'arfa brick stuck in 'is pocket, then 'oofed in the river. 'Appens all the time. If we brung you every one we found, you wouldn't have time to, er...' He scanned the room again. 'Pickle innards.'

Dr Jordan scratched his nose. 'There's an element of truth in that. But the point is that this poor soul was once alive and now isn't, due to—' He bent to make a cursory examination of what was visible of the man's skull, then poked the torn pocket with a pencil. 'What appears to be assault. Therefore someone deserves to face trial.'

'Deserves it for being useless at disposing of bodies,' grumbled the policeman. 'Anyone with any sense woulda chucked it where it would go out with the tide, not dumped it in the docks where it got tangled in all the ropes and whatnot so we have to deal with it.'

'The point is, this man was Jonathan Brown,' said Constable Harris, looking directly at Margaret, 'Dutch Jake's mate from that pub off Duval Street.'

'Good grief! Really?' said Margaret.

'That was another waste o' time,' snorted the other policeman.

'Finding out the truth is never a waste of time,' said Dr Jordan, 'even if the truth is that nothing untoward happened, which was true of Mr Lang. But it's almost certainly not true of Mr Brown here. Leave it with us, Constable Harris. We'll let you know what we find.'

'Thank you doctor.'

After the police had gone, Margaret, Algie and Dr Jordan started the autopsy, but at lunchtime, she had to leave them to continue it together while she prepared for an afternoon at Glassmakers Lane. What little enthusiasm she'd had for the job had long since ebbed away and besides, there no time to do more for lunch than buy a bread roll from the bakery and eat when she could. The whole day seemed to have been such a tearing, unsatisfying rush that she hadn't even read the news to see if there were any mention of Austria.

It wasn't until she was hurrying to Glassmakers Lane for the afternoon surgery that was halted on the final corner by a young boy yelling, 'Read all abaht it! New York sewing machine girls jump to their deaths from the eighth floor!'

Scrabbling in her purse for a halfpenny, she bought the *London Daily News* from him and read the article in horror. '*A ten-storey factory off Washington Square caught fire at sunset yesterday and the appalling number of 150 work people lost their lives... Many of them leapt to the pavement below and were dashed to death. ...*'

Margaret, horrified, had barely shaken the image from her head by the time she went to greet Dr Fernsby.

'Have you seen this?' she said, laying the newspaper down on the desk.

Dr Fernsby nodded. 'Appalling, isn't it?'

'Dreadful.'

'Do you think it will stop the Emperor and Empress of Germany visiting? What incompetence.'

Margaret blinked at her, then looked down at the paper. The next column, in slightly smaller print, was entitled '*The English Spy*', and the article referred to 'sensational hints' in the Berlin press about documents stolen from the German chancellor. How could she have missed it?

Oh God, Fox, please tell me you're still in Austria, she thought. She pulled herself together enough to nod. 'I'm sure that's a misunderstanding. I actually meant the fire in the New York sweatshop.'

'Ah yes,' said Dr Fernsby. 'Tragic. And an incentive for girls like that to better themselves so they're not doing those sorts of jobs.'

'Shouldn't it be an incentive for the factory owner to improve conditions?'

'If all the girls were able to choose better jobs and there was no workforce, the factory owners might think about it,' said Dr Fernsby. 'Why should they otherwise? At least this was accidental and not deliberate. Unlike the malcontents who took a hammer to the sewing machines in a similar place in Whitechapel.'

'Really?' said Margaret. 'I hadn't heard.'

Dr Fernsby reached down awkwardly to pick something up. 'You were away. One of my patients lost their job in consequence. Anyway, enough of the doom and gloom. You haven't had time to tell me all about the sanatorium and the Women's Day March. I imagine it all feels like a long time ago already! Good journey home?'

'Mmm,' said Margaret. If Dr Fernsby wasn't moved by the deaths of the New Yorkers, she'd hardly care about a governess in Switzerland. She glanced at the paper again, wondering how she'd managed to miss the article about the incident in Berlin. Juxtaposed with the one about New York, she'd never expected one page of a newspaper to make her feel so sick.

'The English spy' couldn't be Fox. Fox was retrieving documents stolen from Britain, not stealing them from Germany. Forcing a smile, she recounted as much of her visit to Switzerland as might interest Dr Fernsby before going to her room, reading the article properly, then flicking through the files on her table before looking around the little office in despair. Even a tube carriage full of people had seemed more spacious; a week in the clean, airy space of Switzerland had spoiled her.

The afternoon dragged and the relative freedom of the home visits afterwards couldn't come quickly enough.

Miss Connors was a twenty-four-year-old typist who lodged in a small house off Gerrard Street. A purse-lipped landlady let them in and opened a bedroom door to reveal Miss Connors sitting up in bed with a bowl in her hands. The sour smell of vomit hung in the air and the landlady, with a disgusted tut, flung up the window despite the patient's protestations. A blast of cold air heavily overlain with the smell of London wafted in: petrol fumes, coal smoke and hot manure from the milkman's horse, which was standing directly below. No sooner had the landlady left the room than Miss Connors threw up into the bowl then sat back against the headboard, grey-faced and tearful. 'I've been like this for days,' she said. 'I can't even brush my teeth without being sick. I think the old witch is poisoning me.' She wiped her face with a handkerchief and indicated the green walls. 'Arsenic wallpaper, I'll bet.'

'Have you been licking it?' said Dr Fernsby.

'Of course not,' snapped Miss Connors. 'I need to get back to work: I've been off three days and I can't do without the pay.' Miss Connors looked doubtfully into a glass of water then took a sip before focussing on Margaret.

'This is Dr Demeray,' said Dr Fernsby. 'She may be coming to work alongside me.'

'Oh.'

Margaret took the other woman's pulse and temperature, then ran through questions about the symptoms. She paused. 'May we examine your stomach?'

'Yes, of course. But don't push too hard; I don't want to be sick all over you.'

Margaret pressed and prodded, her fingers gentle, then pulled the covers up. 'May I ask how regular you are?'

Miss Connors blushed. 'I can't keep anything down long enough to—'

'I mean your monthlies.'

'What's that got to do with old Mrs M poisoning me?' She turned to Dr Fernsby for support.

'I'd ask the same.'

Miss Connors sat up, reached for a diary and started to flick through it. 'My last one was … about four months ago.' She frowned. 'That can't be right.' She flicked the pages back and forth, the tiny jottings which recorded her life blurring under her frantic fingers.

Margaret's heart sank.

'Miss Connors, I'll need to examine you more intimately,' said Dr Fernsby. 'Do you understand why?'

The young woman's eyes filled with tears as her gaze fell to Dr Fernsby's stomach. 'I can't be. It was only the once.' Miss Connors's voice was little more than a tearful whisper as she lay back to be examined. 'What'll I do?'

Thirteen

All in all, Monday was a miserable day and it was not until Margaret was home scouring the evening newspapers that the telephone rang and Bert's voice, calm and friendly, came down the receiver. 'The hen coop's secure and in less than twenty-four hours the fox will be on the right side of the water.'

'Wonderful.' Margaret took a deep breath. 'All well?'

'All well, miss. He'll collect you from work tomorrow if you say the time.'

'Five o'clock,' said Margaret. 'And it'll be Tuesday, so I'll be in Gla—.'

'The *other* place?' interrupted Bert. 'Understood. Bye.'

The conversation should have reassured her, but that night, Margaret dreamed of German officials chasing Fox as he tried to board the boat train. When he succeeded, he hid in a carriage papered in arsenic green and a shadowy woman was in the corner, cradling her stomach – or was she holding a heart? Papers rained down on him from a luggage rack full of sewing machines: papers in German, papers in French, death certificates, advertisements for jobs. When she looked closely, all of them were either nonsense, or their words blurred and then burst into flame.

The next day, which seemed to last a million years, was nearly over before she was able to shake the images from her head. Finally, at two minutes past five, the car pulled up outside the surgery.

Margaret had expected Fox to be alone, but it was Bert who emerged from the driver's seat to hand her into the back of the car. To her surprise, he was dressed as a constable.

Fox kissed her warmly.

Margaret giggled. 'Bert might see.'

'I don't care.' Fox gave her another long kiss then settled back with his arm along her shoulder. 'He should be glad I wasn't away as long as I expected to be.'

'What happened?' said Margaret. 'All those reports from Germany—'

'I wasn't in Germany and my time has been frustrating rather than dangerous.'

'Was the mission totally unsuccessful?'

'I met the people indicated, but whatever they're up to doesn't involve British airship designs. As you thought, they weren't so derisive as to suggest a double-bluff, but they were certainly politely dismissive.' Fox stroked the side of her cheek absent-mindedly. 'I was only there a day or so before Hare got word to me that Smith thought I ought to be in Italy. But the whole place is busy with anniversary celebrations, and "taking a military walk" in Libya to "free" it from the Ottoman Empire. They're quite openly warmongering without having to steal anything. Nothing made sense. I decided to come home early and read the original bloody documents for myself.'

'I'm not surprised.'

'It's the way it goes sometimes. How's life at the surgery?'

'Dr Fernsby's straightforward and practical. The work veers between dull and frustrating. And...' Margaret explained her feelings about the fire in New York and about Miss Connors, and Dr Fernsby's apparent lack of sympathy for both.

Fox stroked her shoulder. 'She doesn't sound a kindred spirit.'

'We needn't become close. I can keep my opinions to myself. I don't talk about myself much, and say virtually nothing about you.'

'Because of my job?'

'Not entirely.' Margaret bit her lip. 'I prefer keeping things separate.'

Fox contemplated her. 'Lack of commitment or lack of trust in someone who doesn't think like you do?'

It was a good question. 'I'd rather cut up the murder victim fished out of the Thames than tell a young woman she's "ruined". I've promised Miss Connors I'll find a nice place for unmarried mothers, but I have no idea where to start.'

'You can only do your best, Margaret.' He hugged her closer. 'Who was fished out of the Thames?'

'Someone called Jonathan Brown who'd ingested an absurd amount of chloral, then had been strangled then hit on the head. Depressingly, he wasn't quite dead before the murderer threw him in the river so he died of drowning. Not that he'd have survived all the rest.'

'Did you ever think of taking up floristry?'

'Did you?'

'Does it look as if he was killed for the usual sort of reasons or something else?'

'That's for the police to work out, but unlikely as it seems, the constable who brought the body thinks it's linked with a completely unsuspicious death in January which you've probably forgotten because it happened the day you were knocked down.'

Fox pulled a face. 'January? Nearly three months is a very long time to be in the Thames. How did anyone know who Brown was?'

'He's only been dead a day or so. In January however, he was working in Spitalfields with a man called Jakob Lang.'

'Wait a moment,' said Fox. 'I dimly remember. Wasn't he the one with the letter from Hamburg?'

'Yes. Brown was the man who said that someone fired a gun into the pub where they were working.'

'But there was no proof that they had?'

'None.' Margaret frowned. 'There's no reason for the two things to be related. St Katharine Docks are some distance from Spitalfields.'

'Nearest bit of water, though.'

'That's what Constable Harris thinks, so he'll keep digging, I daresay.'

'Dangerous place to dig,' said Fox.

Margaret looked out of the window and realised they were driving past the British Museum rather than Piccadilly Circus. 'I thought you were taking us home. Where are we going?'

'Hampstead.'

'We can't afford a house in Hampstead, Fox.'

'I know. But I need to speak with some people who can.'

'Anywhere near where you were knocked down?'

'Very. Hence being a police superintendent driven by a constable this afternoon. And I want your brains. What do you make of this?' He passed across an envelope.

'Is this to do with the failed mission or nearly being run over?' said Margaret, extracting a sheet of paper.

'Possibly both,' said Fox. 'That's what Smith deciphered to send me to Austria.'

The contents of the letter were almost word for word the kind of thing that was printed in the popular press, designed to aggravate the least patriotic citizen into mouth-frothing fury at foreign powers who dared to steal British designs to attack its own empire. Some words were clearly in a sort of code with transposed letters, but when Fox handed a crib sheet over, it was easy to see that it was the kind of thing Margaret had invented with her friends when they'd been fourteen. It revealed the names of noble families in both Austria and Italy, often pictured in the illustrated news and society pages.

Fox was right: there was nothing concrete enough to have sent him anywhere, not even specific details of what had allegedly been stolen.

'What about that?' said Fox, tapping the edges of the letter.

Now that Margaret was no longer focussed on the main message, she saw the pattern bordering the edges of the writing paper. She'd thought it was simply squiggles, but now realised that it was both uneven and occasionally repetitive. 'It's rather like Pitman shorthand.'

'You know Pitman's?'

'James tried to teach me it for lectures, but I was too impatient. I made up my own.'

'Any good?'

'Rubbish. I could never work out what I'd written.'

'But this seems meaningless,' said Fox. 'As if Pitman logograms have been applied to nonsense or an indecipherable code.'

'What does Smith say?'

'He can't find a pattern. But this is the thing. We've found out who may have sent the letter - a servant - and that's where you come in.'

'Me?'

'I need a gentle touch.'

'Me?'

'You're a kindly lady doctor assisting the police with interviewing servants.'

'Why would I want to do that?'

Fox shrugged. 'In reality because I want your impressions while I gain my own of her employers. Ostensibly however, the servant's female and young. I want to treat her with sensitivity.'

'No one will believe you're the real police with that sort of attitude. Who is she?'

'A housemaid called Norah Glyn.'

Margaret read the letter again. It was well drafted and literate, even if the contents were nonsense. 'How did you find out she sent it?'

'In late January, Norah Glyn wrote a letter which her employers intercepted and thereafter summoned the local police, saying they thought their maid was being seduced by foreign spies. The police suggested over-imaginative hysteria (I'm not sure on whose part). We've only just found this out, but the letter the employers gave the police had precisely the same writing, the same sort of message and the same sort of squiggles. Will you help?'

Margaret relaxed into his arms. 'Anything to make up for the boredom of general practice.'

'How kind.'

'I'm teasing,' she said. 'But if Norah Glyn sent you to Austria when you could have been with me, I may not be gentle.'

'Of course you will,' said Fox. He paused. 'Other things make it all the odder. That evening I was knocked down: the intended victim was Norah Glyn's employer.'

'What!' Margaret sat up straight. 'At the time, you told me he didn't want to press charges, yet now you're saying that a short while later he was eager to report his maid to the police?'

'Here's another thing, in the part of Abolin's filing system which we couldn't quite follow, are several adventure novels, as well as less gripping books on coal, fossils and various unpronounceable bits of rock. They were to be delivered "with a note" to E at DM, H. The next book due to go was the one on mineralogy that Charles sent you. Now, here we are, going to meet the Edevanes at Deanacre Manor in Hampstead.'

Margaret thought. 'Perhaps Abolin was branching out with his library. Maybe this Norah Glyn was educating herself.'

'Possibly,' said Fox. 'Although then you'd expect G at DM, H. It could be coincidence. It could be nonsense. It could be dangerous. There's still time for you wander on the heath while I talk to them.'

'It's too cold.'

'I'll take that as a yes. So let's go to meet some social climbers.'

The door at Deanacre Manor was opened by a butler.

'Mr and Mrs Edevane are expecting us,' said Fox.

With a sniff, the butler led them into the vestibule and left them, holding the silver tray on which they'd put their cards at arm's length as if they'd infected it.

A few moments later he ushered them into a warm drawing room, where a tall, slender man greeted them and indicated that Margaret should sit with his tall, slender wife before offering them cigarettes, which Margaret declined.

'Thank you for seeing us at such short notice,' said Fox.

'I confess we're rather surprised, Superintendent. We'd been given to understand that we needn't worry about what Mary has been doing.'

'Mary?' said Fox, consulting his notebook. 'I thought she's called Norah.'

Mrs Edevane shrugged. 'I have a set of plain names for the housemaids, regardless of what they were christened. I can never recall them otherwise. They rarely settle.' She turned to Margaret. 'You know how maids are these days. No consideration for others' feelings.'

Margaret caught Fox's glance and smiled as politely as she could.

'The police told us that Norah's nonsense had been nipped in the bud,' said Mr Edevane. 'She insisted a man had made her do it, but couldn't say who. It fizzled into nonsense.'

'Quite,' said Fox. 'But we want to speak with her to establish what made her write the letters, if it *wasn't* a man. I brought Dr Demeray as we felt it might be less alarming for Norah to speak with a lady.'

Mrs Edevane bestowed a sisterly smile on Margaret. 'I'm sure that would be an excellent idea, Dr Debenham, if it weren't too late.'

'Too late?' said Margaret.

Mrs Edevane nodded. 'She gave notice and left.'

'I see,' said Fox. His face and voice were neutral, but Margaret pitied whoever hadn't established this before sending them to Hampstead. 'Perhaps you could tell me where she works now.'

'She was inconsiderate to the last,' said Mrs Edevane dropping her half-smoked cigarette into the ashtray. '*Such* a mistake taking on a workhouse girl. We gave her a home. She left us. Now she's dead.'

'Dead?' said Margaret.

Fox flicked her a warning glance. 'I'm sorry, I don't quite follow. Could you explain from the beginning?'

Mr Edevane shrugged. 'She left our employment after the, er, incident. She was rather impertinent about it.'

'*Very* impertinent,' insisted his wife.

'We were never asked for a reference. She wrote regularly to Nellie – that is the housemaid with whom Norah shared a room. Nellie said that Norah had joined a moving-picture company.'

'Although that's exactly the sort of thing Mary - I mean Norah would say,' said Mrs Edevane. 'She exaggerated so, and we never did know whether half of what she said was true. It was funny to begin with, then rather wearying. But Sarah - I mean Nellie - hung on her every word. We thought the worst, but Norah had made her own bed and it was nothing to do with us. Then a man –almost a gentleman – turned up yesterday with her belongings. He said Norah had called this house the closest thing to home she'd had and perhaps we could dispose of them. So here we are, stuck with a suitcase of clothes. If you police could relieve us of it, we'd be more than grateful. The girl was thoughtless to the last.'

Margaret rose to her feet. 'Perhaps I could speak with Nellie while the Superintendent—'

'While I help with the suitcase problem,' said Fox. 'A very good idea, doctor.'

Fourteen

Nellie, a red-headed girl of about fifteen, was in the dining room polishing silver.

'This is Dr Deben—' began the parlourmaid.

'Demeray,' corrected Margaret.

'Hmph,' said the parlourmaid. 'She does it to everyone. This is Nellie. And just so's you know, my name's not Brown, it's Burlington. Nellie, this lady wants to talk to you about Norah.'

Nellie dropped the knife she was polishing with a clatter. The paste left a white streak on a sparkling spoon, but it was nothing like as white as the girl's face, her freckles standing out as tears started to fall.

'Try not to be scared,' said Margaret, taking a seat beside her. 'I know you were Norah's friend and I'm so sorry to hear she's passed away. I just want to know what she was like. Here, let me do your polishing for a bit while you blow your nose.'

'D-do you know how, madam?' Nellie sniffed.

'I was taught a long time ago,' said Margaret, recalling her aunt's insistence that she and Katherine knew what servants did so that they didn't take them for granted, and then later when their father disappeared, having to help out anyway. Now, she took up the cloth and tried to remember the technique. 'You can watch while you tell me all about Norah. I don't want to make you get behind.'

'Norah was wonderful,' said Nellie, as she dabbed her eyes and watched Margaret grind the polishing paste out of the fiddly decoration on a serving fork. 'She was only a foundling, but she made life in the workhouse sound as exciting as a story-book.'

'Goodness,' said Margaret. 'What was it was like?'

'Oh, there was a time when someone dared her to ask the governors for more food and she was put in a coal cellar and then ran away and was apprenticed to an undertaker. Then she went to live in a fine house and a gypsy boy swore he'd marry her but she said no and he died of sorrow and then his ghost roamed the hills calling for her. Only then the workhouse governors said they was sorry and gave her a roof over her head again, only her own room this time while they trained her up as housemaid until she found a place here.'

'Is that so?' Margaret rubbed harder and vowed not only to give Dinah a tip but also buy some stainless-steel cutlery to replace her silverware. 'Did Norah read a lot?'

'Yes, miss.'

'And you?'

'Not since school, miss.'

'I see. Perhaps you should start. Maybe with *Oliver Twist* and *Wuthering Heights.*'

'I knew she was making most of it up, if that's what you mean,' said Nellie. 'But it was more interesting that way.'

Margaret held out the fork. 'What do you think of my work?'

Nellie wrinkled her nose. 'It won't pass muster, if you don't mind me saying so. I'd best finish it off.' She sniffed and took the cutlery and polish back. 'Norah said she'd get me a job with the studio eventually. I said, "What, me? With my carroty hair and freckles?" and she said, "You won't look carroty in a moving picture and they can cover your freckles," and I said, "My mum don't like painted women," and she said, "It's not like that. It's respectable, they're mostly ladies". Oh, I wish I'd gone with her right off.'

'When she gave notice?'

'Yes, miss. Only she said she wasn't sure if there'd be a place straight-away and she'd let me know. But she wrote regular, and she was having a fine old time. She'd got a starring role – fancy that! I was so looking forward to seeing her when she come back.' Nellie took a deeper sniff, her voice wobbly. 'I never expected her to die.'

'May I ask what she died of?'

Nellie gulped and shrugged her thin shoulders. 'I dunno. She was healthy enough when I saw her a month ago, and she never said noth-ing in the postcard she sent except I wouldn't believe what she'd seen and she couldn't wait to get back.'

'No illness in her family?'

'Who knows?' Nellie shrugged again. 'She was a foundling, like what I said.'

'Here in London?'

'Nah, she said it was much more exotic.' Nellie held out the fork for Margaret's inspection. 'See? That's how you do it.'

'Somewhere in Britain more exotic than London?'

'Yeah, Wales. Norah said it was all mountains and waterfalls and rushing rivers and snow and—'

'Ghosts on hilltops.'

'Yeah.' Nellie sighed. 'I'd love to see it.'

Margaret sat in silence, watching the girl put the cutlery into its tray. How much of what Norah had said was true? Mrs Edevane had confirmed that she'd come from a workhouse. The experiences she'd reported to Nellie were clearly nonsense, but it was true enough that Wales was full of mountains and waterfalls and rushing rivers. It was also full of mines and factories and grinding poverty. Where was the workhouse likely to be?

'But she had a name,' said Margaret. 'So she can't have been completely a foundling.'

'It's not like that,' said Nellie. 'One day, when I was angry cos of Mrs E calling me Sarah, Norah tried to make me feel better.' Nellie rubbed her eyes again. 'Usually she'd tell me a silly story, but this time she just said, "Don't take on so. At least you've got a name what your parents gave you specially. I was dumped with nothing but an old shawl and a Bible. No name or nothing, so the workhouse had to choose one."'

'I see.'

'She said they had lists. One for first names, and one for surnames in Welsh. She said that when she'd been dumped Norah was the next name on the list, and they'd got to Glyn for the last name. She said at least the English could pronounce it. Does that make sense?'

'I think so,' said Margaret, thinking of the idiot on the platform at Neuchâtel. 'The English aren't renowned for learning how to speak other languages.'

'She said they had six surnames to pick from and they were Welsh names but some were spelled in English: Bryn for hill, Glyn for valley, Avon for river, Ford for road, Pontin for bridge, Forest for … well, forest.' A chuckle and a sob choked her. 'Then she stopped being serious-like and told me not to be a goose and when we was rich, we'd call ourselves Lady Ovaltine and Lady Brasso and go to the South of France and tell everyone that Mrs E ain't as much of a lady as she pretends. Which she ain't. I loved Norah. She made a story out of everything. The only thing I got left of her is her letters, and what she left behind for me to look after till she was settled proper.'

Margaret watched the earnest girl as she tidied away her work. 'What did she leave?'

Nellie looked up. 'Some stories. A black printed book in Welsh. And some of her story ideas in a notebook...' A blush clashed with her hair, 'I didn't mean to look, but I missed her. Do you want to see them? They're in my room.'

'Yes, please.'

Nellie's bedroom was in the attics. She'd put her trunk under the small high window, perhaps so that she could kneel on it and look out at the heath in the few hours she had to herself. There was neither fireplace nor radiator. The room was furnished with two metal-framed beds covered with eiderdowns and candlewick bedspreads, a rag rug, and a washstand complete with mirror on which brushes and hairpins were lined up. Nellie's coat and hat hung from hooks on the wall and a well-polished pair of smart boots gleamed beneath.

Between the beds was a chest of drawers, on which stood a water-filled bowl with a night light floating in it.

'I light it with the candle when I come to bed,' said Nellie, noting Margaret's puzzled frown. 'Then I blow out the candle and just have the night light. If I fall asleep before blowing that out, at least it can't set nothing alight.'

Margaret's frown deepened, but she said nothing. The house appeared to be less than twenty years old. It seemed a shame that whoever had commissioned the building hadn't thought that putting electricity in the maids' bedrooms would reduce the risk of fire better than a practice which should have gone out years ago.

'I'm on my own 'cos they haven't replaced Norah yet,' said Nellie. 'It's kinda nice, 'cos I've never had a bedroom to myself before, but it's lonely too. And cold. Me and Norah'd cuddle up sometimes if it got too bitter.'

She opened the chest, lifted out her spare uniform, clean aprons and Sunday dress, and put them on the bed. At the bottom, wrapped in a paisley shawl, were the things Norah had left behind and the letters she'd written since her departure.

Nellie had taken the postcard home to show her mother and forgotten to bring it back to Deanacres. The letters Norah had sent seemed chatty and innocuous, but the diary and the notebook had squiggles throughout. The more Margaret looked at it, the more she was convinced that it was badly executed or deliberately adapted Pitman's shorthand. Dredging through her memory for what James had taught her eighteen years earlier, Margaret tried to work some of the words out but any meaning was elusive. She picked up the black, leather-bound book. It was worn, its tissue-thin paper ready to tear. The words *Y Beibl* were embossed on the cover, barely legible, since any gilt had long worn off. The words inside were in a language Margaret had never learned, but it was clear what the book was. 'I'm surprised she left this.'

Nellie shrugged. 'She said if her Mum had thought that much of the Bible, she'd not have fallen for a baby she had to abandon, or she could at least have left a name inside it. Norah didn't have a lot of time for church.'

'I can understand that.' Margaret put the Bible down and picked up the notebook. 'Did she ever try to find her mother?'

'Yes, even though she didn't get nowhere. It was really sad, but she kept on trying.'

'I see,' said Margaret. 'Did she leave because of the trouble with the police?'

'Yes. No one but me believed that someone made her write those letters— I mean that letter.'

'Someone? Was it a man or woman?'

'A gentleman.'

'Did you meet him?'

'No, but just 'cos Norah was good at stories didn't make her a liar. And she told them she did "I know what you are" before she left. I wish I had the nerve to say that too.' Nellie wiped her eyes again. 'I miss her. And if they don't release that moving picture with her in, I'll never see her again. It's not fair.'

'You don't have a photograph?'

Nellie shook her head.

'Tell you what,' said Margaret. 'Will you let me take these away for a few days, and in exchange, I'll ask if the studio will let you visit on your afternoon off sometime and see what they'll do with the film Norah made? I'd escort you, of course, to make sure you were safe.'

'Would you do that, doctor?' Nellie's eyes sparkled. 'Would you? That would be wonderful!'

'Which studio was Norah working for? British Empire Films? Whetstone's not so far from here.'

'No, doctor.' Nellie wrapped the items up carefully in the shawl and then reached for her prayer book. Inside was a folded piece of paper. 'She sent me this. It was what the film poster would be like.'

It was a rough sketch of a simpering girl peering up at a handsome young man through a posy of flowers, while another handsome man glowered behind them. In the distance was a range of snow-capped mountains below a title in ornate, fashionable script: *Adelheid's Choice*. At the bottom, in smaller, ordinary capitals, were the words *Dysart's Studio, Glassmakers Lane*.

Fifteen

Finding a quiet place to stop the care on the way back to Bayswater, Bert, Fox and Margaret pored over Norah's writings. The notebook held snippets of prose and dialogue, little seedlings which perhaps Norah thought might germinate into a story some day. There were a few swirling doodles and a little more of the shorthand edging the pages as if she had been determined not to leave an inch of paper blank.

Bert flicked through the Bible and scratched his nose. 'This is a job for Miss Hedgehog.'

'Tsk,' said Fox. 'You know she doesn't like to be called that.'

'I'm not surprised.' Margaret frowned. 'You men are so childish. I suppose you call her that because men consider any woman with an opinion as spiky, whereas if she were a man you'd say—'

'We call her Hedgehog 'cos it's her name,' said Bert.

'Really?' Margaret narrowed her eyes. 'I thought you said all the animal names - Fox, Hare, Pigeon - were just coincidence.'

'They are,' said Fox. 'But she really is Hedgehog and I discovered her family even has a coat of arms.'

'Truly?' said Margaret. 'What does it have on it? A ball of prickles on the escutcheon with a lion passant licking its bleeding paw, the motto *celui qui touche sera poignardé* and the battle cry "Who curls up wins"? I swear you're inventing this. How could you possibly know that?'

Fox shrugged. 'A five-minute bit of research which ended up an hour. And then—' He grinned. 'We're teasing you Margaret, her name is really Edwards, but Hare did mishear it the first time and called her Miss Hedgehog and there is something a little spiky about her so as a nickname it stuck.'

'Spiky to the point of scary,' said Bert. 'I can imagine her disposing of a man when he's no use to her any more. Maybe after...' Bert cleared his throat. 'Like a spider.'

'She does give out that kind of aura,' said Fox thoughtfully. 'But I think she's mostly very private. Down to business. Bert is quite right: teasing aside, Miss Edwards is our woman. She speaks Welsh. In fact, she knows a lot of live languages like Gaelic and Basque and so on, which makes her more useful than Smith.'

'The servants haven't got a good word to say about the Edevanes,' said Bert. 'And they've only worked for them since autumn. Inconsiderate, snobbish and in the case of Mrs, inclined to break things and blame it on the servants.'

'Yes,' said Fox. 'She nearly snapped the handle of her tea-cup when I looked through the few rather romantic books in Norah's case and said I preferred thrilling books like Sir Ryder-Haggard's myself, especially *King Solomon's Mines*.'

'Do you?' said Margaret. 'That's the first I've heard of it. I thought you preferred travel memoirs and motor cycling magazines.'

'I do. But *King Solomon's Mines* was one of those delivered by Abolin so I wanted to see if there was any reaction. Mr Edevane did nothing except steady his wife's cup for her then light them both fresh cigarettes. I can't see either of them being readers particularly. The only books I saw were ones with expensive tooled leather covers which looked decorative rather than beloved and a batch of older books that might have been bought to make them look learned. I bet you a pound to a penny they have no idea what's in any of them. She recovered very quickly and her husband said she'd had rheumatic fever in her fingers recently and it had made her a little sensitive to the heat through the fine china.'

'Rheumatic fever in her fingers?' said Margaret incredulously.

Fox shrugged. 'You know what it's like. People are always finding new ailments.'

'Huh.'

'I'll take these papers straight to the office after I've dropped you at the flat, shall I?' said Bert.

'We'll walk from here,' said Fox. 'But yes, if you do that, we'll see what Miss Edwards can come up with tomorrow.'

Later, discussing what they'd found out at Deanacre Manor over dinner, neither Fox nor Margaret were sure whether to be more disgusted by the Edevanes' indifference to Norah's fate or the fact that they hadn't troubled to ask where her grave was. However, having been offered a tour by Mrs Dysart, Margaret thought she might be able to introduce herself at the studio on Thursday afternoon, when she was next at the practice, and somehow get Norah into the conversation. 'Or I could try and get permission from Dr Jordan to go tomorrow.'

'That would look odd and also irritate the board,' said Fox. 'Thursday will do. But when you do go, promise you'll take care?'

'I wasn't going to ask about secret messages or spies, you know,' said Margaret. 'There's nothing to be careful about.'

'Every girl wants to be a moving-picture actress. How did Norah Glyn, a workhouse foundling, land an acting job within days of resigning her housemaid's post?'

'Luck?'

'You don't believe that and nor do I. And eighteen-year-old girls don't just drop dead for no reason. Why are you frowning? Something's bothering you. What?'

'I don't know. It's something Nellie said, but I just can't put my finger on it.'

'Leave it,' said Fox, rising from the table. 'If you don't think about it too hard, it'll come to you. In the meantime, we have some catching up to do.'

While whatever Nellie had said didn't materialise in her subconscious, something else did.

It came to the forefront of her mind when she went to get a book to take with her on Wednesday shortly after Fox left. In a simple frame, propped up on the bookshelf were a part of Charles's note, which she'd folded to display one part of the message:

Don't either of you forget me, but don't mourn me. Go to the music-hall, get a little drunk, go dancing, find justice, then dance some more. Life is too short for weeping.

She traced his handwriting for a second, the grief which had ebbed for a while flowing back. *How did Abolin manage to kill you?* she thought. *Fox said he was smaller than you and mild. You could have overpowered him surely?* She cast her mind back to those dark days in February: the discovery of Abolin's suicide by poison in an alley; a hasty inquest; the case closed by the police with an almost audible snap. She'd imagined Abolin's body, and at the time shocked herself by feeling that whatever suffering the poison must have caused him in his last moments could never balance the pain he'd left behind when he murdered Charles. But now it occurred to her that the reports of the inquest had never mentioned poison at all.

After she arrived at St Julia's, Margaret telephoned the hospital where Abolin had been taken, on the pretext of researching another hospital's approaches to police autopsies. Eventually she was put through to the right doctor.

'What killed him?' he said. 'Any one of a number of things. He'd ingested chloral, there were ligature marks on his neck and he'd died in a wet alley on a freezing night in February. We assumed he'd tried hanging himself and failed, or lost courage and went for an easier way out. We were fairly sure the chloral did for him, but it may have been hypothermia or a combination of the two.'

Margaret tried to keep her voice calm. 'You don't know definitively?'

'The police didn't want us to waste too much time. The man was a murderer and he was dead. He'd cheated the hangman but nothing would alter that. The police just wanted the case closed.'

'Thank you. Have you any photographs of the corpse?'

'Let me see.' Down the line came the flicking of pages. 'Yes. A few of his head and neck. I can get a messenger to bring you the file if you like?'

'Yes please that would be very useful. I'll return them as soon as possible.'

In the evening, Margaret told Fox what she'd discovered.

'The ligature marks were the same as they were on Jonathan Brown,' she said. 'I've been reading up on it and with no sign of a knot and given where the greatest pressure was, they're more likely to indicated someone being strangled by someone else, rather than suicide. There's not enough evidence now to prove anything, but at a guess, Abolin was rendered unconscious and left to die, or perhaps more likely believed to be dead when he was left.'

'You're not saying that Charles took him to some godforsaken part of London, killed him and then killed himself.'

'Of course not Fox,' said Margaret. 'What do you take me for?'

'But Brown's body might never have been discovered while still identifiable whereas Abolin's body was pretty much tripped over a few hours after his death.'

'Whoever killed them wanted Abolin found. Whereas they didn't want Jonathan Brown found.'

Fox perused the photographs and frowned. 'Are you sure?'

'No. But these are the facts.'

'That would mean that someone killed Abolin after Abolin killed Charles. But who?' Fox ran his hands through his hair as if to straighten his thoughts. 'My God. There's an alternative, isn't there? Perhaps Abolin didn't kill Charles. Someone else killed both of them.' He slammed his fist on the table. 'What fools we've been. It was made to look the other way and just as I might have got close to finding out we were looking at it wrong, I'm sent off to Austria by Norah's letter.'

'I'm convinced it's connected,' said Margaret. 'How is Miss Edwards getting on?'

'Slowly. But she's found out where Norah came from and Hare's given her permission to go to South Wales to see if she can find out any more.'

'When is she going?'

'Friday night to stay in Cardiff then going to the town first thing Saturday morning then coming back to London Saturday afternoon.'

'Can you ask if she'll take me?'

'What about St Julia's?' Fox frowned.

'It's only a morning and Dr Jordan had already agreed I could use it for studying at home. If he finds out I went to Wales to do it instead, I'll remind him there's a new sanatorium being built near Brecon and I fancied looking at the area.'

'Norah's home town is miles from Brecon.'

'He needn't know.'

'I can't see it myself,' said Fox. 'But you may be right. The Hampstead police think she might have been behind some other letters, and I'm waiting for them to find them in the archives. If they're anything like the one that sent me to Austria and the one the Edevanes intercepted then it's just nonsense. She probably just liked a good story, thought it was fun and got carried away. It's all coincidence.'

'I thought you didn't believe in coincidence.'

Fox rolled his eyes. 'Do you know how many letters about spies the police receive? Hundreds, thousands. The country's obsessed.'

'So are you.'

'I know what's real and what isn't.' Fox closed the autopsy file and sat back. 'It's shown there's a link between Abolin and the Edevanes. I'll keep digging into that angle. Bert has a lead he and I are following up on Saturday, so go to Wales if you think it's worthwhile. One way or another, we're going to find out who really murdered Charles and why.'

Sixteen

'I hope you're starting to find your feet,' said Dr Fernsby as they stood by her small car on Thursday afternoon. She had demonstrated the accounts to Margaret at length and now, before the evening clinic, there were home visits to do. 'Private practice has a charm of its own and at least someone else gets to cut up the bodies.'

But I like cutting them up, thought Margaret, smiling blandly.

Dr Fernsby put her bag on the back seat of the car. 'I presume a forward thinking woman such as you can drive.'

'I'm fairly competent on a motorcycle.'

'Really?' Dr Fernsby blinked a little.

'My husband wants us to go on a tour one day and I refuse to travel in a sidecar, so if we ever do it, we'll have a motorcycle each.'

'How about a car?'

'I'm learning,' said Margaret. 'My husband's er, chauffeur is giving me lessons.'

'Gracious,' said Dr Fernsby. 'How does a chauffeur tell his employer that she's doing something wrong?'

'He has his own special way,' said Margaret, recalling the time when Bert had told her that she was a menace to humanity before making her do a forty-point turn in a narrow road.

The drivers of a milk cart, a coal wagon and a motor cab, whose progress she was impeding, all added their opinions about women drivers at enough volume for people in nearby houses to peer out at them. But however much her face burned even as she remembered it, Margaret smiled too, because after telling her what a fool she was, Bert had then loudly told the milkman, the coalman, the cabbie and the curtain twitchers precisely where he'd put the crank handle if they didn't leave her in peace to concentrate.

'Let me know when you feel confident enough to try,' said Dr Fernsby. 'It's getting almost impossible to squeeze behind the wheel.' She checked the list in her hand. 'For a wonder, one of our visits is local: the studios. A young artist called Reuben with one of his recurring headaches. It's almost certainly eye strain. Should we do it first or last?'

Margaret's heart jumped. If they left it till later, Dr Fernsby might want a rest before the evening clinic, leaving the patient to Margaret. Then it might be easier to ask random, unconnected questions. 'Last,' she said. 'Let me crank the handle for you while you work out where we should go first.'

Two hours later, as she'd hoped, Margaret entered the studio alone. The outer door banged shut behind her, alerting a young woman reading a Sexton Blake story while seated in a tipped-back chair with her feet up on a desk.

'Hallo!' she said, dropping the magazine but otherwise remaining in the same position. 'Can I help?'

Before Margaret could answer, a young man ambled up with a sheaf of papers. 'Here you are Miss Isaacs, Mrs D says... Oh hallo! Are you the lady doctor?'

'Are you Mr Reuben?'

'Me? No, I'm Ned. Ned Killick, cameraman extraordinaire. I'll take you to him.'

It seemed remarkably informal. The walls were lined with stills from moving pictures, studio photographs of Mrs Dysart in an evening dress and one of Mr Dysart in pilot's gear in the cockpit of an aeroplane. Margaret could only assume he was more competent at flying then editing, since he was alive.

Mr Reuben was lounging in a side office. He had a poultice balanced on his head and was eating a bun until Margaret was ushered in, whereupon he hastily dropped it onto the desk, then realised it had landed on a drawing, picked the drawing up, shook sugar off it and peered for grease, while the poultice slid off his head and onto the floor.

'I'm Dr Demeray,' said Margaret. 'I'm working with Dr Fernsby. I gather you have a headache, Mr Reuben.'

'Don't make it sound so mere,' complained Mr Reuben. 'At the very least it's nervous exhaustion. Here, look at this!' He held up the drawing which was a more detailed version of the one Nellie had shown Margaret. 'They want me to alter her to look like someone else. Is it any wonder my brain is about to explode? And you say "headache" as if I'd stubbed my toe. Perhaps it's something much worse, and I'll die like Norah.' He stabbed at the picture. 'That's her. Or do I mean that is she? I never was good at grammar.' His shoulders slumped. 'I—'

'Stow it, Reuben,' said Ned. 'You're worse than Norah. She could yak for the Empire,' he explained to Margaret. 'Chopsing, she called it. Good word that, chopsing. Anyway, she didn't die of a headache, poor kid.'

'No, but...' said Mr Reuben. He retrieved the poultice and looked hopefully at Ned. 'I suppose you couldn't get someone to warm this up and bring me some coffee?'

'You suppose right. The tea trolley will be round in a minute. And you can't expire, your opinion's wanted on the film. You too, doctor, an independent eye could be just what we need. We'll pay you in buns – there's a couple going begging.'

'I'm happy to do it without the buns,' said Margaret. She waited till the door was closed, then examined Mr Reuben, replacing her instruments in her bag just as someone knocked.

Mr Reuben sighed. 'That'll be the coffee. Shall I live long enough to drink it?'

'There are no symptoms of anything serious,' said Margaret, opening the door and taking two glasses of water from the trolley. 'It's sixpence for the consultation. You need to rest your eyes frequently, and put a cool cloth over them sometimes, but aspirin will help for now. And perhaps drink less coffee. It won't help, Mr Reuben.'

'Just call me Reuben. My surname's quite another matter and I don't use it.'

'Oh. I see.' Margaret waited for an explanation but none came. 'Why not tell me about the film er ... Reuben? That might alleviate the stress.'

'They're not sure whether to finish it or not,' said Reuben, gloomily contemplating the water, then his drawing, and getting to his feet. 'Poor Norah. Her first chance turned out to be her last. She's only in part of it, and they might cut her out or just give up on the film altogether.'

'Oh dear.'

'I liked Norah. When there wasn't much to do we'd have a good old chinwag. I'd be sketching and she'd be writing. She wanted to be a novelist.' He sighed. 'But like Ned says, an outside opinion on the film would be just the ticket. Follow me.'

In a larger, windowless room, painted black and stuffy with cigarette smoke, a group of men and women were standing around as a young man fiddled with a projector trained on the far wall.

'Aren't you dying, Reuben?' said one of the young women.

'Apparently not, Gladys. But the doctor here says I'm prostrated with overwork and I need more pay and a bottle of stout.'

'I said nothing of the kind,' said Margaret. 'You need aspirin, plenty of water and maybe some fresh air.'

'Fresh air? London?' Reuben pulled a face. 'Can't you prescribe Switzerland? Almost everyone went except for me. See what happens when you don't take the lowly artist, Mr Drummond.'

Switzerland? Margaret twisted round to see who Reuben was talking to. Behind her, an older man drew deep on his cigarette, scowling. He'd opened his mouth to speak when he and Margaret recognised each other.

'You were at Neuchâtel with Miss Vale,' she said.

Of course. 'Bryn for hill, Glyn for valley'. That's what's been nagging at me since yesterday. Valley isn't a usual surname, but Vale is, and it means the same thing.

'Blimey,' said Mr Drummond. 'How did you find out she worked for us? Are you here to find out what happened to her?'

'I came to see Reuben. I'm Dr Demeray by the way. I'm working with Dr Fernsby.'

'The other doctor eh? I'm Drummond, the other director.' They shook hands.

'What *did* happen after I boarded the train?' asked Margaret.

Mr Drummond took another drag on the cigarette. 'I went with her to the hospital, and Mrs Dysart wired the money for the burial and I found an English vicar to do the necessary. It took a week, all in all. When I came back her landlady didn't want Norah's things, such as they were, but Reuben remembered that she'd previously lived with a friend and found the address.'

'I thought they were clerk-typists,' added Reuben. 'I don't know why. Something Norah had said. I assumed the address was a block of flats.'

'Yeah,' said Mr Drummond. 'So I took the things there, thinking this friend could use them or pass them on. But it turned out the house is a fancy home with a mob of servants and Miss Pinter's a maid and Norah *used* to be one. The employers didn't want the belongings either. If they'd cared enough to ask where she's buried, I'd have taken the stuff away, but they didn't, so I left them to sort it out.' He exhaled and sighed. 'I'm not only director but actors' manager. I never expected to be undertaker, too.' He shivered. 'Coming back with Norah's things on the sleeper after I'd left her buried among all those strangers...' His face screwed up but his eyes held Margaret's, steady and assessing. 'I can give you the employers' address, if you like.'

'Yes, please,' Margaret handed him her notebook and watched him write the Edevanes' address. At least now she'd have a logical reason to request that Nellie visit the studio. 'I've been waiting for Dr Gilliand to send me the results of the post-mortem.'

'It was hyper-thingy-thing-thing. Hereditary.' Mr Drummond wrinkled his nose.

Margaret frowned. 'Just like you said.'

'Just like *she'd* said.'

Margaret nodded as if it all made sense. *How would Norah have known?*

'I thought Dr Demeray could give us an outside opinion on the film,' said Reuben.

'Not that you want your poster saved,' said Mr Drummond, grinding his cigarette into a bucket of sand and shoving his hands in his pockets.

'What will you do with the film if you don't use it?' said Margaret.

'Same as we do with most things we edit out – keep it in case we can splice bits of it with something else to make it longer,' said Mr Drummond. 'You'd be surprised what people don't notice, even when it makes no sense. Let's see, shall we? Crank it up, Killick!'

The lights were extinguished and with a spatter of flickering numbers, letters and meaningless symbols, a film was projected onto the wall. There was no apparent attempt at a narrative. It started with Swiss scenery: mountains, snow, pretty little houses and churches. Even with the film in black and white, sitting in a room full of smoke, Margaret could smell the clean, cold air. She coloured the scenes with her imagination, half-waiting to see herself and Fox kissing on the hillside.

Now there were a series of scenes depicting a young woman with one or other of two young men: dressed in mufflers and overcoats, their faces barely visible; leaning against a wind whirling with snowflakes; kissing one, then being kissed by the other; then waving one of them goodbye. Then the girl was running hatless through a meadow, her fair hair flowing behind her, briefly glancing over her shoulder towards the camera: a young woman bursting with life, her eyes sparkling, her full mouth ready to smile or laugh.

The images disappeared, to be replaced with more flickering nonsense.

'There you go,' said Mr Drummond. 'That was Norah filmed out-doors in Switzerland, bundled up in scarves and hats and whatnot. And *this* is what we've filmed in the studio so far with Gladys.'

Now the film showed the other actress in a scene with one of the men, her hand to her brow then her breast as only his embrace stopped her from fainting. She was shorter than Norah, her hair finer and her figure possibly fuller, but otherwise they were very similar. And the actor, Margaret realised, was the young man who'd arrived on the platform at Neuchâtel with Mr Drummond when she was with Norah.

'We're trying to decide if the average viewer would realise we've switched actresses,' said Mr Drummond, 'because if they would, the whole thing will be so much wasted time and money.'

'How very inconsiderate of Norah to die before you'd finished making the film,' muttered Margaret.

Mr Drummond grunted. 'This is a business. If I'd known she had a hereditary heart condition, I wouldn't have let her do all that running around.'

'I thought you said you knew.'

'Mr Dysart told me *after* she'd done all the running,' said Mr Drummond. 'Anyway, what's your view? It doesn't make much sense when it's all out of order, but hopefully you get the gist.'

'I think so.'

'I was never sure about the expense of the whole Swiss thing, but the Dysarts want to make films that are a bit out of the ordinary and Norah's story seemed good, even if her acting wasn't up to much.'

'Norah's story?'

'You've read *Heidi*?' asked Mr Drummond.

'Of course.'

'Well, this is supposed to be what happens when Heidi grows up and has to choose between Peter and some bounder called Hans. Norah wrote it. It's sentimental, derivative codswallop.' He chuckled. 'Which makes it absolutely perfect for a moving picture. We might change the names though, in case anyone accused us of plagiarism. Mrs Spyri's dead, but we can't afford to get done. No one understands British copyright. Gawd knows if anyone understands Swiss copyright.'

'I see your point,' said Margaret. 'But if it helps, I don't think there's enough of Norah's face in the Swiss scenes to compare with Gladys's later, especially if there will be a lot of Gladys. And it would be a shame to cut Norah out altogether.'

'Yeah,' said Mr Drummond, and Margaret sensed him shiver again. 'And after I spent all that time with her body, she might haunt me.'

Seventeen

The following morning, Margaret took a small overnight case with her to St Julia's ready to meet Miss Edwards at Paddington after work. Investigating Norah's origins seemed like a step in the right direction, but all the same, Margaret felt unable to wait until Monday before she could find out more about the London angle.

At one o'clock on the dot, she left St Julia's for Glassmakers Lane, under the pretext of using her lunch hour to organise a date to combine the promised tour of the studio and Nellie's visit, and telling Dr Jordan that since Dr Gilliand hadn't written, she wanted to ask more questions about Norah, while also checking to see that Mr Reuben had recovered.

'It's your time,' said Dr Jordan, 'although I hope you remember to eat. You're looking far too thin.'

Gloomy under grey skies and speared by a bitter breeze, Glassmakers Lane was its usual self-contained self. The busyness of Shaftesbury Avenue seemed a hundred miles away rather than under a hundred yards.

As Margaret looked about, a sense of discomfort grew. She'd felt like this before, usually in the East End, when people were watching her covertly. But in Glassmakers Lane surely pockets, purses and person were of little interest to anyone. The street was quiet. The only people on the street were those hurrying home for lunch. A window cleaner up his ladder paused in his whistling to ask a tiler on a nearby roof if he fancied going for a pint. Miss Burton was turning over the sign on the chemist's door and gave her a small but friendly wave. Margaret glanced at the surgery, but since it was lunch time, no one could be seen at the waiting room window. Dr Fernsby was no doubt dining alone at the rear of the building as she usually did.

Dysart's studio doors were shut and Margaret hesitated. She had no plan of what to do next, and wished she were less impetuous. *If they're in, won't they think it odd that I couldn't wait till Monday to speak with Mrs Dysart and even if they don't, how on earth am I going to initiate a conversation about Norah when I have no reason to ask? And who's really going to believe I'm worried about Reuben's 'nervous collapse'?*

As if summoned by her thoughts Reuben himself strolled out of the studio, looked at her in delighted surprise, tipped his hat and walked up.

'How nice to see you! I didn't know you worked here on Fridays!'

'I don't. But I remembered something I forgot to ask yesterday.'

'About my head?' said Reuben. 'It's quite all right today. I daresay it was worry about the film. Now they've decided to go ahead, I feel a hundred times better.'

'I'm very glad to hear it. Is Mrs Dysart in today?'

'Not till later. Mr D is in though. Dysart that is. Drummond also.'

'Oh. Thank you. That's a shame, I was hoping to speak with her.' *Now what should I do?* 'You seemed fond of Norah,' Margaret hazarded.

'Very.' Reuben's eyes flickered for a second and his smile dimmed a little. 'It's nice that you care. I sometimes feel like I'm the only one who does.'

Margaret seized her chance. 'Perhaps grief caused your headache. Would you like to tell me about her? Perhaps we could have lunch in Soffiato's or somewhere?'

'What a—'

Reuben's words were interrupted by a yell and running footsteps on the pavement coming from the dead end of the street. As they turned to see what was happening a young man in rough clothes barrelled between them, nearly knocking Margaret backwards and tangling with her in a brief, absurd dance before dashing on. Mr Reuben remonstrated loudly, shaking his fist.

Margaret stared after the running man, her hat askew. Something buzzed painfully in her ear and a strand of hair came loose. Over Reuben's yells and the startled exclamations of Soffiato's customers and the Burtons, who'd all come outside to see what was happening, she heard a series of strange, sharp, hollow noises.

On the pavement ahead, the man stumbled, fell, staggered to his feet and fell again.

'He's been shot!' shouted the waiter from Soffiato's.

'Where from?' called Mr Burton.

'Get indoors, doctor!' said Reuben.

Margaret ran towards the man. He was clambering to his feet again, clutching an arm, and blood oozed through his fingers. 'Go!' His voice was hoarse. 'Leave me be.'

'Let me see,' said Margaret. 'I'm a doctor.'

'Get out of the street!' someone shouted from a doorway.

'Let me see,' Margaret repeated. 'You're hurt.'

'No!' the man hissed. 'I need to get away. No one's safe in this street. Anders will see to that, especially when he can't get what he's after.'

He limped as he tried to pull away and Margaret steered him sideways into the shadows. There was something familiar about his face, pale under a shock of dark hair and beetling brows.

'Let me go!'

'You're hurt. Your leg and your arm.' She caught at his grey jacket and the edge of something yellow flashed from its inner pocket - a leaflet perhaps, a starched handkerchief - before he shifted and it disappeared.

'I twisted my ankle,' he growled. 'That's all. The arm is just a scratch.'

'It's more than a scratch, and you've been shot in the leg too. Please. I'm a doctor. What's your name?'

'No.'

'Please let me look.'

'No. It's not safe.'

Wrenching his injured arm away, he pushed Margaret with the other and she overbalanced. As she righted herself he limped off at more speed than she'd have thought possible, turning onto the main thoroughfare. Reuben made chase, returning after a few minutes with a constable. 'I don't know how, but he's gone,' he said, shaking his head. 'I've got a policeman.'

'What's all this about again?' said the constable. 'You were talking that fast, sir, I couldn't make head nor tail. Guns? Here?' Then he turned to Margaret and paled. 'Cor, I didn't know it was a lady what got shot. Here, sit down afore you faint.'

'What?' said Margaret, but Mr Burton and Reuben had paled too.

'The top of your ear's bleeding,' said Reuben.

'It was a horse-fly,' said Margaret. 'It bit me or stung me or whatever they do.'

'Blimey,' said the constable. 'If that's the case, it must be a new breed. We'll need to get armour on the horses.'

'What?' Margaret unpinned her hat. Through the narrow brim was a neat, round hole, and when she touched her ear it was sticky with blood.

'I want you to give up,' said Fox an hour later at St Julia's, watching Margaret rearrange her hair for a fifth time in front of the mirror in her office.

'I can't go out in public with my hair down. I'm not fifteen. Then there's the hat. What will I tell the milliner about the hole, when I'm still not convinced it was made by a bullet?'

'It wasn't a bloody clothes moth that nearly took your ear off,' snapped Fox. 'What I mean is that I want you to give up asking questions. I want you to give up working in Glassmakers Lane and stay here.'

Margaret let her hair drop and stared. 'Don't be ridiculous.'

'The man who they were shooting at said Anderson was making it unsafe.'

'He didn't say Anderson, he said Anders.'

'Are you sure?'

'I'm sure he didn't say Anderson.'

'Why are you frowning, then? You're not sure.'

'He could have said Andrews,' said Margaret. 'But there was definitely no "son" at the end.'

'Maybe it's another name change. If so, he's got too close to you. I want—'

'I don't care what you want, Fox, I need to get back to work. Dr Jordan needs me.'

'You should go home and rest.'

'I've lost a quarter of an inch of skin, Fox. Dr Fernsby put enough antiseptic on it to shrivel my ear, but I'm not about to die.'

'Shock.' Fox folded his arms, his face grim. 'Blood loss. At the very least, I'd like you to stay away from Glassmakers Lane from now on.'

'No. You know why I need to work with Dr Fernsby, and while I'm there I can help you too. Reuben will speak with me, I know it.'

'I can get someone else to go undercover and do that. We'll just lose a few days.'

'Why?' Margaret slammed the hairbrush down. 'You have me. I'm not so obviously connected with any sort of intelligence department.'

'I want you safe.'

'I want *you* safe, but I can't imagine you listening to me if I told you to stop. I want to help. I want to know what Norah was writing and I'm not happy about her death and if it's connected with Abolin, it's connected with Charles and I want to stop Anderson doing whatever he's doing. Do you agree with the board and think I should give up doing everything requiring my brain and spend my days dusting and doing good works simply because you've put a ring on my finger? I don't belong to you. I—'

'Have I ever suggested I think any of that?'

'Then why are you trying to stop me doing as I choose? Just now, I choose to help you.'

'You've just been shot.'

'You said the police said Mr Nierling junior was firing at a burglar.'

'Robber. And Mr Nierling junior will be lucky if I don't find a new home for his rifle.'

'So it's unconnected, and I have a reason to be in Glassmakers Lane, which you don't. If it isn't, then the surgery remains an alternative to sitting at home darning your slippers if the hospital dismiss me. I have no idea what I'd do without a career.' Margaret stalked over to the bookshelf and poked through the volumes, but she couldn't see any of them. All she could see was the whirl that kept her awake: leaving St Julia's for another hospital so badly run it was desperate enough to employ a married woman, Dr Fernsby's little practice with its dull routine and duller accounts, a sanatorium with its echoes and misery, unspecified research in an unspecified location which kept popping into her mind as a garden shed... She calmed her voice. 'Maybe this is the last time I can help you, Fox, and I'm going to whether you like it or not.'

Fox ran a hand across his brow. 'I'm not asking you to stop doing your job. I'm asking you to rest this afternoon and *then* stop helping me, because I'm putting you in danger.'

'I wasn't being shot at,' said Margaret. 'It was the man who ran off who was being shot at. I don't need to rest, so I'm going back to work. I'm not going to stop helping unless by doing so I put *you* in danger. I thought we were supposed to be a partnership.' Her ear stung and her head ached. Fox was irritated with her, but she hoped he was also irritated with himself for being overprotective. If he had been the one caught in crossfire, she would want to hide him away too;. but she would never hobble him by saying so. That was the difference.

They took a step towards each other. After a few seconds, they embraced.

'I love you,' he said.

'I love you too.'

'So stop standing in the way of bullets.'

'I will if you will.'

He kissed her. 'I'll go back to Glassmakers Lane to see what the police are doing. If it's nothing to do with Anderson, I'll leave them to it. If it is, I'll see what I can do to take over the investigation. I wish you'd at least go home tonight rather than to Wales. I'd like to be able to take care of you as well as Juniper.'

'I'll be fine. Do you have the other letters from Hampstead police yet?'

'I was about to start looking at them when you telephoned.'

'I should have kept quiet, shouldn't I?'

'Good God,' said Fox. 'Promise you'll never do that.'

'Everything will be all right,' said Margaret. 'Whatever Norah was doing, I don't feel it was with malice. The people who were close to her, loved her. I think she was being used. And I want to find out why.'

'What if there's nothing to be found?'

Margaret remembered Norah's huddled form on the platform in Neuchâtel. 'I feel as if I'm letting her down. Isn't that how you feel about Charles? What if you never track Anderson down?'

Fox scowled. 'There is no "what if" about it; I'll do it if it kills me.'

'It had better not,' said Margaret. 'Because I want to see you in one piece and a more modern frame of mind tomorrow evening.'

'Will you darn my slippers?'

'The best you'll get is cocoa at bedtime.'

'Only cocoa?'

'Not even that, if you don't stop behaving as if I'm made of china.'

Eighteen

'I wouldn't be here if I didn't feel fit to work,' Margaret told Dr Jordan and Algie after Fox had gone and she'd entered the laboratory, realising even as she said it that if Fox hadn't fussed so much, she'd probably have asked to go home with her mounting headache and the sick relief that she hadn't been standing an inch or two to the left.

'I'm sure if it were *my* ear that had been shot, you'd have started making sketches by now,' said Algie, head on one side like a hopeful puppy.

For the first time in what seemed like days, Margaret forgot her indignation, her misery and her shock and burst out laughing. 'Scientists are heartless beasts!'

'You are, too,' said Dr Jordan. 'And not heartless, not really. Just curious. It's for the common good.'

Algie examined her with professionalism, more delicate in removing the sticking plaster than Dr Fernsby had been in putting it on. 'I think the wound has clotted sufficiently now. I'll just clean the dried blood off so that we can see properly. If it starts bleeding again, I can put a stitch in – if there's anything to stitch together, that is. Let's get you into the light, then Dr Jordan can photograph the wounds and I'll sketch them. I don't suppose you feel like lying down?'

They all looked at the laboratory table, scrubbed to within an inch of its life and stinking of disinfectant, but somehow nevertheless haunted by its last occupant.

'No' said Margaret.

A few moments later, they compared Algie's sketches to the photographs of Jakob Lang. There was too little damage to Margaret's ear to compare with whatever had scraped along Lang's head. The abrasions were similar, perhaps although the amount of flesh affected was much smaller and the tiniest bit of ear had gone. It proved nothing about whether Lang had been shot. Margaret looked at the sketch and then in a mirror; she hoped it was her headache making her feel nauseous.

Dr Jordan focussed on her face and frowned. 'I wonder if you should—'

It had only been a couple of hours ago, but it felt like weeks. Mr Reuben fussing over her; the police constable trying to interrupt the jabbering witnesses to instruct someone to telephone the police station; Dr Fernsby's robust cleaning of the wound; taking a cab to St Julia's and getting a message to Bert. She'd never expected Fox arrive in a temper. It was hard to know which had hurt her head more: the bullet which had skimmed the top of her ear, Dr Fernsby's scrubbing, Reuben's wittering, or the questions – *Where were you standing? Where was he standing? What did you hear? What did you see? Did you turn? What angle must it have come from?*

The laboratory felt stuffy and airless and as she looked back, the events unfolded as if they were part of a moving picture she was watching from a distance. *Glassmakers Lane settling down for lunch, a woman in a nice hat chatting with a young man, another man barging through and the woman startled. Why did he push between them rather than go round them? Was he injured as he did so, or afterwards?*

Margaret rewound and replayed the 'film', and couldn't decide. Then she 'watched' for the hundredth time and imagined Fox there instead of a woman. Fox, standing just a little to the left, and... Now she wished she'd responded to him differently. Little slivers of rainbow light flickered in the corner of her eyes, and her nausea returned.

'You're looking rather grey,' observed Dr Jordan. 'Matron asked me to tell you something but...'

'I'll be all right.' Margaret wanted more than anything to lie down and go to sleep. The floor would do. Even the mortuary slab seemed suddenly appealing. 'What was it?'

'Frimley San telephoned to say that Mrs Balodis - I'm sure you remember her - is very close to death.'

'So she won't live till Easter.'

'No. The san wrote to her children but had no reply. Matron wondered if you knew whether they might have moved.'

'I suspect they may have.'

'You met them—'

'I met her daughter.'

'Anna, wasn't it?' said Dr Jordan. 'And the son was Anders?'

'Andris...' Margaret felt her voice fade as she said the name.

'Dr Demeray, are you quite all right?'

The headache ran onstage, and Margaret's mind whirled as it tried to recall the exact name which the man who was shot in Glassmakers Lane had said.

The man hadn't said Anderson but Anders, she was certain of that. But that wasn't what had puzzled her, and what she now realised.

The injured man had looked so very like Anna.

Miss Edwards was not the short, stout older woman with grey hair that Margaret had expected, but tall, slender and in her early thirties. Despite the time of year, her skin appeared a little tanned and her eyes were dark brown with thick lashes. It was impossible to tell what her hair was like. She sat, straight-backed opposite Margaret in the dining car of the train, having propped her man's umbrella beside with a glare suggesting that it had better not move if it knew what was good for it and placing a portmanteau in the adjacent seat. She wore a long coat in mouse grey and a hat which somehow conveyed disapproval through the large plain button adorning the front.

'Here we are, doctor,' she said loudly. 'Have you been to Wales before?'

'I'm afraid not, Miss Edwards.' Margaret rather wished the other woman would drop her voice. The migraine had all but gone but she felt a little delicate. 'My family holidayed in Sussex or occasionally Hampshire.'

'You're missing a great deal.' Miss Edwards shoved her gloves into her coat pocket then, ignoring convention, removed her hat too, revealing frizzy blonde hair barely controlled by a fine net. Because of its bulk it was hard to be sure of its length, but it looked as if it would barely touch her shoulders if the net were removed. 'But please don't take the town we're going to as a reflection of the country as a whole. You'll find it ugly.'

'I know the East End well,' said Margaret. 'It can't be uglier than that and it's humans that cause ugliness not nature.'

'True.'

'I know what a mining town looks like. But I also know there's a great deal of beauty to be found nearby. I was thinking of visiting Brecon at some point.'

'For a holiday? Brecon is pretty.'

'To see a sanatorium.'

'Ah. Not so pretty.'

The waiter came to take their order and after he'd gone, Miss Edwards put her head on one side. 'I suppose Fox told you they nicknamed me Miss Hedgehog.'

'Er yes.'

'He's a fool, Dr Demeray. But he's more competent than most, so I don't mind it from him. Or Bert for that matter. Now woe betide if Smith or his ilk tried it.' Miss Edwards twinkled a little and grinned as she perhaps envisioned her revenge.

'Please call me Margaret.'

'Certainly. I'm Elinor. Were you followed?'

'Should I have been?' said Margaret. In the aftermath of a migraine, she hadn't been as observant as she might have been on the journey to Paddington. On the other hand, Fox had been there to see her off and he would no doubt have noticed anything.

'I don't know,' said Elinor. 'You listened to a man who'd been shot today. Perhaps whoever shot him didn't want you to know what he told you.'

'He didn't say anything that meant anything.'

'They don't know that.'

Margaret's hand trembled a little as she poured the tea brought by the waiter. The vestiges of the migraine attempted a curtain call. Anders, Anderson, Andris... 'It's a waste of energy to fuss about it until I have to.'

'I'm glad you're a capable woman,' said Elinor. 'I can see you're feeling a little under the weather, but you're still here. Fox is worried sick about you. Men get more ridiculous every day. I'm waiting for the day when science will advance enough to replace the male reproductive function with some sort of pill.'

'I should introduce you to my friend Phoebe,' said Margaret.

'Please do.' Elinor opened the portmanteau and placed Norah's Bible and notebook on the table, opening the latter and putting a lens on the page.

'Those squiggles look like Pitman's.'

'They are.'

'But they don't make sense.'

Elinor peered through the lens. 'They do to me.'

'Really?' said Margaret, squinting. '"Nid"? Who's "Nid?"'

'What, not who. In context, broadly speaking, it means "not". It's Welsh. Norah adapted a phonetic system which was designed for English as best she could, given that I suspect she could speak and possibly read Welsh but not write it – it's discouraged to the point of punishment in school – and Welsh has sounds which English doesn't.'

'I see,' said Margaret. 'So anyone taking a cursory glance would think it was just a pattern because it's so small, and anyone realising it might be a script would think it was code as it doesn't make sense in English.'

'Or you could be Smith and think it's Phoenician,' muttered Elinor. 'If Hare had a brain he'd have put me in that post.' She flicked through the pages, tracing the shorthand on the edges. 'Most of the passages are sketches in words. They're very witty with just the tiniest hint of mockery. On some days she wrote a great deal: funny little observations of the household; lyrical sketches from walks on the heath; news from two women called Esther and Bronwen, who appear to have grown up in the workhouse with her. Some days she wrote little, except to say how exhausting the day had been. Generally she was cheerful and positive, but every now and then she'd record that another advertisement in a personal column had failed.'

'What sort of advertisement?'

'Here's a clue.' Elinor pointed at a paragraph of scribble. 'This was in October, a short while before she went to work for the Edevanes. It says, broadly speaking: "Maybe Bron is right and I should try outside Wales. Maybe my mam is in service. Or maybe my da got work somewhere else. I could try Bristol or Birmingham maybe. Bron says to try a London paper. That seems so big. But what if I don't, and my mam or da are right here under my nose? But like Esther says, they're probably both dead, and if they'd wanted me they'd have come for me years ago, and I should give up wasting my time hoping for something which will never happen."'

'Oh poor Norah. She was trying to find her parents.' Margaret's heart constricted. In her working life she'd spent far too much time in workhouses, treating people, arranging for them to be moved to hospital, watching them die. Workhouses performed a function, but that function was as impersonal as a machine: men and women were separated even if they'd been married their entire adult lives; young boys were taken from their mothers to be put in with the men; or-phaned siblings separated. Heartbreak, shame, empty eyes, broken bonds, hardening souls. Norah was lucky to have emerged with her spirit intact.

'Yes,' said Elinor. She opened a notebook of her own. 'I spoke with the workhouse and the records simply state that on Friday 7th April, 1893 a baby girl was abandoned on the doorstep within hours of birth, wrapped in towel and paisley shawl with Bible tucked inside. There was no sign of her mother, nor any note. She was named Norah Glyn from standard lists. No one ever came to claim her.'

'How terribly sad.'

'It's only natural that she wanted to find her mother. Although what she'd have said if she'd found her I can't imagine. The workhouse educated her, trained her for domestic service and even let her do a short course in office work. She was a healthy girl, inquisitive, a little rebellious. She didn't contact them after she left and no one has asked about her. They had nothing else to add.'

'Then what do you think we'll gain by going to her town?'

'Background.'

'Fox thinks none of the letters she sent relate to anything important. He thinks Norah just liked making up stories.'

'That doesn't explain what she wrote on the letter margins. Including the one that sent him to Austria.'

Margaret leaned forward. 'Of course, they had shorthand on them too. What does it say?'

Elinor consulted her notebook. 'On the one her employers intercepted: "I'm no longer sure any of this is true. I don't know who to believe. He says I don't have to write these any more." On the one which propelled Fox to Austria: "I'm sorry if it's lies. He says it's true. I don't know. Please help me."'

'So someone *had* told her to write them.' Margaret frowned. 'Why Norah, particularly?'

'That's what I think is worth discovering,' said Elinor. 'Maybe it's a family link. The workhouse doesn't know about. Norah's mother must be at the town. Or was there in 1893. And presumably her father too. Just because Norah couldn't find them, doesn't mean I can't. Digging is what I'm good at. It's why I'm letting the census record me tomorrow regardless of what some in the suffrage movement say. I like information. One day someone might need to know where I was in 1911, hard as it is to imagine. You?'

'Yes,' said Margaret. 'But some of my friends aren't.'

'That's their business of course. But I hate incomplete records.'

Margaret smiled vaguely, determining under no circumstances to let Elinor see her filing. 'If the workhouse has no information, and the mother chose to keep quiet or wasn't local, how will we find anything out? Perhaps no one knew.'

'I'm betting someone knew.' Elinor's face was grim. 'Norah should have looked through her Bible.' She opened the black book and turned the pages. In the latter part, here and there, the word 'Mair' was underlined.

'How do you say that? Mare? What does it mean?'

'The best pronunciation you English can manage is Myer,' said Elinor with a sniff. 'It's Welsh for Mary.'

'So that's what her mother named her.'

'Perhaps, but more importantly, maybe it's the mother's name.'

'That's not much help.'

'I'm taking a stab in the dark. There were several instances of the word bara – that's bread – and baker, also underlined.'

'So Bara's a surname?'

Elinor shrugged. 'Unlikely. But I wondered if Mair was connected with a baker.'

'And do you think you're right?'

'We'll have to wait till tomorrow to find out.'

Nineteen

They arrived in Norah's home town at ten the following morning. It was raining with a steady, exhausting persistence. The sky was grey, the houses were grey, what was visible of the mountain was grey. The very drizzle seemed full of coal dust.

Standing in the main street, Margaret and Elinor looked up at the workhouse. The massive building loomed over the town like workhouses always did, but the town itself was already both cowed and belligerent. Rows upon row of terraced houses stood in the shadow of the mountain and the slag heap, straight and regulated as cog teeth. But all the doorsteps and pavements were scrubbed clean and the gutters swept clear. Small women, thin but neat and proud, watched in open curiosity, shawls pulled over their heads against the rain.

Elinor spoke with one of them in Welsh and the other woman pointed, her eyes still fixed on Margaret and asked something herself which Elinor answered.

'What was all that?' said Margaret, seeing Elinor's suppressed scowl as they walked in the direction given.

'She thought you were a school inspector and when I said you were a doctor she said "I've heard everything now. Aren't we good enough for a man then?"'

'I sometimes wonder if I should give up.'

'Don't be absurd. Now there are two bakers here. We're looking for either Jones the Bread or Evans the Bread.'

'Who?'

'It's a Welsh thing: Jones the Bread for the baker, Morgan the Milk for the dairyman, Fox the Secrets for the spy. You get my drift.'

'What if they both have Mairs?'

'We'll cross that bridge when we come to it. Here we are - you take Jones and I'll take Evans. It'll save time and look less odd - perhaps. Don't worry, they won't eat you. Even you're taller than most of them.'

Margaret entered a small bakery and two women chattering inside fell silent as she stepped over the threshold. Her intention of greeting them brightly in the Welsh for 'good morning' as Elinor had taught her, seeped away as she realised she'd have no idea what to say if they replied. So she greeted them brightly in English instead. The women replied in unison as if they were a school class then glanced at each other with half shrugs. A man, presumably Mr Jones the Bread, a sour-faced man of about sixty, was serving a mother with a child tucked into her shawl. A woman, presumably his wife was a sharp-angled woman somewhat younger who had just finished dealing with an old lady and turned to Margaret.

'Go on then madam,' said one of the women by the door. 'We've been served. We're just having a bit of a chops out of the rain.'

Margaret approached the counter and asked for two penny buns. Then as quietly as she could, she added. 'May I see Mair? An old friend's asked me to look her up.'

Mrs Jones went very pale. 'I'm afraid can't help you, madam. That'll be tuppence please.' She took the coins, then beckoned the next customer with a smile that looked like it was poisoning her.

Feeling foolish, Margaret made her way to the door but as she passed the two women, one of them whispered, 'Mair's up by the Ebenezer.'

'Is that a pub?' Margaret whispered back.

'There's the godless English for you.' The other woman rolled her eyes. 'Pub? It's a chapel.'

'I'm terribly sorry,' said Margaret. 'I didn't mean to offend. Which house by the Ebenezer?'

'House?' whispered the woman. 'Mair's in the graveyard.'

Margaret and Elinor stood under the umbrella staring at a well-scrubbed tombstone. A posy of flowers stood brave under a Welsh inscription. 'It says, "Mair Jones died 8th April 1893 aged seventeen",' said Elinor.

In 1893, Margaret had been nineteen and carefree. Now, thinking of the stranger buried under that grey mountain, her throat constricted and tears filled her eyes. 'Surely someone must have known. Surely...' The sense of being watched trickled down her spine and she turned.

Mrs Jones was nearby, wrapped in a thick overcoat and staring. 'Who *are* you?' she said. 'You're too old to be ... her.'

Elinor dug about in the portmanteau for Mair's Bible and paisley shawl and held them out. Mrs Jones touched both for a moment before looking back down into town. 'Tell her she can't come. If my husband found out, he'd show her the door and maybe me too. He won't stand for sin or the evidence of it.'

'So you knew,' said Margaret.

Mrs Jones touched the shawl again. 'Near the end I guessed. Mair said nothing to me, and what could I say to her, knowing what we'd have to do?'

Margaret shook her head. 'Throw your own daughter out?'

'Robert Davis was long gone and it was too late for him to make a decent woman of her: everyone would know and we wouldn't be able to hold up our heads.' Mrs Jones knelt and tidied the posy of flowers. 'That night it was raining-pouring. I found Mair in the kitchen, shivering and sodden, and crying silent... I never saw anyone cry without making a noise before. It was the worst thing.'"

'*That* was the worst thing?' said Margaret.

'The doctor wrote she died of pneumonia.'

'That's ridiculous,' said Margaret. 'He should be struck off.'

'Should he?' said Mrs Jones. 'He couldn't save Mair, but she could save our reputation.'

'You must have known a baby had been abandoned at the workhouse. You could have offered to adopt her to – I don't know – replace Mair.' Margaret tried to keep her voice steady.

Mrs Jones shook her head. She looked Margaret in the eyes with a pleading expression for a few moments, but then self-righteousness closed her up again and she turned away. 'She'll just have to find Robert Davis if she wants a family.'

'And where is he?' said Elinor.

'He went to London.' Mrs Jones turned to leave.

'Wait a moment,' said Margaret. 'Were there any heart problems or people dying young unexpectedly in your family or Mr Davis's?'

'No.' Mrs Jones stared as if Margaret were mad. 'Goodbye. Go away now.'

Elinor scowled as they watched her walk out of the graveyard with her head held high. 'So Norah's father came to London. Maybe he's the connection?' She shook her head. 'It'll be near impossible to find someone called Robert Davis after nineteen years.'

'Near impossible,' said Margaret. 'But perhaps not completely impossible.'

'Whether he has anything to do with Fox's search for Anderson is another matter,' said Elinor.

'Maybe he has nothing to with it at all,' said Margaret. 'But I still think Norah's letters are linked. The only problem is working out how.'

It was late afternoon when Margaret returned to a London that was just as resolutely grey and miserable as the mining town, rain getting heavier by the minute. But she decided to go to Glassmakers Lane before going home anyway.

It too was dreary with drizzle. Watched perhaps by the silhouettes lunching behind the grey net curtains in Soffiato's, only a few determined shoppers with umbrellas scurried between puddles like tiptoeing ink-cap mushrooms, briefly brightened as they passed Burton's Chemists, where the huge apothecary jars in the window glowed and lured with red and blue ghost-light.

At the far end of the street Nierling's lurked, greyer than ever in the wet murk.

Margaret glared at the shop. If there was time, she might give Mr Nierling junior a piece of her mind to add to the piece of ear he'd shot off.

In the studio, no one was on the desk, and Margaret made her way to Reuben's room, tiptoeing for reasons she couldn't quite explain to herself. The door of a side office was ajar and she could see Mr Dysart within, standing with his back to the door as he spoke on the telephone. 'You can't blame *that* on me... No, of course he's not happy, but I'm sure he'll track it down in time.... We'll have to discuss how with her later... Yes ... no... Perhaps *you* should do it, darling, if *you're* so much more competent... Goodbye.' He slammed the receiver onto the rest and the telephone onto the table. 'Bloody women.'

Margaret crept by. Voices murmured from various parts of the building and she wished she knew where they edited the films, although it sounded as if things weren't going to plan.

Reuben was in his room, pulling a face and putting the final touches to a poster.

'I came to see how your head is,' she said.

He looked up and blinked, clearly too deep in art to remember there was another world around him. 'What head? I mean, I'm fine. You're the one who's been injured. Are you well enough to be here?'

'Yes, perfectly. Is that for Norah's film?'

'Yes,' said Reuben, beckoning her over to look at his design. 'I had to change it to Adelaide, which was a palaver, and half the audience will call her Addle-head with either spelling, but who am I to judge? What do you think?'

'It's wonderful.'

He traced the picture of Adelaide without touching the paper. 'This'll have to go off to the printers now. It's no longer quite Norah. Not that it ever would have been, but...' Reuben scratched his nose. 'She'd lent me a story she was writing about a lady detective. I showed it to Mrs D and she's dramatising it. It's all I could do in her memory.'

'I'm sure Norah would appreciate it.'

'We're all behind, otherwise we wouldn't be working so late. I'm almost looking forward to going home for dinner and my landlady can't cook. I just hope I don't drown on the way. At least I don't have to help edit. All that fussy cutting and sticking just so – it gives me headache just thinking about it.'

'Where do they do it?'

Reuben waved an arm vaguely beyond the wall. 'I can show you if you like, but it's probably best to ask first. And I'm not sure a lady should hear the language they use.'

'I'd survive,' said Margaret.

'Why are you asking?' said a voice from the doorway. It was Mr Drummond. 'We've got things to do and you're wasting our time.'

'Just curious,' said Margaret. 'The whole thing is quite fascinating.'

'Hmph,' said Mr Drummond. 'You're really here to ask about Norah again.'

'It's hard not to be interested in her,' admitted Margaret. 'Every time a patient dies I feel sad. And besides, I specialise in chest ailments. When did Mr Dysart tell you she had a condition?'

Mr Drummond frowned. 'I—'

'You must be very desperate to know about Norah to come out in this weather.' Mr Dysart had entered, hands in pockets. He appraised Margaret with his head on one side, his blue eyes taking in her dripping raincoat and wet shoes. 'I didn't see you come in.'

'I was passing,' said Margaret, then remembered how unlikely that was.

Mr Drummond grunted.

'Mrs Dysart offered me a tour,' she continued. 'I was at a loose end and thought I'd see if I could arrange it.'

'I'm afraid she's not here and we'll be all going home shortly,' said Mr Dysart. 'She'll be sorry to have missed you though.'

'Maybe I'll see her next week,' said Margaret. 'I'm sorry to seem so curious about Norah but I've been refreshing my knowledge of aortic stenosis and it seemed too good an opportunity to miss.'

'Ah.' Mr Dysart stroked his chin. 'I suppose you don't know. Norah was a foundling who'd been trying to find her family. While we were in Switzerland, someone purporting to be her father wrote to her care of the studio and the letter was forwarded to our hotel. The writer said he hadn't been aware of her existence until recently, and said her mother had died of an inherited heart defect.'

'I see. Do you have his details?'

Mr Dysart shook his head. 'Norah confided in me, but never showed me the letter. I had to come home earlier than everyone else but I advised her to wait till she was home and I'd help. Of course the letter was presumably with her things.'

'Hmph,' said Mr Drummond. 'Then her former employers have it now.'

A distant voice shouted 'Telephone call for Mr Dysart!' and he withdrew.

'Never mind,' said Margaret. 'Nothing can be done about Norah. But I shall enjoy my tour when I have it.' She kept her voice light, but Mr Drummond's glare was enough to turn her to stone and her heart was thumping. He turned on his heel and stamped out of the room. 'Er, how do you find Mr Drummond, Reuben?'

'Usually on set.'

'Ha ha. I mean as a person.'

'He's a bit ratty at the moment because he can't find something he needs. But generally he's all right. Just doesn't pull punches; he spends half his time telling people that squirrels could act better. He doesn't much like being bossed about by Mrs D, but he has to acknowledge that she's good and gets the best out of people, rather than being good but making them resign. Although he did all right in Switzerland when she was sick and couldn't go.'

'Is she often sick?'

'Mrs D?' Looking up from his poster, Reuben looked puzzled. 'Normally she's as strong as an ox.' He bit his lip. 'I never knew Norah had found her father after all these months. She'd been trying for a year. And I still can't believe she's dead. I thought Norah was as strong as an ox, too. I never thought she'd die.'

Twenty

At home, Juniper met Margaret with contempt, pointedly coiled round Fox's legs for a while then went to sit on the windowsill, miaowing in disgust at the road outside, now slick, dark and running with rain.

Margaret changed, then settled with Fox by the fire to explain about her day. She waited for him to say that going to Wales had been a waste of both her time and Elinor's but he simply hugged her and sighed. 'That's the way it goes sometimes.'

'Yours too? You said Bert had a lead. What happened?'

'We went to meet someone in Spitalfields prepared to give information.'

'About Charles or Anderson?'

'About Abolin. We were to meet him in a pub called the Dolphin - the sort of low establishment where your corpses like to die.'

'Go on.'

'We weren't familiar with the pub; we just knew it was somewhere near the market. Bert asked directions from a woman who was wearing insufficient clothes for the weather and shivering so much, I was afraid the wall might disintegrate around her. Once she realised we weren't trade but willing to give her a sixpence anyway, she nodded down the sort of narrow, twisting, stinking alley that makes a diseased intestine look appealing.'

'I suppose it's pointless asking if you had anyone in the area ready to help if there was trouble.'

'Yes, it's pointless.'

'And you took directions from a woman so far down the order of loose women that she plies her trade in daylight and is satisfied with a sixpence.'

'I'm not sure that street has seen daylight in a hundred years,' said Fox. 'And sixpence is sixpence. But just as we were about to head off, she asked if we were looking to shiv or to get shivved. I found another sixpence and she said, "It makes no odds to me, but someone built like a brick karzy is waiting in the back alley behind the Dolphin. He told me to sling my 'ook unless I wanted to get blood on my fol-de-rols, so I did."'

'Why did she warn you?'

'She was annoyed because it was usually good business down there. She said the pub had changed its name and a couple of regulars have died, so it's considered haunted. Fear of seeing a ghost adds to the clients' excitement, which speeds things up for her. "People dropping dead is one thing," she said, "but people being shivved or beaten to a pulp is another. I don't mind being haunted by people I know, but not by strangers. Especially such nice strangers." We gave her another sixpence and she thanked us kindly and said now she had enough to go off duty, get a drink and something to eat. I suspect she may forget the food, but there's nothing I can do about it.'

Margaret stared at him. 'And you still have the nerve to worry about me.'

'Bert and I can look after ourselves against a lump of muscle, but I wasn't walking into anything near blind and want to speak to Bert's source to get things clear.' Fox rolled his eyes. 'Only he's gone to ground.' He shook his head. 'I feel a fool. The man we were told to ask for was called Bookie Brown. The name rang a bell, but it was only afterwards I remembered the man your friendly policeman fished out of the river was called Brown. It's a common enough name, but if we'd gone into the pub and asked for a dead man, we'd have been marked out straight away.'

'Oh Fox.'

'We'll go again tomorrow, and see if by any chance there's anything worth finding out. Bert went to sort out arrangements and I came back here to seek something I fear isn't there.' He pointed to a pile of letters on the dining table. 'It's been a thoroughly disagreeable day.'

'Are those the ones Norah sent? I think someone was making her write them. Possibly her father.'

'I still can't see anything important in them.'

'How many are there?'

'Six. The first is dated 3rd January and the last one - the one the Edevanes found - is dated 23rd January. Most of them say things like "while decent Englishmen are tried in Germany for protecting us, German spies hide nearby masquerading as men in your club or ladies in your church. They may seem just a little too English. Seek them out before they destroy us".' Fox had adopted the shocked tone of an outraged alderman.

'Oh dear.'

Fox laughed. 'I know. I mean everyone knows that's true, and we have just as many people being just a little too German across the channel. But this letter's more detailed and is the one the police paid attention to.' He rose, collected the letters and brought them over.

20th January 1911

Dear Sirs,

In Whetstone, you will find a stationer cycling into the countryside after dark. Where is he going? Whom does he meet? Why does he have a printing press running at night in a shed?

If you want to find the spies in Hampstead, look no further than the incomers.

Shall we speak of Toad Hall Street? There is a certain academic who purports to do nothing but read books and study the stars. What do his staff believe he does in the locked room which they may not enter even to dust? I shall tell you. He has created a listening device, and he has it connected to every telephone and internal communication tube. If you do nothing else, warn them to be careful of the secrets they share over the wire or speak of in their private quarters.

'Good grief,' said Margaret. 'Is that possible? And where's Toad Hall Street? I've never heard of it.'

'The device may be possible,' said Fox, flicking through the letters. 'But it seems unlikely that anyone could connect it to houses in Hampstead without anyone noticing. As for Toad Hall Street, it doesn't exist, or at least not in Hampstead. However, there is an area called Frognal. Deliberate misdirection?'

'Or association of ideas from the children's book that came out a few years ago.'

'Which one?'

'*Wind in the Willows*. There's a Toad Hall in that.'

'How do you know?'

'In Father's head I'm still eight. He bought it for me. It's good.'

'I take everything back. You're quite useful,' said Fox. He shook his head. 'Why is everything about this to do with books and names that everyone gets wrong?'

'Never mind. What did the police discover?'

'A stationer in Whetstone turned out to be printing leaflets for a rather peculiar religious sect. Nothing illegal, but rather at odds with his role as churchwarden. Which could also be said about his cycling out at night to meet a widow, though he swore that all they do is play chess and drink cocoa.'

'Why can't they do that in daytime?'

'Who drinks cocoa in daytime?' Fox grinned, then sobered again. 'However, using more initiative than I might have given the police credit for, they connected Toad Hall with Frognal, where they found one gentleman who matched the description given. They were quite triumphant until he turned out to be a perfectly innocent elderly widower who'd decked out a room with things belonging to his late wife, and liked to sit in it playing gramophone records and thinking of her. He didn't want the servants rearranging anything, so kept it clean himself. He was most distressed by what happened and complained not only to the police but anonymously in the local Gazette newspaper.'

'I wonder if that's why Norah started to doubt what she was writing.'

'It's possible. After that, she wrote the letter which the Edevanes intercepted.'

'Was that in the same vein?'

'See for yourself.'

23rd January 1911

Dear Sirs,

You should have arrested the stationer, apparently. And you went to the wrong house when seeking the telephone spy. Try again. Someone is listening in, perhaps to those with new houses and new wealth, who have come from some distance and are trying to charm their way into the best

circles, even though the trade which made their money is nothing if not
dirty?

'"Apparently"?'

'Interesting adverb, isn't it?'

'Mmm,' said Margaret. She perused the letter again and compared it with the earlier letters. While the writing in the first ones was confident – the letters well formed and the ink dark – the later ones were less certain, the script fainter and more angled. The last was almost scrawled: the word 'apparently' had a fine line through half of it and there was the scribbled, agitated shorthand all around the edge of the paper which Elinor said indicated that she was doubtful about what she was writing.

'I think it was the last sentence that worried the Edevanes,' said Fox. 'They're incomers. If they were also spies, presumably they'd have destroyed the letter and perhaps Norah too. But as it is, they were worried enough about someone listening to their conversations to ask the police to do something about it. Then it all turned out to be nothing.'

'It's all very strange,' said Margaret.

'What are you thinking?'

'What if it's not just the part about incomers that bothered the Edevanes? What if it's the reference to dirty money.' Margaret frowned. 'Nellie said Norah told them that she "knew what they were". I thought she meant snobs and social climbers but now you mention it, they didn't seem unfamiliar with running a home with servants, just nasty. They seemed perfectly used to wealth.'

'Dirty money?' said Fox. 'Gained by blackmail or immoral earnings you mean? There's immoral like brothel-keeping and then there's immoral like running a sweat-shop or badly regulated factory.'

'Or a mine,' said Margaret slowly.

'What?'

'A badly regulated mine.'

'Of course,' said Fox. 'All those books Abolin was delivering - books on mineralogy and novels like *King Solomon's Mines* which upset Mrs Edevane so much. Is there a connection? Even a well-regulated mine is dirty by nature of the end product.'

'Were the Edevanes Welsh? Do they come from the same town as Norah? I know they have an English accent but they could have cultivated that. I can imagine her wanting to have a dig at them: they're pretty loathsome. But this is rather an odd way to go about it.'

'It is. And then, of course, six weeks later, after she'd left the Edevanes and started with Dysarts, she sent a final letter to Scotland Yard which had nothing to do with Hampstead and simply said that the expert with a telephone device had used it to steal airship designs and sell them abroad, which led to me running around like a fool in Austria and Italy.' He heaved a sigh. 'Just a moment.' He went to the telephone and asked for the office number. Once connected, he said, 'Get Hedgehog to discover E origins, when and how DM purchased. Yes… Yes tomorrow. Goodbye.' He replaced the receiver and stood for a moment hands in pockets, staring into the fire.

Margaret stood beside him and pulled his face towards hers to kiss. 'We're on track again now. If you can find out if there's anything significant about the Edevanes, I can talk to Reuben about Norah, maybe I can find out why she sent the letters.'

'Elinor could do that.'

'Out of the blue? I know Reuben.'

'What about the man who was shot yesterday? Didn't he tell you Glassmakers Lane wasn't safe?'

'It wasn't. An idiot was firing down it. And if it's not safe for me, it's not safe for Elinor.'

'It's part of the risk of her job. It's not part of the risk of yours.'

'I've been wondering if that young man was Andris Balodis. Perhaps he'd heard Nierlings was a soft touch. I suspect he and Anna have done a flit, so they're probably homeless. I've asked Constable Harris to track them down, if only to tell them their mother won't live till Easter.'

'They won't be homeless if Andris filched the hundred pounds the Nierlings said he did– they could buy an entire house!'

'A hundred pounds?' exclaimed Margaret. 'I can't believe there was that much money in the shop. I bet they don't make that much in six months.'

'Another good point. Incidentally, Nierling junior offers one of his less dubious second-hand books, which he values at ten shillings, as compensation for your *very* minor injury.'

'How kind.'

Fox pulled her into his arms. 'I'd still be happier if you weren't working in Glassmakers Lane.'

'It's in a much nicer area than St J's.'

'I just have this feeling...'

'You and your feelings,' said Margaret, kissing him. 'If it helps at all, I won't be back in Glassmakers Lane till Tuesday. Dr Fernsby isn't running the clinic on Monday afternoon and has asked me to work there all day on Thursday while I work at St J's all day on Monday.'

'Good. I'm beginning to wonder if you're having an intrigue with Reuben.'

Margaret was aghast. 'He's only about twenty-two.'

'So if he was older like the other two...'

'Good grief,' said Margaret, pulling a face. 'Mr Dysart's the right age but I prefer someone with a spine and Mr Drummond is over fifty and I prefer someone who doesn't constantly glare. I'll have to make do with you.'

'Thank you.'

'I think we both need cheering up. Do you love me very much?'

'Seems so.'

'Do you really want to go all these letters again?'

Fox raised his eyebrows. 'At the moment, I want to chuck them in the fire.'

'Then let's go to the hotel for the night. Let's get dressed up and go dancing and eat a fancy dinner and dance some more. And afterwards you can show me why making do with you is worthwhile.'

'If my lady insists,' said Fox, with a deep, insincere sigh, 'I'll try my best.'

Twenty-One

By the time Margaret woke on Sunday morning, it felt as if it had been raining for a year. She was surprised she hadn't dreamed that the hotel was Noah's Ark, floating along in vain hope of land. Even nearby church bells sounded as if they were tolling underwater.

Fox was curled around her and she turned in his arms to face him, stroking the light stubble on his cheek. He stirred, then, without opening his eyes, kissed her and ran his hand down her back.

The telephone began to ring. 'Damn and blast!' Fox muttered through the kiss.

'Ignore it,' said Margaret.

The telephone kept ringing, and Fox pushed her away gently. 'Botheration. It might be important.'

With a groan, he threw back the covers and lifted the receiver. 'Hallo? Oh, hallo Bert. Good. Why...? Oh God... Yes, I will. Goodbye.' He replaced the receiver with a bang, his face solemn and pale. 'Bert's found his source. He's been badly beaten and is scared rigid. Someone said they'd tell his highly *un*lawabiding neighbourhood that he was a nark unless he lured us to The Dolphin. We'll have to question him, then get him out of London altogether, even though the prospect of that will probably terrify him almost as much as staying put.' He paused to kiss her. 'I'm sorry.'

'When you say "question him" and "get him out of London"...'

'He'll be in better condition afterwards than he is now. Don't worry. But I might not be able to tell you any more.'

'I understand. Can you take me home before you go into the office?'

'Of course, or would you prefer Katherine's? Aren't we supposed to be having a family lunch there?'

'It'll be too early and I'd rather change first.'

As they drove them back to the flat, Margaret flicked through Norah's letters again.

'Do you really think there's a connection to anything important?' said Fox. 'Abolin was sending obscure books to the Edevanes in Hampstead. Norah was trying to get the police to investigate spies in Hampstead, yet all the leads were nonsense. It seems more like threats than anything.'

'But then how did she end up at Dysart's? I can't imagine it's that easy to get into moving pictures.'

'Yes. With every respect to the poor girl, Norah was a nobody.'

Margaret pondered. 'You're right: that's exactly what she was. Perhaps the person who asked her to write the letters knew that, and used it to his advantage.'

'How would he know?'

'I have no idea.' Margaret picked up the notebook even though she still couldn't read the shorthand. 'What surprises me is that there are no diary entries after this one in November. She seemed so intent on writing everything down. Was there another in the suitcase Mr Drummond gave to the Edevanes?'

'There was nothing in there but clothes, a couple of popular novels, her toiletries and some costume jewellery. No letters. No diary.' Fox slowed the car as the rain grew heavier. 'What did the shorthand on the letter that sent me to Austria say again?'

'"'I'm sure these are lies. Please help me.'"'

'If only we'd known that and about the Hampstead letters. Maybe we could have found her. The stress must have made her heart fail.'

Margaret shook her head. 'I'm not so sure it was that.'

Fox sped up a little. 'I'll have to get a move on. God knows where we're going to find a safe place for Bert's informant. But he can't stay in London. What he'd consider his reputation is now irreparably lost, so he's now useless. Here we are at the flat. Do you have to go to Katherine's?'

'I can't tag along with you, and I'm not staying inside all day waiting for you; I'll go insane. If you're worried about someone waiting for me to get into the way of a bullet, they're not going to come out in this weather to do it.'

Fox grunted. 'Hopefully I'll get to Katherine's for lunch. I'll call if I can't.' He held her tight and kissed her.

'Please stay safe,' she said.

'You too. Keep your wits about you.'

Margaret stood on the pavement and watched the car until it was out of sight.

Stay safe. Keep your wits about you.

Unnerved, Margaret went in to her flat and changed. 'This'll never do,' she told Juniper. 'I can't just sit about till lunchtime while everyone else is doing something.'

There was no point trying to go and see Nellie, who would no doubt be accompanying the Edevanes to church, then helping with an elaborate meal and the consequent clearing-up. And the Edevanes themselves would find it very odd if Margaret arrived with no excuse whatsoever on a Sunday.

She thought about going to the studio and interrogating Reuben again, but hadn't he said the studio would be closed today? And besides, she didn't have the energy to counter Mr Drummond's scrutiny.

On the other hand she could try and speak with Constable Harris by telephone, not only as the link to the Balodis family but also Jonathan Brown.

He was surprised but pleased to hear from her. 'I was just about to go on my beat, doctor,' he said. 'Is there anything more to tell us about Brown's body?'

'Not exactly,' she said. 'Do you know any more about the murderer?'

'It's taking some digging,' said Constable Harris, 'but he'd been meeting strangers since before Christmas so it must be one of them.'

Margaret thought of Bert's source. 'Could he have murdered for being an informer? Didn't he tell you that he thought Lang died because of mistaken identity? Maybe what he meant was someone was after him – Brown, that is – and shot at the wrong man.' She realised she was touching her ear as she said it and felt absurd.

There was a pause. 'So when Brown tried to get us to investigate, it was to get the people off his back? Could be. Anything else?'

'Jakob Lang was known as Dutch Jake,' said Margaret. 'Did Jonathan Brown have another name?'

'Mostly Jonathan or Jonny Brown. A few had started to call him Bookie Brown recently because he'd begun a sideline in second-hand books: he had a stall. Why?'

Margaret's scalp prickled. 'Did he do any private trade?'

'Think it's important?'

'It might be.'

'Anyone in mind?'

'Abolin.'

'The murderer?'

'Yes.'

She could hear Constable Harris scribbling with a pencil. 'Thanks doctor, very useful. I'll let you know. Mind how you go.'

'What do you think, Meg?' said Margaret's father after tea at Katherine's house. 'Wouldn't my stories make excellent films?'

'Of course they would Father,' said Margaret, half-listening and half-wondering what Fox was doing, He'd telephoned to give his apologies for lunch and say he'd collect her as soon after afternoon tea as he could.

'Now you're working near a moving picture studio, perhaps you could introduce me.' His voice was a little cunning.

Paying attention now, Margaret had an image of herself being given a tour by Mrs Dysart with both her father and Nellie in tow. She wasn't sure which of them would be harder to control. 'I don't *work* at the studio,' she said. 'I can't just march in and make odd requests out of the blue.' *Even though that's exactly what I'm doing about Norah.*

'Of course not, dear.' There was a worrying glint in her father's eye as he stared into the middle distance. 'And there's a very interesting-looking bookshop down there.'

'How do you know?'

'I visited Glassmakers Lane because Kitty told me you were working near a studio. It was shutting up unfortunately.'

'Good! The bookshop's filthy and dark and the owners are idiots.'

'Those sorts of places always turn up something unexpected.'

'You can't imagine how true that is,' said Margaret. *The young man rushing, the bullets firing, a sharp pain...* She touched her ear and caught Katherine's inquisitive frown.

Before Katherine could ask any questions, Margaret's nephew Ed entered the room and stood by the fire, shuffling a pack of cards. At sixteen, he had reached a stage of adolescence where (when he remembered) he'd viciously squash any boyishness into his idea of sophistication. He'd started to oil his abundant curls flat and sometimes effected an indifferent expression and slight drawl to demonstrate his maturity. Worst of all he had dropped calling her Aunt Maggot as he had since babyhood, in exchange for her proper name. All of this irritated Margaret intensely. Today, fortunately for her current levels of agitation, he had been behaving more naturally

'Oh Meg.' Her father fussed. 'It's a new bookshop! Or new to me, at least. And we haven't been book shopping together for ages. And I'm sure them say they'd there ought to be a new copy of *Erewhon* there. And it couldn't be missed as it had a yellow cover. I've lost mine. And its cover was very dreary. When can we go?'

'What's an erewhon?' said Ed. 'That's a stupid title.'

'It's an anagram of "nowhere",' said Margaret. 'About a place that seems perfect but isn't.' *The young man falling, blood on his sleeve... a flash of yellow?*

'Talking of books,' her father continued before she could catch hold of the thought properly. 'Your flat is rather too small for a married couple, Meg. You want somewhere big enough for Fox's books to be added to yours.'

'We're trying to find somewhere bigger, Father, but we've both been caught up in other things and can't quite agree on the right place.' She rolled her eyes a little. 'At the moment, I think Fox wants to put me in a castle with a moat and dragons.'

'Hasn't he already got a dragon of his very own?' said Katherine.

'You can talk,' retorted Margaret.

Their father was too deep in thought to pay attention. 'I've, er, I've been wondering if perhaps you'd both like to come and live with us, Meg. There's plenty of room, and we could have lovely evenings in front of the fire, reading to each other.'

Katherine choked down a snort.

'May I show everyone some card tricks Mother?' asked Ed.

'Please do,' said Katherine. 'It'll distract your grandfather from his mad ideas.'

'You could become another Houdini, instead of becoming a policeman,' suggested Margaret

'I want to join the army now Aunt Margaret,' said Ed, the veneer of adulthood descending. 'One has to be prepared for war.'

'I do so wish you wouldn't keep saying that Ed,' fretted Father. 'Who would dare threaten the British Empire?'

'Germany. Haven't you read the papers Grandpapa?'

'I prefer to read of lovely things.'

Margaret shivered. She heard the doorbell, then Fox's voice in the hall and then he was being ushered through the door, his mouth smiling, his eyes tired.

'But Germany can threaten all they like,' Ed continued. 'We could wipe them out in no time, couldn't we Fox?'

'I think you mean *Uncle* Fox,' said Katherine.

'Fox is fine,' said Fox sitting on Margaret's other side and giving her a quick kiss. 'But I'm rather too tired to talk any more politics today. What were you all doing before planning how to defeat the Germans?'

Ed's face dropped. 'Card tricks.'

'Wonderful,' said Fox. 'I could do with something cheering. Can you show me? Go on. Do your best one.'

'Honestly?' Ed was dubious. 'It's just kid stuff.'

'But they're wonderful tricks,' said Margaret. 'I've seen you or James do them so many times and I can never see how they work.'

After a pause, Ed started to shuffle the pack of cards, his confidence returning. 'Anyone can do it if they know how, Aunt Maggot. It's just a question of making people look anywhere but the right place.'

'Is that right?' said Fox leaning forward and nudging Margaret. 'The wrong anywhere instead of the right somewhere.'

'Or do you mean nowhere,' said Ed.

Trying to stop the young man running away, his jacket falling open a little, a flash of yellow…Not a leaflet or handkerchief… a book.

'Father,' said Margaret, 'when did you go to Nierling's?'

'Late Friday afternoon. They were closing up and wouldn't let me in.'

'And they told you about *Erewhon*?'

Her father squirmed. 'Not precisely. I'd just poked my head round the door to see what was there and heard them talking to a customer. I wasn't eavesdropping you understand. He asked why *Erewhon* in the yellow cover wasn't where it was supposed to be and they said it wasn't their fault it wasn't there, and maybe there would be one in the next consignment of old books. At least I think that's what they said. The customer was somewhat rude about it and talked about thieves. Quite unnecessary. I'm sure when it doest come in, they'd rather sell it to a gentlem—'

'Did you see the customer?'

'It was far too gloomy, dear. Someone tall and dark. Then an old chap came and shut the door and told me to come back another day. Shall I try tomorrow do you think?'

'The consignments come on Fridays,' Margaret prevaricated. 'I'll go and ask when I can.' She forced a smile into her voice. 'Come along Ed, show us another trick.'

Fox raised his eyes at her and whispered, 'What's all this about?'

'*Erewhon*,' she whispered back. 'Andris didn't steal money. He stole a book. He said Anders would be angry because he wouldn't get something he was after. Mr Drummond is angry because he can't find something. I'm sure this is it. We have to find Andris.'

Twenty-Two

Margaret arrived at the mortuary wing early on Monday. Having instructed Pigeon to see if he could track down Anna and Andris, Fox had left the flat very early on the trail of the Edevanes. There was nothing to do but be patient.

'Oh! Good morning, doctor,' said the clerk. 'I'm glad you're feeling better. We thought you might not be in, so I gave your post to Dr Jordan.'

'That's quite all right Mr Holness,' said Margaret.

There was nothing on her desk when she hung up her outdoor things and donned an apron, but when she joined Dr Jordan and Algie in the laboratory, three letters were on the bench beside the microscope they were peering into.

'Good morning,' said Margaret.

The men turned. 'What did I tell you, Mr Hardisty?' said Dr Jordan.

Algie's expression was relieved, but his gaze was focussed on Margaret's ear. 'No fever, no sickness?'

'Er, no. Are those my letters?'

'Yes. Sorry.' Algie handed them over. 'Is your ear all right?'

Margaret looked up from the uppermost envelope. 'It's perfectly healthy. I've cleaned and redressed it twice a day.'

'Mr Hardisty was concerned that the wound might be infected. We were looking at the piece of your ear he removed on Friday.'

Margaret put the letters down. 'How could you remove some of my ear without my noticing?'

'I did ask,' protested Algie. 'It was just a loose bit of skin which looked odd. Maybe you didn't quite hear me – you seemed a little distant – but I thought it might show us something useful. For forensic purposes, that is.'

'You can check the wound for yourself if you like, Algie,' said Margaret, lifting her hair enough for him to remove the small piece of sticking plaster. 'I can't see how there could be an infection. Dr Fernsby cleaned it before I came here.'

'It appears all right,' said Algie. 'I don't suppose I could remove more tissue?'

'It'd prefer it not to look as if it's been gnawed by a starving rodent, thank you. Now I'll have to re-dress it.'

'Sorry, doctor.'

'Let's see what you saw.' Margaret peered through the microscope's lens at the culture plate below. There were definite signs of bacterial growth – but everyone had done nothing but fuss and prod from the moment she'd found out she was bleeding. 'Perhaps I lifted the edge of the original dressing just enough to let something in whilst travelling about. It's hardly difficult to pick up a germ, and I seem to recall that it kept catching on my hair. I'll find some more sticking plaster and come back.'

She returned to her room and opened the first letter. It was from a disinfectant manufacturer asking Margaret, as a 'beautiful lady doctoress', to endorse their product which they claimed helped ladies achieve 'feminine freshness'. They'd managed to combine delicate coyness with avaricious money-grubbing, but her reply would do the reverse, giving case histories of women damaged or killed by such 'freshening' techniques in lurid detail, and saving what coyness she could muster for hints as to where their 'attractive fee' would best placed.

Casting the letter down in disgust, Margaret looked at the second one, a reply from a laboratory, offering her a selection of dates on which she might visit to discuss a position. She wasn't ready to deal with that, either.

Then there was the third letter. It was flimsy, typed, and battered, but the postmark was indisputably Neuchâtel.

Her heart beat faster. What did she really want to read? That Norah had died naturally, or that there was foul play? It hadn't occurred to her until now that if it had been the latter there would surely have been a criminal investigation, and she would have been contacted as a witness.

The letter paper inside was tissue-thin and the words hard to read, combining Continental script with the traditional doctor's poor and impatient handwriting. Fortunately, Dr Gilliand's English was impeccable.

My dear Madame Doctor Demeray,

Please accept my apologies for the late despatch of this letter. In the last weeks there have been outbreaks of both diphtheria and measles among my patients. In consequence, as you may understand, I have been too exhausted to write.

What I have to tell is brief. Having confirmed that life was extinguished, I and the police officer whom you saw accompanied the body of the young woman, Miss Norah Vale, and Mr Drummond, who said that he employed her, to l'hôpital Bon Berger. There I spoke with the pathologist, providing my observations and the statement of Mr Drummond as to her family history. I felt that these two things were not entirely in accord, but left it to the pathologist to undertake a post-mortem to establish the facts.

Thereafter I was neither consulted by the hospital nor approached by the police, and therefore assumed that they were satisfied as to cause of death.

However, now that the sickness among my patients is under control, and recalling your request, I telephoned to my colleague at l'hôpital Bon Berger and from him ascertained that the girl had been in possession of a letter from her estranged father. This, among other things, alerted her to heart disease within the family and said that she should be careful.

Since this gentleman was resident in a Paris hotel, my colleague put in a trunk call and spoke with him later that day to establish the nature of the hereditary illness. The father said that he and his young daughter had only recently been reunited, and expressed his distaste at the thought of her dissection while accepting that the police might deem it necessary. The hospital, being under pressure to treat the injured from a motor-car accident, was disinclined to undertake a post-mortem unless the police demanded one. I believe the police interviewed Mr Drummond, who revealed no reason for Miss Vale to be intentionally hurt, since she was universally liked but of no great importance to anyone (except perhaps her father in Paris). They decided that since there were no injuries on the body and everything pointed to a congenital defect, there was no reason to waste the hospital's time. Her body was therefore released to the English church for burial.

I have since spoken with the pastor, who showed me where Miss Vale was laid to rest. He said that Mr Drummond was in attendance, but the father had been prostrated by grief and warned not to travel. The father had asked for his letter to be returned and said that he would pay for a small headstone.

Although both you and I were puzzled at the time, I hope that what I have discovered puts your mind at rest. Should you ever return to Neuchâtel, I would be more than happy to renew our acquaintance and compare the experiences of a busy London doctor and a busy country doctor. I suspect that I have the better view on my daily walk, and maybe the better air!

Please accept, Madame, my best regards

Alphonse Gilliand

So this was proof of the estranged father Mr Dysart had spoken of. But if it were Robert Davis, who'd left the mining village to seek his fortune, he must have done very well to be living in a Paris hotel, and Elinor was looking in the wrong place. Or else it wasn't him at all. But either way, the indications were that this man hadn't been the one who prompted the letters.

He must have contacted Norah through the newspaper advertisements, thought Margaret, *and she'd presumably given the studio's address for further correspondence because she wanted to feel safe while she made sure it was true. After the debacle with the letters about spying, perhaps she'd learned to be cautious.*

But it was still a puzzle. Nellie and Reuben had seemed of the opinion that Norah's search for her father had been fruitless and Norah seemed open with both of them. Perhaps, after so many disappointments, she'd kept it to herself until she was sure. That made a little sense. But what *didn't* make sense was the studio forwarding the letter to Switzerland when it might miss Norah altogether. Why not just keep it for her return? And that aside, 'gentleman' suggested rank and wealth. How often did a man of that kind want to be reunited with a by-blow who'd been abandoned to a workhouse in babyhood? It was like something from a sentimental novel.

At lunch time, Margaret went to the hot, stuffy café. She wished Fox were there to talk to and managed to turn her frustration into an imaginary, tetchy conversation with him.

'There you are,' he'd say. 'Natural causes. You can forget about it.'

'But it felt wrong,' she'd say. 'And I'm sure Dr Gilliand thinks so too.'

And Fox would say...

As she took a sip of coffee, she glanced at a table nearby where a couple held hands, whispering with furtive intensity. 'She doesn't understand me like you,' the man murmured. 'She doesn't deserve you,' the woman replied.

They reminded Margaret of when her dead husband said he was going away on business before slinking off to his mistress. The coffee tasted colder and more bitter than ever before.

She pushed her plate and her half-drunk coffee away. *Stop it Margaret. You know what Fox's job is and why he can't always tell you what he's doing. He's nothing like Owen.*

Having returned to the mortuary wing, she turned her mood into an acerbic reply to the disinfectant company and was halfway through when Algie came to say she had a visitor.

Her heart leapt until she recalled that apart from one occasion the previous summer, Fox never visited her in the mortuary wing, and in any event he'd have telephoned or wired first. 'Who?'

'Constable Harris.'

'Another murder victim's body?' Her heart sank, imagining Andris found dead from bullet wounds.

'No, or at least, not exactly.'

'Honestly, Algie, you're going to have to develop a little more clarity.'

'It's about a crime, but the victim's not dead yet. They're in the London. The body that is. I mean the victim. Still alive, but too injured to move. And the London specialises in injuries and we generally don't.'

'Why is Constable Harris here, then?'

'He didn't say.'

'Show him in please, and ask an orderly to bring us some tea. That should give me enough time to straighten things up.'

By the time Constable Harris arrived, she had tidied her desk and dusted both the skull and the plaster sculpture of an open chest with removable parts which sat on top of her filing cabinet. Students, or maybe just Algie, occasionally put old hats on the skull and cheap jewellery on the torso when she was away from the hospital. They often managed to do it when she was feeling despondent over a case and it made her laugh and feel that things weren't so bad. She would miss the students if she left.

Constable Harris took a seat warily. Perhaps he was worried the chair might be infected. He cheered up when she offered him tea. 'There's not many offer us anything,' he said, holding up a hand after she'd put a fourth sugar lump in. 'An inspector might get given a brandy at a murder in a rich cove's house, but that's usually the culprit trying to fog his brain. No one never gives a constable nothing. Your tea looks better than the usual institutional lily-livered stuff.'

'I'm very particular,' said Margaret. 'And no one argues with me about it.'

'I can imagine.' Constable Harris caught sight of the skull, blanched, then took a deep draught from his cup. 'Ahh, that hits the spot.'

'I hear there's a victim of crime at the London. Where does St Julia's come in?'

'Not St J's,' said Constable Harris. 'You. The victim asked for you, Dr Demeray.'

'What?' Margaret jumped to her feet and reached for her coat. 'What happened to him? Is he badly hurt? Why didn't you come sooner?'

Constable Harris looked at her in surprise. 'It's not a he, it's a she. Letitia Connors.' Margaret frowned and reseated herself. 'She was found at early light. She hasn't said much that made sense apart from her name, but we did catch "Dr Demeray". There can't be many, so I offered to come and see if it was you. I didn't realise you had any living patients. Is she yours? Not that she seems chesty.' He blushed. 'I mean, no more wheezy than you'd expect in the circs. All that rain yesterday, it's a wonder she weren't drownded. If the cosh doesn't do for her, pneumonia might.'

'Is she in her twenties? Brown hair, brown eyes, average height, buxom, pregnant? I mean, I hope she's still...'

'That's her. It's miraculous about the baby. The whack on her head should have done for it, as much as what she'd planned.'

'What she'd planned? Where did you find her?'

Constable Harris pulled a face. 'Down one of them alleys where there's a woman who'll help a girl in trouble for a few shillings. We've never once caught her at it, but we know her all the same. You know what I mean, and you know the sort of help she offers.'

'I do.'

'I ain't judging,' said Constable Harris. 'But it's against the law. And she's a dirty drunken old witch. Half the women die a short time afterwards, but they'll never point the finger even when they're dying.'

'Poor Miss Connors. I was going to see her to discuss where she could go to have the baby safely without anyone knowing, if that's what she wanted or needed...' Margaret stared into her tea, wishing she'd gone sooner, remembering the horror and distress on the young woman's face when she'd found out she was pregnant.

'Will you come and see her? Maybe she'll tell you what happened.'

'Of course I will. Mr Hardisty can explain to Dr Jordan.' Margaret rose again and donned her coat and hat. 'I'll pay for a cab.'

'Thank you, doctor, that'll save us all some time. She's pretty bad, but she might pull through. The baby too, they hope.'

'I'm glad. Hopefully I can help reassure her.'

Why go to Whitechapel? she wondered as they climbed into a motor cab.

'Why there, though?' said Constable Harris, echoing her thoughts. 'There are women offering the same services everywhere, and Miss Connors doesn't look so poor she couldn't have found someone cleaner and safer elsewhere.'

'Safer for the operation?'

'Safer in general. Even the tarts usually go in twos near Duval Street, except for Mad Minnie.'

'Mad Minnie?'

'She swears the pub where she plies her trade has been haunted since they changed its name from the King's Head in January.'

That's it, thought Margaret. *The pub, Dutch Jake, Bookie Brown, the prostitute desperate for sixpence.* 'Is it called the Dolphin now?'

'How'd you know?'

'Someone I know was asked to meet Bookie Brown there, but I think the woman you called Mad Minnie warned him off.'

'Gawd,' said Constable Harris. 'He's lucky. Who gets *invited* to a place like the Dolphin? The person he was most likely to meet would have been his maker. Is that why you were asking Brown's nickname yesterday?'

'Yes.'

'He wasn't peaching for us.' His voice dropped a little even though the chances of the cab driver hearing were negligible.

'You said he was meeting someone. Do you know who?'

Constable Harris squirmed and then said 'One name is Moishe or Mosher, an anarchist who disappeared like any number of them not long after the Stanley Street siege. Another is called Piccadilly.'

'Because he's very rough, or very posh?'

'Posh, I think.'

'Anarchist?'

'Not sure. And you were right about the connection to Abolin. Brown sold him books. Not many. And he also sold them to a shop called Nierling's in—'

'Glassmakers Lane.'

'You know it? It's been under observation for trading in mucky books and anarchist literature. I'd have thought you'd pick somewhere nicer to buy stuff.'

'I've never been inside.'

'Best don't. Another thing: you remember the letter Dutch Jake had? I had a butcher's at the file. Dutch Jake's missus said it wasn't nothing to do with him, and there was no envelope.'

'Was there one in his pockets?'

'Nope, but in the pub there was a book, even though the regulars can barely read and it was the sorta book that woulda needed more reading that most.'

'What was it? Anything to do with mines?'

Constable Harris screwed up his face in recollection. 'Pope? Pope Alexander? The Dunce or something.'

'*The Dunciad* by Alexander Pope?'

'Could be. Is it religious? The sarge thought maybe Brown was shot at by someone who doesn't like Catholics or Germans. Plenty of both about.'

'Or by people who don't like poetry.'

'Yeah,' chuckled Constable Harris. 'I'd shoot the teacher who made us memorise *The Lady of Shallot* in an instant.'

'I think it's something else,' said Margaret.

'Me too.' Constable Harris sobered. 'But so help me, I dunno what.'

Twenty-Three

At the London Miss Connors lay half-conscious, her head wrapped in bandages, her face grey. Like all seriously ill people in hospitals, she looked smaller than she really was, but uncorseted, the curve of her pregnancy was visible under the tight bedclothes. A nurse stood guard alongside, lips narrow, making notes in a file.

'Hallo, Miss Connors,' said Margaret, her voice low. There was no response. 'It's Dr Demeray. You asked for me.'

The other woman's eyelids flickered and she looked up with an expression Margaret couldn't read. Relief, mixed with fear, mixed with shame? But Miss Connors was being sedated as much as the doctors dared. Perhaps the expression was nothing but weariness.

'Bad woman.'

'No.' Margaret took her hand. 'I'll help you, once you're well enough to leave.'

Tears appeared on Miss Connors's lashes. 'Went to Dr Fernsby.'

'Yesterday? Sunday?'

'Is it Monday now?'

'Yes.'

'Was desperate. Wouldn't help. Asked for you. Then...' Her eyes closed again and she winced.

The nurse tutted, and muttered, '"Whatsoever a man soweth, that shall he also reap."'

Margaret glared at her. "'Let he who is without sin cast the first stone.'"

The nurse put her nose in the air and shut the file with a snap.

Miss Connors took a sobbing breath, her eyes still closed. Under the covers, her hand reached for her stomach.

'Then what?' said Margaret. 'Can you tell me? Who told you to go to that street? It's such a dangerous place.'

Miss Connors opened her eyes again and frowned. 'Don't remember being anywhere. Not safe.'

'You are,' said Margaret. 'I promise. Now go to sleep. If anyone is unkind to you, I'll let Matron know who to put on a month of bedpan cleaning.' She gave the nurse a final warning glare and went to speak with the ward doctor. He was not entirely confident that Miss Connors would survive; her responses were becoming less coherent. He would have sedated her more if it hadn't been for the baby, but as it was, he anticipated she would slip into a coma shortly.

The sooner someone asks Dr Fernsby what had happened, the better, thought Margaret.

None of it was any of her business, but she felt some responsibility for Miss Connors, and Glassmakers Lane wasn't under the jurisdiction of the City of London Police. Constable Harris might not be able to ask questions, but she could.

Margaret tried to telephone Dr Fernsby but there was no response. Presumably Miss Hill had been given the afternoon off since there was no clinic. Sending a telegram seemed unnecessarily dramatic, so she explained the situation to Dr Jordan. In the circumstances, knowing how ill Miss Connors was, he was more than happy that she leave St Julia's early to speak with Dr Fernsby.

Margaret arrived at the surgery at four p.m. A maid let her into the building and she made her way to the floor where the consulting rooms were alone. The waiting area felt strange without patients or Miss Hill, and eerily silent. Perhaps Dr Fernsby had long since withdrawn to the part of the building which was her home, and the maid hadn't realised. Margaret was about to summon her, when she heard a crash coming from Dr Fernsby's office and what sounded like a cry. She rushed to the door just as it opened and a woman in a beige coat and large flower-covered hat backed out. 'It was a stupid thing to do,' she said, loudly. 'I can't believe —'

Dr Fernsby stood just inside the door, her usually mild eyes flashing. Seeing Margaret, she blinked, and the other woman turned. It was Mrs Dysart.

'Oh,' she said. 'Dr Demeray. I mean, good afternoon. I, er, I heard what happened on Friday. I'm glad to see that you're quite well. Or at least, I assume you are. You look quite in the pink.' She attempted a smile, but she was breathing rapidly and her cheeks were blotched with red.

'I am,' said Margaret. 'And you're right, I am due tomorrow rather than today, but I need to speak with Dr Fernsby about a practice matter.'

The two women stared at her, then at each other. With one so pale and blonde and the other so dark-haired and rosy, the fairytale of Snow-White and Rose-Red slipped into Margaret's mind, and she wondered if she'd taken leave of her senses.

'I shall leave you both to it,' said Mrs Dysart.

Margaret shook her hand. 'I'm sorry if I interrupted a consultation.'

'Not at all, I was just leaving. And I'm perfectly in the pink too. I'm so sorry I keep missing you. I'm looking forward to giving you the guided tour. Could you come the day after tomorrow? I'm sure the practice can manage without you that afternoon, can't it Dr Fernsby?'

'Dr Demeray doesn't work here on Wednesday afternoons. It'll be the hospital's decision.'

'And did I hear Norah's little friend wanted to come? Bring her too if her employers will allow it,' Mrs Dysart's smile seemed more natural now, her breathing calm. 'Toodle-oo Dr Demeray. I shan't see you about the place tomorrow as my husband and I are visiting possible outside locations. And tonight we're closing early to celebrate finishing *Adelaide* against all the odds. Good evening, Dr Fernsby. I shall consider what you said carefully. I daresay you are quite right.'

Mrs Dysart and Dr Fernsby shook hands, and the former left without a backward glance.

'I'm sorry for interrupting,' repeated Margaret as she followed Dr Fernsby into her office. The wooden cat family was scattered about the floor. 'Oh! What happened?'

'I knocked them off with my skirt as I passed,' said Dr Fernsby. 'I'm so bulky.' She made to bend.

'I'll do it,' said Margaret. 'You look a little - er - tired.'

'Thank you.' Dr Fernsby took a deep breath. 'What did you hear?'

'That she's sorry about something.'

'So she should be. Mrs Dysart is your patient as much as mine. She is forever taking herbal remedies that upset her stomach. She tends towards hypochondria. Dramatic temperament, I suppose.' Dr Fernsby rang for a servant and sat down awkwardly. 'I sometimes believe I'm expecting an elephant.' She sent the maid for tea and gestured for her to shut the door when she left. 'It's nice to see you have no ill effects from Friday Dr Demeray, but what did you mean about coming here to discuss a "practice matter"?'

'It's about Miss Connors.'

Dr Fernsby's irritated frown returned. 'That silly woman. Has she been bothering you?'

'She was found in a back street early this morning—'

'What a foolish girl.' Dr Fernsby shook her head.

'It's touch and go whether she'll survive.'

'Survive?'

'She asked the police for me.'

'For you? How strange. How coherent is she?'

'Not very. The last thing she recalled was seeing you in desperation and she's feeling guilty. The police think she might have been seeking a woman who performs illegal operations. At any rate, she was robbed and left for dead.'

'Oh my,' said Dr Fernsby, running a hand over her face. 'I feel terrible.'

'Why?'

'She came here at teatime on Sunday, when we were having a little family party. I might have been short with her, but when begged me to...' Dr Fernsby touched her stomach protectively. 'Quite apart from the legality, I suppose I'm sensitive on the subject, but I should have been more compassionate. I simply said that I couldn't contemplate doing what she wanted. She offered me all her savings and I still said no. And then she asked where you worked.'

'To see if I had a different view?'

'I assume so. But I told her you wouldn't help, and nor would any respectable doctor.'

'And then?'

'And then she left.'

'I don't suppose you saw *how* she left?'

'I had the impression she was walking home.'

'I gather the father won't help.'

Dr Fernsby shook her head. 'He made all the usual promises to get what he wanted. Then afterwards she discovered he was already married and ended things between them. She thought she'd got away with it. "Only the once", she said. "He said nothing could happen the first time." And her parents wouldn't help, apparently. I told her you were looking for homes for unmarried mothers but she said she'd heard terrible things about them. If I'd explained that you'd find the nicest place you could, it might have made all the difference. I thought I'd talked her into waiting till she heard from you, but evidently not. And now she's going to die. What a waste.'

'She might not,' said Margaret. 'And the baby is still fighting too.'

'I wouldn't be too hopeful,' said Dr Fernsby. 'A head injury like that is likely to be fatal. But I have no idea how Miss Connors got to be in Whitechapel, let alone near the King's Head.'

Margaret opened her mouth to correct the name to the Dolphin, then realised she'd mentioned neither Whitechapel nor a pub nor the injury. She realised, that far from being upset about Miss Connors, Dr Fernsby was furious – but why? And now that she thought about it, Dr Fernsby's expression was now the same as when she'd been angry with Mrs Dysart. 'You're probably right,' she said. 'Miss Connors is in a coma and perhaps unlikely ever to regain consciousness.'

Dr Fernsby relaxed. Perhaps she intended to look sympathetic, but there was no mistaking the suppressed smile playing on her lips.

Fox telephoned Margaret at home later that evening. 'Thanks for the letter.'

'Letter' was their code word for information; they avoided talking about Fox's work more than necessary over the telephone. Margaret had contacted his office by telegram before returning to St Julia's asking if she could meet Elinor, but the person who 'accidentally' bumped into her as she rounded the corner near the mortuary entrance was Pigeon. In the polite exchange of apologies, he'd muttered 'Miss H is off on a job for a few days' and she'd passed him a note about the putative father in Paris and the summarised the other information for Fox:

Dolphin near Duval St was the King's Head in January where Jakob Lang died. Might Mad Minnie's ghosts be JL and Bookie Brown? PC Harris says January letter to JL from Hamburg had no envelope and wasn't his, but there was a book near where he fell. Poetry not minerals. BB had been talking to two men - one Moishe/Mosher/Masher, the other Piccadilly.

'Interesting connections,' said Fox now.

'Yes.'

'You sound upset. What's wrong?'

'One of my patients has been hurt.'

'Badly?'

'Very. Dr F doesn't care.' Margaret imagined how it would have been a year earlier if the same thing had happened. She might have told Phoebe or Katherine what she could. More likely, she'd have told Juniper and lain awake, seeing that sad, desperate face in the hospital bed and wondering what she'd tell the poor woman's parents if she died, whether she should mention the child or keep it secret, and what would happen to Miss Connors and the baby if they survived. Now, if Fox had been home, she'd curl up in his lap and tell him. Or maybe she wouldn't straightaway, but he'd be ready to listen, when she was ready to talk. 'I'm missing you.'

'Me too. I should be back tomorrow night. Have your plans changed at all?'

'No,' said Margaret. 'They're precisely the same. I, er... I heard from the doctor I'd written to at last.'

There was a brief pause while Fox presumably dug around in his mind for what she was talking about. In the background, the music she'd been dimly aware of stopped and with a whirr and a slight screech, another tune started. Someone was operating a gramophone. It couldn't be Fox as it was too distant. 'I recall,' he said, his voice perhaps wary, perhaps indifferent. 'Your hypothesis proved?'

'No.' If he'd been there in person, he'd have known that one word was full of doubt and perhaps disappointment. He'd never be able to tell over the wire. 'But it did reveal someone I didn't expect.'

'Someone or something? The line's not clear.'

'Someone.' She waited for him to tell her to stay home or at St Julia's or to take care, but he didn't.

'I trust a doctor to know when to stop cutting into a wound.'

'I'll be careful, I promise.'

'Good.'

'Any news about the people sought?'

'Not yet. They've gone very thoroughly to ground. Or he's dead. And you might be mistaken.'

'I'm not.'

The record came to an abrupt stop halfway through the tune, and Margaret was sure she heard someone giggle.

'Where are you, Fox? I mean, what sort of place?'

'Somewhere quite safe where I'm unlikely to be shot at or tempted to take up acting.'

'Ha ha.'

'Take care, keep your wits about you and don't go expressing your opinion of booksellers in their own shop.'

She laughed. 'I'll try not to. I love you.'

'Me too. See you soon, preferably with no more bits missing.'

Twenty-Four

I t was bitterly cold the following day.

Glassmakers Lane seemed fragile in the chilly spring sunshine, with no trace of the deluge at the weekend. The maids were sweeping and wiping, the waiters polishing, the pharmacist's jars gleaming.

Dr Fernsby had recovered her temper and was rearranging her office when Margaret arrived. 'Any news of Miss Connors?'

'I telephoned before I left home. She hasn't regained consciousness and has signs of pneumonia, but her heart remains strong and the baby's still alive.'

'I'm sorry if I seemed angry yesterday,' said Dr Fernsby, rubbing the small of her back. 'Mrs Dysart irritates me immensely, and when you told me what happened, I felt annoyed with myself for not seeing the signs that Miss Connors intended to take drastic action. It happened once before: a poorer, younger girl went to some vile woman in an alley off Fashion Street. It's why I thought of Whitechapel, even though you never did say where Miss Connors was. You must have thought me quite mad.'

'It's easy to connect ideas,' said Margaret.

After a pause, Dr Fernsby sighed. 'Sorry as I am for her, she's been a fool. Now, do sit down and go through the visit book with me. You'll have to do it alone today. It feels as if my hips are dislocating every time I walk any distance, and my bladder— I do apologise. All of this is probably putting you off motherhood.' She contemplated Margaret with her head on one side. 'You can take my car if you feel confident at driving it.'

Margaret flicked through the book. 'I'll be fine on foot. It's far simpler.'

'I'm not sure you should be carrying a heavy bag all that way.'

'Why ever not?'

'You're looking pale.'

'I didn't sleep terribly well last night.' Margaret reread the addresses and plotted a logical order and route which would get her back in time to have some lunch. 'I'll manage. Tomorrow I'll bring my bicycle.'

'You'd be better learning to drive a car. It's getting quite dangerous to ride a bicycle around London. In the future, I doubt anyone will do it.'

The morning went smoothly. Reuben had made an afternoon appointment to discuss his headaches, which saved Margaret having to make up an excuse to visit him. The morning patients were interesting and the home visits were over quicker than anticipated. Margaret wondered whether Bert or Pigeon had spoken to Constable Harris about Dutch Jake, and what Constable Harris had thought if so. It wasn't something she could ask him directly.

During lunch in Dr Fernsby's quiet dining room at the back of the house, Margaret talked through the case notes and then they fell into a general conversation about current affairs over coffee. Margaret watched for any more sign of that strange smirk but Dr Fernsby was her usual serious self, a little guarded perhaps but nothing more.

While warm from a fire, the room was dark, despite walls decorated with cream paper patterned with pinkish leaves in a never-ending swirl. It was hard to imagine how the large oak furniture had been brought into this townhouse with its narrow doors and staircases. On the walls were rural scenes in ebony frames. Sunlight was doing its best to shine into the garden over the roofs of the houses beyond, and when the conversation lapsed, Margaret could hear sparrows bicker and pigeons coo, and somewhere not too far away, children playing.

'I'm sorry I still haven't met your husband,' she said. 'Should he be away so often, with you in your condition?'

'I have several weeks to go,' said Dr Fernsby. 'And he gets terribly bored at home. Shall I arrange a small dinner before the confinement? Then I can meet your husband too.'

'That would be lovely,' said Margaret, wondering how she'd get out of it.

They fell into a silence broken only by the baritone clunk of a sleepy mantle clock and the squabbling sparrows. Margaret glanced round at the walls again. No portraits. No photographs. 'May I look at your pictures before I go?'

Dr Fernsby shrugged. 'If you like. They mostly belonged to some dusty ancestor, and they're rather dreary and old-fashioned. I keep meaning to modernise this room. I daresay it'll all come back into fashion one day and the boys might be glad we didn't get rid of the furniture, but it's hard to imagine.'

Margaret rose and studied each painting in turn. Old and smoke-damaged as they were, they were hard to decipher: mostly hunting scenes depicted in rich browns and greens with the odd splash of red, but not English and certainly quite old. Hunter and prey lurked in dark forests made dingier by age, forever hiding from each other, never to catch or be caught. It was easy to imagine Hansel and Gretel or Sleeping Beauty lost in those shadowy dells.

The clock cleared its throat and after a second's hesitation struck two.

'We'd better get back to work,' said Margaret.

'Yes, of course: although there are no patients booked until three. I know you're keen to familiarise yourself with my accounts and filing system but I'd like to discuss a patient's heart first. You may have some expertise from your work at St J's to offer.'

'Of course. What does he suffer from?'

'Angina. Not the same as the Dysarts' Miss Vale.'

'How do you know about Miss Vale?' The words were out before Margaret could stop herself.

'Mrs Dysart will talk about anything,' said Dr Fernsby, rolling her eyes. If she thought Margaret snappish, she gave no indication, simply pouring herself more coffee. 'And I gather that your journey from Switzerland involved finding Miss Vale dead. You never mentioned it.'

Margaret made an apologetic shrug. 'I didn't realise until much later that it had any connection with Glassmakers Lane. I didn't think you'd be interested.'

'I assume from the garbled description it was subaortic stenosis. So cruel. A disease striking down the young and apparently healthy.' Dr Fernsby rose awkwardly to her feet. 'And I gather Miss Vale had a great deal of potential.' She put on a rapid, affected voice: a shadow of Mrs Dysart's. '"I was *so* sorry I hadn't been with them when it happened, though I don't know *what* I could have done, and also I'm *glad* I wasn't with them when it happened, as I wouldn't have known *what* to do, and *could* you check my heart to make sure I don't have the same disease? And it's *such* a pity that Norah died. She wasn't the best nor the prettiest actress, but she *was* my best scriptwriter and had endless ideas, even if she did talk rather a lot." As if Mrs Dysart could throw stones.' Dr Fernsby chuckled. 'She's not so bad when she's not worrying about her health or tipping into girlishness. I suppose after having to be more masculine than the men all day, it's an inevitability.'

'I never get girlish, and you haven't met the hospital board.'

'I bet your non-working clothes are very feminine.'

'Mmm.'

'Anyway, irritating as Mrs Dysart is, it's good to meet another woman who is making her way against the odds, isn't it? I gather the very best in the moving-picture business are women and they're directing and running studios very successfully. When you and your husband come to dinner, I'll invite the Dysarts too. It'll be an interesting evening.'

Uneasy, Margaret discussed the patient with angina and then went to her consulting room on the excuse that she wanted to continue to familiarise herself the accounts and more importantly the case notes for the afternoon's surgery.

Her mind drifted to Fox, wondering where he was and what he was doing. Surely it couldn't take two days to find out where the Edevanes had come from before arriving in Hampstead? Bert had simply told her that what he was doing was less risky than usual, and not to worry.

When the telephone rang, she fell upon it in relief. 'Hallo?... Oh Reuben!... Yes, I'm quite all right, thank you for asking. I thought you were coming for an appointment later. Has something happ—... my father? What do you mean, my father's at the studio?' She closed her eyes and counted to ten. 'Let him talk till he runs out of steam, then sit him in a corner. I'll be there in two minutes.'

She went to tell Dr Fernsby, and stood outside her consulting room irresolute. If she left without explanation, Dr Fernsby would wonder why she thought it acceptable to disappear, and afterwards no doubt Mrs Dysart would pass this snippet of gossip on too. But if she stayed to explain, it would take too long and who knew what her father would do during the delay.

From outside the room however, she could hear Dr Fernsby talking, presumably on the telephone since Margaret could only hear one voice which suddenly raised enough for words to be made out. 'I wish you were here,' she snapped. 'It's getting too close... I can't leave it all for her to manage on her own... And she needs instructions...'

She's arguing with her husband. She's more worried about the confinement as she's been making out.

Leaving a note on her own desk to say that she was pre-empting Reuben's appointment by visiting him at the studio, Margaret rushed across the road.

Miss Isaacs, engrossed in another Sexton Blake, blinked in Margaret in surprise. 'You got shot last Friday, didn't you?' She swung her feet down and flung the magazine aside. 'How exciting! Can I see the hole?'

'My hat took the brunt. Thankfully there isn't much damage to my ear.'

'Pity,' said Miss Isaacs, without irony. 'You have such nice hats, too.'

'Is there an elderly gentleman here with Reuben?'

'He's ever so sweet. He asked if I was a star. I said, "No such luck with a phiz like mine, I'm just a secretary and *that* makes it sound fancier than it really is", but then he said, "You have the profile of a Greek goddess; I shall tell them to cast you as Athena". I never knew Greek goddesses had snouts like mine!' The young woman threw her head back and laughed. 'Have you met him?'

'Oh yes.'

'You know where Reuben's cubbyhole is, don't you? If they're not there, they'll be in the projection room. I'll bring you some tea.'

'Should you just be letting people in willy-nilly?' said Margaret. 'Isn't the equipment here rather expensive?'

'You can't get to anything important without getting past Morrie, Stew and Norb, and that's like trying to get past elephants. Morrie's right fist is bigger than all three of their heads put together. It's probably got more brains, too. All anyone could steal this end of the place is Reuben's posters, the petty cash tin, and me, and all I can say is that if they want bits of paper and three shillings and sixpence, it's no skin off this Greek goddess's nose, but no one's nabbing the goddess herself without a fight. Go on through, doctor. I'll bring biscuits too.'

Twenty-Five

There was no one in Reuben's room, so Margaret made her way to the projection room and knocked on the door. When no one answered, she let herself in.

In the darkness, she could just make out her father seated on a chair, mesmerised by the flickering screen before him, where Adelaide swooned in the arms of a handsome, brooding man, watched by another handsome man with clenched fists. It looked similar to the scene on Reuben's picture but without the likelihood of the young woman coming to her own rescue.

A title card replaced the image:

Unhand her, you fiend! Adelaide is mine!

The film resumed to reveal the two men fighting.

Adelaide lay in an elegant pose on the carpet, at risk of being trodden on, and giving the impression that Mr Brooding had dropped her to deal with Mr Fists. The men struggled with each other, to-ing and fro-ing and knocking ornaments from a wobbling table. Adelaide remained unconscious and Margaret's professional mind thought *If she doesn't come round soon, there could be all sort of medical consequences,* while her instinctive mind thought *For pity's sake, woman, get up and decide which of those two moronic clodhoppers you want to breed with.*

Illogical as it was, Adelaide seemed to read Margaret's thoughts. She came to her senses, sitting up and lifting her hand to her brow before turning to see the fighting men, pulling herself upright using the now rock-steady table, and swaying in a particularly feeble manner just as Mr Brooding got Mr Fists by the throat. Two more title cards appeared:

No, Hans, no! I love Peter! I shall never be yours!

I shall never give you up, Adelaide! I shall take you to my cabin in the mountains and you will be mine — forever!

The film resumed.

Mr Brooding had nearly bested Mr Fists, but Mr Fists found a final burst of energy and fought back, and when he had Mr Brooding half-tipped backwards, Adelaide picked up a miraculously unbroken vase from the carpet and hit Mr Brooding resoundingly over the head.

'Bravo!' cried Father, jumping up in his chair. 'Bravo, Adelaide!'

Another title card:

Oh my beloved! Let us ask the pastor to marry us immediately! I shall never let you out of my sight again!

It was unclear who was making what sounded more threat than promise but the final frame showed Mr Fists and Adelaide in the doorway of what appeared to be a small Swiss church, kissing fondly. The scene changed to one of a range of mountains and then faded to:

The End

'Bravo! How wonderful!' exclaimed Margaret's father as Mr Drummond turned the lights on. 'So romantic! It's brought a tear to my eye! And the heroine! Determined and brave, yet delicate, ladylike, sweet and feminine! How like my own dear daughters!'

'Good grief, Father,' said Margaret.

'Meg! You're here!'

'Yes, but why are you?'

'You said you couldn't introduce me, so I came myself. Have you seen this film?'

'No one outside the company has seen the whole thing before now,' said Mr Drummond. 'But it's always nice to have an opinion.'

'It's wonderful! Meg, you must see it from the start!'

'Not just now. Let's—'

Miss Isaacs poked her head round the door. 'Tea in here or in your room, Reuben?'

'My room, I think,' said Reuben, interpreting Margaret's look. 'Are there biscuits?'

'Of course.'

'Then let's go. May I help you, sir?' He assisted Margaret's father to his feet in a way which made Margaret ashamed of her impatience, then led them to his room.

'Why are you here, Father?'

'I have a book which you must read,' he replied, pulling a package wrapped in brown paper from his briefcase. 'And I thought while I was here, that I might just pop into this studio first.'

'Your father wonders if the Dysarts would like to adapt any of his travel memoirs,' said Reuben, 'or take his more recent fiction and branch into films for children.'

'I see.'

'Before I have any tea, might I, er...' Father rose to his feet, blushing a little.

'Oh!' said Reuben. 'Down the corridor, third door on the left.'

He waited until Margaret's father had gone. 'I'm not sure there's any money in children's films. What do you think?'

'I bet there is,' said Margaret. 'And Father's stories are very good. Plenty of excitement. A girl who's every bit as adventurous as the boys...'

'You mean Meg!' Reuben's face lit up.

'You know them?'

'Norah loved his books. She used to read them to me. I never associated them with you until your father arrived today and I realised the surname was the same. I'm such a fool.'

'Not at all.'

'Only...'

'I'm sorry my father's so presumptive,' said Margaret. 'He has no idea when he's being embarrassing.'

'He's delightful,' said Reuben. 'And Mr Drummond's told him to write to Mrs Dysart. But there's something I wanted to ask you.'

'Of course, your headache. Since I'm here...' Margaret realised she hadn't brought her doctor's bag and grimaced.

'My head's fine.' Reuben stared down at his desk, fiddled with a pencil and dropped his voice. 'It's about Norah.'

'Oh?' Margaret tried to sound nonchalant.

'I've been reading the stories she left... It helps keep her alive in my head.' He looked up again. His eyes sparkled.

'The detective ones?'

'There's more than those.' Reuben twiddled the pencil again and snapped its point on the desk. He traced the lines of the woman's face on the poster. 'You saw her – her body. Do you think she died naturally?'

'There's nothing to say that she didn't.'

'Ah.' A frown overlaid the pain and grief. 'So you have doubts too.' Margaret said nothing, aware she was holding her breath. 'Can I trust you?'

'Yes.'

'Before Norah left for Switzerland, she asked me to look after things for her.'

'Her stories?'

'And a diary.' Reuben dug about in a drawer and brought out an envelope just big enough for a slim exercise book. 'She said if anything happened to her, I should put it somewhere safe then give it to the right person as soon as I could. When she... when she died, I didn't know what to do. I mean, she's... She was an orphan. I knew she had some friends but which of them was the "right person" I've no idea. And to me her death seems wrong. She was full of life.'

'Reuben...' Margaret hesitated. She could hear her father approaching and she didn't want to rush the young man into taking the wrong action, but professionally she felt she should be honest. 'When someone dies, it often seems impossible to the people they leave behind. And the condition they said she died from can kill suddenly when no one knew anything was wrong. Yes, I wish I knew more about her death, but it doesn't automatically mean it's suspicious.'

'They why did someone go through her room both before and after Mr Drummond took her things?' said Reuben.

'They did?'

'The landlady blamed the maid but the maid denied everything. There was even a floorboard lifted. And when I heard you ask Mr Drummond about Norah's heart condition, I thought about the way Norah said "If anything happens to me" and it made me wonder.'

'Have you read the diary?'

Reuben shook his head. 'It felt too personal. I know you work at a hospital and I know hospitals help the police with suspicious deaths. I wondered if I should take the diary to them, but now it seems like fate: you asking about how Norah died and turning out to be the daughter of an author she admired so much.'

'Mmm,' said Margaret, as vaguely as possible, trying not to push at the wrong moment. 'You hadn't thought about keeping it here till you decide?'

'I had,' said Reuben. 'But I keep coming in and finding my things disordered.' He peered round at piles of paper, half finished drawings and open books. 'I suppose you don't believe me, and I know it looks chaotic, but I know when things aren't where they're supposed to be.'

'I do believe you.'

'Then will you take it?'

'Yes and I'll keep it safe.'

Reuben passed over the envelope and watching Margaret tuck it in the depths of her handbag, his shoulders relaxed. 'I can't imagine why, but everything seems ... hallo Mr Drummond, how can I help you?'

'Your visitor got lost. Here you are Mr Demeray. I should have guessed you were related to the doctor. A million unexpected questions. Ha ha ha.' His voice was cheery, his expression suspicious.

'Dear sir! Thank you so much for letting me see the film,' said Father, oblivious. 'It's quite wonderful how you made me believe everything was taking place in one place when half the time it was somewhere else. I must ask—'

'Come along Father,' said Margaret. 'I think you've bothered the people here long enough. Let's get you in a cab to Katherine's.'

His face dropped into a petulant scowl. 'But I wanted to meet Mr and Mrs Dysart and I wanted to go to the bookshop to see if —'

'I told you I'd ask and besides, you've forgotten that Tuesday is when Katherine's cook makes that really rich chocolate cake,' Margaret tempted.

'Marvellous!' Father stopped sulking and turned to leave. 'What are we waiting for?'

Margaret returned the surgery at ten to three.

The waiting room had started to fill and Dr Fernsby was talking with Miss Hill. She turned as Margaret entered. 'I saw you from the window coming out of the studio and heading for the main road. I wondered what on earth you were doing. You hadn't taken your doctor's bag.'

'I forgot,' said Margaret. There was no point in making anything up. 'My father had turned up there. He's developed a fascination with moving pictures and has been asking me to take him to visit the studio ever since he discovered it was here. He's eighty-one but full of surprises. Reuben asked me to intervene.'

Dr Fernsby's eyes dropped to the envelope. 'Reuben? Is that a present from him?'

'Goodness no. It's from Father. He tends to push books onto me that he thinks I'll enjoy without asking whether I want them.'

Dr Fernsby frowned. Perhaps no one ever dared offer her anything she might not welcome. 'How strange.'

'I'd hate that,' said Miss Hill. 'I'd rather choose my own books. I like romances. He didn't buy it from Nierling's did he?' She wrinkled her nose.

Margaret hesitated. 'I - I don't think so.'

'I hope not,' said Dr Fernsby. 'It's far too insanitary for a man of his age.'

'What did he give you?' asked Miss Hill.

'I rather dread to open it,' said Margaret.

'Go on, doctor.'

With a room full of people watching, she had little choice without making an unnecessary fuss. Knowing her father, it could be anything, from the latest children's book to esoteric verse to a new philosophy. It could be pristine or falling apart. It could have come from Foyles or a street trader like Bookie Brown. She unwrapped the parcel to reveal a brand new copy of *The Spell of Egypt* and relaxed.

'Is it a romance?' asked Miss Hill.

'It's a travel book.'

'Oh.' Miss Hill was disappointed.

'Mmm,' said Dr Fernsby, smiling. 'That doesn't look as if it came from Nierling's. Might we have a word, Dr Demeray?' She strode towards her consulting room.

Margaret followed in her wake feeling felt irritated and frustrated. There was next to no time to look at Norah's diary before clinic. And now she she was being treated like a naughty schoolgirl about to be admonished for daring to go outside without asking permission. She prepared to defend herself.

'I thought you'd gone to see Reuben to stop him wasting your time in clinic,' said Dr Fernsby. 'But you didn't take your bag.'

'I meant to,' said Margaret, her arms folded. 'But my primary concern was stopping Father from bothering anyone and sending him home and in my rush, I—'

'You needn't be defensive,' said Dr Fernsby. 'I can see your dilemma, even though my father was quite a different sort. And I don't think there's anything wrong with Reuben's head, do you? I think he just likes to make a fuss and be comforted, like a spoiled child. So pre-empting him was a wise decision.'

Margaret subsided a little. 'He suffers from eye strain as you thought. I've reassured him that there's nothing seriously wrong.'

'Good. Now then, I'm six weeks away from going into confinement and I wanted to say that I like working with you and I'd welcome a formal application for a partnership.'

'Thank you.' It hadn't been what Margaret expected.

'It would be good to have you on hand more,' said Dr Fernsby then chuckled. 'And at least I'd have an idea where you might be at any given moment.'

'Ha ha.' Margaret forced a laugh. 'That's me. Now you see me now you don't. One minute in Whitechapel, the next in Hampstead!' Did Dr Fernsby's eyes flicker? It was impossible to be certain.

Twenty-Six

In the twenty minutes which should have been Reuben's appointment, she was finally able to read the diary. The entries started with Norah beginning work at Deanacre Manor, making friends with Nellie and using her half-days to attend a course to improve her type-writing.

Norah recorded in detail not only all her fruitless attempts to trace her parents but the equally fruitless attempts to obtain an office job. Finally she recorded a triumph - winning a story competition in the local Gazette under the name of Miss Vale. The prize was five pounds, equalling nearly six months of Norah's wages, and publication of her story about a little orphan called Marietta in four instalments leading up to Christmas.

Then:

Saturday 10th December 1910

I had a letter about Marietta! It was from someone called Mr Friend saying he was an orphan too and it touched his heart. The Gazette had given him my address and he wanted to know if I wanted a writing job!

Margaret sat up straight. Newspapers wouldn't just give out addresses like that. But presumably Norah didn't realise. She should have been suspicious yet...

I was so excited till I realised I haven't got any references for writing. I wrote back and explained that I'm just an amateur but if he could let me know what the job entailed I'd consider it. I told him to address the envelope to Miss Glyn and hope he'll imagine she's my guardian or something and has to read my letters. I spent the day making up a story in my head about a lady detective. And I broke a vase so I'll have something docked from my wages, but it doesn't matter since I've got the five pounds.

Monday 12th December 1910

Mr F wrote back. He put a letter to Miss Vale in an envelope inside another envelope addressed to Miss Glyn, with a note asking her to pass it on. He wrote about being in an orphanage and feeling alone and said it would be nice to give the job to someone similar. He asked when and where we could meet. I wrote straight back saying I could manage Friday at 2 o'clock in the parish church. I didn't say it was my half-day because he needn't know I'm a maid. (Church seems the safest place as if Mr F's not to be trusted I can call the verger for help. And if anyone sees us they won't tell Mrs E because we'll just look like worshippers.) I caught the 9.30 post and he replied in the last post this afternoon and said he would!

Friday 16th December 1910

There was a letter in the lunchtime post from Mr F. He said something had happened and he couldn't meet me, and asked if I read the papers. He said he'd write about another meeting when he could. I'm not sure what to do. And I'm not sure what papers he means. I decided not to go out for my half-day. It was raining, anyway. I stayed in my room and wrote some more of the lady detective story. Everything is going wrong for her, but she'll live to fight another day.

For the next few days, the diary simply recorded preparations for Christmas and how Norah's book was progressing. The lady detective seemed to have hit a streak of violence, laying out three assassins in one chapter and fielding a speeding bullet with her umbrella in another.

Margaret felt profound pity for this young housemaid who wanted not only a better life but to feel of value to someone and just as it seemed both were about to happen, the mysterious Mr Friend let her down just as everyone else had.

Thursday 22nd December 1910

Mrs E gave all the servants the afternoon off for Christmas shopping on a whim. I bet she'll say it's our Christmas present to save giving us anything.

The others went home. N invited me for tea with her family and so did B but I didn't want to intrude, so I said no.

I went up town to see the lights and displays, but it's not the same when there's no one to share it with. Everything was all crush and bustle and I had nothing to buy since I got N's present a while back. There were some good films showing, but I'm not going into a picture house alone after the last time. I had tea in a Lyons, only I had to share a table with sweethearts and they didn't want to chat with me, just each other. I rather wished I'd gone with N after all.

After sunset, I took the tube back to Hampstead. I didn't feel like going to the house before it was time to go on duty, so I went to see the decorations in the church instead. Matron used to say churches are popish compared to chapels, but I can't see why God should care if there's stained glass or plain. Isn't what's inside people more important than what's inside a building?

Anyway, it was beautiful. Flickering candlelight was reflecting off the brass and the gold on the Bible verses and curlicues, and off the holly and off the windows, and it felt like a magic forest. I was inventing a story where the lectern eagle woke the stained-glass birds and they flew around my head up to the rafters, glittering like rainbows and singing like angels, when a man sat beside me and made me jump.

'I'm so sorry we couldn't meet last week, Miss Glyn,' he said. 'I'm Mr Friend.'

My heart raced like a millstream. He's not a bit how I imagined him from his letters. He's rather old – around forty, I should think – nice-looking but not flash. The sort of man you mightn't notice. The verger was tidying hymn books, so I knew I was safe. Besides, Mr F seemed too ordinary to be afraid of and didn't seem interested in me <u>that</u> sort of way. It wasn't what I was scared it might be after all.

'How did you recognise me?' I whispered.

'Only an author stares up at ceilings in a dream.' He has a kind smile. 'You have the skills the King needs, if you're willing. There's no pay, I'm afraid, but you could help save the country. If you'd rather not, you needn't. Others might do, but I wanted to offer you the chance first. We orphans ought to stick together, don't you think?'

Well, if the King needs me, then I know my duty, and Mr F seems so nice and brotherly. I just know I can trust him.

This finally seemed to explain why she might have written the letters. Maybe it would explain who Mr Friend was. So far he hadn't claimed to be Norah's father.

Margaret turned the page.

The remainder of the diary was written in Norah's Welsh short-hand. Without Elinor's help, it was meaningless.

Margaret clasped her bag to herself as she made her way to the tube. Much earlier, after she'd found her father a cab, Margaret had sent a telegram to Fox's office to ask for someone to meet her at Oxford

Circus. She felt increasingly nervous about having the car associated with her in Glassmakers Lane, but she also felt vulnerable as she rushed through the throngs of commuters. Perhaps she should simply have got a cab. She took a convoluted route to Oxford Circus, switching back and forth a number of times, but finally in a crush of passengers emerged onto the pavement. Bert, in his chauffeur's garb was waiting for her and asked her to drive while he took the diary and flicked through.

'Miss H is still off digging,' he said. 'And Smith hasn't managed to learn either Welsh or shorthand, so we'll have to wait, but thanks.'

Margaret winced as she crunched the gears and steered to avoid a cyclist whose skills were worse than hers.

'You should ask for a lift more often,' said Bert. 'Who knows what might get robbed from a lady's handbag if she got accosted on the way home.'

'Is that likely?'

'It's possible. Have you told anyone who didn't already know where you live?'

Margaret thought. 'Not specifically. But I'm in the telephone directory.'

'Modern life's a trial,' said Bert. 'How's anyone supposed to keep stuff secret? Right ho, you'd best drive home now. Just to let you know, we've had someone on watch and we'll keep it that way, but I don't reckon anyone would attack you there when they could get you much less obviously somewhere else.'

'Somewhere else. Everything and everyone seems to be somewhere else,' Margaret muttered. She pulled up outside the flat, peered into the dusk to see if anyone was visible and parked the car. 'Is there any news on when Fox or Elinor will be back?'

'Tomorrow I reckon. Right, out you get and keep your wits about you.'

Inside the flat, Margaret changed and looking out of the front window again, was unnerved by the third stranger of the week to visit Mrs Winson. She chided herself for being foolish and nosy and settled down with Juniper to read her post. One was a bill. The other, addressed in a careful print, was postmarked Hampstead. It was from Nellie with another letter folded and placed inside.

Dear Dr Demray, Thank you for offering to take me to the studio where Norah worked. Don't worry about the short notice. I'm thrilled. I usually don't get to go nowhere. Mrs E's let me change my half day, so I'll be at Tottenham Court Road station at two o'clock. I have something else for you too. The housekeeper wanted to inspect our rooms so I moved the furniture to give the floor a good clean and found something sticking up between the boards under Norah's bed. I'm sending it to you cos I don't understand it and don't want to keep it neither in case the police ask me questions. If they do, will you come with me?

Yours truly Miss N Pinter.

Margaret extracted the other envelope. It was typed, and the post-mark, though smeared, was clearly WC1. Inside was a short typed letter.

Dear Miss Glyn

I am sorry to hear that, due to a misapprehension, you have vacillated to the point of uncertainty as to how you might support the cause. I hope that this is simply youthful irresolution rather than abnegation, since the consequences of the latter are momentous for all concerned. However, I wish you well in your new endeavours and shall take a keen interest in your progress. I hope that the one thing you understand is that you should say nothing about my requests since there really are spies everywhere and they will not think a young girl too unimportant to dispose of. I also

sincerely hope, for your own good, that you have hidden nothing from
me.

Yours, advising caution,

Mr Friend.

Twenty-Seven

O n Wednesday morning, Margaret telephoned the London from St Julia's. Miss Connors remained incoherent and they had moved her to a side-room away from the brightness of the ward. Constable Harris had asked to be informed of anyone asking to visit, but no one had.

When she explained about Nellie, Dr Jordan approved her request to take leave that afternoon and then said she'd been asked to attend a board meeting. Despite his previous assurances, there was a coolness in the atmosphere.

'I gather you've been invited to visit a laboratory with a view to research, and offered a partnership at a private practice as well as invited to apply for a position in a Swiss sanatorium, Dr Demeray,' said the chairman. 'And I also hear from Dr Jordan that you've visited South Wales to see where a new sanatorium is planned. You seem very popular.'

'Yes sir,' said Margaret. 'I have skills to offer which—'

'Your skills are without question,' interrupted the chairman. 'The issue remains as to whether you can utilise them here while fulfilling your wifely duties and whether you *should* utilise them at the expense of a young man who will have a family to support eventually. If other places feel differently, perhaps you'd be advised to take them up on their offers.'

Seething, Margaret returned to the mortuary wing. Today was clearly not the day to discuss working additional hours at Glassmakers Lane. *Not that I want to*, she thought. *I don't want to admit it to Fox, but I don't feel safe there.*

Checking herself in the mirror, Margaret saw a woman in a boring dress who looked grey under the eyes, a little hollow in the face and bad tempered. A tumble of thoughts span. *'You're skilled but we don't want you,' said the board. 'I like to know where you are,' said Dr Fernsby. 'I can't always tell you where I'm going,' said Fox. 'She doesn't deserve you,' said the girl in the café. He and Elinor will be back today. Why am I thinking of them in the same sentence?*

There was a knock at the door and an orderly stepped inside. 'Telephone call for you doctor.'

'Thank you.'

Margaret smoothed her hair and went to the front desk, feeling her heart lighten. But it wasn't Fox. It was Elinor.

'Can you meet me for lunch?'

'Of course. There's a café opposite the hospital.'

'Not there. Do you know the Gardenia Restaurant near Covent Garden? Can you manage that?'

'It would be better actually. Will Fox be there?'

'Doubt it. I can't see him eating vegetarian food by choice. See you at one.'

Margaret arrived at the Gardenia with her heart pounding from rushing and feeling a little nauseous.

The restaurant was beloved by suffragettes and its tables were packed mainly with women, some chatting amiably and others more intense, poring over leaflets or maps. Many wore a Holloway badge, and several of them were presumably not long released from prison. They looked gaunt and exhausted, sipping tea but ignoring the stands covered in cakes and sandwiches.

'Good day, madam,' said a waitress. 'We're rather busy, but if you're prepared to share, I'm sure I can find you a seat.'

'I'm meeting a friend, thank you.' Margaret scanned the room, wishing she'd asked Elinor to wear a hat that was easy to pick out, although it was hard to imagine Elinor having the patience for frivolous hats. Finally, she spotted her and wound her way through the tables as quickly as possible.

'We don't think anyone's watching your usual café,' said Elinor, beckoning the waitress and ordering more tea and a selection of sandwiches and cakes, 'but it's wise to be cautious. And it's noisy enough here to talk without being overheard since most of the ladies here are busy planning campaigns. Did you know some of them roller-skated all night at the Aldwych Rink on Sunday to avoid the census enumerator? I like that kind of initiative. While planning to thwart the government, why not have fun too? Not that I can roller-skate. Can you?'

'Yes.'

'Interesting.'

'Did you and Fox have a successful digging expedition?'

'I did. Can't speak for Fox. I hadn't started looking for Robert Davis, so your information won't go to waste, although I somehow doubt the man in Paris was him. Anyway, it'll have to wait. I've been translating the diary all morning.'

'That's quick.'

'It's not too bad when you have the knack and while it's sometimes long-winded, it's not long. And I dictated to Smith as I went along and he had to type it all up for me which was very satisfactory.' Elinor smirked. She took out the original diary and a pile of typescript.

There was a great deal of it. Much as she wanted to know what it said, Margaret's heart sank, wondering how late she was going to arrive at Tottenham Court Road in time to meet Nellie.

Elinor lifted the top sheet of neat typescript and handed it over. 'This is a summary. I doubt you have time to read the rest just now and we really do need to go through it thoroughly, but I thought you'd like to know the gist.'

Facts:

- Norah Glyn placed advertisements in various newspapers seeking her natural parents. These were anonymous, inviting replies to be sent care of the papers. No replies were received.

- Between 3rd and 23rd January NG posted a number of anonymous letters to Hampstead police asking them to investigate local spies.

- NG stopped when discovered by her employer.

- NG joined Dysart's Studios as an employee a few days later.

- In early March, a letter in the same style as NG's was received by Scotland Yard who forwarded it to Hare resulting in an abortive mission to Austria.

- NG went with the film crew to Switzerland in March and died on the way home.

Apparent facts:

- NG started letter writing after a man calling himself Mr Friend said the Gazette gave him NG's address and asks her to write the letters as a patriotic duty.

- Friend encouraged her by offering to help find her parents.

- NG doesn't appear to question any of this. She appears to think him 'posh' enough to know what's what but not 'too posh' to trust.

- NG stopped writing when she began to doubt that either what she was writing or the reason she'd been asked to write was genuine. She wondered if it was a convoluted ruse to discredit her employers whom she despised but didn't know why they should be discredited.

- NG was afraid but believed she was relatively safe with the studio crew. However she was afraid enough to note that should anything happen to her, there was important information in another place.

- NG was recorded to have died of an inherited heart problem, which none of her friends knew she had.

Critical entries in Norah's diary:

9th January: Another book arrived without a stamp. Mr E snappish. Mrs E cried.

10th January: Mr E's car stolen last night and found in a ditch. They've arrested someone.

18th January: The letter Mr F wants me to write is sillier than any story. Am I distracting the police from something more important? Mr F was not happy when I said I want to find another way to be patriotic. He scares me a little. Mrs E had another book in the post - *King Solomon's Mines*. She gave it to me. After, when I was cleaning the grate I found a bit of half burnt paper with '...leave the mines but the mines won't leave...' written on it there.

23rd January: Mr F asked me to write 2 final letters. One of them is about airships. He said not to date them and to give them to him to post. I don't understand. What if it's all lies and someone gets hurt, or someone is looking in the wrong place for something again? I won't do this anymore. Mr E gave me a shilling and a few hours off work to hide a big envelope. His hand was shaking. He said it needs to be safe but not in the house, and he'll need it back some time. I don't know who to believe. I might tell the police.

24th January: The E's told on me and the police came. I don't know who to trust. I hope Mr F loses interest in me. I hid the photographs like Mr E asked but after the way the police talked to me, I'm not telling them anything.

25th January: Mr F wrote and threatened me. I'm hiding his letter in case anything happens. It may have finger prints on.

30th January: I was sitting in a Lyons writing a story to take my mind off things when a lady asked what I was doing. She said there was a job going in a film studio and a writer was just what they were after. She was like an angel. I'm handing in my notice.

1st March: Good news and bad. I had a letter which if it's true might change everything. Have I really found my da? I'm going to think about it before I reply. And I saw someone in the lane who looks a bit like Mr F and a bit different. Please God he doesn't follow me to Switzerland. I just wanted to do the right thing. I just wanted to find my parents and ask why they didn't want me. I just want to be more than an orphan without a name.

'What about the envelope she hid?' said Margaret. 'I'm really worried for Nellie. She forwarded me the threatening letter from 25th January. It had been hidden under a floor board in the house. What if Norah hid the sealed envelope in the same place even though Mr Edevane had said they should go elsewhere?'

'Do you have the threatening letter with you?'

'No, I was keeping it to give to Fox. Since you're back, I assume I'll see him later.'

'I couldn't say. But it'll be interesting to see if there are fingerprints.'

'It'll be smothered with Nellie's for a start.'

Frowning at the pages in the soft light of the restaurant, Elinor said, 'Girls are generally very silly, but I have the impression Norah wasn't. The sealed envelope will be somewhere else.'

'Everything seems to be somewhere else. Including Fox.'

Elinor raised her eyebrows. 'It's his job. It's my job. He possibly tells you too much as it is. To tell you more could put both of you in danger. I assumed you understood that when you married.'

'I did.' Margaret shifted in her seat. The other woman's serious face was warmer in tone than Margaret's. It was unfashionable but attractive. 'But staying away in hotels with—'

'Temptation?' Elinor snorted a little. 'Charles enjoyed that perhaps. Fox is a little bit of a flirt when it's useful but that's all. He married you. That should tell you everything.'

'Mmm.'

'Going back to business. Wasn't Fox knocked down by a car in Hampstead on the evening of 9th January?'

'About then.'

'Does he look anything like Mr Edevane?'

Margaret pulled herself together. 'In the dark I suppose he might. They're the same sort of build, at least. That's...'

'Odd? Frightening? Who sent Fox there?'

'I think it was Smith. What does Smith look like?'

'Men are all much of a muchness to me,' said Elinor. 'Didn't you say your friend Phoebe feels the same?'

'She doesn't want to marry one,' snapped Margaret. 'It doesn't mean she can't tell them apart.'

'Hmph, well, Smith is...'

'Nondescript, quite nice looking, forty-ish?'

Elinor considered. 'Nondescript yes. Nice looking, I suppose so. But I doubt he's thirty, although he has a middle-aged way about him. On the other hand how old was Norah?'

'Eighteen. Anyone over twenty-one is ancient when you're that age.'

'That's very true,' said Elinor. 'But if what you're implying about Smith is also true, I've just read out all of Norah's diary to him. I need to get back to the office and talk to Hare. And someone needs to get Nellie out of that house.'

Margaret checked her watch and rose. 'I have to go. I'm meeting her in ten minutes.'

'Take her somewhere safe, Margaret. Don't let her go back.'

'I'll be chaperoning her in Dysart's studios for an hour first.'

Elinor tapped up the transcript of the diary. 'That should be all right. Norah felt secure there. She was happy.'

'Yes,' said Margaret. 'But then she died.'

Twenty-Eight

Nellie emerged from the tube in a neat moss-green outfit and a brown hat. With her pallor and red hair, she looked like a shy dryad who'd wandered from a London park. She gripped a capacious hand-bag as if it contained the Crown Jewels. When Margaret offered to shake hands, she unpeeled her fingers with mild trepidation for just long enough to do so, then re-clasped the handle.

Margaret, who had assumed Nellie was quite used to travelling the underground alone, was worried. Had the girl been followed? 'Did anyone trouble you on the tube?'

Nellie looked baffled, shook her head, then let loose a nervous blast of questions.

'It is quite respectable, isn't it? Don't they wear paint on their faces? My mum says painted women are loose women, and she won't be happy if I go somewhere full of loose women. But I'm not sure about men. Can you have loose men? Did they look down on Norah because she was a maid before? Will they look down on me? Will they think I'm just a kid because I'm only fifteen? Will they give me strong drink? Mum made me sign the pledge. Do I look all right? Will they—'

'They're perfectly respectable, and looking forward to meeting you,' said Margaret. 'And there will be tea and buns; they seem to live on them. All those I've met liked Norah very much, thought she was very skilled, and think it's a great pity she's gone before her time.'

Nellie nodded. 'There'll never be anyone like her. Despite every-thing, she just kept trying. And now no one will ever see her act.'

'They've kept some of her in the film,' said Margaret. 'You'll see the whole thing today. And whenever you see it again in the cinema, you'll know she wrote it.'

'Yes, doctor. Thank you for bringing me, doctor. You won't leave me, will you, doctor?'

'Of course not. I have a feeling I wouldn't like to get on the wrong side of your mother.'

Nellie laughed. 'You don't bring up ten kids without being tough as old boots, do yer?'

'Which one are you?'

'Third. Whenever I go home, I've got the four littl'uns crawling over me. I love it.'

'You don't want your own yet, I hope.'

'Cor lummee, no, doctor. Are you mad? But I'd like to be a nursery maid. I had hopes of Mrs E, but she's not showing any signs of it. Probably as well – I'm not sure her nerves are up to it these days. And she'd never remember their names. Oooh, is this it? It doesn't look much from the outside.'

Margaret opened the door of the studio and ushered Nellie inside. Miss Isaacs put down her latest magazine and greeted them with a grin. 'Pleased to meet you, Miss Pinter. I'm Miss Isaacs. Hallo again, doctor. I'll get Reuben. He's put on a special waistcoat and tie to give you a proper tour, and there will be tea and buns waiting in the projection room at the end.'

'Told you,' Margaret whispered to Nellie.

'Did you bring your dad, doctor?' asked Miss Isaacs.

'Er, no.'

'That's a shame.' Miss Isaacs got to her feet, stretched, and led them in the direction of Reuben's room.

'Your dad?' whispered Nellie. 'Oh! Is he Mr Roderick Demeray? He was one of Norah's favourite authors! What a small world! Does he work here too?' She scanned Margaret, her expression suggesting it was amazing that anyone as old as Margaret could have a parent still alive.

'Not if I have anything to do with it,' muttered Margaret. 'Here we are. Miss Pinter, this is Reuben – apparently it's all he'll answer to. Reuben, this is Miss Pinter, another of Norah's good friends.'

'Delighted to meet you,' said Reuben. 'Now then, Miss Pinter, where would you like to start?'

'Call me Nellie, do. It's making me all nervous everyone being so fancy.'

'A woman after my own heart,' said Reuben, tapping his nose. 'All the best people stick to first names. What do you know about films? Have you a favourite?'

'How can I choose? There's so many! But I was so looking forward to seeing Norah's film about Heidi.'

'Ah,' said Reuben. 'And, as the fairy godmother would doubtless say, you shall see the film. Or is it "will"? Are you any good at grammar? Anyhow. The title's changed to *Adelaide's Choice* and I'm afraid you can only see Norah from a distance, but the story is her very own. And I've something else to tell you, though you'll have to wait a moment. Do you want to see the poster?'

'Ooh, yes please!'

'Would you like to put your handbag down?'

'No, thank you.'

'You don't need to fend anyone off, I promise.'

Nellie glanced from Reuben to Margaret. 'It's not just that. I mean, it's not that.'

'Well, if it makes you feel happier, but you'll have to let go when the buns come round. Actually no, don't. Then I can eat yours.' Reuben winked and with a flourish unrolled the printed poster. Norah and Gladys had had enough similarities in their features that anyone who loved them would only see the person they knew, and each young woman would think it was an idealised version of herself. Margaret, who'd only seen Norah lifeless and Gladys briefly, wouldn't have been sure which it was.

'Ooh, it's wonderful!' said Nellie.

'This one's yours,' said Reuben. 'I kept three back. One for you, one for me and one for luck. You can leave that here for now.' With a flourish and a bow, he ushered them through the door. 'Follow me, ladies. Or rather, come with me. Follow the sounds of whirring and mild cursing – cover your ears if necessary – and I'll take you to the set.'

'What was it you wanted to tell me, Mr – I mean Reuben?' Nellie tucked her arm into Margaret's as they made their way down a corridor towards the back of the building, heading for a stout-looking door.

'They're filming Norah's lady detective story.'

'But—' Nellie bounced. 'But I didn't think she'd finished it!'

'She hadn't,' said Reuben. 'But as the film will be less than half an hour long, Mrs Dysart took the highlights of what we had so far and made up an ending. I'm sure Norah's would be better, but Mrs Dysart wants this to be the first of a series and insisted on the Lady Detective having a sweetheart who could save her from time to time.'

Nellie pulled a face. 'She could save herself.'

'Cinema audiences prefer it when women are helpless.'

'I don't.'

'Don't worry, she's still pretty fierce. Come in and have a look.'

Behind the doors, a set portrayed the inside of a drawing room. Gladys, wearing cycling clothes, held a large umbrella en garde as she faced a towering man in a cape and a top hat who was pointing a pistol at her. They were poised, their weapons trained on each other. In the background, a maid cowered.

In front of them, the film crew stood also poised: one man holding the camera, prepared to start winding the handle, Mr Drummond with another man to the side. Mrs Dysart, hands on hips, sized up the scene.

'And ... action!' she said.

Gladys and the actor began to circle and the camera whirred, Gladys flicking out with the umbrella just as the villain was about to shoot. Their feet clunked over the stage as they declaimed stilted dialogue which would never be heard, but had to be brief enough to put on title cards for a potentially slow-witted, semi-literate audience to read.

'You've been uncovered, Lord Tapington, there is no escape. Surrender now!'

'To a mere girl? Mwahahahaha!'

'Coo,' whispered Nellie. 'I know this bit. It's the bit when everything looks as if it's going right and then goes wrong, just before the ending Norah never got round to writing. The Lady Detective nearly gets Lord Tapington, but then he escapes and she thinks she's failed. That's right, ain't it Reuben?'

'It is. They've been trying to get it right all morning. But don't worry about the ending. Mrs Dysart wrote a thrilling one with a car chase through a Sussex village which we filmed last week. Ducks flying out of the way and everything. Although it was quite hard to get the ducks to keep doing it. Some of them were intent on suicide after the fifth take, which is rather how we all felt, I think.'

Nellie stared. 'You filmed the ending last week?'

Reuben nodded. 'There was a break in the weather so we could film outdoors. If we'd known it was going to be dry today we might have filmed the beginning, but everything was set up to do this scene. If everything goes well today and the weather stays fine, we'll film the beginning tomorrow. Otherwise, we'll do the middle here instead.'

Nellie nudged Margaret and whispered, 'It's all in the wrong order. How can they stand it? And that maid wasn't in the story. Norah would never have written about a maid that was so useless.'

At that moment, just as the Lady Detective knocked the pistol out of the villain's hand and had him at the mercy of her umbrella, a door in the back of the set burst open and two square-set men in check suits leapt across the room. One wrestled the trusty umbrella from its owner's hand, pushing her with such force that she fell to the ground. Gladys slammed her head with an audible bang and swore fruitily in the very act of feigning unconsciousness, while the maid winced as she rushed out of the door at the back of the set. The other thug helped the villain to his feet, and as the three men looked down on the apparently lifeless form of the Lady Detective, the villain snapped the umbrella in half and threw it down.

'And ... cut!' shouted Mrs Dysart. 'Well done, everyone.'

The cameraman stopped turning his handle and straightened up from looking down the lens. Gladys sat up, rubbing her head and swearing with more vigour.

'Cor,' whispered Nellie. 'I hope that maid's gone for help, the useless lump. If that was me, I'd have tripped them men up as they come through the door, then biffed them with something.'

Mrs Dysart turned. 'Ah, you must be Miss Pinter. How nice to meet you. I'm so glad Dr Demeray was able to bring you. What do you think of things so far?'

'Peculiar, if I'm honest, ma'am. Middles, then endings, then beginnings. How can you make sense of things if you've got the order wrong?'

Mrs Dysart chuckled. 'Yes, it does seem strange at first. One has to re-order it afterwards. Then sometimes when you look at it, you see things you never expected. It will be a challenge when we can make longer films, but I'm sure we'll manage. Come and see the editing room where we put things together: we have a film from a while ago which we'd put aside for a bit. Then we can have tea and watch *Adelaide's Choice*. How does that sound?'

'Very nice, ma'am, thank you.'

'You needn't call me ma'am, you know. We're all quite equal here. Call me Mrs Dysart.'

'Mmm,' said Nellie, clasping her handbag tighter, her face inscrutable.

'I suppose you'd like to be a moving picture actress too.'

Nellie, watching Gladys, now brushing herself down while cursing the man who'd pushed her over, scrunched up her nose. 'Not so sure, M-Mrs Dysart. Now I've seen it, it looks a bit of a muddle and not that exciting.'

'As with everything, from wine-making to cooking a stew or even writing a story, there are a lot of messy steps and times when you want to give up because it doesn't seem right, but in the end, it's worth it. Come to the cutting room and see where the magic starts.' She steered Nellie out of the room.

'Come on,' said Reuben. 'We can't leave young Nellie with Mrs D for too long or she'll have her head turned.'

'I doubt it,' said Margaret. 'Nellie's young, but she has a solid level of common sense that I'm not sure I have now. I certainly didn't have it at fifteen.'

'Common sense is a curse to a creative person,' declared Reuben. 'All one needs is a sensible friend to look after one while one lets one's imagination fly free.' He increased his pace.

Margaret was about to do the same when someone cleared their throat behind her. She turned to find Mr Drummond standing four-square in the corridor. 'Why are you *really* here?'

Twenty-Nine

'I'm chaperoning Miss Pinter.'

'I mean generally. In Glassmakers Lane. At Dr Fernsby's. In the street getting shot at. Isn't there enough work at the hospital?'

'Need I stay in the same job forever? Have you?'

Mr Drummond grunted. 'Obviously not. But no one's shot me ... yet.'

'They were aiming at a robber ... burglar ... the man who stole from the bookshop. I can never remember which is the right term.'

'So they say.' Mr Drummond raised his eyebrows. 'This girl...' he nodded in the direction of the cutting room. 'Should you be bringing her here? Reminding her of Miss Vale? Getting her upset?'

'I'll make sure she isn't,' said Margaret. 'This may help her come to terms with the death.' She paused. Nellie was with Reuben. There was a little time to prompt something else. 'I can't help feeling sad myself. It's a shame her father couldn't attend the funeral with you.' She watched the man's face as she said this. The eyebrows lowered in a scowl and even in the darkness of the corridor, she could see his cheeks redden.

'How'd you know about that?'

'You saw me give my card to the doctor on the platform. He wrote to confirm the death was deemed to be of natural causes, and explained what happened next. It seems a shame that the father in Paris...'

Mr Drummond extracted a case from his breast pocket and took out a cigarette. He thrust it into his mouth, replaced the case and dug a matchbox out of another pocket. 'Him? Her father? A likely story. He'd have seen the advert, and thought, "where there's desperation, there's money". Wrote and found out she was a young girl. A girl without friends or family, all alone in the world, easy pickings. Maybe she'd get rich through the films, and her "father" would rake in the cash. Or more likely, since no one's ever going to get rich from moving pictures, he planned something worse. Wouldn't be the first time, would it? So in the circs, of course he didn't turn up. I bet if she'd gone to that hotel but told him she was bringing a guardian, he'd have scarpered.'

'Had you suggested that to her?'

Mr Drummond struck the match and lit the cigarette. 'I knew nothing about him till after she was dead. If I'd known beforehand, I'd have told her to give the letter to the police. What's any of it to you?'

'Professional curiosity,' said Margaret.

'Yeah?' Mr Drummond took a drag from his cigarette and nodded towards the cutting room. 'The poor kid's dead and buried. You'd best go and chaperone the living, then take her home and tell her to forget Norah. And maybe you should do the same.'

Before she could respond, Reuben sauntered up. 'Are you coming, Dr Demeray? I think you'd better. Nellie's all excited again. Turns out editing is as thrilling as giving the laundry cupboard a good sort out, only with less lavender. And she's given her professional view on how servants really behave, and given Mrs D ideas for a whole new set of comedies.'

Nellie was tearful when they left. She clutched her handbag, risking damaging the poster inside.

'Before I go back on the underground, can I talk to you on your own if it's not too much trouble?'

'It's no trouble,' said Margaret. 'I'll get a cab and take you home and we can talk then.'

'Coo - I've never been in a motor car. They'll think I'm a bit above myself turning up in a taxi.'

'You're still on your half day. Why don't I take you back to your mum's for a bit?'

'Coo - can I? Are you sure?'

'Of course I am. Where's your home?' Margaret hailed a cab.

'Cricklewood.' Nellie gave the address and climbed inside. She was shaking a little but settled back cautiously to have her first motor-car ride, grabbing the strap as they swerved to avoid cyclists and horse-drawn vehicles, then relaxing enough to start enjoying it. She half-unrolled the poster and sniffed. 'I can't thank you enough, Dr Demeray. It's been one of the best afternoons of my life. I shan't never forget it. Norah would be so proud, and so she should be. I can't wait for the film to come out so I can take Mum. She said Norah could talk the hind leg off an 'orse and most of it nonsense too, but she loved her, she really did. She always liked it when I brung Norah back. She'd read stories to the little 'uns and it was lovely. It's a shame Norah's not in more of the film. I mean, that Gladys is pretty but she's not a patch on Norah.' Nellie sighed.

'Are you tempted to go into acting too?'

'Not me,' said Nellie, swallowing a last sob and sitting up straight. 'I couldn't be doing with all that fuss and make-up and things out of order. A nanny, that's what I want to be one day. And I want to be brave like you and Mrs Dysart, not a wet weekend like Mrs E. Mum says she drinks,' said Nellie.

'What?'

'Mrs E. Mum says she reckons that's why she's always crying and she broke a perfume bottle right in front of Martha.'

'It's possible. But you ought to be careful what you say to people.'

'I can trust you, though, can't I?'

'Yes of course, but—'

'It's recent, though. The crying. She got really flustered after Christmas when books kept arriving that she hadn't ordered.'

'Do you know why?'

Nellie considered. 'I think they had messages in. Amony... anomy... not signed anyway I don't think. We'd find burnt bits in the grate.'

'Were they rude? Accusations?'

'N-no. I don't think so. They were like orders: "You must", "Don't forget", "We want".'

'I see.'

'She was all right when they stopped. Then she was a bit funny when Norah left and then she was all right again, and now she's a state every morning. The amount of powder she puts on. More than Gladys even.' Nellie paused. 'It was a lovely visit to the studio, but something made me feel twitchy. My gran was Scottish, and Mum says I've inherited the sight from her. It's in the ginger hair.' She attempted a laugh.

Margaret gave her a hug. 'My husband gets that too; he calls it "tingling". Try not to worry. Will you trust me?'

'Yes.'

'When we get you home, I want you to stay there for a few days.'

Nellie gasped. 'I can't do that! I'll lose my job.'

'I'll go straight to Deanacre Manor myself and explain. But maybe you should give notice and try to get into nursery work if that's what you really want. I have just the friend who could help you start. If you can manage her little boy you can manage anyone.'

'But why?'

Margaret hesitated. *If I say too much you could put her in more danger.* 'You remember the letter you forwarded to me that you didn't understand?'

'Yes.'

'I think it was from the man that asked Norah to write those letters which got her into trouble. I'm worried he might come looking for it and pester you. I don't think he's very nice. I mean, he may look nice, but isn't and the police are after him.'

'Oh gosh. Mum wouldn't be happy if I got mixed up in that.'

'I'll explain it to her that you're best out of it at home for a day or so. If you lose your wages, I'll make it up to you and as I say, I have a friend who'd be happy to hire you. Will you trust me?' As she said it, Margaret imagined Maude's face if she was suddenly provided with an extra maid out of the blue. Much as she - not to mention her nanny - would be glad of the help with her youngest child, Maude was a journalist. She'd smell a story within seconds. It would take a lot to keep her from asking questions.

Nellie chewed her lip, and fidgeted with her handbag. 'Yes. I found another letter to give you. I don't understand that either. After the last one, I wondered if there was anything else hidden under the bed and as soon as I had the chance I got the floorboard up.'

Margaret felt both relieved and a little deflated. 'A big envelope' was how Norah had described it. Why would you need a big envelope for a letter? But Norah had hidden it at Deanacre after all and Nellie was in danger.

'Can I see it?'

'I posted it to you.'

'But you could have brought it with you this afternoon!'

'Mum says that anyone can get their handbag stolen but no one dares to interfere with the Royal Mail.'

Margaret bit back a swear word. They had arrived at Nellie's home, a neat terraced house with a sparkling doorstep. Lace curtains in every nearby front window lifted as the taxi slowed and in one, an older version of Nellie peered out with her mouth dropping.

'Oh my!' exclaimed Nellie. 'That's Mum. What'll I say to her? You won't tell her about the police will you? What am I going to say?'

'I'll tell her there's sickness at Deanacre.'

'But there isn't, so that's a falsehood. Mum doesn't hold with fibs.'

Nellie's mother had appeared at the door and was staring out in astonishment.

'Hasn't anyone got anything wrong with them?' said Margaret in exasperation.

'Martha's got neuralgia.'

'That'll do. It's not a fib. Just say it might be the first sign of chicken pox and don't go into detail. I'll come and explain to your mother and then I'll go to Deanacre to get your things and explain there. I'll make sure you don't lose your job unless you give notice yourself.'

Nellie's job was in the balance anyway. When Margaret arrived in the taxi at Deanacre Manor, the servants were staring out of the windows and there was a small crowd on the pavement staring into the capacious drive.

Bert and Fox were there with their official car and several real policemen were putting Mr and Mrs Edevane into a Black Maria.

A movement in the crowd made Margaret look. A man who had been scanning the scene turned. He saw the taxi and strained to see its occupant. Without a second thought, Margaret ducked out of sight and told the taxi driver to drive on, then head back into London.

She knew that man. She'd only seen him once, behaving like a fool on the platform at Neuchâtel. But now, the last thing he looked like was a fool.

'Where to now, missus?' said the taxi driver.

'Just carry on for now,' said Margaret.

'I don't blame you for not stopping. Who wants to get caught up with peelers if they don't have to?' He launched into a rambling story about the iniquities of the police, speed traps and unreasonable fines.

Margaret checked behind them, but nothing seemed to be following. With any luck, the taxi had looked as if it were slowing to see the disgraceful activity outside Deanacre before moving on. The man from Neuchâtel, even if he'd seen her, couldn't have had time to catch them up before they'd disappeared.

'What you reckon they're being nicked for?' said the cabbie.

'I can't imagine.' Her mind whirled. The logical thing was to go home and collect her post and telephone Fox's office. Or telephone Maude, make something up to explain Nellie, bracing herself to counter sarcastic comments about presumption, then take the girl to Maude's Marylebone home where no one would look for her. Or perhaps she should go directly to Fox's office. No, that was no good. They'd recently moved premises and it was now doubtless harder to find than before. She gave her address. 'Can you hurry?'

But at home, there was no letter from Nellie. No post of any kind, just a telegram which had been handed to Mrs Winson and had come from Dr Fernsby.

Presume you remember promising to help with an additional evening surgery. I expect to see you at half past five.

Margaret could recall no such thing.

Thirty

S he telephoned Fox's office and heard herself gabbling.

'Slow down Mrs F,' said the person at the other end. 'Least said soonest mended remember.'

'Yes of course.'

'You staying or going?'

'Going. To the other place.'

'Right ho. I'll get Miss H to meet you.'

Margaret arrived on the corner of Glassmakers Lane at twenty five minutes past five. She brushed herself down and straightened her hat before walking briskly but calmly to the surgery.

Elinor had got on the tube at Piccadilly Circus and sat next to her, then taken out some knitting and let her wool roll about Margaret's feet. In the chaotic retrieval, she listened to what Margaret knew, took a slip of paper with Nellie's home address and muttered that she'd collect Nellie's belongings from Deanacre and that Fox would be waiting for Margaret in Glassmakers Lane at seven, before gathering her own things together, giving Margaret a dirty look, and storming off to find another seat.

At the surgery, Dr Fernsby greeted Margaret with relief. 'I thought something had held you up; you're usually early. I hope your afternoon with the tour and the maid and everything was more relaxing than mine.' She looked weary, her usually upright frame slumped.

'What happened?' said Margaret. 'If you're done in, I can manage the appointments alone and you can go and rest.'

'Nonsense.' Dr Fernsby straightened up. 'Pregnancy is no excuse for idleness, and one must be an example to one's patients. As for the appointments, you can't possibly manage them alone, unless you want to be here till eight o'clock.' She contemplated Margaret's face. 'Which I can see you don't. I shall be all right.'

'Has Mrs Dysart been troubling you again? She seemed perfectly well when I saw her earlier.'

'No. Although she did invite me for tea after you'd left the studio to show me her film and tell me how talented she is.'

Margaret frowned. Dr Fernsby was clearly one of those people who viewed other people's enthusiasms as showing off, when there was nothing boastful about Mrs Dysart's pleasure in the work that her studio had created. She itched to ask why, if she felt that way about the other woman, Dr Fernsby had gone to tea with her.

'Today Mrs Dysart seems quite devoid of ailments,' said Dr Fernsby, getting awkwardly to her feet and walking round the room, straightening things. 'I gather Miss Vale's young friend enjoyed herself and you took her back to her employers. I thought that might be why you were late.'

Margaret glanced at the clock. She wasn't late at all, but Dr Fernsby didn't seem in the mood to be disagreed with. 'I took her to visit a friend.'

'I'd have thought all Miss Pinter's friends would be in service too.'

'They are,' said Margaret, without the remotest idea.

'It's a shame you didn't arrange to bring your father at the same time and save him coming yesterday. Has he given you any more books?'

'No. Why?'

'And you talked him out of visiting Nierling's I hope.'

Margaret frowned. 'I wish I could be sure. He heard a rumour - goodness knows where - that there's a book he wants there. I'll have to track a copy down elsewhere and buy it for him, although how I'll manage a yellow one I've no idea. Although that might not stop him. The older and more chaotic the bookshop, the more fascinated he is.'

Dr Fernsby paused in levelling the spines of books on the shelf. 'Yellow?' Her tired eyes glinted and bored a little.

Curious, thought Margaret and said as disinterestedly as she could, 'Father talks about so many books so often, I've just realised I'm not quite sure which it was. But it can wait. You seem very anxious. Did something happen this afternoon?'

Dr Fernsby seated herself and laid her hand on her stomach. 'The baby has been sluggish for some days and hadn't moved at all today until about half an hour ago. That was enough to start with.'

'You should have asked me to come over while I was at the studio! I'd have listened for the heartbeat.'

'It would have wasted your time. What could you have done if it had been absent?' She sighed. 'I shall be glad when it's over. I feel far too old to be doing this again.'

'I'm sorry.'

'Well it's hardly your fault. But just as I was managing to have a rest, your assistant telephoned from St Julia's and asked for you to make contact as soon as you could.'

'Algie?'

'He wouldn't say what it was about. I do wish you'd told him your arrangements for today.'

'I'd never expect him to call me here.'

'I told him to telephone you at home later.' Her eyes challenged Margaret. 'I also reminded him that you're working here tomorrow morning in lieu of Monday afternoon.'

Margaret's surprised irritation blurred into fear. A missed letter. A missed telephone call and a request to work an extra evening and a change in schedule which she didn't remember agreeing to. She could argue or she could play along. The latter seemed safest. 'I'm sorry you didn't have the rest you'd hoped for, but I think it's rather unreasonable to be annoyed that the hospital where I hold a senior position might not telephone me once in a blue moon. I'd taken an afternoon's unpaid leave today and Mr Hardisty knew I'd be in Glassmakers Lane. Perhaps he thought I'd come here after going to the studio. If you still want me to undertake your work after the baby is born then naturally any calls I have won't trouble you, and if we decide to go into partnership thereafter, I'll have my own receptionist if necessary, and certainly my own telephone in my consulting room.'

Dr Fernsby's shoulders lowered a minuscule amount and she rubbed her temples. 'I apologise; I'm being irrational. It's hard to sleep this late in a pregnancy and one's mood does fluctuate. I suppose you could speak with him now. But you'll have to choose between Miss Hill's desk or mine and put up with either the waiting room or me listening in.'

'I'll do it from here. Thank you.'

Margaret waited for the connection, slowing her breathing to sound calm, half turned away from Dr Fernsby.

'Hallo,' said Algie. His voice was wary. 'Did I get you into trouble?'

'No. What is it?'

'I could have had a wire sent, but I wasn't sure where you'd be.'

'Don't worry,' Margaret glanced at the clock, wishing he'd get to the point.

'Constable Harris came looking for you. He wanted to give you a message.'

'Oh no.' In the last few hours, Miss Connors had slipped from Margaret's mind. 'The poor woman. I hoped...'

Instinctively, she turned to see Dr Fernsby listening. The other woman mouthed 'Miss Connors?' and raised her eyebrows.

'She's still alive,' said Algie. 'But Constable Harris says someone tried to make sure she wasn't.'

'What?'

'The hospital is giving out that she's not expected to regain consciousness or last the night.'

'That's so sad.' Margaret turned her back on Dr Fernsby again.

'It's not true,' said Algie. 'She did, for a bit. She gave a description of the last man she remembered seeing. Constable Harris got permission to stay with her for a few hours to see whether she said any more, but while he was off the ward briefly, a man talked his way in to see her, asking if she'd been given digitalin.'

'But—'

'There's nothing wrong with her heart. I know. Apparently he forced his way in to see her. She became agitated and one of the nurses got Constable Harris back to intervene. There was a medicine bottle in this Oswald Durrell's pocket.'

'Who?'

'Sorry, I can't read my writing – it's Drummond. He's refusing to explain his presence and they've arrested him for attempted murder.'

Mr Drummond, standing over Norah at Neuchâtel, indifferent and irritated. Mr Drummond, more or less insisting she go away. Margaret was about to express her delight when she realised Algie's voice was not as triumphant as she'd have expected. Her heart sank.

'And then?'

'Miss Connors is back under sedation, but she's on the mend. Only...' Algie still sounded conflicted, uncertain.

'What?'

'Constable Harris said to telephone him tomorrow but keep it quiet for now. No matter who asks. He thinks someone else is involved.'

'I see.' Margaret frowned. 'Thank you for letting me know. Goodbye.'

'Miss Connors?' asked Dr Fernsby.

Margaret nodded. The other woman's eyes slipped from hers to the clock, then back, boring into Margaret's. Speculative. Waiting. As indifferent and uncaring as Mr Drummond's had been.

'She's not expected to regain consciousness or last the night.'

Dr Fernsby nodded with a sigh. 'That's very sad.' Her shoulders straightened, one hand touched her hair to check it was tidy, and this time, she made no attempt to hide the tiny smile flickering on her rose-red mouth.

Fox was waiting as promised when Margaret finally left the surgery. He pulled her into an enveloping hug and his lovely, familiar scent made her heart lurch, unsure whether to race or calm. 'I can't leave you for five minutes can I?' He said.

'Five minutes?' said Margaret, extracting herself from the hug to kiss him. 'It's felt like five years.'

'Will you drive us home? Bert says you're good enough for us not to shout at each other but you still have to practice.'

'I'm too tired, my mind's running in circles and it's getting dark.'

'Then you need to wake up and concentrate and if you crash the gears I'll slap your hand.'

'I haven't felt so nervous for my knuckles since I was learning to write on a slate.'

They changed seats and Margaret pulled slowly away from the kerb.

'Concentrating on driving will stop you trying to untangle your thoughts,' said Fox. 'But apart from having to make Nellie disappear, why's your mind running in circles?'

Margaret gave a brief summary of the previous two days ending with her suspicions about Dr Fernsby and Mr Drummond.

'At least he's under arrest, but I can't work out what Dr Fernsby wants. It could be pregnancy making her irrational and unsympathetic with Miss Connors, but it doesn't feel that way.'

'Which bothers you more? The way she responded to the news about Miss Connors or the duties you don't remember agreeing to?'

'Both.'

'What does Miss Connors have to do with anything?'

'I still don't understand how anything has to do with anything,' said Margaret. 'But it does. And I'm scared of the man I saw in the crowd when I arrived at Deanacre just as the Edevanes were being arrested. I'm sure he couldn't see me clearly, but I know it was the man I saw the day Norah died.'

'Coincidence.'

'Doesn't exist, and you know it.'

'But from your description after Switzerland, he sounded like the sort of rich man who'd live in Hampstead, so maybe he does.'

'Yes but he didn't look the archetypal British idiot abroad today. Is Nellie safe?'

'I think she's safe enough where she is for the time being,' said Fox. 'Everyone's focus is on Deanacre.'

'Who's going to explain to Nellie's parents that she can't go back tomorrow? Especially when they might see the Edevane's arrest in the papers.'

'It won't be reported.'

'Oh.'

'Elinor will speak with her parents, don't worry.'

'What's all this about, Fox?'

'All? I'm not sure yet. But I know some of it.'

'Is Smith involved?'

'We're not sure if he's an intelligent fool or a double-agent. He's under observation to see what he does. Hare has him working round the clock to stop him leaving the office while we try to establish the facts.'

'Aren't you worried?'

'Of course. But if he's a double-agent, he won't be the first, simply the first to have fooled Hare so comprehensively. Here we are at home. I've organised for the Black Lion to deliver a hot dinner shortly.'

'How wonderful.'

Fox chuckled as he handed Margaret out of the driver's seat. 'I thought you wouldn't mind. I bet there's nothing in the pantry anyway, but more to the point I'm starving and you're exhausted.'

Margaret snuggled into him and closed her eyes. 'I'm not only exhausted. I'm scared.'

Thirty-One

No post had been delivered. The last delivery was due just after they got home at a quarter to eight, but nothing arrived except for the meal from the Black Lion.

'Nellie's letter's been intercepted, hasn't it?' Anxiety and weariness mingled. A migraine threatened.

'Not necessarily,' said Fox. 'If the daft girl only posted it on the way to meet you, it might easily not arrive till tomorrow.' His words were light, but she could sense his frustration. 'And you said it was a letter, when Norah's diary said large envelope. So perhaps it's just another threat from Mr Friend.'

'Oh God, I hope so.' Margaret took a mouthful of food and willed it to taste of something other than worry. 'Why have the Edevanes been arrested? It's seemed like they were victims rather then perpetrators.'

'Because the books comprised veiled threats?' said Fox.

'There were messages inside. Nellie thought some were instructions.' Margaret frowned as she said it, the word resonated. 'Was *Erewhon* another that was due to be sent?'

'Maybe. It fits with our view that it was blackmail or coercion,' Fox continued. 'Finding out which has been what's taken all this time. The police arrested them on our intelligence and we got back in time to take charge as we needed to.'

'And you had to leave London to gather that intelligence.'

'Elinor discovered the main facts. I had to establish the detail. I've been in the Forest of Dean. Nice hotel surrounded by trees, very refreshing now that everything's finally turning green. They said there will be bluebells everywhere in a week or so.'

'Elinor didn't mention any of that.'

'Any of what?'

'All the trees and bluebells.'

'I'm not surprised. I doubt there were any of either where she was.'

'I thought she was with you.'

Fox looked blank. 'Hardly. Hare wouldn't pay for her to stay in a hotel again. The last time was only because she could speak Welsh and there was a possibility of a lead. She's spent the last two days trailing back and forth by train visiting ports and harbours and sifting through dusty records in dreary offices looking for details of boxes of books coming and going. It's what she's good at. Anyway, the Forest of Dean is lovely as I say. We ought to go there together one day. Maybe in the autumn, when those leaves turn and it must feel like the world's afire with colour.'

'That's nice but irrelevant. Why were you there?'

'Looking for bombers.' Fox sat back and folded his arms. 'Aren't you going to eat your dinner?'

Margaret put her wine glass down. 'Never mind dinner. Bombers? Are there many anarchists in the Forest of Dean? It sounds more like somewhere you'd find wizards and elves.'

'Perhaps you can. But that doesn't preclude anarchists or people intent on threatening the country's stability on behalf of an enemy power, the same as anywhere else. Not everything's pretty. There are mines too, big and small. Iron smelting. It's a busy little place, but secret somehow. You drive for miles through forests, seeing nothing, then there's a little cottage, then a small town, then a mine, then nothing but trees again. If you stop, you feel as if you're being watched, although it's hard to know what by. There are wild boar roaming free, so ten to one it's that. The people are extremely friendly.'

Margaret thought of the Balodis children, their sense of injustice bubbling into fury. 'But there's unrest there? Miners threatening strike action? I don't associate miners with bombs.'

'Working class unrest is always the assumption, isn't it?'

'Half the country is on the verge of upheaval at the moment, even if the other half is oblivious. The Singer factory workers have been on strike for nearly three weeks.'

'This is nothing to do with striking or anarchy,' said Fox. 'It's to do with destabilising London with a bombing campaign. The very plot that Charles and I were trying to uncover in January.'

'You've lost me, Fox. If it's all to do with London, what were you looking for in Gloucestershire?'

'The Edevanes.'

'The Edevanes? They live in Hampstead and seem too stupid to destabilise more than a bottle of gin. You still haven't explained why they've been arrested.'

Fox wagged a finger. 'Good things come to girls who wait. We thought Norah's letters were all nonsense but—'

'*Norah* thought they were nonsense, and she was writing them.'

'What if they weren't? We did some more digging. Mr Friend dictated his letters to Norah and she wrote them down in shorthand then transcribed them later. She wrote down Toad Hall Street and the police thought it was Frognal because of association of ideas. But what if the name was *nearly* Toad Hall Street, misheard by a girl still engrossed by children's books, who came from another part of the country and was still unfamiliar with London accents? Or even possibly couldn't read her own shorthand.'

Margaret racked her brain. 'I don't know Hampstead well enough to guess where it could be.'

'It's not Hampstead. It's Westminster. Tot Hill Street.'

'But the letter said—'

'The letter never said the person in Toad Hall Street was in Hampstead. In Tot Hill Street, we found a man with very dubious equipment and some interesting notebooks. It's doubtful he'd get as far afield as Hampstead, because why bother with some semi-retired colonel nearly in the countryside when he could theoretically walk up the road and tap any number of government departments.'

'My God.'

'Quite.'

'And the cocoa-drinking printer with a chess-playing widow friend?'

'In the clear so far. That leaves the "incomers" to Hampstead.'

'The Edevanes.'

'Or rather, the Vallance-Smyths. In fact, strictly speaking they're simply Smiths. They added her maiden name on marriage and made his look less plebeian. I can't imagine what kind of idiots would do that.' Fox grimaced.

'Nor can I, Mr Foxcroft-MacSionnach.'

'The Vallance-Smyths bought the Hampstead house in that name.'

Margaret sat up. 'Are they any relation to your Smith?'

'No.'

'Go on.'

'You remember the mention of dirty money in the letter Norah had sent? The books on mines and minerals and so on?'

'They're mine owners,' said Margaret.

'As you suspected. Once we had their name and where they'd come from when they purchased Deanacre, we could work out who they were. I went to look for their coal mine. There are several collieries of various sizes in the Forest of Dean. Most seem well-enough run. The Edevanes have control of one that isn't. Or wasn't last autumn.'

Margaret cast her mind back. She recalled a series of headlines and a brief flurry of newspaper horror which dissipated as soon as public interest waned. 'Not the one with the explosion and seven killed?'

'Four of whom were under seventeen. Yes, that was theirs.'

'So they sold the colliery and moved?'

'No. They hired a manager to run it and moved. I think they preferred a house with windows.'

'You need to explain.'

'The union and the inspector of mines argued the explosion was caused because the Edevanes weren't following safety legislation,' said Fox. 'The Edevanes argued that they had, only the miners had failed to follow the rules designed to protect them. The coroner found for the Edevanes, who gave gifts of money to the families of the bereaved as gestures of goodwill... then cut the wages of the workforce so they didn't lose any profits from the gifts, recovering the bodies or reopening the shaft. I think it's safe to say it didn't go down well.'

'That explains Mrs Edevane's anxiety.'

'Or shame. The evidence that went before the coroner wasn't sound. Those miners were murdered.'

'Manslaughtered,' said Margaret. 'Murder requires malice aforethought.'

'The explosion was caused by a bomb.'

'They bombed their own mine? Killed their own men?' Margaret felt nauseous. She saw the vapid faces of the Edevanes before her and tried to imagine them – or perhaps just one of them – sitting down calmly to plan action which would kill seven innocent men and boys. Mrs Edevane couldn't remember the names of people she thought inferior; perhaps they wouldn't matter to her. But surely it would matter if she lost money and face. 'That makes no sense whatsoever. Weren't they insured?'

'Yes, but not enough to make it worth the risk.'

'Then why do it?'

'I found papers in Mr Edevane's former office suggesting it was a trial of a new kind of explosive. Something easily transported and detonated that could be used to attack government buildings or the underground or what-have-you and destabilise everything.'

'That's not new. People have been trying to do that since, well, Guy Fawkes at least.'

Fox stared at her as if she was dim. 'I know. And it's my job to stop them. Once that information was given to the police, they made the arrests.'

'And you honestly believe the Edevanes were clever enough to develop a "new" explosive, prepared to risk their reputations by trying it out on their own colliery, but too stupid to destroy incriminating paperwork?'

'Don't be ridiculous Margaret,' said Fox. 'Of course I don't. They're brainless snobs who can't run a bridge party without help. These are the facts: a mineshaft at the Edevanes' colliery was deliberately blown up in October. The Edevanes, formerly known as Vallance-Smyth, moved to Hampstead in November, seemed happy enough to begin with, and settled into the part of local society populated by social climbers, incomers and foreigners who don't mind a lack of letters of introduction. Norah's diaries establish that in mid-December the Edevanes seemed a little less happy. This unhappiness increased until mid-January, decreased after Norah's departure, and—'

'Something puzzles me about that,' interrupted Margaret. 'They didn't press charges on the man who'd been hired to knock Mr Edevane down, presumably to keep the police at arm's length, but then they reported Norah, a day or two after she'd been asked to hide something. That would risk them looking into everything.'

'They thought the police would just look into Norah and those who were using her would back off. To some extent it seemed to work. But of course the blackmailers were just rethinking their approach. According to the staff, their misery has increased to a much greater degree recently. Some incriminating paperwork in Gloucestershire baffled the manager who, without saying it in so many words, indicated that Mr Edevane took little interest in the colliery and was nothing but a hindrance when he did. But this is the most significant thing: when they were arrested, they both seemed almost relieved.'

'Relieved? Have they any idea what prison is like?'

'Possibly not, but even what idea they may have seemed more appealing than staying in the house where they feel under siege.'

Margaret ran her fingers in circles on her temples. The headache hadn't quite materialised. She needed to think. 'So the letters...'

Fox reached to stroke her hair. 'I believe they had two purposes. One: to coerce or blackmail the Edevanes into keeping their mouths shut about letting their mine be used to test the explosive. Two: to distract the intelligence services. The only problem with two was that the police didn't pass them on to the intelligence services until recently. And it was only at that point that it worked.'

'Yes,' said Margaret. 'Like Ed saying a conjuror makes the audience look in the wrong direction. We've been looking in the East End among the poor and we've been looking in Hampstead among the rich.'

'Exactly. And finding nothing concrete. The police, have turned Deanacre upside down and interrogated the servants. Fortunately, the housekeeper was happy to tell the inspector that Nellie Pinter was barely more than a dim-witted child and not to be harassed by a bobby, giving me the chance to say that I'd question the girl myself and report back. The inspector wasn't happy, but I outrank him. I just hope to God they don't find anything in her room. The servants were only allowed to take their clothes. Every letter, every book – even their prayer books and Bibles – had to be left behind.'

'If only—' The doorbell rang. 'Who's that at this time?' Margaret could feel her heart hammer.

'I'll go. Keep back.' Fox rose to his feet, slipped his right hand into his jacket pocket and went down the stairs to the front door.

Thirty-Two

Regardless of his plea, Margaret waited at the top of the steps to watch, holding her breath.

'Good evening sir,' said a male voice. 'I'm dead sorry to be so late. A couple of posties are off sick today and we're all behind like a cow's tail at the Post Office. Just a letter for Dr Demeray.'

'Thank you. I hope your evening improves.'

'Thank you, sir. Good night.'

The door closed, Fox smelled the letter, then bounded up the stairs and handed them to Margaret. 'Is this what you're expecting?'

Margaret breathed out. 'Yes.'

The envelope was addressed in Nellie's careful script. It contained two photographs, both wrapped in tissue and a note in Norah's writing: 'Photographs borrowed from those Reuben took for his art. In case they're needed'.

The first had been taken from a distance in a dilapidated street. But one thing was certain.

'That's the man I saw at Deanacres earlier!' said Margaret. 'The one from Neuchâtel.'

'Are you sure? His clothes don't look like they belong to anyone who could afford a tube ticket, let alone a sleeper to Switzerland.'

'Clothes are easy to change. And there's Mr Drummond in the background – I'm sure it's him – talking to Anna Balodis.'

She turned it over. Written on the back were the words *Why here?*

'Mr Friend?'

'Mr Drummond can't be Mr Friend. Norah would have said something in her diary. So it must be the Neuchâtel man, and this must be a moment she realised they knew each other. Now do you believe that her death wasn't natural?'

'Granted, Mr Drummond might have killed Norah somehow, although how could he mimic a natural death?'

Margaret frowned. 'When he went to see Miss Connors, he asked about digitalin. Heart medicine. He had something in his pocket. I bet he was going to try it again on Miss Connors.'

'Miss Connors again.'

'Maybe she's not connected with Anderson, just Mr Drummond.'

At that moment, the telephone rang.

'Oh God,' said Margaret, going to it. 'What if they've found Nellie?'

'We're keeping the house under surveillance.'

'Hallo?'

'Hallo, Dr Demeray? It's Constable Harris here. Sorry to call you at home and so late too.'

'I thought you wanted me to telephone tomorrow. Congratulations! I—'

'It's all wrong,' said Constable Harris. 'Someone confirmed Mr Drummond's alibi for Sunday night. We've had to let him go.'

'But Miss Connors—'

'She's recovering slowly, but until we've make a secure arrest the hospital is giving out that she has no chance. I'm sorry doctor. We're still on the case.'

Margaret expressed her fury, while Fox, hand poised to extract the second photograph, listened with raised eyebrows and an irritating expression of polite doubt.

'You can't keep people in custody without evidence,' he said.

'Aren't you taking anything I say seriously? I saw that man' – she stabbed at the photograph – 'at Neuchâtel and outside the Edevanes' house. He was standing over Norah seconds before I was. Then that man' – she stabbed at Mr Drummond – 'sauntered up as if a dead eighteen year old in his care was less interesting than lettuce in a sandwich. Why don't you believe me?'

'I do. And I think you should stay away from him.'

'But I'm working in Glassmakers Lane tomorrow,' said Margaret.

'Why the hell are you going back? You hate practicing your bedside manner and you don't trust Dr Fernsby.'

'No. But I need to find out what she's hiding.'

'I don't want you any closer to this damnable case than you already are,' snapped Fox. 'This Mr Drummond you think killed Norah works just across the road. If he has any inkling you suspect him, what will he do? The police think the restaurant is full of German spies, the bookshop is a nest of vermin – some literal – and it definitely has a rifle. Go back to St J's and stay there. I'll manage the book situation. It's bad enough you're tangled up with Nellie.'

His change of mood shocked her into fury. 'I can't not go to the surgery tomorrow. And who will ask the questions I should? Elinor?'

Juniper, watching them from the sofa, leapt down and hid under it.

'Elinor?' Fox gawped.

'It used to be Bert or Pigeon and now it's Elinor!'

'Only when it's translation or digging through files. What are you implying?' His face flooded with colour, his eyes blazed. 'I couldn't wait to get back to you here.'

'Back here? Not back home?'

'Anywhere with you in it is home. What's got into you?'

'What's got into *you*? Last year you wanted my help. A few weeks ago, you wanted my help. Now you don't. Is it because there a woman who's free whenever you need her while I'm caught up most of the time with working where—'

'Where you're surrounded by men. Many of whom are decent, attractive and can sit by the fire every evening rather than disappear without saying where they are.'

'Yes but... they're not you.'

'Exactly. And no other woman is you. Oh God Margaret.' Fox ran his hand over his face, his voice dropping, hoarse. 'I didn't wait all those years after Cynthia died to pick a wife I didn't want with all my heart and wouldn't be faithful to. I've told you before: I'm not Owen. I'll never be Owen. Why won't you ever believe it?' They fell silent. The fire crackled and the clock ticked and Juniper gave a tiny mew from under the sofa. 'Why are we fighting? Isn't there enough trouble to deal with? Do you honestly think I'm attracted to Elinor?'

She stepped forward and leaned into him. She mumbled, 'She's pretty.'

'So are lots of women. I can't make love to all of them.' His arms came around her but her tension wouldn't leave. 'Besides, I dread to think what would happen to *any* man who made advances to her. Even one as irresistible as me.'

Margaret chuckled a little. 'I'm sorry. Things have got out of proportion and I can't see straight. When you're away, I... no I shan't say it. Never mind.'

'When I'm away you what? Flirt with doctors? Wear trousers? Dance on stage? Come on, tell me.'

'I worry I'll never see you again. And I know... I know it'll be worse than what Owen did to me. And I'm afraid I could cope better with the kind of pain I've survived before than knowing something terrible has happened to you. I - I shouldn't tell you this because it's like a ball and chain and—'

'It's not,' Fox kissed her head. 'Knowing someone would grieve if I didn't come back means everything to me.'

'But your colleagues would—'

'We can't afford to get too close to each other. Look at Smith. But you can't stop me worrying about you when you're worried about me. And this case is the devil.'

'It is.' She put her arms round him and let herself relax into the embrace. *Why, when we're both worried, do we start arguing?*

'It's not just the case though is it?'

'I feel useless, Fox. Dr Jordan is trying, but I know St J's won't keep me on. I don't trust Dr Fernsby but I need to know what she's doing. Am I just so caught up in your case I'm seeing everything she does as suspicious? What if she's just a manipulative woman? And if you don't want my help. I feel like I may as wrap put my self-respect in tissue and hide it in a bottom drawer for a day that'll never come.'

He stroked her hair, held her tight and gave her a small shake. 'What have you done with the woman I married? Margaret Demeray wouldn't let me or a board of idiots or a woman who's left it till the last moment to get a partner tell her what to do. We wouldn't have got this far without your work. I'm sorry about what I said. It's just that after my best friend was murdered, I couldn't bear losing one more person I loved and feel that I want...'

She lifted her head and looked at him. 'You want me in a castle with a moat and dragons.'

He chuckled gently. 'The real Margaret Demeray wouldn't let a dragon tell her what to do either.'

Margaret wiped her eyes. 'Oughtn't we look at Norah's other photograph? I don't understand why the Edevanes would want her to hide the first one. Maybe the second will explain it. I'll pour us some wine.'

She went to the table while Fox extracted the second photograph. He gasped.

'Margaret!' His voice was sharp, but there was something pained in it too. His face was white.

'What is it?'

Fox was staring at the photograph in his hand and after a second, passed it over. In what appeared to be an East End Street, the man from Neuchâtel, in the same rough clothes as before was deep in conversation with Charles. 'If that's Mr Friend - one minute dressed like this in Whitechapel, the next a smart man in Hampstead, what is Charles's connection to him? They're laughing, sharing cigarettes.'

'Charles was undercover,' said Margaret.

'I know, but he told me his source said that Anderson was nothing but a petty criminal hanging onto the tails of anarchists and dissidents, then found a man who he said was Anderson but later turned out to be Abolin who was being run by someone to threaten the Edevanes.'

'Then the person running him must be Anders.'

'If he knew Piccadilly was a link to everything else, Charles would have told me,' insisted Fox. His face was greenish white, as if he felt nauseous. 'Unless Charles was working for Anders himself, hiding something all the information we needed to stop anything from happening.' He slammed his fist on the table, then put his head in his hands. 'This is why we don't get too close to each other.'

'Fox,' Margaret put her hand over the photograph. 'We don't know when this photograph was taken, under what circumstances, or how Norah got it from Reuben. For all you know, this was taken just before Charles was murdered, before he had a chance to tell you anything.'

'Charles was killed in February. Norah left in January. She'd have had no chance to leave anything at Deanacres after that.'

'She could have gone back to visit Nellie,' said Margaret, holding his hand. 'You knew Charles. *I* knew Charles. He would never double-cross you. You said yourself just now that you can't convict someone without evidence.'

Before she could say any more, the telephone rang.

'For pity's sake!' growled Margaret, snatching up the receiver. 'Hallo?'

'Dr Demeray?' It was Pigeon. 'We got what we were looking for. Can I speak to his nibs?'

She passed the telephone to Fox who listened, then said goodbye and replaced the receiver.

'You were right. Andris stole *Erewhon* and now the book's in our hands. There's a letter inside from Hamburg addressed to what appears to be M Anders. The envelope's a little smudged. The letter is in code.'

'So they've found Andris?'

'Not yet. His sister gave the book to someone in their anarchist network only thankfully for us, he's in our network too. It'll be decoded tonight and tomorrow, we'll get it back to Nierling's. We'll just have to put it somewhere it might have been overlooked.'

'Do you know if Andris is still alive.'

'I get the impression he is, but Anna was very scared.' Fox sat very still. 'You were right. I'm sorry. I ought to go to the office...'

'You're exhausted,' said Margaret. 'Nothing will change if you have a good night's sleep and like it or not, this is your home. But tomorrow, we'll carry on untangling this and we'll do it together.'

Thirty-Three

F ox rushed to his office early the next morning and half an hour
later, Margaret left for work by bicycle.

Arriving in Glassmakers Lane at a quarter past eight, the bicycle
tyres slipping on its cobbles, she cycled the length of the waking street,
as it opened up for a working day. Her body was warm from exercise,
but her hands and face were chilled by the bitterness of the air and
the sense that while the street appeared peaceful, throbbing under
the small morning sounds heralded the calm before the storm: the
breath-holding pause before battle.

At the dead end of the road, Margaret made to turn. A scrawny,
elderly, rather doddery man, presumably the older Nierling, turned
cloudy eyes on her and arranged a box of battered books on a table
outside the front door.

Whether he knew Margaret was the woman whose ear his son had
accidentally caught with a bullet, it was hard to tell. He seemed intent
on straightening his scratched and damaged volumes as if, despite their
aged and jaded appearance, he wanted them to look their musty best
to attract new owners.

Margaret braked, checked her watch and dismounted. Propping
the bicycle against the wall, she peered through the dusty shop window. She could see why her father had been enthralled. Novels, plays,

poetry, travel books, ranging over two centuries, and in states from near pristine to disintegrating were spread in disordered display.

'Shee anything you like, madam?' said the old man, whistling on the sibilant, his accent a curious amalgam of cockney and something else.

'Can you tell me if that's *Delightes for Ladies* by Sir Hugh Plat?' said Margaret, pointing at a small volume opened to display an elaborate title page with curlicues and old-fashioned long S's.

Mr Nierling senior hobbled up and peered in with cataract-whitened eyes, leaning his forehead against the window and shielding his gaze. 'Could be. Could be. Come shee.'

He made to usher her indoors, but just then two men sauntered up, arguing in the kind of sustained, friendly way that old friends do. Catching sight of Margaret, both tipped their hats, then started rummaging in the box of books, to Mr Nierling senior's consternation. He wrung his hands. 'Careful! Careful!'

'Sorry, old chap,' said one of the men, flicking through the volumes more slowly but with some force.

Mr Nierling turned to Margaret with a pained, apologetic expression. 'I'll help you shoon,' he said and hobbled back to supervise, giving the impression that he'd snatch the books to his bosom if the mishandling got worse.

The other customer mounted the steps of the shop. The newspaper under his arm was bulkier than normal, as if it held something inside its pages.

Mr Nierling flicked agitated attention between the two men and Margaret.

The first man let one of the books in the box slip onto the pavement and a page drifted loose, to Mr Nierling's cry of grief. 'Sorry, old chap,' said the man, digging into a pocket. 'I'll pay, of course. Sixpence? Let's see...'

'A shilling,' snapped Mr Nierling. 'It's very valuable. You don't appreciate good things.'

As they bargained, the man with the newspaper opened the shop door, slipped into grimy gloom and turned right to the place where Father had said he thought the tall, dark man had been looking.

'I'll come back at lunchtime,' said Margaret, collecting her bicycle. Mr Nierling seemed too agitated to care, but the man with the loose change met her eyes for a second before glancing up at the shop. His shoulders were tense, relaxing only when the shop door opened and his companion came bouncing down the steps holding aloft a book with a highly decorated cover.

'And *that*,' said Mr Nierling, 'is *three* shillings.'

'Come now,' the other man said. 'The flyleaf's gone.'

'Maybe it never had one.' snapped Mr Nierling.

'Here's a shilling for mine,' interposed the man standing by the box of books as Margaret made to leave. 'Otherwise I haven't anything smaller than a half a crown. Unless you'll take that for both.'

A few moments Dr Fernsby greeted Margaret with raised eyebrows.

'Had you forgotten you'd asked me to do an extra duty?'

'Not at all.' Dr Fernsby's eyes scanned Margaret and frowned at her cycling skirt. 'So you cycled here rather than come by tube.'

'It'll make the rounds easier.'

'That skirt unbuttons up the back.'

'People ought to be too sick to care what I'm wearing.'

'You must learn to drive.'

'I will,' said Margaret. 'But a bicycle is a lot simpler for getting about and cheaper to replace if someone steals it. And it's fun.'

Dr Fernsby shrugged. 'You may be right.' The seriousness on her face became wistful and a small smile appeared. 'I recall the freedom of my first bicycle. Do you? It was 1890 or '91 and I was in my twenties. What a scandal to my parents! But they couldn't stop me.'

'I remember it vividly,' said Margaret. 'I was sixteen. It was wonderful.'

For a brief moment the shared recollection made her forget everything else, but then the awareness of her suspicions and the excessively tidy consulting room, with its books and its prints and the wooden cat family, Margaret felt trapped, encoffined.

Perhaps Dr Fernsby could read her mind. The smile vanished, her gaze became speculative and she heaved a sigh, rubbing the small of her back as she straightened up. 'I telephoned the London to ask after Miss Connors this morning. Did you?'

'Not yet,' said Margaret. There had been no time to telephone anyone. 'What did they say?'

'Fading fast poor thing.' Dr Fernsby's uncharacteristically soft expression appeared to be painful to maintain.

She's been practicing in a mirror, thought Margaret, but she echoed the other woman's words. 'Yes indeed, poor thing. By the way,' she added as she stood to leave for her own consulting room, 'did you tell Mr Drummond I also work at St Julia's?'

Dr Fernsby's almost compassionate expression dropped to be replaced by a flicker of confusion and then a frown. 'Mr who?'

'Drummond. He works with Mrs Dysart. Perhaps you told her and *she* told him.'

'I've no idea who you mean,' said Dr Fernsby. 'And I can't imagine why you think I'd tell anyone anything about you. Perhaps when your father went to the studio he told him.'

'Of course,' said Margaret. 'That'll be it. How is the appointments list? If things become too much for you, please let me know so I can take over.'

'I shall be fine I'm sure, but —' The telephone rang and Dr Fernsby answered it. Her frown lifted and a natural smile brightened her face but all she said was 'excellent' before replacing the receiver.

'Miss Connors?' asked Margaret.

'Someone different,' explained Dr Fernsby. 'But all's well. Nothing you need worry about.'

The morning was busy, and concentrating on the cases before her, Margaret pushed all thoughts aside apart from the task in hand. But as the morning drew to an end, she realised that even if her suspicions about Dr Fernsby were groundless, neither her heart nor her skills lay in a private medical practice. She missed the space and airiness of the laboratory. She missed the simplicity of a tissue sample or a corpse. It might be hard to discover their secrets sometimes, but nowhere near as difficult as finding out what was wrong with someone who was alive but intent on hiding crucial clues because of embarrassment, shame or ignorance. She could not save the corpse on the slab, but her research might save someone else.

'I'll have half an hour's rest on my bed before lunch,' said Dr Fernsby at twelve o'clock. 'I'll ask the maid to take you through to my sitting room and bring you coffee. I'm sure you'll find it a comfortable place to read.'

'Thank you,' said Margaret, 'but I have an errand.'

Glassmakers Lane was now fully awake. Soffiato's had put tables and chairs on the pavement. Two couples and a lone man sat warming their hands on cups of coffee and eating hot pastries.

Dysart's seemed to have emptied onto the pavement. A charabanc was being loaded with equipment under the ineffectual eyes of Mr Dysart and the critical ones of Mr Drummond, who looked angrier than ever. Margaret shuddered. She cast her mind back to the time at Neuchâtel when she'd thought him indifferent. But he'd been angry too. How could Margaret prove what he'd done? And why had he tried to kill Miss Connors? Margaret looked back at the surgery. Someone was in the window of the waiting room to the left of the entrance. Because of the way the sun shone, they were impossible to identify inside the building though they themselves would be able to identify Margaret quite easily. When Miss Connors had been there on Sunday, what had she seen Mr Drummond doing?

Reuben sauntered over as Margaret thought. 'Fancy a trip?'

Margaret forced a nonchalant smile. If only she were free to do as he suggested and keep an eye on Mr Drummond. 'Where are you going?'

'St Katharine Docks. We're filming another bit of the Lady Detective. Whatever would Norah make of the adventures she wrote about being changed from the high and mighty, unmasking dastardly aristocrats in castles, to hoi polloi in the grubby end of town? I'm glad you're here. I wanted to speak with you, but with them dragging me off I couldn't come over. I'm not even sure why they need me, but Mr D's insisting I go.'

'Dysart?'

'Drummond. I suppose I can do some sketching or take some photographs.' Reuben lifted a small folding Kodak out of his satchel. 'The latest model. Cost just over a pound. Worth every penny.'

'Are you making pictures of Mr Drummond?' Margaret looked over at the man in question. He had dark shadows under his eyes and pulled at his hair in exasperation, remonstrating with one of the other men through the cigarette clamped in his teeth as a tripod was wangled into place.

'Of the docks,' said Reuben. 'They might come in handy for something. I prefer sketching to photography. It gets my mind clear sometimes.'

'Me too.'

'I had no idea,' Reuben looked at her speculatively. 'We'll have to compare sketches. It'll be as good an excuse as any to talk. By the way, is the - er - item I gave - er...'

'It's in the right hands,' said Margaret.

'The police?'

'Yes. You were right to keep it safe.'

'I thought so.' Reuben put the Kodak back into his bag.

'Do you have many photographs?' said Margaret.

'A few. I take them of people when they're not paying attention to get their natural poses right. You know - gesticulating, lighting cigarettes, funny expressions etc. Norah used to like looking through them. She borrowed a couple I think, though I couldn't tell you which. I was going to teach her how to use the camera.'

Seemingly aware of someone's scrutiny, Mr Drummond's gaze moved around until it lighted on Margaret. His eyes narrowed.

'Mr D isn't portrait quality today, is he?' asked Reuben.

Margaret decided to take a chance. 'You seem very busy on this film. I suppose you work night and day when you can.'

'Hmph.'

'Were you all here on Sunday?'

'We don't normally work on Sundays and it was too wet anyway,' said Reuben. 'I was so afraid to leave the house for fear of drowning, I stayed in to suffer the landlady's boiled beef and carrots instead of going to a chop house. Funny you ask though... Oh, watch out.'

Mr Drummond stalked over. 'Why are women so contrary?' He ground out his cigarette and lit another. Either the cold was making him shiver or his hands were trembling.

'Dr Fernsby needs my help today.'

'Humph. Did the maid get back safely?'

'Yes.'

'She needs to forget Norah and forget all this.' He drew angrily on the new cigarette, then waved it to encompass the studio, its staff and perhaps the street before exhaling with force and glaring harder. 'If I were you, I'd have my father try another company for filming his stories.'

Margaret felt her face burn. How dare he? Much as she wanted to distance her father from Glassmakers Lane, his stories were no more mad than Norah's, or any of the others that made popular films.

She refocussed enough to realise that Mr Drummond's expression had changed from anger to resignation. 'You don't want his stories set in the wrong places, do you?' he said. 'Because that's where they'd end up. Same as Norah's. This is supposed to be her film, but I'm sure she didn't expect it to be filmed in so many odd places. Righto, this won't get the baby a new bonnet. We need to get off before the light goes, and it'll be dark enough down by those warehouses anyway. Shadows all over. It's enough to make an artist curse.' He stamped back towards the charabanc and waved the actors aboard.

'Are you sure you can't come?' said Reuben.

'No,' Margaret replied. 'I've just enough time to get a book from Nierling's.'

Reuben frowned at the shop and then around the street. 'I'm going to sketch it out doctor,' he said. 'You do it, too. Then let's compare sketches as soon as we can. I can't get it right in my head at all. Can you?'

Thirty-Four

Walking to the bookshop, Margaret told herself that the sense of being watched was imaginary: part concern, part suspicion, part threat. Just as she had all those months ago in Myrdle Street, she turned to face it. But this time no one was following, no one obviously looking at her. The charabanc was loaded and they were leaving. Yet the uneasiness remained.

Margaret continued the last few yards to Nierling's. The bell on the door brought no one. She could hear voices overhead, and someone walking above with what sounded like heavy boots. Little bits of plaster fell from the ceiling onto her and the dusty floor. The shop was every bit as dark and dirty as it appeared, but not as damp. She could imagine Father happily lost among the shelves, poking around the disorganised wares. Books of all sizes, from chapbooks and pamphlets to tomes and immense Bibles, were squashed or lolling in rows, some spines absent, some peeling, some with the gilt titles long rubbed off. She felt the familiar tingle she always felt in the air of bookshops, one of the few things she'd inherited from Father, and the books whispered *I am a new world for you to discover ... choose me, choose me.*

The entire history of sedition might be found hidden amongst the novels and sermons. It might include things long since normalised or legalised – but it was impossible to imagine how long it would take to track it all down.

Margaret made a brief foray into the back of the shop where Fox had said there was contraband literature, but the sheer darkness discouraged her. She sensed she was not alone and wondered if Mr Nierling senior was snoozing behind the desk, but when she stepped closer no one was there. A rusty cash tin complete with key lay on the counter.

Every now and then she heard a noise. Pausing till it came again, she realised it was a tiny gasp as someone refilled as much of their lungs as they needed to. They were trying to hold their breath.

The hairs rose on the back of Margaret's neck as she made for the front of the shop. Gripping her handbag a little harder, she considered humming, but feared it would come out sounding as quavering as she felt. Her knuckles started to ache, so she loosened one hand enough to lift a curtain behind the window display. Just as she did so, a man popped his head round a shelf to her left. 'Hallo-allo-allo!'

She stifled a squeak.

'Sorry, d – madam, did I startle you?'

It was Pigeon, barely recognisable in a smart suit, carrying a cane under his arm. He wore a bowler, shoved to the back of his head. She'd never seen him out of motorcycle clothes.

'I thought the shop was empty.' Margaret shook her head as she said this and Pigeon jerked a thumb at the shadowy realms beyond the nearest bookshelf in tacit agreement. 'I, er...- If I hold the curtain, could you get that book for me?' She pointed at the one she'd seen earlier. 'I'm not sure I can reach it, and Mr Nierling seems to be elsewhere.'

'Novel?' said Pigeon. 'Ladies like novels.'

'Don't men?'

'Different sort. More danger, less romantic nonsense.' Pigeon winked, then reached out with the handle of his cane, hooked the book and drew it towards him.

All the time they were speaking, he was as tense as she was, listening. She held the curtain and flicked her gaze around the room, but the light from the window had blinded her to anything in the shop. Pigeon, she noticed, had kept one eye shut.

'Oooh, something's gone in my back,' he moaned, as he came back through the curtain, holding his back, closed the eye that had been open and opened the other. 'Some posh cove nabbed *Erewhon* just after I arrived and went upstairs with N,' he whispered. He straightened, handed her the book and raised his voice. 'Here you go, madam.'

'Thank you, sir.'

'Is it what you were after?'

Margaret examined it. 'Yes, though it feels spongy.'

'Best leave it then, madam,' said Pigeon.

A thump from overhead brought down another shower of ceiling plaster, including a sliver of ornate moulding which fell between them.

'Be careful,' said Margaret.

Pigeon pushed his bowler forwards and patted a chest that was, now she thought about it, rather bulkier than normal. 'My hat's better than yours,' he said, and winked before ambling round the corner of the bookcase.

Remembering Dutch Jake, Margaret picked the shard up. It was sharp but easy to crumble. It might have hurt if it had caught her, but not as much as the bullet. Surely not enough to make anyone fall. She put it and the damaged book on the nearest shelf and checked her watch.

She'd missed Fox; either he'd been there before Pigeon or he'd arrive later. She stepped out into the cold sunshine, then walked slowly towards the surgery, brushing the dust of the shop from her gloved hands. There was nothing more she could do except try to find out if Dr Fernsby's amusement at Miss Connors's fate was because of disapproval or something else. And Margaret had a feeling that would prove hard.

She felt the patter of someone running up behind her before she heard it. Her heart hammered and she half-ducked. Then someone barged into her, knocking her slightly sideways, and her handbag fell from her grasp. The oldest trick, and she wasn't ready for it. She trod firmly on its handle and braced herself for an assault, but none came. A hand touched her arm. 'Ssssh, it's me. I'm not going to hurt you.'

Margaret looked up into the face of Constable Harris.

'I didn't know you'd be here,' he said. 'I'd left a message at St Julia's. Miss Connors is starting to remember. She's scared for you. She says you need to stay away or they'll get *you* next time.' Raising his voice, he said, 'So sorry, madam, let me help you. Here's your bag.'

'Who'll get me? Mr Drummond? Is that who you're following?'

'Mr Drummond unnerved Miss Connors but she isn't scared of him. You remember I said Bookie Brown had been dealing with someone known as Piccadilly? He's been sighted and I followed him here. But he's disappeared.' He glared at the buildings as if they'd absorbed his prey and blanked their façades to spite him.

'Be more careful next time,' said Margaret loudly, brushing her handbag down.

'I'll pay for any damage, naturally.'

'So I should think. Here's my husband's card.' She dropped her voice. 'Tell him what you know. He's a superintendent.'

'Delighted,' said Constable Harris, glancing at the card. He tipped his bowler and sauntered off.

Dr Fernsby kept to herself for the rest of the day, but a typed letter from Fox arrived for Margaret marked 'private' saying he'd meet her at the tube station after work.

The afternoon dragged, and as Margaret reviewed the notes of the patient she was due to see last, Miss Hill knocked, entered and handed over another file.

'Miss Waters sent a message to say she's better, which is just as well, since Mrs Dysart has arrived demanding an appointment.'

Mrs Dysart seemed her usual cheerful self when she sat down a moment later, having given Margaret no time to scan her file.

'I asked for you especially,' she said, before Margaret had a chance to speak. 'It's just a simple request and you seem sympathetic.'

Margaret ignored the implied criticism of Dr Fernsby. 'What seems to be the matter?'

Mrs Dysart seemed no paler than normal, nor lacking in her usual sparkle. But she was breathless, and when she removed her gloves, despite her general slenderness, her hands appeared swollen, the fingers bulging around her rings. She looked round the room with sardonic interest. 'She's given you quite the cupboard, hasn't she?'

Margaret took the opportunity to glance at the main notes. *Date of birth 5th August 1875. Arrhythmia. Six pregnancies, three live births: 1897, 1898, 1901. Dysmenorrhea. Occasional gastric problems. Prescribed medication:*

'...so I do feel a fool. I thought you might be less scathing.'

Margaret realised she hadn't heard the beginning of the sentence and decided to grope her way towards working out what it had been. 'Anyone can make a mistake.'

Mrs Dysart pulled a face. 'I can't even begin to say what she said the first time I lost those tablets. Although it's not as if it's in my interest to do so, is it?'

Remembering Dr Fernsby's irritation, Margaret hazarded a question. 'Have you been trying a herbal alternative?'

Mrs Dysart gave a slight giggle. 'I'm not that silly. Pain is one thing, dying is another. Will you give me another prescription?'

Margaret, took the deep breath people always took when considering a question, glanced down again and read on.

Prescribed medication: digitalin. Tendency to self-prescribe cannabis, coca extracts and black cohosh preparations.

She blinked. Mrs Dysart had lost a supply of digitalin. Twice. She turned the page to find the record of prescriptions made. The last had been in mid-March, only a week after the previous one, with a note alongside to say the earlier bottle had been smashed and its contents lost.

'Did you smash another bottle?'

'I didn't smash the first one,' confided Mrs Dysart. 'That's just what I told Dr Fernsby. It was in all the fuss when we were going to Switzerland, and at the last moment I felt unwell and they had to go without me. I didn't realise the bottle had fallen out of my bag until it was found in the gutter just before they left, with half the contents down the grating and the rest sodden from rain. Just as well, since if anyone picked any up, they might get sick, I suppose.'

Margaret blanched. 'Digitalin is a poison!'

'I've been very careful since March,' said Mrs Dysart. 'I lock the latest bottle up at home and take the old one with just a few tablets in it when I'm out and about. I lock *that* up in my office at the studio when I'm there.'

'So what happened?'

'I forgot to take it home with me yesterday evening. When I went to get it today... Well, I'm not sure what's happened, but it wasn't as topped up as I thought and some of the tablets are different. I don't know if it's all right for them to be touching other drugs and I daren't go out to the shoot.' She handed over a small ridged bottle. The label was blurry, its contents and the name hard to read. Inside were six tablets, four different in size and colour to the others.

Margaret had no idea which were digitalin, and what the others might be. She frowned.

Mrs Dysart waved a hand. 'I know Dr Fernsby thinks me an utter hypochondriac because I try to manage my other ailments without resorting to a doctor, but I'm hardly likely to do that with a tricky heart, am I? I am fond of being alive. I have things to achieve. I have the studio, three children and a husband to consider.'

'Let me examine you,' said Margaret. Beyond a slight murmur, Mrs Dysart's heart gave no cause for immediate alarm. 'Have you mixed up some of your other preparations with the tablets?'

'I suppose it's possible.' Mrs Dysart looked confused. 'I'm sometimes in rather a hurry, but I'm not stupid. Even Mr Drummond, who tends to say exactly what he thinks, didn't call me that when he found the bottle in March.'

Mr Drummond. He'd taken the tablets in March and he'd taken them last night. And he'd replaced some of them with something else, but why? To confuse her? To kill her? 'Leave these with me,' said Margaret. 'I'll ask Mr Burton to confirm what they are, and if necessary destroy them. Go home, and make a note of how many you have in the bottle there.'

'But I need to go to St Katharine Docks and direct the filming! Can't you prescribe just two tablets to tide me over? I can take that bottle and ask Mr Burton to do it myself.'

'Best not,' said Margaret. 'This bottle may be contaminated. I'll write a prescription for two tablets to put your mind at rest, although you seem quite fit today. Please promise you'll keep them safe at all times, and yourself too. How are you getting to the docks? It's not really the sort of place where you should wander alone.'

'Driving. Morrie will be with me.' Mrs Dysart heaved a sigh but gave Margaret a broad smile as she took the prescription. 'Thank you, doctor. I can't have Mr Drummond directing the last part of my film.'

'You mean Norah's film,' said Margaret.

Mrs Dysart paused as she prepared to leave. 'Of course. Norah's film.'

Thirty-Five

Margaret arrived at the tube station shortly after five. Workers were heading home at speed, heads buried in newspapers and books. One of them ambled up and dropped his newspaper. 'Hallo, wife.'

'Hallo, husband. Where are you taking me?'

'Firstly, to Waterloo to leave your bicycle and then on the tube to find two young people who seem to think south of the river constitutes out of London. Pigeon tracked them down.'

It was impossible to say anything more in the crush of people and it wasn't until they were on the last underground journey that Fox cuddled her close so they could talk in low voices as if they were whispering sweet nothings.

'Your constable seems a sharp type,' he said. 'I approve. Even if he's under the false impression you'll listen to me. He has doubts about Mr Drummond's guilt.

'Even though he went to harass Miss Connors, or worse?' argued Margaret. 'But he had Mrs Dysart's digitalin, I'm sure of it. And he's put other things in the bottle too and left them where she'd get them today.'

'There *were* tablets in his pocket which he said he needed to keep. Constable Harris's sergeant took that to mean he'd drop dead any moment if he didn't have it to hand.'

'What about the label?' said Margaret.

'The label was a printed one from Burton's Chemist, but it had got wet and the bits written in ink were smudged. Name began with a D. Whatever it was supposed to contain also started with a D. By that time someone was looking into his alibi, and the sergeant let Drummond keep them rather than have a death in custody.'

'And then they released him.'

'Had to. He'd told them that on Saturday evening, he'd taken the boat train to France and didn't get back till Monday morning, and the port records confirmed it. He wasn't in the country when Miss Connors was injured, or even when she was found.'

'Could he have falsified that? I mean, are they sure it was him and not someone using the same name?'

Fox shrugged. 'He could have, but I don't think he did. The case against him was built on assumptions. He arrived and spoke to Miss Connors and she was upset. He was uncooperative and bad-tempered and rude. He had a bottle of pills in his pocket. So Constable Harris, the nurse and the sergeant thought he meant her harm, although how you'd get a tablet into someone thrashing about I've no idea. Being uncooperative, bad-tempered and rude doesn't mean you're guilty though, does it? It may just mean you're that way by nature. Plenty of the most successful criminals are nothing but charming. But the clincher came this morning. Hang on, here's our stop.'

The tube station was busy and they fell silent as they made their way into the open air. Outside, people rushed by without heeding them, avoiding a beggar and a grubby flower seller, pausing only to snatch up an evening newspaper from a barefoot boy. Despite the temperature, a hokey-pokey man wheeled his cart of ice-cream up and down in the vain hope that someone wanted to be as cold inside as they were outside.

'And the clincher?' prompted Margaret.

'Miss Connors came round this morning,' said Fox, as they started walking. 'She's still a little vague about Sunday and Mr Drummond's visit seemed like a bad dream. She says she wasn't scared of him but of what he said.'

'A threat?'

'You tell me. He said, "Which one of them did that, and why? Tell me. Did they give you something?" Then he said, "As soon as you can, get away and stay away". She said she sensed his anger, but it wasn't directed at her. She says the only strange man she remembered from Sunday was fair-haired and a bit stupid-looking. Amiable. She says she remembers rain and feeling safe, then knowing she wasn't, and then more rain. But she says she knew Dr Demeray was in danger and someone wanted her dead only it's still a blur as to who.' Fox paused. 'I don't think Mr Drummond's guilty of anything, Margaret, except maybe being stubborn. Perhaps if someone asked for his help rather than made him feel under suspicion, he'd have given useful information. As it is, he thinks the police are stupid, and doesn't know why you - as a private individual - are asking questions.'

'He's trying to work it out alone.'

'Stubborn is as stubborn does. I think he's your kindred spirit.'

'Thanks.'

In a low voice, she explained what she'd found out that day. 'I thought you'd be in Nierling's.'

'Hardly,' said Fox. 'We have a series of men going in and out, although we can't do too many, since I doubt they're used to much in the way of trade. I gather you know *Erewhon* was returned successfully.'

'I also know that it's been retrieved.'

'Yes. By your Neuchâtel man.'

'Then you can arrest him.'

'You're always in such an ungodly rush, Margaret,' said Fox. 'Where's your subtlety? If we pounce on him, we'll only get *him*. Maybe we could squeeze the information we need out of him, but more likely not. He'll either be too wily to talk, or like the Edevanes, too scared.' Fox paused. 'But it's a moot point. He got out of the building without being seen; the Nierlings came downstairs without him. The police did another convenient raid and searched the place top to bottom, but found no one else there. It's an old building, and it's possible to get from its attic to the one in the house next door, so presumably that's how he did it. He's got away ... this time. We sent Smith under observation, but nothing happened on his watch. Just now, he's back in the office being generally useless, reading some Sumerian love poetry he bought there.'

'You don't seem very upset about it.'

Fox pursed his lips. 'We've been feeding Smith duff - or at least useless - information for a while. That's the only way we can see if he's a double agent or a fool. If he's simply a fool, we'll have to work out what to do, since he knows *some* things, even if not many things. It's irritating we couldn't follow your Neuchâtel man. The one talking to Charles.' His jaw set. 'But we will intercept them both soon.'

'Fox, I keep telling you, it doesn't mean that Charles—'

'And in the background is your other man, Drummond, talking with a girl who looks like this Anna Balodis, who's an anarchist. We've deciphered the letter that was in *Erewhon*. It's in two parts. The first part appears innocuous, but I don't think it is.' He pulled Margaret out of the flow and frowned as he remembered. 'This is the gist: "We're awaiting new films by 10th. It's necessary to change dates. Masses for Bartholomew, Thomas, Guy, Julia, must now be on 13th and those for Saviour and Queen, Mary O and Katharine on 14th."'

'Say all those names again.'

'Saviour, Queen, Mary O, Katharine—'

'Dutch Jake – remember the letter he had from a religious aunt, written in German, telling him to say masses for Our Saviour and Queen of Heaven and Maria and a lot of relations. The translator hadn't translated any of the Christian names into English so I assumed they were people. But could it be a reference to docks? Mary Overie, St Saviour, Queenhithe? St Katharine? And then—'

'Bartholomew, Thomas, Guy, Mary ... Julia.'

'London hospitals?' Margaret swallowed. 'It's about the bombing campaign you were trying to stop. And 13th is a week tomorrow. Good Friday. What if they hadn't received that letter? And how would they know where to find it in the chaos. If I recall it, the first one said...' She wrinkled up her nose in thought. '"Nowhere would there be a change."'

'The letter was in a book called *Erewhon*. Isn't that an anagram of "nowhere"?'

'And it was wrapped in yellow to be easily found.'

'If they bombed those hospitals the day before they bombed the docks, not simply would there be the loss of life and the disruption to the roads round about and so on, but the loss of medical skills in the capital just when the docks were attacked.' He reached for her hand. 'Of all the things I assumed you'd be in danger of, Margaret, it wasn't that. Come on, let's hurry.'

He tucked her arm into his and made for the tube. 'The second part is different,' he said, his voice low. 'It's a message. "Why did you allow them to refuse to hand over the photographs? They won't have destroyed them. Be sure to visit them as soon as the second reel is complete. All must be in place by 8th. Find the maid's friend and find out what the maid saw or worked out."'

'Oh no! Nellie!'

'We've sent her to visit a Norland nanny training college for her own safety. But the poor kid knows nothing at all. Norah didn't tell her anything of interest and as you know, she didn't entrust the diary to her. All Nellie had were the photographs and the letter that Norah received.'

'But should you have let that man collect *Erewhon* with that letter inside? Especially given that you didn't stop the man who collected it.'

'I'm not worried we've lost him today, since I'm sure he'll be visiting at least one of the Edevanes in the next few days, "when the reel's complete". And clearly the photographs are important.'

'They have to be different photographs. They can't be the ones of Mr Drummond and Charles.'

'I know. So what are they?'

'Photographs of what really happened in the mine? Photographs of the landmarks they plan to bomb? The Edevanes seem to idle to go round London doing that sort of thing and too fancy to visit the docks.'

'We'll have to ask them. And we'll have to put them on an extra watch, since there's always a guard willing to be bribed. Always. So that leaves the reel.'

'Mr Drummond is pushing to finish a moving picture. Although... it doesn't quite fit.'

'What's it about? Interesting facts about London industry and charity?'

'It's a silly story in the style of Sexton Blake, featuring a fearless young woman armed with nothing more than an umbrella who solves crimes and rights wrongs.'

'Oh, that thing. I didn't think it would feature St Katharine Docks.'

'I don't think it was supposed to, but now it does. Will we have time to go to there? It's not far is it?'

'Not if you're a raven or a duck or you fancy a swim. Did Drummond set that up?'

Margaret thought back to the conversation she'd had with Mr Drummond earlier in the day. 'I-I'm not sure. He implied that Norah's story was being changed and he wasn't happy about it. He insisted Reuben go with them, even though there's no reason why. Reuben wasn't happy about that, either. He kept saying I was looking the wrong way at things.'

'Reuben?'

'Mr Drummond.'

'And your impression?'

'I don't know. I need to have those tablets analysed.'

'Do you know if he can speak German? I mean, do you think Mr Drummond wrote the letter? It was in code, but based on German.'

'Judging by how he was at Neuchâtel, I'm sure he can't speak much beyond English. Who decoded it? Smith?'

Fox shook his head. 'We gave copies to our three best people. Two came up with almost identical versions, but Smith's was different. Not wildly so, but enough to mislead us if we'd listened to him. He doesn't know we'd asked the others.'

'Like his view on Norah's letters.'

'Perhaps he's incompetent,' said Fox, as they entered the tube.

'But you don't think so.'

'No.'

Margaret pondered. 'Did Mr Drummond say why he took the boat train? Where was he going?' She wasn't sure why she asked when she already knew.

'Neuchâtel,' said Fox. 'Apparently he said, and I quote: "I wanted to see if there was a headstone like the bastard promised. But there wasn't, and that means that I was right about him, and maybe that bloody doctor is right about Norah, poor sodding kid. And Gawd knows, if she keeps asking questions, she's gonna get more than a bit of her bleeding ear shot off." You owe him an apology. He's worried about you.'

'Yes,' said Margaret. 'And now I'm worried about him.'

Thirty-Six

Windmill Walk felt more than a few miles from the gentility of Glassmakers Lane.

Despite its pretty name, the road was little more picturesque than Myrdle Street: the same grime and litter, with windows bare or curtained with rags. Women sat or stood in doorways, lolling, observing with covert interest. Children, playing with a deflated ball in the road, watched them pass with open curiosity. Two boys ambled over to walk alongside, getting closer and closer, working up to the moment when their little hands could slip unfelt into pockets and bags.

'New 'ere, mister? Dahn on yer luck? Looking for a gaff for the night, mister? We know just the mansion for this fine lady right dahn 'ere. One room for the two o' you. Only a tanner.'

'That's a pretty flar on yer brooch, missus.'

'Them's nice shoes, mister. That's a nice weskit. Wot's the time? Show us yer pocket watch, will yer?'

'I can show you a trick if you like, missus. Pick a card, any card and it'll be the queen o' 'earts, just like you. Garn, pick a card.'

'Why you stopping 'ere? 'Oo you after? What they done? Is there gonna be a stabbing? Can we watch?'

'Tell you what,' said Fox, digging in his pocket. 'I've got fourpence here for you to share now, since you've been such good company. There's a couple of men going to turn into this street in the next minute or so. One's got a green checked suit and the other's got shiny brown boots. If you can send them off somewhere else and tell them we went another way, I'll give you sixpence later.'

'Each?'

'Don't push your luck.'

The boys scampered off as Fox pulled Margaret into a crumbling doorway. 'They're living here.'

'Were we really being followed?'

'I think so, but they got caught up in traffic crossing the road outside the station. And we were walking more quickly.'

'And don't my feet know about it,' said Margaret, wincing. She looked at the door's peeling paint. 'Is this a lodging house? Or rooms?'

'Rooms,' said Fox, opening the door. 'Who knows how many the landlord's crammed in.'

Anna's room was on the top floor at the rear of the building, in an attic which had been divided into badly plastered partitions a fraction of the size of the room she'd had in Myrdle Street. Nothing covered the window except the soot on its outer panes. Inside was a trunk and a narrow metal-framed bed with its legs in dishes of vinegar, piled with clothes and blankets. There was no fireplace. The room was bitterly cold and stank of turpentine and Lysol. From outside came a constant rumble of trains.

But Anna had retained her defiance. Wearing a faded brown outfit, she stood with arms folded, and scowled at Margaret. 'How'd you find me? Who told on us?' She scanned Fox from head to foot. 'Is he a copper?'

'It's not like that, Anna,' said Margaret. 'I'm asking for help, not looking to hand you in.'

'I ain't peaching on no one.'

'No one's asking you to peach,' said Fox. 'We know you and Andris allegedly destroyed the machines in that sweatshop.'

'Yeah, so you don't know nothing.'

'I said "allegedly". No one on the force knows where you're living and I won't tell unless there's a good reason. And putting you in the way of Sullivan isn't a good reason.'

Anna subsided. 'Yeah, well. Someone else smashed up those machines to try and get us arrested. All we want is to save up enough to get to a country where they're not stuck in the past. Australia, America, New Zealand. Only Ma... Anyway, I ain't helping the doctor till she's helped me. Here.' She indicated the bed and drew back a thin blanket. Under the jumble of cloth was a man. His face was as grey and blotchy as the stained shirt he wore, his breathing shallow.

Margaret turned to Fox. 'It *is* the man who was shot at by Mr Nierling. Anna, is this Andris?'

'He told me you tried to help him, even though they'd shot at you too,' said Anna. 'Said you were a doctor and described you and I put two and two together. Can I really trust you?'

'Yes. He looks very ill.' Margaret handed Fox her bag, pulled down the makeshift covers. 'Andris, can you hear me? I'm just going to examine you. Don't be alarmed.'

Once the covers had been fully removed, Andris moaned 'Hot,' then fell silent again. He was ice-cold to the touch. His trousers had been removed and his long underpants cut off at the knee on his left leg. The cut fabric had been used as a bandage. Margaret removed his sock to reveal bluish, blotchy toes, and then took off the bandage. There were two wounds, one little more than a graze and the other deeper. Both were swollen and though clean, pus was seeping out.

'I've been doing my best,' said Anna. 'I got the bullet out using tweezers I'd boiled up. I lug boiling water up all them stairs three times a day to clean that wound and I'm putting powders on, but it ain't done no good.'

'Fox, can you give me the stethoscope? It's in my bag.' She took Andris's pulse and listened to his heart. His arms flailed as he tried to fight her off, moaning that she was trying to kill him. 'Shh, shh.' She covered his chest again, then stood up. 'Anna, you've done a wonderful job, but his blood has become poisoned. He's extremely ill and he needs to be in hospital. Even there, it may be too late.'

Anna's stern face crumpled. 'But I—'

'It isn't your fault,' said Margaret. 'It could have happened if he'd been living in Buckingham Palace. He might have a chance if he's somewhere as sterile as it can be, but I'm afraid that despite all your efforts, that's not here. Have you any clean dressings?'

'Here,' said Anna, digging a parcel of brown paper out of an oilskin bag.

'St Thomas's is no distance,' said Margaret. 'I know some of the doctors there. I can explain—'

'But he can't go to the hospital. They'll find him.'

'The Nierling's?'

'Them?' Anna snorted. 'What for?'

'Stealing from their shop.'

Anna drew a breath, then narrowed her eyes at Fox. 'We're not thieves either.'

'You gave someone a book. It came from Nierling's, didn't it?'

'I—' Anna closed her mouth with a snap. Fear and indecision flickered across her face then settled into pride as she lifted her chin. But her voice trembled. 'They have to be stopped. Whatever they're planning, it'll be anarchists what get blamed.'

'The Nierlings are planning something?'

Anna snorted. 'What them? They're are as scared as anyone.'

'Of Anderson?' said Fox.

'Anderson?'

'Let me get away,' whispered Andris, pulling his arms free of the covers and staring blindly at Margaret as she redressed the wounds. 'No one's safe in this street. Anders will see to that.'

'Anders, then,' said Fox.

Anna bit her lip.

'It's not peaching if they nearly killed Andris,' said Margaret gently. 'Tell us who they are.'

'I don't know who they are,' said Anna. She had more control of her voice now. But she looked down on Andris with indecision. 'But Andris said they might be in Glassmakers Lane.'

'They?' said Fox. 'Is Anders more than one person? Or is it a gang?'

'There's two of them in charge,' whispered Andris. 'And people working for them. Some gents, some thugs, a clerk. That's all I know.'

'He can't go to hospital,' said Anna. 'They'll see a bullet wound and get the police involved, and then Anders will find out.'

'No they won't,' said Fox. 'I'll see to that.'

'You got that kind of clout?' Anna sneered.

'Yes.'

'He does,' said Margaret. 'You can trust him. What he most wants to do is find Anders and stop him.'

Anna sat on the edge of the bed and picked up Andris's hand. He calmed as she stroked it. 'What do you think you're stopping exactly, mister? Moshie thought Anders was anarchists. Well, I'm an anarchist. Andris is an anarchist. We want a world without empires and monarchs, without dictators and presidents who've got there because of money or bribery, without people getting wealthy off the back of other people. We want a new start. That's all.'

'And what does Anders want?'

'The German Empire to swallow up the British one,' croaked Andris. 'And Germany winning the war that'll come.'

'I see,' said Fox. He glanced at Margaret.

'I don't want a war,' whispered Anna. 'I *wanted* to smash machines, but I never done it. I just want life to be fair. And I want a voice.' She stroked Andris's brow and heaved a sigh. 'I'll trust you this once, doctor. But how we gonna get him to hospital?'

'I'll carry him until we can get a cab,' said Fox. 'We'll get his trousers on then wrap him in my coat.'

'Thank you for trusting me,' said Margaret. She looked round the mean room as Anna collected her coat from the trunk and wondered whether the photograph of the Balodis family in happier days was in the trunk, with Anna's silver-grey dress and the few belongings they'd had in the other room, or whether they'd had to sell it all to secure this sordid space for a few weeks.

'Yeah, well. It's not many people would come in a place like this and sit on that bed. You said you wanted me to help. What is it?'

Margaret took the photograph from her bag. 'You're in this,' she said. 'You probably didn't realise it had been taken. We just wondered if you knew who the other people are. Is that one of the Anders?'

'I told you, I don't know who Anders is.' Anna buttoned her coat, took the photograph, and peered at it. 'I remember that day. It was after you visited to tell me about Ma. Him' – she pointed at Mr Drummond – 'he was trying to get me to sign up as an actress. Saw me carrying *The Freedom Press*, asked if I was a good reader, then said he needed someone who looked like me to be a villainess. I didn't know if he was being straight or if he was after something else. Things hadn't got that bad. They still ain't.'

'I believe he was being straight,' said Margaret. 'He really does work for the moving-picture company, but I think he thinks there's something wrong about what happened when Andris was shot. I don't know quite what he knows, or suspects – yet. What about this one?'

'Him?' said Anna, looking at the man Margaret had met in Neuchâtel and seen outside the Edevanes' house. 'He's the one what I'm scared of.'

'Because he's Anders?'

Anna shook her head. 'I think he works for him. High-up. He kept coming round Whitechapel saying he knew someone offering work, and no one does that. It was odd. You said Anderson before, didn't you? One of the jobs this bloke knew about was pretending to be someone called Anderson for a couple of months. You'd get three quid for every month you could keep it up, and if you got arrested, you'd get a shilling for every day you were inside. The bloke what took it got arrested, then murdered someone, then topped himself.' Anna blinked a little and sniffed.

'You knew him?' said Margaret, waiting to see what the young woman would say.

Anna looked at her with narrowed eyes. Then at Fox. 'I bet you know I did. Peter Abolins. He was my Dad's cousin. Soft as butter. He wasn't the murdering sort nor the sort to give up. Never. He just wanted out of Whitechapel to run a business and it was hard to get going, but he wouldn't have murdered for it and we don't believe he'd do himself in either. We think they did for him. That job is why he'd died.'

'Who told him about the job?'

'Piccadilly,' gasped Andris. Anna showed him the photograph. 'He's not Anders. Does their dirty work.' He submitted to having his trousers put on. When he sat up to have his coat put on, he collapsed.

Anna went pale. 'Oh, Gawd. Is he...?'

'He's fainted,' said Margaret. 'Try and keep his head low, Fox.' She was torn between wanting to help and wanting to prompt Anna. 'We'll get him to the hospital in one piece, I promise.' She swallowed. 'How about the man he's talking to?' She pointed to Charles.

Anna checked for herself that Andris was breathing, then moved the photograph into the light. 'Looks like Moshie. His proper name was Miroshnik. We thought he was one of us for ever such a long time. Once we cottoned on he was a copper or something, we strung him along a bit, but we made it clear we weren't like Gardstein's lot in case he lumped us all in together. If we were going to get arrested, it wasn't for being cop killers. Now that I remember, *he* was looking for someone called Anderson. Gawd, I wonder if this Piccadilly is telling him where to find cousin Peter. No one's seen him for months. I hope he's all right.'

'Who?' said Fox. 'Who hasn't been seen for months? Piccadilly?'

'Miroshnik,' said Anna.

'He's dead,' said Fox. 'Murdered.'

'Gawd,' said Anna. 'I'm not sure about the hospital now. Piccadilly or one of the Anders will find him. I —'

'If you trust me and Dr Demeray, we'll do everything we can to keep your brother's identity secret and give him a chance of survival.'

'It's Piccadilly's fault cousin Peter is dead. It's his fault Andris got hurt. *And* you, doctor.'

'How?'

'We were keeping our heads down out of the manor. We got kitchen jobs in the Strand. Then Andris saw Piccadilly. He was dressed different. A proper swell. So he followed him. Thought Piccadilly would take a cab and he'd lose him but it was worth a try. Only Piccadilly walked. He stopped at a book stall near Covent Garden and Andris sneaked up close and heard the stallholder whisper "it's delivered. It's in a yellow wrapper. It'll be on the right-hand side." And Piccadilly walked on, only Andris was too far behind and when they got to Glassmakers Lane, Piccadilly had disappeared. Then Andris saw the bookshop and wondered if that's where cousin Peter got his books and that's how Piccadilly knew he might be good to use. Andris went in but no one was around, so he poked about on the right hand side and saw this yellow book with Earywon on the front and peeked inside and there was a letter for Anders in it. He nabbed it just as the Nierlings came out from the back and saw him.'

'And then shot him when he ran off,' said Fox.

'No,' Andris had come round. 'Not them. Wrong window.'

Thirty-Seven

By the time Andris was safely at St Thomas's, it was too dark to find out if the film crew was still be at St Katharine Docks. After being checked for vermin, Margaret and Fox were driven back to Bayswater by a convoluted route, stopping for an early dinner at a quiet restaurant.

They were silent for most of the journey. Margaret held Fox's hand and put the information buzzing round her head into some sort of order.

Miroshnik. She'd had no idea of Charles's Whitechapel name, one which would set him firmly within one group and outside another – except for bona fide anarchists perhaps who were more tolerant of each other because of their shared goal and desire to shed the shackles of tradition. Over the meal, she and Fox talked of anything but moving pictures, anarchism, foreign aggression. She knew that he was as exhausted as she was, his mind was also trying to put the pieces together.

As the savoury was removed, Fox put the photograph of Charles laughing with Piccadilly on the table. 'I'm still not sure. Just because Anna liked him, it doesn't mean he was only on our side. He could have been on both. How do I know he wasn't complicit in setting up the whole Anderson thing to distract us?'

'Because you know Charles.'

'That's the skill, Margaret,' said Fox. 'Being utterly believable. Charles was a risk, with parents who had been born in a country which is tangled up with both Russia and Austria. They may have connections among enemies. Charles worked in newspapers before joining us. He had contacts, he'd know how things worked so he could manipulate someone like Norah. Charles could turn his hand to anything, be anyone. What if he fooled us - me - as much as he fooled people in Whitechapel?'

'This whole thing is so poisonous.' Margaret glared at coffee which was too bitter again.

'I'd feel better knowing that Charles wasn't the Mr Friend who had Norah writing letters,' said Fox.

'But that's Piccadilly.'

'Is it?' Fox's voice was hesitant.

'Norah wrote "why here" on the back of the *other* photograph,' Margaret insisted. 'The one with Piccadilly and Mr Drummond. *Not* the one with Piccadilly and Charles. She knew Mr Drummond and she knew why he was in Whitechapel so she can't mean him. But what if she knew Piccadilly too and didn't expect to see him in Whitechapel dressed like a tramp because she was used to him well-dressed elsewhere. And her diary said she'd seen Mr Friend "in the lane" after she started work at the studio. That could mean an alley in the East End or it could mean Glassmakers Lane.'

Fox pondered. 'According to the bits of the diary you haven't read, she asked Mr Friend why he picked her and he said it was because he'd heard about her intelligence and capability. He said something about Wales and about her mother. She wondered how he knew.'

'The Edevanes. It can't be Charles.'

'And even after she'd left, she posted those letters which led me to Austria and Italy. Although...'

She looked at Fox and simultaneously, they said, '*He* posted them.'

'Mr Friend said not to date them and that he'd post them himself,' said Margaret.

'On the grounds that they needed to be sent on a certain day, but he understood how hard it might be for her to go to the postbox all the time.'

'Exactly. Has anyone checked the dates on the letters?'

'If not, they will now.'

'So that means Mr Friend *couldn't* have been Charles. Because Charles was dead by the time those letters were posted.'

For the first time in a long while, Fox smiled properly. 'Come on, Mrs Fox, let's get you back to the den. I need an early night.'

'Exhausted?'

'Not yet.'

Margaret rose early the next morning, long before she needed to leave for St Julia's. Leaving Fox asleep, she bathed and dressed, made tea and sat with her sketchbook in the sitting room. Her last drawings were observations from Switzerland. There were views; images of people waiting on country platforms; the melée at Paris as passengers alighted and separated for the next stage of their journey; the dark sea of the channel, dotted with shadowy vessels and their spots of light.

Now she turned to a blank page and started to pour the things in her mind through the pencil: people, buildings, scenes.

Juniper jumped onto the windowsill to inspect the neighbourhood and settled into a conveniently majestic pose until Margaret began to draw her too, whereupon she leapt down and stalked off to investigate Fox. A muffled yelp indicated that Juniper was checking he was still alive by digging her claws into his chest and purring into his face.

Fox, tousle-headed, joined her a few minutes later, wrapped in his spare dressing gown, and looked over her shoulder. Margaret had drawn a plan of Glassmakers Lane and was tapping her teeth with the pencil. 'Something bothering me about Nierling's.'

'Everything bothers me about it.'

'Seriously, what were your observations?'

Fox scratched his nose and pondered, looking round Margaret's sunny sitting room until his gaze settled on the bookcase. 'You're the bookshop aficionado,' he said. 'But I thought the point was to keep most of the stuff in groups. I mean, you've left a few books lying about, but broadly speaking' – he pointed – 'medicine, science, history, travel, religion, poetry, novels, things you can't classify. Is that right?'

'Yes. At worst, Nierling's ought to be the same, and yet there's no discernible order. That's partly why Father would like it. It would be like a bran tub – pay a penny, plunge your hand into a barrel, pull out a parcel and it could be anything. But *Erewhon* was easy to find; it stood out because it had a bright-yellow wrapper. All you'd need to know was which bit of the shop it was in. And yet you said there's a room at the back which has two specific subjects: pornography and anarchy, both potentially illegal.'

'And in better order. But that way, if there's any trouble, the police will only ever look in the back for reprehensible literature and the customers who buy it.'

'Even though there's barely any evidence of sales.'

'Except in cash,' said Fox. 'The search the other week revealed a lot of it on the premises. The police obtained a warrant to look at their bank accounts. Money goes in and comes out in bits and bobs at irregular intervals. It looks legitimate but it's untraceable, so the chances are that it's about as illegitimate as it can get. The books are better recorded. Boxes regularly come and go. Some are full of obscure, odd or boring, mostly old books. The dates of those match with boxes going to and from Germany. We believe it's a way to get messages back and forth inside volumes which no one was going to investigate because they'd be too busy looking for normal mail or telegrams or telephone messages.'

'And Abolin and Bookie Brown?'

'We think Bookie was collecting them then passing them on through his stall. Who'd notice a man like that or his customers? Apart from your father, most people would go to him for the popular books and ignore the obscure ones. If anyone tried to buy the one he needed to pass to a specific person and they didn't ask the right way, he could just say he was saving it for someone. Only that day back in January, it looks like Bookie Brown was having second thoughts. Perhaps he'd found the letter and shown Dutch Jake who translated it and made him wonder. Maybe he didn't pass it on as he should have and someone really did try to shoot him, startling Dutch Jake enough to trip and fall. Abolin? I think he was hired to threaten the Edevanes. He just wanted the capital. I daresay the minute the two of them wanted out, that signed their death warrants.'

'Like Norah.'

'Presumably,' said Fox. 'They took a bit longer to get to her and Bookie, but they did it. And I believe Charles had half worked out that Abolin was just being used.'

'Why didn't he tell you?'

'Because he thought Abolin was somewhere safe and he thought he'd get everything straight before he sent us down another wrong alley. He liked to be thorough.'

Fox turned to her sketchbook. Margaret had drawn the people from Glassmakers Lane and the man from Neuchâtel. Under the sketch she'd made from memory of Dr Fernsby and Mrs Dysart, she'd unconsciously scrawled: Snow White and Rose Red.

Fox read the names aloud. 'Who are they?'

'Two little girls in a fairy story named after the rosebushes outside their mother's cottage. One is dark haired with rosy cheeks and lips, the other fair and pale.'

'These aren't little girls, though.'

'No. The blonde one is Mrs Dysart and the brunette is Dr Fernsby.'

'I hadn't realised they were sisters.'

'They're...' Margaret looked at her sketch again. It was an accurate likeness. The two women were ten years apart in age; it was obvious in the lines around Dr Fernsby's eyes and the softening of her jaw. Their colouring was quite different, too. Dr Fernsby's dark hair, threaded with a few grey hairs, was dressed in a style from a few years before. Her eyes were brown and flashing under thick, dark lashes, her lips narrow and red. Mrs Dysart's fair hair was in the latest fashion, her eyes pale and smiling. She was slighter than Dr Fernsby, her frame narrower, her lips fuller and her mouth more naturally smiling, but Fox was right. There was a strong resemblance in the line of their noses, how their eyes were set, the way they held their heads. 'I hadn't realised it either. They've never said. I've only seen them together twice and the last time, they were arguing.' Margaret looked up at Fox, frowning. 'I thought they didn't really like each other. They've never given any indication they're related. Quite the opposite - that they'd only recently become acquainted through pure proximity.'

'Do sisters automatically like each other? Or were they just doing the sort of incomprehensible bickering that you and Katherine do?'

'Sisters don't have to like each other. But no, it sounded worse than bickering.'

'Perhaps the stakes were higher.'

'If they're sisters, they've made every effort not to have it known. And if Dr Fernsby's involved in something then...'

'Tell me about it.'

Margaret made a rough sketch of the scene while she described it. Mrs Dysart emerging from the consulting room, backing away from the cold anger on Dr Fernsby's face as she apologised for buying quack medication. Or had she?

'It was a stupid thing to do,' Mrs Dysart had said. Dr Fernsby had said she was talking about herself. But now Margaret thought, it wasn't apologetic: it was angry. It wasn't remorseful, it was accusatory. They were both angry about what someone had done.

'And this was the day after Miss Connors visited the surgery,' said Fox.

'Yes.'

'And a few days after you'd been shot by Nierling.'

'If I *was* shot by him.'

'He said he was shooting.'

'Andris said he wasn't. There's something else.' Margaret retrieved the book, turned the pages again and tapped at the sketch map of Glassmakers Lane. 'Mr Drummond said I was looking the wrong way. I thought he meant at the problem – he probably did – but I think he meant something else too. Everything seemed so sudden; it happened all at once and I couldn't swear to the order. I was standing here, looking that way' – she added a small cross with an arrow – 'talking to Reuben who was looking at me' – another cross and arrow – 'and

Andris pushed between us from somewhere. Reuben and I turned, and ... I never had my back to Nierling's.' Margaret touched her ear. The thought that she no longer knew where the shot had come from hurt a good deal more.

Fox picked up the sketch. 'If you were standing there, the shots came from either the surgery, the studio, or Soffiato's.'

'Soffiato's is the most obvious. They're of German descent, pretending to be Italian. But I can't believe it.'

'Nor me,' said Fox. 'We've investigated them, and their loyalties are to King George. They're scared of the way things are going and keeping their heads down, just making a very bad job of it.'

'But Dr Fernsby... How could someone shoot from the surgery without her knowing?'

'That building has at least five storeys. He could have shot from another floor, although the angle...'

'Or... Dr Fernsby knew,' whispered Margaret. 'What if Anders is controlling her, as he is the Nierlings? What is he using against her?'

'And is he using her sister too?'

'Perhaps Mrs Dysart trying to stop her? And someone's trying to tamper with her medicine so she can't. And they used it to kill Norah. If it wasn't Mr Drummond, it's someone else. In either case, it's more likely that a doctor could get hold of digitalin than anyone else.'

'You don't know Norah was killed that way.'

'Not yet,' said Margaret, rising. 'But I'm going to discuss it with Dr Jordan, and I'll send a telegram to Dr Gilliand on the way.'

Fox stood up and pulled her into his arms. 'I'll see what we can get out of Edevane and what I can find out about Dr Fernsby and Mrs Dysart's background. Will you promise to stay away from Glassmakers Lane?'

'Will you?'

'No.'

'Neither can I.'

'Sometimes I think Charles was mad not to want to get married,' said Fox. 'And then...'

'Now you know how I feel every time you disappear.'

'If you do go there, don't eat or drink anything, don't trust anyone, don't turn your back, and—'

'Wear my thickest coat and hat.'

'That'll keep you perfectly safe,' said Fox. She could tell he was trying to smile, but his mouth twisted in worry even as she kissed it.

Thirty-Eight

It felt as if she'd been away from St Julia's for weeks rather than days.

Dr Jordan agreed with her hypothesis about Norah. 'Even a healthy young girl would die very quickly, with every appearance of having suffered natural cardiac arrest. If you or Dr Gilliand had known what she'd been given, and it wasn't too long afterwards, an antidote could have been injected to restart her heart and she might have survived.'

'Oh, don't,' said Margaret, closing her eyes briefly. 'I wish I'd had enough time to examine her properly.'

'You left her in the care of another physician and have nothing to blame yourself for. If you're right then... oh that poor girl.' Dr Jordan removed his glasses and polished them. There was a thin film of moisture on his lashes. He cleared his throat. 'Can your suspicion be proved?'

'It would depend on an exhumation, then whether it's possible to get any evidence from the body.'

'An exhumation may not be easy to obtain.'

'I know,' said Margaret, feeling her shoulders sag. 'I telegraphed Dr Gilliand to ask if he could explain the Swiss protocol by return, and warned him to expect a letter from me. I couldn't put the whole thing in a telegram.'

It was hard to concentrate during the morning. The smells in the laboratory were overpowering. Either the time she'd spent away had made her nose more sensitive, or they'd changed the disinfectant. When Margaret sat down in her office with a pot of tea at ten o'clock, she opened the window to let in some fresh air, but finding it not only cold but tainted with petrol and acrid smoke, she closed it again.

The telegram from Dr Gilliand, which came at eleven, simply said, *'Entendu. Répondrai bientôt.' Understood. Will reply soon.* It arrived shortly before Mr Drummond, who walked up to the desk while she was folding it back up. 'Oh,' she said. 'Er...'

Mr Drummond shoved his hands in his pockets and scowled. 'I've come to stand you lunch.'

He made it sound enough of a threat that the desk clerk stopped pretending not to listen. 'Dr Demeray, Dr Jordan wants to see you.'

'It's all right,' said Margaret. 'Mr Drummond's bark is worse than his bite. I think.'

Mr Drummond marched her to a nearby licensed restaurant where he ordered steak pie with chipped potatoes and half pints of stout for them both. To his obvious disgust, Margaret changed her order to a pot of tea and some ginger biscuits.

'It's a bit early for lunch,' she explained.

'I suppose so,' said Mr Drummond. 'But the studio has a picnic planned, and it's not picnic weather.' He studied her for a moment. 'I've been asking around about you. I daresay you have about me too.'

Margaret considered denying it, but decided to tell the truth. 'I discovered you'd asked a young woman in Whitechapel to come and act for the studio. I think you wanted the femme fatale type.'

Mr Drummond frowned, then nodded. 'That was Dysart's idea.'

'Mr?'

'Theoretically. But not really.'

'Whose, then?'

'Mrs D's the one who comes up with things. They're getting madder by the minute. We've been filming all over: hospitals, museum steps, docks, outside people's houses. I've seen maps for Nottinghamshire, Yorkshire and South Wales – all the coal-mining bits. Not pretty. She says it's to film *Robin Hood* and *Wuthering Heights* and *Camelot*.'

'Camelot's in Cornwall and none of them involve coal.'

'Yeah. I reckon she's found out what really happened to Norah was murdered and it's sent her barmy.'

The waiter arrived with their food.

'Did you recruit Norah, too?' said Margaret.

'No,' said Mr Drummond, shovelling in steak pie. 'She was just there when I came back from scouting for locations, chewing everyone's ear off. The rest... Well, you know the rest.'

'So what did you find out about me?'

'That you're in Glassmakers Lane by some bizarre coincidence. Never believed in coincidences before, but I suppose you have to start somewhere. All this is wasting time. I want your advice.'

'Mine?'

'It goes against the grain, but there you go. Here.' Mr Drummond pulled a sealed envelope from his inner pocket. It was creased, as if it had been there a long time. It was addressed in Norah's handwriting, to a Mr Robert Davis in Clapham, and bore unfranked Swiss stamps. 'She gave it to me to post that day. I couldn't work out why she didn't just post it herself,' he said. 'Then after she died there was all that stuff about her "father" in Paris. I wondered if this was the same geezer, or the same sort of geezer, trying to do the dirty on her. I kept thinking I ought to open it, then that I ought to post it. And then you came along with your suspicious little mind, and I wondered if you were trying to get it from me. There's something wrong about the whole thing.'

'I agree.'

'What do you reckon, then? Open it?'

Margaret thought of her father, who'd say that it was against the law to open someone else's mail, then of Fox, who'd say she ought to give it to his department for analysis. 'Yes. You need to hold it—'

'By its edges. Thanks for suggesting I'm an idiot.' Mr Drummond picked up a dessert knife and slit the envelope. Inside was a letter and another smaller, sealed envelope. Mr Drummond slid the letter onto the tablecloth and flipped it open with the knife. He turned it so that they could both read it.

Tuesday 21st March 1911

Dear Mr Davis,

After all this time maybe I've found you, but I don't feel I can call you Da or even Father yet.

Thank you for saying you'd meet me with your wife wherever I suggested so I'd feel safe. I'd like to bring my friend Reuben, and maybe my friend Nellie's Mum because she doesn't take any nonsense from anyone, and maybe even Mr Drummond who's my boss and an old grump but looks out for us girls like we're his daughters. I'd like to meet you at Alan's Tearooms, Oxford Street. It'll be full of suffragettes but they are my heroines because they fight even when they're in a corner.

I hope you don't think this means I doubt you. I'm excited, but I'm not ready to trust anyone without checking. What you wrote about you and my mother made sense. And from the way you described the town, I know you grew up there and came away for the same reasons I did. So I'll trust you, because you're not telling me I'm cleverer or more important than I am. You know what I am and where I'm from. I wish my mam was still alive.

I'm sending this from Switzerland because you said your little boy collects stamps. I'll write again on Thursday when I'm back in London. I suppose that letter might get to you first. This may sound very strange, but if you don't hear from me by Saturday 1st April, please will you post the other letter that's in with this one. She will know what to do.

Yours sincerely, Norah Glyn, or maybe Norah Jones, or maybe even Norah Davis. Or maybe – if I were named for my mam instead of the next letter in the alphabet – Mair.

'Gawd,' said Mr Drummond. 'Do you reckon this Davis was genuine?'

'Yes. What about the other letter?'

Mr Drummond extracted the other envelope. It was addressed to Nellie's mother.

'Shall we?'

'In for a penny, Mr Drummond.'

'In for a pound, Dr Demeray.' He worked the letter free.

Dear Mrs Pinter

Thank you for being the only one apart from Nellie who believed that Mr Friend existed. I know you're right and that he played me for a fool, but I'm scared. I thought he was ordinary and unimportant. I thought I'd seen the last of him, but I've seen him since and I don't think he's how he seems. Once I saw him sneaking about in Glassmakers Lane after dark, dressed to the nines. Then I saw him in Whitechapel. But this time he was dressed like a beggar talking to someone I've never seen before. My friend Reuben took a photograph which I've borrowed and put under the floor board in our bedroom in Deanacres.

I'm not sure if Mr Friend knows I saw him in Glassmakers Lane, but I saw him yesterday in Switzerland, and he's on the train today, and I'm scared. If anything happens to me, please tell the police to ask Reuben for

*my diary and unscrew the top right knob on Nellie's bed at your house.
I'm sorry, but it was the only place I could think of.*

*Thanks for all your kindness, Mrs Pinter. Thanks for treating me
like another daughter and saying I could call you Mum when I felt
ready. I'll never forget it.*

Margaret stared down at the letter, willing the tears to recede. When
she looked up, Mr Drummond was grinding his thumbs into the
corners of his eyes.

'It's too late,' he said.

'If you and I hadn't distrusted each other from the start we might
have got there quicker, but we'll get there now. My husband's in the
... police. He'll help.'

'Who do you think she saw in Glassmakers Lane?'

Margaret pulled the sketchbook from her bag and turned to a page
where she'd made a drawing of Charles early in December 1910. Mr
Drummond looked blank and shrugged. Then she turned to the page
where she'd drawn the man from Neuchâtel. 'What about this one?'

Mr Drummond frowned. 'That's Mr Fernsby.'

'Mr Fernsby?' The bile rose in Margaret's throat.

'Yeah, your mate's husband. He owns half the street, including the
studio. He's like Will o' the Wisp, though. One minute you see him,
then he's gone. Likes slumming it in Whitechapel. There's lots of
reasons why he might, but I've never been convinced it's the obvious
one.'

'He was at Neuchâtel looking at Norah's body when I got to it and
then he wandered off. Didn't you see him?'

'No,' said Mr Drummond. 'But I was in third class. He'd have been
in first, like you. And I never got off the train till I was looking for
Norah. What are you telling me?'

'I think he killed her.'

'Gawd, and all this time I thought it was Dysart.'

'Mr Dysart?'

'He's scared of his wife, but not of the actresses. Thought maybe he'd been too familiar and Norah was going to tell Mrs D.'

'Would Mr Dysart kill her for that?'

Mr Drummond waggled his head. 'Well, she's dead. And we had him with us, grumbling about cheap hotels and travelling third class. He went home on the earlier train so he could stop off in Paris and do some business. Sell films, you know. So when there was that letter in Norah's pocket and the "father" in Paris, I thought Dysart had given her something to kill her slow so he wasn't around when it happened and was answering all those telegrams from some swish hotel.'

'Is he capable of murder?'

'Maybe.' Mr Drummond took a mouthful of stout. 'Here's a thing: just before we left for Switzerland last month, Mrs D's tablets ended up down the drain and she couldn't go because she could die without them. It seemed like an accident but ...'

'What tablets?' said Margaret carefully.

Mr Drummond rolled his eyes. '"What tablets?" she says. Hippocratic bloody oath. I bet you know perfectly well she what she takes. Heart tablets. I never made any connection with Norah's death till you started asking questions, then I started to wonder if Mr D had pinched some of them, knocked the rest down the drain so no one would know they were missing and used them to kill Norah. Could that work?'

'It depends on the drug. Have you - er - even seen the label?'

'Funny you should say that,' said Mr Drummond, scowling into the middle distance. 'When I fished it out the gutter for Mrs D, I saw they were digitalin. That's foxglove isn't it? Then... A bit after you left the studio with Nellie and just after Mrs D had gone home to see to her kids, the police came round asking if anyone had seen a young woman in Glassmakers Lane on Sunday afternoon.'

'Did they?' Margaret put on a neutral face but Mr Drummond snorted.

'Don't come the innocent with me. Didn't you say your husband's in the police? The woman ended up in some godawful alley and then in the London, didn't she? Well everyone at the studio said no, we hadn't worked then, but afterwards I heard Dysart whining on the telephone. "I got drenched that Sunday getting her out without anyone seeing me while you were sitting round having tea with your sister like the Queen of Sheba," he said. Then he whined "She should have been done for. Why do *I* have to make sure that everyone's dead?"'

'Did you tell the police?'

'Waste of time. I went to warn the woman but she wasn't quite the ticket and I got arrested, and searched, then released. You probably know that too. I recognised the bottle in my pocket as soon as I saw it. I said the tablets were mine so I could get them analysed myself. Took them back to the studio the next day, hung up my coat meaning to take them to Burtons at lunchtime; when I looked later, they were gone. Then *I* felt a fool. Could digitalin have done for Norah?'

'It could,' said Margaret. She rose. 'I need to telephone my husband. Let's hope whatever's in that bed frame links directly to Mr Fernsby or Mr Dysart, otherwise I can't see how we can prove anything.'

Mr Drummond looked at his watch. 'They'll be waiting for me. I'll quiz Mrs D on the way.'

'Be careful, Mr Drummond.'

'Nah. I'll be in a crowd.'

'Where are you going?'

'Brooklands. It's a race track and —'

'Aerodrome!' Margaret rose to her feet. 'And Mr Dysart can fly, can't he? Go on ahead. I'll join you before you leave to tell Mrs Dysart that I want to accompany her as a physician.'

'You mustn't come back to Glassmakers Lane. Someone took a pot-shot at you a few days ago.'

'You sound like my husband.' Margaret put on her coat and picked up the sketchbook and letter.

Mr Drummond heaved a sigh and rolled his eyes. 'Let me guess. When you got married, you didn't promise to obey him, did you?'

'Certainly not.'

'Flaming women,' he said, flinging the necessary coins onto the table. 'What did I ever do to deserve five contrary daughters, three addle-headed actresses, and you?'

Thirty-Nine

A fter telephoning Fox's office and explaining to Dr Jordan that she needed to collect more information about Norah, Margaret was collected by Bert and Elinor at a quarter to twelve.

'I used to hide things in the bed frame when I was a kid,' said Bert, when she explained. 'Lost a few things that way.'

'Me too,' said Elinor. 'Let's hope we can get at what Norah hid easily. I suspect Mrs Pinter won't take kindly to us taking the bed apart.'

'Tell her it's for the Empire's sake,' said Margaret. 'That might work.'

'Aren't you coming?'

'No, I need to get to Glassmakers Lane. Drop me here and I'll get a cab.'

'Fox would want us to take you,' said Bert.

'There's no time. What's he's doing?'

'Looking for Mr Friend,' said Bert. 'If only someone neutral had seen Norah with him and we could be sure whether he's Piccadilly or Smith or someone else entirely.'

Margaret frowned. 'There was something in the diaries...'

'You haven't read the whole translation,' said Elinor.

'Not the one in Welsh,' said Margaret. 'The one in English.' She concentrated. 'I remember she arranged to meet Mr Friend in the parish church because the verger would be there to protect her if necessary. Maybe he noticed.'

'Stone me,' said Bert. 'You're right. We'll send a telegram on the way to Cricklewood. Someone needs to get to that verger before the same thing occurs to whoever Mr Friend is.'

Margaret arrived outside Dysart's at a quarter past twelve. The studio people had left early. The only people remaining were Miss Isaacs, Morrie and Norb, and carpenters who were creating props. As she left the studio and stood on the pavement wondering what to do next, Margaret peered up at the surgery. On the floor above the waiting room, someone tall and dark had opened the sash and was looking out. Something flashed as the sun caught it and Margaret's heart started to pound.

'Oh, doctor, I forgot.' Miss Isaacs called from the doorway and then joined her on the pavement. 'Reuben said he thought you might turn up and said if you did, could you to look at his latest artwork. Do you want to do it now?' Across the road, the window closed and the person inside the building withdrew from sight.

Heart slowing, Margaret followed Miss Isaacs into Dysart's then went through to Reuben's room alone. At least it gave her some breathing space. If the flashing light meant someone had trained a gun on her from the surgery, she needed to find a different route out of Glassmakers Lane.

She examined the clutter on Reuben's desk remembering that he'd said there was order in the apparent chaos but wishing he'd left something to indicate what she was supposed to be looking at. There was a sketch for a poster: a blonde girl walking the upper wing of a biplane, flailing an umbrella, which pointed at a pile of half-finished sketches but particularly at an even less finished one of Margaret with a series of ornate arrows alongside. Turning over the sheet of paper at which the arrows pointed, Margaret found a sketch map of the street, with tiny figures representing herself and Reuben and Andris. He'd come to the same conclusion.

Her brain told her to leave, but her senses told her to stay. Looking down at the desk again, she saw an open book with an engraving showing Glassmakers Lane about forty-five years earlier, before most of a higgledy-piggledy jumble of insanitary-looking buildings had been replaced with elegant neo-classicism.

Margaret's receipt for the sixpenny consultation had been shoved in as a bookmark elsewhere and when she turned to the relevant page and moved a scrawled reminder to buy a new rug, there was another engraving of the street after all the buildings but for what was now the studio, Nierling's, and the building next to Nierling's had been demolished. The road was full of deep holes. New sewers were being laid, the road was being stabilised for the underground passing beneath. It was possible to see into some of the original cellars on both sides of the street. Never mind the attics joining, it was possible some of the cellars did.

Margaret put the book down and looked around the room. The desk was pulled back, more of the floor exposed. Was the rug slightly kinked? She bent to lift it, expecting a trapdoor, but only found dust and a folded piece of paper. She was about to drop the rug again when she had second thoughts, picked up the paper and unfolded it. Inside, in Reuben's scrawl, was a note: 'We're taking reels to the aerodrome! Are they going to fly far away? Join us! Bring a pal!'

She had to contact Fox. Cursing herself for not keeping Bert at hand somehow, Margaret returned to the foyer. Miss Isaacs, feet on desk, was buried in another penny dreadful. 'Is there a garden?'

'Is there a what?' said Miss Isaacs, looking up from her book.

Margaret gave the first reason that popped into her head. 'I want to sketch the rear of the building.'

'Takes all sorts,' Miss Isaacs swung her feet down. 'Mind you, having met your dad... This way.'

She led Margaret through the building into a small dark space where two carpenters were sawing and hammering. 'There isn't much to see.'

There wasn't. It was a mossy, cobbled space with a tumbledown shed. 'I think it was let as a sort of lodging once,' said Miss Isaacs. 'Sort of place bad girls get murdered in, if you get my drift.'

But the shed was next to a gate which, if nothing had changed since that old drawing, led ultimately to Shaftesbury Avenue. Was that how Mr Dysart had got Miss Connors out without being noticed?

Margaret willed Miss Isaacs to go back indoors. All she needed to do...

'Hey, Miss Isaacs!' called a voice from inside the building. 'Where are you? Is the doctor still here?'

'Yes!' Miss Isaacs yelled back. 'What's happened?' She turned to Margaret. 'You'd better come. They've probably just got a splinter, but you never know.'

'But I—'

'Quick!' Morrie appeared at the back door. 'It's Dr Fernsby. The baby's coming.'

'What?' said Margaret. 'It's not due for at least six weeks.'

'Seems no one's told the baby that. Miss Hill's out for lunch, but the maid said you'd come in here. Best hurry. My missus always says early babies come quick.'

Margaret felt her heart race again and nausea churned in her stomach. What had Mr Fernsby done to his wife? How could she get word to anyone now? And to make things worse, it had been years since she'd delivered a baby. 'Miss Isaacs, I need you to come with me.'

'I don't know anything about childbirth!'

'I'm not asking you to help, I want you go through Miss Hill's books till you find out how to contact the midwife and then ring the police.'

'Why?'

'Because I say so.'

They ran across the road, dodging a car and a motorcycle. Leaving Miss Isaacs rooting through Miss Hill's desk, Margaret dashed upstairs to the living quarters. Low moaning came from the dining room where Dr Fernsby lay on the floor, with a maid mopping her brow.

'I can't get her to move, doctor. She says her back's hurting her.'

'Where's your master?' Margaret crouched and picked up Dr Fernsby's wrist.

'We can't have a man in here! She's having a baby!'

'He's in the house, then?'

'Yes ma'am, I mean doctor. He's the one who knew where to get you from.'

So it was him in the window, thought Margaret. 'Go and get him. Then we can move Dr Fernsby somewhere more comfortable.'

'But—'

'Do as I say. We can't leave her here.'

'Cook's got water boiling and towels coming.'

'Do as I say!' Margaret bellowed.

'Get out!' shouted Dr Fernsby. 'I just want the doctor here.'

'But ma'am—'

'Out! Go to the kitchen and stay there. The doctor will ring when she wants you.'

The maid appealed to Margaret, and after a pause, Margaret nodded.

'It's too soon,' groaned Dr Fernsby when the maid had gone. 'It's too soon.' Her face was paler than normal but there was no sheen of sweat or grey under her eyes.

'Shh,' said Margaret, taking the other woman's pulse and trying not to hear her own instead. She leaned in close. 'What did he do to you?' she whispered.

Dr Fernsby groaned more loudly.

Calm down, Margaret told herself. *Remember what to expect, what to do.*

But Dr Fernsby's pulse was lower and more steady than Margaret's. Her heartbeat was regular and slow, and so was the baby's. Even though Dr Fernsby groaned at regular intervals, when Margaret put her hand on her belly there were no contractions, just the awkward fidgeting of a seven-month baby in the womb, twisting nonchalantly in its confined space. The head, as far as Margaret could tell without closer examination, was not engaged.

Dr Fernsby's groans stopped. 'A false alarm, I think.'

As their eyes met, a slow, insolent smile crossed Dr Fernsby's face. She sat up, and a shadow fell over them.

Margaret turned and looked up.

The man she'd seen at Neuchâtel, hands behind his back, stood over her, looking down as if she were an interesting specimen. His face was no longer cheerfully vacant but bore an expression of sardonic intelligence. 'I'm *so* sorry we've wasted your time, doctor.'

'One can never be too careful,' said Margaret, rising slowly to her feet and glancing at the door behind him. She wondered which of his hands held the gun, and which way to trip him before she ran. 'I've sent for the midwife.'

'She'll be out on her rounds,' said Dr Fernsby.

'And the police.'

'They'll be too late.'

Behind Margaret, Dr Fernsby's voice was different. She must be standing now, and perhaps her smile had widened.

Mr Fernsby put his head on one side. 'Nice to meet you again Dr Demeray.'

'Why did you kill Norah?'

'Me?' said Mr Fernsby. 'What did she die from?'

'Digitalin.'

'And how was I supposed to get that?' He chuckled.

Margaret narrowed her eyes. 'Your sister-in-law seems to be rather clumsy. Her husband's rather good at sleight of hand.'

'How did you—' Dr Fernsby snarled.

'Poor little orphan Norah,' interrupted Mr Fernsby. His face shifted; now he looked shy and coaxing, his accent changing subtly. 'Just one more letter for King and Country, then you'll be better than all those people who looked down on you and I'll help you find your mother. Just one more.'

'The stage is missing an actor,' snapped Margaret. 'Why did you choose Norah?'

He shrugged. 'The Edevanes were being difficult. We tried several things to pressurise them and wondered whether there was a way through their servants. We looked into each one's background and it didn't take long to work out Norah's pitiful campaign to find her parents. When she won the competition in the Gazette, it was the perfect pretext to contact her. Not only could we distract the police from us, but we could play on the Edevanes' paranoia at the same time. It was a godsend.'

'I don't think God has anything to do with what you were planning.'

'I'd be careful what you say if I were you,' said Dr Fernsby.

'Don't let him manipulate you into supporting him,' said Margaret. 'The police know what he's done.'

'Do they really?' said Dr Fernsby. 'You know, I quite liked you, Dr Demeray. I thought you of all people wouldn't automatically assume it was men behind this plan with their little wives trotting on behind. Why couldn't it be women, with men following on?'

'You?'

'Why not? I was pleased a woman could look after the practice while I had this baby and make it look quite normal if I sold it on once our plans succeed. It's a shame I picked a police spy. Never mind.'

'Your plans won't succeed. Someone will be here soon.'

'The midwife isn't coming, my dear,' said Dr Fernsby. 'And neither are the police.'

'Miss Isaacs—'

'I told her I'd deal with it,' said Mr Fernsby. 'Which I've accidentally forgotten to do. Perhaps I should have sent for a surgeon. He'd be more useful.'

Margaret felt something hard dig into her spine. She twisted and found Dr Fernsby holding a pistol to her back. 'It might be too late by the time he finds her, Leopold. And perhaps we shan't dump her body in Whitechapel this time. It seems far too law-abiding.'

'Dysart said it was just bad luck that the woman wasn't dead before she was found,' said Mr Fernsby with a sneer.

'Incompetence, more likely,' snorted Dr Fernsby.

'You were involved in the attack on Miss Connors?' cried Margaret. 'She came to you for help!'

'If she'd waited till opening hours, she wouldn't have heard Mrs Dysart accusing me of incompetence.'

Margaret swallowed. 'So it was you who shot the young man?'

'No, Leopold shot him. I was shooting at *you*. Unfortunately for her, Miss Connors overheard my … Mrs Dysart referring to my failure to do anything but wing you. I suppose I should have known better than to let you go back to the hospital where they'd clean the wound again, after I'd dressed it with a nice little bit of infected gauze. Now then, doctor, let's move very slowly down the stairs to the motor car. All the staff are so inconveniently out. You will support me as if I'm in labour, and Leo will encourage you to keep your opinions to yourself with the pistol. And then we'll—' Her eyes widened. 'Leopold! Behind you!'

Instinctively, Margaret twisted to face Mr Fernsby again. His face was white with fury. Holding a gun to his temple, stood Fox.

'Check, Dr Fernsby,' he said. 'Or should I say, Dr Fernsby, born Caroline Anderle half-sister to Marianne Anderle. Your move.'

Dr Fernsby snorted. 'The elusive husband. I wondered when you'd break cover.'

Margaret was unable to suppress a squeak as the pistol jabbed harder and deeper. The nausea she'd felt earlier started to well up again and small, sharp pains zig-zagged across her lower stomach.

'I suggest you drop your weapon, doctor,' said Fox. 'Then I'll drop mine and we'll have a nice chat.'

'That's the difference between you and me, Mr Demeray,' said Dr Fernsby. 'I'm fond of Leopold, but I'm willing to sacrifice him for the Empire. Are you willing to sacrifice your wife? Frankly, I'm happy to shoot all of you if necessary. The main difficulty will be clearing up the mess afterwards.'

Mr Fernsby's eyes goggled. 'Caroline!'

'I take it we're speaking of different empires?' said Fox, still not looking at Margaret. His expression was cold and detached, and only someone who knew him well would realise he was furious.

'Of course. Although yours will part of ours in a few years, by hook or by crook,' said Dr Fernsby. 'Now, I suggest you drop your weapon and stop leaving a dent in my husband's face. The quicker you do it, the less painful your wife's death will be. I can't speak for yours.'

Fox started to lower his hand. Margaret tried to plead with her eyes, but he still wasn't looking at her. But he gave a tiny shrug of his shoulders and Margaret twisted, ducked and knocked Dr Fernsby off balance. The pistol fired into one of the dreary landscapes, then something heavy clattered to the floor. Margaret turned, ready to grapple with the other woman, only to find that Bert was gripping Dr Fernsby's arm and holding a pistol to her head.

'I don't know how painless your deaths will be, either,' said Fox. 'But if by some travesty you escape justice, then next time you try this sort of thing, picking a room with only one entrance might lead to greater success. Ah. Here are some friends of mine who want to take you away and ask you a few questions.' Three police constables entered the room.

'I'm pregnant,' snapped Dr Fernsby, squirming in Bert's arms.

'So is Miss Connors,' said Fox. 'And she can remember everything. Come on, lads, let's take them in.'

Mr Fernsby drew himself up to his full height. 'You can't prove anything,' he snapped. 'I can afford the best lawyers, and once they've finished with you two, you'll—'

'Save your breath for the station,' said Fox. 'Let's see whether you feel the same if your wife remains determined to sacrifice you for the other Empire.'

The police escorted the Fernsbys away, leaving Fox and Margaret behind. For a few seconds, they stood holding each other, and Margaret was unsure where her trembling stopped and his began. Then she pulled back. 'We have to go. It may already be too late. We have to get to Brooklands aerodrome. The Dysarts have taken the film crew there.'

Fox nodded. 'Another film of the approaches and the layout of all the places which will be useful for the enemy to know, under the disguise of being part of a moving picture.'

'They've taken reels of film they've already made. Reuben thinks they're going to be sent abroad.'

'How long ago did they leave?'

'Nearly an hour ago. How are we going to catch up?'

'Motorcycle. Pigeon and I can drive faster than a charabanc.'

'You and me.'

'Me and Pigeon.'

'Me and you.'

'In that outfit?'

'Fox, if Dr Fernsby was willing to sacrifice her husband for her empire, I'm willing to sacrifice my dignity for mine. I'm coming with you. Pigeon can help Bert round up the evidence and telephone Brooklands, or telegraph, or whatever you do.'

'But... Oh, very well. But I'm not darning any holes in your stockings afterwards.'

Forty

The motorcycles outstripped every vehicle in their path and once out of London, it was possible to reach full speed. They were stopped by two police traps but were waved through when Fox produced his card, even though they were clearly baffled by Margaret, with her skirt hitched up and Pigeon's goggles loose on her head.

They slowed down on the approach to Brooklands, as the lanes grew less even and more narrow, and they were finally able to communicate.

'So this is one of their potential targets,' said Fox. 'An airfield; that's smart thinking.'

'The field itself, or the planes?'

'I don't know. Have they been to any coal mines yet?'

Margaret shook her head. 'Mr Drummond said they would next week. Why? Because of the Edevanes?'

'Because of what Norah hid in the bedpost. They're photographs of plans of large mines, which Mr Edevane took on the Anders' behest at some beano hosted by the Mine Owners Association.'

'Why did he do that?'

'The usual. Blackmail. If they'd followed the legislation in their mine, no one would have been able to lay a bomb, and even if someone had, no one would have been hurt. So their negligence resulted in murder. And the bomb itself was a test: a small explosion in an insignificant mine. The Anderle sisters were under orders to distract the government by causing disruption in London docks and hospitals – enough to create fear, and put the blame on anarchists or Fenians. But in the meantime, the main plan was to bomb the biggest mines in the country. With only half the usual coal production, Britain would grind to a halt for weeks, maybe months, even if it eventually bought in from abroad – Germany being the major market. Edevane worked it out and found just enough courage to hold out but not enough to hide the photographs himself. Here we are. Is that them?'

The charabanc was parked near to the airfield and Ned was setting up the camera near a two-seater Blériot monoplane while Mrs Dysart pointed directions at the actors.

'I can't see Mr Drummond,' said Margaret. 'Or Reuben. Wait – there's Reuben sitting on the grass, drawing, and Mr Dysart is by that other plane. They're helping someone into it.'

'Could that be Mr Drummond?' Fox passed her some binoculars.

'Yes, that's him. He looks unsteady. And there's a box in there – it looks like one for putting film reels in.'

'Hopefully Bert has got word through. All you need do is stay here and watch. Take photographs when you can, for evidence.'

'How am I supposed to do that if I'm not standing still? I'm not staying back here. Mr Drummond looks ill.'

'If Dysart helped kill Norah and attacked Miss Connors, he won't stop at you. There are only so many times in one day I can face seeing you in danger.'

'Once this is over, I'll stay away from your work for a while. I promise. But I'm involved in this case and I will be forever. Maybe I could have saved Norah in Neuchâtel; I'll never know. But I can help find justice for her now. And I can't just stay back here and watch someone try and kill you. Besides, I'm a terrible photographer and nothing will be clear from this distance.'

They ran the motorcycles as slowly as they could to keep the engine noise low, then left them in the grass and walked forward. The film crew was its usual noisy self and oblivious: Gladys and the other young women shrieking and giggling and flirting with a blushing pilot, the actors striking poses, Mrs Dysart shouting instructions and Ned swearing about the light.

Beyond them out two men were coming near. They moved in a nonchalant manner, but she could tell they were together and watching what was happening. She wished she had asked to take Bert's pistol, even though she had no idea if she could use one in earnest. Her stomach clenched again and she gritted her teeth. 'Did you find the verger in time?'

'Yes. He gave a positive identification of Mr Fernsby. He'd never seen Smith. Smith is a different problem entirely.'

'Good. I think. What do we do now?'

'I'll see what's in the plane. You distract Mrs Dysart.'

'I love you.'

'Likewise.'

Fox ambled over to the plane as if he owned Brooklands. No one noticed but Reuben, whose eyes briefly frowned then focused on the sketch he was making. Margaret, brushing her skirt down and pushing the goggles to the top of her hat, walked up to Mrs Dysart. Her legs wobbled. Ned's swearing intensified, then the sun popped out from behind a cloud and flooded the airfield with light. He cried out 'Hallelujah!' and, catching sight of Margaret, made a thumbs-up and grinned.

Mrs Dysart turned. In her apricot outfit, her hair golden in the sunshine, she glowed like ... like an angel. First like one full of sweetness and light and then, as she recognised Margaret, like one full of fury and revenge. Mrs Dysart, who'd tempted Norah with a job and harangued her sister after – what? The failure to kill Margaret? And then the failure to silence Miss Connors?

Mrs Dysart, who'd sent her husband and brother-in-law to Switzerland with a handful of pills.

'I thought I'd come and see you were all right,' said Margaret. 'And tell you that your sister went into labour.'

'What? I mean, it's very early.'

'Shouldn't you ask me which sister?'

Mrs Dysart shrugged. 'You've clearly worked it out. Surely you didn't leave her to labour alone?'

'Someone else took over, and Mr Fernsby's with her. I'm sure she's fine.'

'And she's really in labour?'

'She was rather large. Perhaps she mistook her dates.'

'She's a doctor.'

'Even doctors make mistakes and behave in an un-doctorly manner.'

'As long as she's in good hands,' said Mrs Dysart. She looked over Margaret's shoulder towards the plane, frowned then looked into Margaret's face. 'Why precisely are you here?'

'I'm worried about your health. All those pills that keep getting lost. So easy for you to die if you don't have them when you need them.'

Mrs Dysart raised her eyebrows. 'That's very kind of you, but as you can see, I haven't.'

'And it's also very easy to kill someone with them if they're taken by accident. Or deliberately given in lieu of something else. Or turned into a solution and injected.'

'That's very concerning. Do you think someone stole mine for that purpose?'

They locked eyes.

'Mrs Dysart,' called Ned, 'the light won't last forever. What do you want people to do?'

'Perhaps you'd like some tea from the flask now that you're here, Dr Demeray,' said Mrs Dysart. 'I'll just get this scene set up and then we'll have a chat.'

'Thank you.' Margaret took the proffered flask and poured some out. It smelled strange, but then everything smelled strange at the moment. 'I'll just go and look at that plane. I've never seen one up close.'

'Maybe later you could even have a joy ride. My husband can fly you. But do drink up, you look rather cold.'

'Mrs Dysart!' shouted Gladys. 'Shall I climb into this plane now? Shall I fight Bob? What do I do?'

'What am I supposed to do, Mrs Dysart?' shouted one of the actors. 'Shall I stare into the sky?'

'Mrs Dysart, what do you think about this?' called Reuben, walking up and waving his sketchbook.

While she was distracted, Margaret pretended to sip her drink and ambled towards the plane. Fox was deep in conversation with a mechanic. Mr Dysart was in the pilot's seat with Mr Drummond slumped behind him. Another man spun the propeller.

'Stop!' shouted the mechanic, rushing over. 'What are you doing?'

'Chocks away!' shouted Mr Dysart, and the man removed the blocks from under the wheels. The plane started to move forward, gathering speed.

Suddenly Margaret felt a shove and stumbled into the plane's path. She struggled to right herself, dropping the flask and dancing sideways awkwardly, her ankle twisting.

'Dr Demeray!' cried Mrs Dysart, pushing and pulling at her. 'Whatever are you doing? Have you been drinking? Get out of the way immediately.' She gave another shove and Margaret's ankle gave way.

Fox and the mechanic rushed forward, jumped, and caught hold of the starboard wing, steering it away from the two women. Mr Dysart increased its speed. A grimace twisted his mouth beneath the goggles. Margaret couldn't make out his eyes, but she stared into them, willing them to see her as she struggled to her feet. She mouthed *Norah*. The plane was bearing down on her, moving off course with the mechanic hanging on its wing. Fox had managed to swing himself up and was crawling along the wing. She could get out of the plane's way even with a twisted ankle. But Mrs Dysart had also managed to swing up onto the port side and tumbled on top of Mr Drummond. 'Just take off, will you!' she shouted.

'We can't,' yelled Mr Dysart. 'Not with three of us in here and him on the wing!'

He tried to accelerate, but the weight unbalancing the plane and Fox was distracting him. Mr Dysart lashed out, making the plane swerve towards Ned, who'd set the camera up and was filming. Then he produced a revolver and fired at Fox.

'Don't be such a fool!' yelled Mrs Dysart. 'You might damage the wing. Just take off and he'll fall.'

Margaret hobbled forward to pull at the tail fin. The two men she'd seen earlier ran forward and pulled on the wing with the mechanic. The plane started to slow, and turn.

Mrs Dysart reached for her husband, then fell back. 'What the—'

Mr Drummond had lifted himself up. Shoving Mrs Dysart sideways, he punched Mr Dysart firmly in the back of the head. The plane slowed to a halt.

Fox pulled himself along the wing and held his revolver against Mr Dysart's temple. 'Drop - that - gun - now.'

Mr Dysart dropped his pistol over the side of the cockpit.

'Can't I trust you to kill anyone?' snarled Mrs Dysart. The two men who'd come down the hill dragged her out of the plane and held her arms behind her back.

Margaret limped round to face her.

'My sister and her husband are very rich,' snarled Mrs Dysart. 'When I tell them you've interfered with my film and damaged this plane, their lawyers will—'

'As I told you earlier,' said Margaret, 'your sister and her husband are being very well looked after just now. The people looking after them are all wearing blue. Or is it black? I'm not one hundred per cent sure what prison officers' uniform is these days. You'll have to let me know.'

'I tell you what,' said Mr Drummond later, having emptied his stomach but still distinctly green around the gills, 'we'll make more money out of that bit of film than any of the fictional stuff.'

'Do you think so?' said Margaret. She was mortified at the sight of herself: face grimy from motor-cycling, skirt muddy, hair coming down. Fox had merely bemoaned his motor-cycling cap, which had a hole in it where Mr Dysart had missed his head.

'Maybe,' conceded Mr Drummond. 'I despair of the public, I really do. It's not so much that they prefer fiction to fact, but they'll believe any sort of twaddle if it's fed to them the right way, and dismiss the truth out of hand if it doesn't fit with how they want things to be.'

'I'm afraid that unless someone manages to blur some of the faces, the film will never be seen by anyone except a closed court,' said Fox.

'I suppose those faces include yours,' said Mr Drummond gloomily. 'How am I supposed to make a living? It'll be enough of a fight to buy the innocent bits of the stock and start again. Not that I'm entirely sure who I'm buying them off. I hope the film you've confiscated is enough to convict the Dysarts of trying to kill you two, not to mention poisoning me and whatever they planned to do with me once we were airborne.'

'That and treason,' said Fox.

'Treason?'

'Those film canisters won't only include melodramas and comedies. From what you've said, there will be enough extra footage of the most inconspicuous way to approach key buildings in London and the best places to leave bombs.'

'What bombs?'

'We've found quite a cache in the cellar of one of Fernsby's Soho properties.'

'Blimey.'

'And then, quite apart from her efforts to poison you and kill me,' said Fox, 'there's Mrs Dysart's part in a conspiracy to murder, if we can work out who actually gave Norah the digitalin. Dysart is adamant he had nothing to do with it, only arranging for the letter purportedly from her father in Paris to be waiting in Switzerland for Norah and then staying in the Paris hotel to "be the father" if necessary for a few days. If only we had evidence that Mr Fernsby did more than stand over her on that platform.'

Margaret flicked backwards through her sketchbook as they talked, looking at the drawings: Mrs Dysart and Dr Fernsby; the man she now knew was Mr Fernsby; Reuben and Mr Drummond; Norah huddled on the platform; a rough pencil impression of the platform just before Norah was found, with people spilling out and getting in each other's way. If only it had been a photograph... 'Wait a moment. Did Ned set up the camera on the platform?'

Mr Drummond, clearly trying to make sense of the sketch upside down, nodded. 'We had twenty minutes or so. It was a lot of palaver, but you never know when a bit of film of people milling round a station will come in handy so we thought... Hang on.' He snatched the sketchbook and spun it round so he could see it properly. 'I like your thinking, Dr Demeray, I like your thinking. Thank Gawd you ain't as daft as you're belligerent.'

'Will you still have it?'

'Course we will,' he said. 'It's like string; you don't throw the odd bits away. So now we'll go and find out what's on it.'

Bert appeared in the doorway waving a slim notebook. 'Fox - we've found this in amongst the Penny Dreadfuls belonging to Miss Isaacs. It might speed things up. Organisation might be their downfall. There were extra payments "for security" to Stewart Jones and Norbert Floyd. I think the dates match the day Charles Craven died and—'

'Let me see.' Fox strode over.

'I keep telling him that being tidy is overrated,' said Margaret.

'Ha!' said Mr Drummond then winced as he rose slowly from his seat. 'If I hadn't had the pie at lunch, Gawd knows what that tea would have done to me. Even though you looked at it as if it was poisoned. The pie, I mean.'

'It looked lovely, apart from the mushrooms.'

'You don't strike me as the picky sort.'

'I love them, normally, but somehow—'

'No appetite, not liking the taste of things, and covering your nose outside.'

'Mr Drummond,' said Margaret, 'what are you talking about?'

'I know it when I see it. I've got five daughters, Gawd help me – worse than herding cats – three grandchildren, and one on the way. And it's stout you want in your condition, although ginger helps at the beginning. Call yourself a doctor and him a detective.' He walked out, chuckling.

'What is he laughing about?' said Fox, returning to her side.

'Oh,' said Margaret. 'Oh my word. I've been too busy to pay attention.'

'To what?'

'I think I'm expecting a baby.'

Forty-One

Robert Davis was of middle height and blond, with grey eyes. 'Thank you for telling me what happened, doctor. I'm not sure why you invited me here, though.' He stared around the studio's projecting room with interest and confusion.

'Norah was happy here,' said Margaret.

'What did she look like?'

'She was fair haired like you and pretty.'

'Aye? A bit like both her parents, then.' He sighed. 'Mair was pretty as they come but her hair was raven-black, like, and her eyes blue as speedwell. I wish I'd gone back for Mair, but there you go, I didn't. If I'd have known about the baby, I would have gone back, isn't it? But we was just kids who didn't really know what we was doing. She just wanted to get away from her mam and da for a few hours now and again, and who wouldn't? Cold as the grave, them two, but me all warm and loving. What we did just come natural. No one never told us nothing. So we didn't know what might happen, and she never wrote...'

'It's possible she didn't know herself till the very last moment, and then perhaps she was too scared.'

He sighed. 'We was only seventeen. No one would give us permission to marry, and I couldn't wait another four years to leave that stinking hole. I asked Mair if she'd come anyhow - I'd have married her soon as we got somewhere we could lie about our ages, but she wouldn't, or perhaps she couldn't. I thought: "Fair play, maybe she doesn't love me. No point in holding grudges". But I'm not ashamed to say that six months after, when I heard she was dead, I cried like a baby. It had been a bad, damp, lung-clogging winter, but Mair was strong as iron so I was surprised. I would have visited her grave, but I couldn't face going back to that fuss-arsing, mutter-mumbling town to have them sneer at me 'cos I hadn't made my way yet after all my big words. The only thing there worth anything was gone, and me seeing her grave wouldn't bring her back. And since then, I can't complain, is it? I found another lovely girl and I got my family in the end. I've had a nice life. But if only someone had known about the baby, they could have got her and brung her up proper with people what loved her. Poor little scrap.'

'Mair's mother knew.'

'And she never went and got her?' Mr Davis punched his palm. '*Duw anwyl*, heart of stone that woman: all mourning clothes and sewn-shut lips and pouncing in judgement. Or was it Mair's da stopped her?'

Margaret thought about the fleeting emotion in Mrs Jones's eyes: doubt, guilt, sorrow, shame, fear. Too many years had passed to know which had been the strongest. 'Maybe. But in the end, she made her own choice. And that was to pretend none of it had ever happened.'

'I'd have got Norah myself if I'd known. Dunno what me and a baby would have done up here in the smoke, but I wouldn't have left her. You've got to believe me.'

'I do.'

'So what was Norah like as a person, then?' he said, looking up at Reuben and Mr Drummond. 'It's pointless now, but I'd like to know. The truth, mind. No gilding it.'

'She was chopsy,' said Reuben. 'Does that sound right? Talkative, anyway. Imaginative, lively, impatient, clever, slapdash, funny...'

Mr Drummond added in a gruff voice. 'Sometimes a little annoying.'

Mr Davis laughed for a second. 'Like me in that way, too.'

'She wrote stories and poems,' said Margaret. 'She wanted to be a novelist or a playwright.'

'*Duw, duw*, what a waste. And now no one will ever know.'

'They will,' said Fox. 'Show him, Margaret.'

She reached into her bag. 'My cousin Nathan Lawrenson has a printing press. He normally just prints pamphlets and newspapers, but he's turned Norah's writings into a book. I had a feeling you might want one. And her friends gave me photographs to copy too.'

His eyes filled with tears and he rubbed them angrily away. 'Have you given anything to her grandparents?'

'Not yet.'

'Good. Don't. Do you know how if a book publisher would take these? Make something of them?'

'I'm finding out, and there are two people happy to finish some of the things she was working on.'

'Thank you. So you say Norah was happy here. What did she do?'

'She was, very briefly, a moving-picture actress,' said Margaret. 'Mr Drummond was allowed to save the film she was in. Another actress takes the role on part-way through, but it still makes sense somehow. And it was Norah's script.'

Mr Davis laughed again, his humour twinkling through the tears. 'You gotta tell her grandparents that! They'll be horrified. They'll wonder the rest of their miserable lives if they could have saved her from the sin of acting if they'd taken her in. Blood of theirs in the moving pictures. I loves it.' He blew his nose. 'Can I see the film, like?'

'Of course.' Mr Drummond's voice was unsteady. He leaned in to Margaret. 'Reuben changed some of the title boards, and with a bit of jiggery-pokery, I changed the ending.'

The lights dimmed and the projector rolled and the short melodrama played out in all its magical nonsense. Mr Davis chuckled a little, and sniffed a little more.

But this time, as Adelaide's true love clasped her in his arms, the title board simply said

My love! You are mine and I am yours! Let us be free and happy forever!

And in the last frame, Norah ran in the meadows of those impossible Swiss mountains, looking over her shoulder, laughing and full of life.

As the image faded, Mr Drummond whispered, 'I got photographs made from that too. I thought he might like one. It was the least I could do. Was I right, do you think?'

But Margaret was too choked-up to answer.

The short piece of film from Neuchâtel was enough to add Norah's murder to Mr Fernsby's indictment. He approached her on the platform as soon as she alighted from the train, grasped her arm, and steered her into the crowd before she collapsed. Then he walked away, coming back when Margaret appeared. Precisely how he'd administered the poison was unclear, and he refused to admit it. Whether he'd be convicted was immaterial from a legal point of view, since there was more than enough evidence of treason to execute him, along with his wife and the Dysarts, but Margaret felt vindicated.

'What will happen to the Fernsby and Dysart children?' she asked Fox a few days later, over breakfast. She was still surprised he hadn't been angry that she hadn't recognised her own pregnancy, but his reaction had been pure joy, wonder and excitement with perhaps a little of the fear she felt herself. The board at St Julia's was another matter, but at least it had agreed to keep her employed in pathology until July or when it became unhealthy for her to continue, and hinted that they'd welcome her back as a tutor a few days a week after the baby was born if she so chose.

'New names, and they'll go to distant relations in other countries,' said Fox. 'Not Germany of course. And the trail there has gone cold. It's a worry. Even the ten year old is aware of what's happened. They might grow up ashamed, or angry, or vengeful: there might be seeds for treachery sown in them already. But when the baby comes, it will be adopted and hopefully never find out that its mother was executed for betraying her country, shooting you, and drugging Miss Connors so that Dysart could kill her in a back alley, with her name tarnished in every way imaginable. It's just as well they had to use him rather than Norb and Stew. She'd have had no chance with them, just like Charles and Abolin and Bookie Brown.'

'Poor woman; she just wanted someone to talk to. If Dr Fernsby hadn't refused to tell her I worked at St J's, Miss Connors wouldn't have gone back to try again and overheard them talking about the attempt to kill me.'

'And in the end her parents are more than willing to support her.' Fox tapped the letter which Miss Connors had sent. 'It's just as well Constable Harris persuaded her to contact them.'

'Talking of Constable Harris, I hear some generous soul is paying for him to do evening classes so that he can put in for promotion to sergeant.'

'Mmm,' said Fox. He got up, went to the front window and looked out. He stood with his hands in his pockets, watching Mrs Winson's son load the very last of her belongings into his motor car.

Margaret joined him. 'The other thing I kept forgetting was that Mrs Winson was thinking of selling up. Every time I saw a visitor I was afraid they were looking for you or me. I never thought   to ask and now she's moving away.'

Fox put his arm round her. He was every bit as tense as he had been before he'd proposed. Perhaps it was unsurprising; the question of a home for both of them would become pressing soon. Margaret's only preparation so far for the baby was wondering how much it would cost to renovate the attic rooms and hire Nellie as a nursery maid. But if they were going to have to move...

There was a light, hesitant tap at the flat's front door.

'That'll be Mrs Winson coming to say goodbye,' said Margaret. She welcomed the older woman in and shook hands. 'I'll be sorry to lose you as a neighbour.'

'I'll miss you too,' said Mrs Winson, with a shy twinkle. 'A great many of my friends are desiccating with boredom, but you have kept me intrigued and entertained for eight years. I've asked Humphrey to buy some ragtime recordings just to remind me of you.'

Margaret laughed. 'I thought I was scandalising you!'

'My dear, I lived in the colonies for many years and nothing shocks me. At least you weren't doing one thing and pretending to do another. Perhaps you'll write me a letter to tell me what time you're getting in and how many times a mysterious motor car arrives to collect you and how often you have to run for the tube. And talking of letters, here's one the postman delivered to the wrong address. Just a bill, I'm afraid.'

'Thank you,' said Margaret, taking the envelope. 'I promise to write. I hope the person who's bought your flat will be as forgiving of me.'

Mrs Winson chuckled. 'Oh, you are funny.' Then she turned to Fox. 'Here you are, Mr Foxcroft-MacSionnach,' she said, and handed over her keys. 'I don't know how you'll bring it all back together, but I'm sure you'll manage.'

Margaret stared.

Fox gave her a winsome grin. 'I still haven't got round to buying an engagement ring. I bought a flat instead. Between us, we seem to own a family home.'

Newsletter

To get news about my books and others, as well as the first chance to read Advanced Reader Copies of any new releases, please sign up for my newsletter at

https://paulaharmon.com/newsletter/

Historical Note

This book was prompted by research into early 20th Century British intelligence organisations.

In July 2020, during lockdown, I 'went' on a virtual online walking tour around London called 'Secrets and Spies' organised by Footprints of London. A book was mentioned, called 'Odd People' by Basil Thomson, which I subsequently bought. In it, the author describes investigations into possible spying before and during WWI. One of the cases was one where a maidservant was reported by her employers for sending malicious letters about non-existent listening devices, saying that she had been told to do it by a mysterious man without any evidence that he existed. I thought, 'What if the maid was innocent and there was more behind the story than an overactive imagination? What if the employers were covering something up?' And Norah popped into being.

1911 was an eventful year. In Britain, there was a Festival of Empire to celebrate the coronation of King George V and Queen Mary and a visit by Kaiser Wilhelm II and Kaiserin Augusta of Germany. There were social reforms to help the poorer members of society; the launch of the Titanic; a Circuit of Britain Air Race and the first airmail service. But there was also huge social unrest with several riot and strikes (including the one at Singer Factory in Edinburgh). Tensions in Europe were starting to escalate, with treaties forged between some

European countries preparing for attack by other European counties. There was fear of anarchy within Britain and accusations of espionage and counter espionage between Britain and Germany. Further afield, there was European aggression in north Africa and Turkey and revolutions in Mexico and China.

The following events referred to within this book really happened:

The murders of Sergeants Tucker and Bailey and Constable Choateby gunned down in Houndsditch on the night of 16th December 1910 while trying to thwart a burglary. The murderers were alleged anarchists led by George Gardstein. He subsequently died while the others escaped.

The finding of Leon Beron's body on Clapham Common on 1st January 1911. A man called Steinie Morrison was later convicted of the murder, which appeared unlinked to anarchy.

Bomb making equipment was found in lodgings connected to the Gardstein gang and the alleged murderers were tracked to Sidney Street, leading to a decision by police on 2nd January 1911 to cordon off the area leading to a siege the following day. The film of the siege (including Winston Churchill) can still be found on the internet. The besieged gunmen were killed and a fireman died as a result of injuries sustained when a wall collapsed.

International Women's Day Marches in Switzerland, Austria, Germany and Denmark on 19th March 1911.

The Triangle Shirt-Waist factory fire in New York on 25th March 1911 in which 146 garment workers died. (And for the record, the London Daily News really did put an article about it right next to one about an alleged British spy in Germany.)

The 1911 Census on 2nd April was hotly opposed by many suffragettes and some did indeed spend the night roller skating at Aldwych to avoid the enumerator.

Both Alan's Tearooms and The Gardenia existed and were popular with suffragettes.

The Freedom Press, an anarchist paper, was founded in Whitechapel in 1868 and still exists. It denounced the murders of the policemen in Houndsditch.

By 1911, several film studios had been set up in London, including the Ideal Film Company in Soho in 1911, not far from the fictional Glassmakers Lane. All the films listed in chapter seven (except for The Cockney Connection as far as I know) were real films, some of which you can still find clips of online.

There were several female directors in the early moving picture era - Alice Guy-Blaché for example. It was only when the industry really took off that they were pushed further into the background.

https://en.wikipedia.org/wiki/Siege_of_Sidney_Street

https://www.thecinetourist.net/straight-out-of-whetstone.html

https://www.messynessychic.com/2016/09/22/the-girls-we-shou ld-thank-for-kickstarting-hollywood/

https://womanandhersphere.com/2012/09/03/suffrage-stories-th e-suffragette-1911-census-boycott-where-and-what-was-the-aldwych -skating-rink/

Acknowledgements

With many thanks to Liz Hedgecock and Sim Sansford, for their eagle-eyes.

About Paula Harmon

Paula Harmon was born in North London to parents of English, Scottish and Irish descent. Perhaps feeling the need to add a Welsh connection, her father relocated the family every two years from country town to country town moving slowly westwards until they settled in South Wales when Paula was eight. She later graduated from Chichester University before making her home in Gloucestershire and then Dorset where she has lived since 2005.

She is a civil servant, married with two adult children. Paula has several writing projects underway and wonders where the housework fairies are, because the house is a mess and she can't think why.

https://paulaharmon.com
https://viewauthor.at/PHAuthorpage

https://www.facebook.com/pg/paulaharmonwrites

https://www.goodreads.com/paula_harmon

https://twitter.com/Paula_S_Harmon

Other Books By Paula Harmon

THE MURDER BRITANNICA SERIES

Murder Mysteries set in 2nd Century Britain

https://mybook.to/MurderBritanniaSeries

THE MARGARET DEMERAY SERIES

Historical Mysteries set in the lead-up to World War 1

https://mybook.to/MargaretDemeraySeries

THE CASTER & FLEET SERIES

Historical Mysteries set in 1890s London

https://mybook.to/CasterAndFleetSeries

THE BOOKER & FITCH SERIES

Contemporary Mysteries set in an English riverside town

https://mybook.to/BandFSeries

OTHER BOOKS BY PAULA HARMON

https://paulaharmon.com/books-by-paula-harmon/

SHORT STORIES BY PAULA HARMON & VAL PORTELLI

https://viewbook.at/PHWeirdandpeculiartales

AUDIO BOOKS BY PAULA HARMON

https://paulaharmon.com/audiobooks/

Also short stories in the following anthologies:

DORSET SHORTS

https://mybook.to/DorsetShorts

WARTIME CHRISTMAS TALES

https://mybook.to/WartimeChristmasTales

Printed in Great Britain
by Amazon